UNLIKELY

RETURN

A NOVEL

NINA ATWOOD

Published by Nina Atwood Enterprises, LLC
Dallas, Texas

Cover art by LLewellenDesigns.com

ISBN-13: 978-0-9702809-9-2 (Trade paperback)
ISBN-10: 0-9702809-9-8 (Trade paperback)
ISBN-13: 978-0-9702809-5-4 (E-book)
ISBN-10: 0-9702809-5-5 (E-book)

PROLOGUE

THE WAVE

The ocean swelled, cerulean waves moved endlessly, peaking and troughing. One wave, traveling hundreds of miles, crossed another, and the two continued as one, larger wave. Later, that wave crossed two more, growing increasingly larger, and so on, until a rogue wave was formed.

Largely considered a maritime myth, now more than 125 feet tall, trough to crest, the rogue wave moved with alarming speed, despite its casual appearance. Traveling at over 44,000 feet per minute, the wave moved with urgency, but with no destination.

It encountered little. Larger fish dove deep, sensing the disturbance above. Dolphin and other intelligent creatures moved laterally in advance of the wave, recognizing and adroitly avoiding the danger. Smaller fish were borne upward to enormous heights and violently returned below. Sea birds flew away, later winging back to follow in the wake of the wave and take advantage of the feast of small, stunned fish floating on the surface.

The vast ocean around the growing wave lay undisturbed as the behemoth continued to gain power. It had come together without warning—no storm, no shifting of tectonic plates beneath the sea, no resulting earthquake. Here, on the open ocean, no oceanic devices captured the journey of the wave. No one saw, and no one knew.

Ahead, completely oblivious to the enormity of the danger approaching, the passengers of the *Princess Rose* drifted serenely on the open ocean—eating, drinking—believing in their supremacy and, therefore, their safety.

That would all change in an instant.

PART ONE

THE BOAT,
THE ISLAND

CHAPTER ONE

Jack faced the men he would host for the next few days. The tall guy with salt-and-pepper hair, Paul, stood behind the other two. Jack guessed him to be in his early sixties. He was slender, with intelligent eyes that scanned the boat with interest.

The second guy, Stuart, looked around 40, lean but muscular, also on the tall side, the kind of guy who seemed totally at ease in his own skin. He displayed a languid posture with hints of aggressiveness, like a great cat at rest, reserving strength for the sudden burst of predatory energy. He had dark blond hair, light gray eyes, and a direct gaze that was not challenging, not exactly open, but somewhere in between—the kind of guy who didn't miss much.

The third guy, Ben, was not so tall, with a runner's body, eyes averted as if attempting to avoid too much human contact.

They were the usual clients—guys who spent the majority of their lives behind desks. They chartered boats like Jack's for a couple of days at a time because they wanted a vacation from their lives. There was a primal need to see, feel, taste, and smell things in the natural world, and that need eventually called people like Jack's clients into his world.

Jack understood that need better than they ever would. He enjoyed feeling the way he did when the boat was far from land, far from the comforts of everyday life, where the people on his boat, whether they realized it or not, needed him for their very survival. Where he could compete with nature—the ocean, the waves, the weather.

The place where he felt truly alive.

Out there, their smartphones ceased to operate. They were unplugged—and they said they wanted that. But they were not prepared for it—for the utter quiet, the gentle sway of the boat, the absence of the roar of civilization. The inability to check in. No email, no social media, no calls, no voice mails.

Jack's clients typically filled the silence and space with too much alcohol, backslapping, and locker room humor. He put up with all of it because it paid well. Quite well.

When they set foot on his boat, Jack was the Captain, and their business and financial status no longer mattered. He was in his element, and they were out of theirs. He enjoyed that shift in power, though he never abused it.

He got their attention with a nod.

"To make this trip more enjoyable, there are a few things that you need to know. Once we get to the reef, we stop and fish today for three hours. That's about all the time we'll have before sunset. We don't fish at night. We have dinner, we socialize, and we sleep.

"You are free to stay up as late as you want," he continued, surveying the men, making eye contact as he talked. "We have beer on board, plus whatever you brought with you—but realize that if you get dehydrated from too much alcohol, you won't have any fun tomorrow. You won't realize how strongly the sun is affecting you until it's too late. Drink more water than you think you will need. If you don't have sunscreen on already, put it on, and keep applying it.

"We start tomorrow early, before sunrise. I will give you one wake-up call. We fish for several hours. We stop around 1:00, have lunch, before going back to fishing. We spend another night on the water, then head back on Thursday.

"I suggest you use lunchtime to rest and hydrate, so you'll be ready for afternoon fishing. Can't tell you the number of times people ignore this advice and end up spending the rest of the trip in their bunks.

"Don't wait if you start to pull in a big one—ask me or Tony to help. It doesn't work to try and be a hero and end up losing the gear or getting pulled overboard.

"In case of emergency, follow my instructions to the letter. Wear your lifejackets at all times.

"Bottom line: we're here to have fun, so be safe, be smart, and we will all have a great time. Any questions?"

No one asked anything. "Okay, let's get started."

Tony, Jack's stand-in Deckhand, stood nearby, arms crossed. He was short, wiry, but with a small beer belly. He wore a torn sleeved white tee shirt and sported a shaved head, scraggly goatee, and multiple tattoos, including a scorpion, which crawled along the side of his neck. His stance was cocky, which only served to make him look punk. Jack sighed inwardly, gesturing to Tony to get rolling. Tony ambled over to help start the boat on its three-day journey.

Their vessel, a 50-foot yacht, the *Princess Rose*, was Jack's pride and joy. They cast off and slowly idled out of the harbor. The sky was a rich blue with the occasional white puffy cloud. With so little wind, the water was calm. It was a spectacular day to head out for sportfishing. Their destination—the waters off southern Baja, where the yellowtail was found in abundance, or so they hoped.

The three clients turned to each other as the boat got underway. They introduced themselves and engaged in small talk. They were put together by Captain Jack because they all wanted the same thing—three days of sport fishing on a chartered yacht. Although most charter groups are composed of friends and family, in this case, not so.

A couple of hours later, they were safely anchored not far from a well-known reef. Jack had set up the three guys with bait, lines, tackle, and sinkers, all designed for going after yellowtail. The water was gentle, and the silence supreme.

Not for the first time, he wondered if it was a mistake hiring Tony. But it was last minute due to his long-time Deckhand's abrupt move away from the area, and he hadn't had the time to do a thorough search. Tony's attitude was poor. He seemed off-key toward the clients, almost contemptuous.

When Jack reminded Tony that morning that he would sleep on the sofa in the main salon that night, he'd acted angry and surprised, as if Jack hadn't already covered that when he interviewed him for the last-minute job. He'd claimed he knew sportfishing and boating well, but Jack had already caught him leaving out steps in their preparation for launch.

Thankfully, it was only a three-day fishing excursion. He could get by with Tony for this trip, but he'd have to find someone new for the future.

He was interrupted in his reverie by the older of the three guys, Paul.

"Captain," he greeted Jack, smiling.

"You can call me Jack. Can I do something for you?"

"No, not really, but I have to say, this looks like a great boat. Can you tell me a little about it?"

Jack rarely got an opportunity to talk about his pride and joy, and Paul seemed genuinely interested, so he took it.

"It's a Silverton, 50-T Series, twin inboard diesel, built for sportfishing or cruising, depending."

Jack had risked his entire meager fortune on the boat, buying it at auction in the depths of the Great Recession for $289 thousand, a steal. Since then, he'd done fishing and cruising charters on a weekly basis, living in the garage apartment of a small cottage in Chula Vista, owned by Melanie, an attractive widow. She was generous with her home, opening the kitchen and main living areas for Jack's use at any time, in return for which he did minor maintenance and repairs on top of rent.

She seemed lonely and appreciative when Jack was around, grateful for his company and help around the property.

Jack didn't need anything more—the boat was his life. It was paid for and heavily insured. It was the one thing he would regret losing. He began the tour for Paul, who offered a stream of questions about the boat.

Jack started with the cockpit. It was small but nicely finished, with stations for fishing, a small fold-away kitchen with sink, grill, and ice maker, plus seating. From there, they climbed the short stairs to the enclosed main salon, with leather sofas, burled wood appointments and tabletop. There was a granite countertop in the galley, with double sink, refrigerator/freezer, and cooktop. The salon also featured a built-in flat-screen TV with a hidden electrical panel.

They climbed to the bridge deck, which was enclosed, with twin helm seats and top-of-the-line instrumentation. Paul showed more interest here, asking more questions. He seemed to have both a fascination with and knowledge of mechanics. Next to the helm was a spacious enclosed seating area.

They stopped at one point, and Paul shifted a bit uncomfortably.

"I know I've taken up a lot of your time, but mechanical things fascinate me." He shrugged. "My wife says I ask too many questions. That I make people uncomfortable. But we're separated now," he shared, looking down.

Jack said nothing. He didn't ask the obvious next question, silently declining to delve deeper. A brief, awkward silence stood between them.

"Hey, thanks for the tour," Paul said, looking up and brightening. "Your boat is great."

"No problem," said Jack. Paul nodded and wandered off.

When Jack first began taking people out on his boat, he engaged them in conversation, asking questions to elicit their stories. But over time, he'd realized his error. Most of them weren't there to openly share about their lives. Most of them were on the boat trying to forget.

Couples and friends were different. When he took them out, usually four to six people at a time, they knew each other, were familiar with one another's stories. They bantered easily and filled the air with conversation, mostly oblivious to Jack's presence. That freed him to focus on taking care of things in the background while they conversed with one another.

He was far more comfortable that way. Not being particularly extroverted in the first place, Jack found it tedious to have to engage in conversations, working hard to figure out the right questions to ask. Now, he focused on the boat, on the fishing, on safety, and on the water. No one ever seemed bothered by his long periods of silence, and that suited him perfectly.

Ben slowly raised his rod, patiently reeling in the line. They used chunk bait—mackerel and sardine—80 lb. line, heavy tackle, and 14-ounce sinkers. Their target was the large yellowtail jack, a beautiful fish with a distinctive yellow stripe, the love of sport fishers because of the fight they provided. Ben didn't care—yellowtail, any tail, any fish. He let the line drift.

He wasn't sure why he was here. He'd been feeling lost, drifting like the line in the water, and one day he picked up a brochure at a restaurant at the marina. What the heck. At least he'd be away for a while, and maybe he could forget, just for a couple of days.

They'd been at it for over an hour, and he hadn't had so much as a tug. He felt the gentle sway of the boat, heard the small slaps of the waves against the sides, and he found it soothing. He used the downtime to look at the guy closest to him—Stuart. He'd been the first to start on the beer, and he took a pull from the bottle in his hand now.

Stuart glanced over at Ben and nodded. He seemed intense, though Ben couldn't say why that was his impression. Ben figured Stuart would be competitive about the fishing, trying to land the biggest fish the soonest.

He returned Stuart's nod and turned back to the water. He

refocused his eyes on the most distant part of the horizon, allowing his vision to fuzz. His breathing slowed, and he felt almost sleepy.

"Any action?" It was Tony, the Deckhand. He'd approached Ben from behind. Tony carried himself with a swagger that Ben found irritating.

"Not yet," Ben told him.

Tony lingered. "This your first time out?"

"Yup."

"Want some help with that?" He smirked at Ben.

Ben was silent for a beat or two.

"I'm good," he said carefully.

"Yeah, first time out, guys find out just how strong those fish are, get their poles pulled out of their hands, look like idiots. I can show you how to cast and hold it, so that doesn't happen. I've been on hundreds of these fishing trips," Tony boasted.

"No, thanks, man," Ben said, turning away.

"Sure, okay," Tony huffed, and wandered off, approaching each of the men on the boat, probably asking the same question.

Ben turned his attention back to the water, the horizon, and the slow play of the line.

It had been a couple of months since the divorce from his wife, Michelle, was finalized. The recognition that the damage of his one-night stand was permanent was still a hard pill to swallow.

He blamed Michelle's sister, Liz, for the fact that he was now a divorced, single Dad, living separately from his children, forced to negotiate visitation with his ex-wife. It still seemed surreal. Yes, he'd screwed up, big-time. It was the worst kind of screw-up. But he might have had a shot at repairing the damage if it hadn't been for Liz.

After their separation, Ben had called Michelle every couple of hours for three days straight, but his calls went to voice mail. He left

long, pleading messages, but got no return call. He sent desperate texts, long emails. No answer.

Finally, on the third day, Liz answered Michelle's landline home phone.

"Hello?"

"Liz. Um, I'm calling for Michelle."

"So?" The cold tone of her voice told Ben she knew everything. Liz had always been his champion. That was clearly over.

"Can you just put her on the line, Liz?"

"Nope."

"Liz, I need to speak to my wife, so put her on the line, now."

"Hey, Ben?"

"What?"

"She's not going to be your wife much longer, and if you have anything to say, you can tell me, or you can tell her lawyer."

"Put her on the line. I'll tell her myself."

Liz hung up.

It took three more calls, Liz answering and hanging up immediately, before Michelle took the phone away from Liz and spoke to Ben, barely.

"Hello, Ben." Her voice was flat, disengaged, almost a whisper.

"Michelle," he breathed. "I miss you. Please, baby, let's get together and talk. I don't want to be separated from you."

He spoke quickly now, filling in the silence with his fear and loneliness. "I know I screwed up, Michelle, but I love you. I never meant to hurt you. I want us back together. We can make this right, I promise you. Let me come over. See you. Hold you."

She was silent for so long that he thought she'd hung up. Finally, she answered. He heard a sniffle.

"I don't think that's a good idea." He heard her softly crying now.

"Oh, baby, I'm so sorry. I know you're hurt..."

"Hurt?" she sounded more energized now, angry. It was better to him than the sadness, which tore away great chunks from his chest.

"Of course, you are, and you have every right to be. I'm hurt, too, Michelle. I can't sleep, I can barely eat. I just want to see you, so I can make this right again. I miss you, and I miss the kids. I want to be home again with you."

"You are hurting. You can't sleep. You want." Flat, dull again. "Ben, I don't really care how you feel. It seems to be all about you, doesn't it? Well, no matter how much you are hurting, it's a grain of sand compared to how I feel. You wrecked our life together.

"I wish you had never told me! If you had to go and screw someone else, why didn't you keep it to yourself? Why on earth did you think I needed to hear that?"

Stunned, he tried to explain.

"I couldn't live with it, baby, with the lie between us. We promised each other we would always be truthful."

"Faithful, you jerk! We promised we would be faithful! Why didn't you keep that promise?" She began crying, her voice fading away, and Ben was suddenly confronted with Liz's voice again.

13

"Ben."

"Liz? Is Michelle okay?" He paced around his motel room, frantic. "I'm coming over there!"

"Listen to me, Ben. Don't you dare come over, and don't call again and talk about your stupid feelings! Do you understand? No one gives a rat's ass how you're feeling! No one gives a shit how you're doing. Just stay away!"

Shocked, Ben asked, "Were you listening, Liz? I'm trying to have a private conversation with my wife! Put her back on the phone, now."

Liz laughed contemptuously. "Too bad. Like I said before, you can talk to me, or you can talk to her attorney." She hung up. He felt like someone had blasted a shotgun through his chest.

After that, it was all downhill. Michelle had filed quickly and asked for everything. An attorney, she'd known exactly how to work the family court system in her favor, and Ben had chosen not to fight. She'd gotten everything she wanted; he got some of their assets and, most importantly, regular visitation with his children.

The only other thing he cared about was lost to him forever.

Ben felt a strong tug on the line. He began reeling in the line, and the tug turned into a monster pull. The rod bent into a deep arc. Ben launched into action instinctively, pulling with all his might.

The fish gave Ben a run for his money. He strained hard, trying to keep the rod in his hands, while gradually getting in a reel here and there. He pulled with all his might, suddenly needing to land this big fish. He *needed* a win.

It was slow going, and after a few minutes, he could feel the burn in his arms and shoulders. He stopped pulling and allowed slack for a moment.

Looking briefly behind him, Ben saw Tony watching. Tony mimicked reeling in the line, with a smirk. "Watch out, that fish ain't dumb. He's trying to break the line, wrap it around the reef or the rocks down there."

Ben pulled again, hard, taking up the slack. It hurt like hell, but this time he didn't slow down. Slowly, he pulled the fish closer, and now it was close enough to pull into the boat.

Ben jerked his head, signaling he needed help. Now that his catch was so close, Ben realized he didn't have a clue about how to bring it onboard.

Tony took his time ambling over, then waited for the last possible moment, stepping in and gaffing, then helping to swing the fish—a large yellowtail, probably 35 pounds—into the boat, deftly separating the hook and line from the fish's mouth.

The fish was so beautiful, with a bright, lemon-yellow stripe running from eye to tail, that Ben momentarily felt regret about bringing it in, oddly empathetic about the plight of the sea creature that would soon be their dinner.

Tony told Ben to hold the fish up for a photo, but Ben shook his head no.

Captain Jack approached, eyed the fish, looked at Ben admiringly. "Nice catch," he said, nodding to Ben, "especially for your first time." He eyed Tony for a moment, then said, "Next time, make sure you're helping." He walked away.

Tony saluted Jack's back with an "Aye, aye, Cap'n!" and muttered something under his breath. He spat on the deck and sauntered away.

Stuart rolled his eyes at Tony's retreating back, catching Ben's eye. He held up a beer, silently offering one.

Ben shook his head and turned away, saying nothing. He went to bait his hook again, ignoring the pain in his arms and shoulders. He cast, and he waited, allowing his mind to wander as the line played out.

That evening, the men sat in the main lounge enjoying beer and cocktails. Their haul was modest—15 yellowtail, ranging from 15 to 25 pounds, Ben's first catch by far the largest. They caught other, smaller, fish, mostly bass and a couple barracuda, but threw those back.

Captain Jack cooked one of the smaller yellowtail, starting with a mix of peppers, onions, and vegetables, which he stir-fried with spices before adding the fish. Ben declared the resulting savory meal was one of the best he'd tasted. The others concurred over huge mouthfuls of food.

Jack stayed in the background, cooking, cleaning, quietly observing.

Stuart spoke loudly, chugging one beer after the other. He was entertaining, Ben would give him that. He pantomimed his struggle to bring in his sixth small fish of the day, a bass, which he now pretended to haul up and at which he gaped.

"Might as well throw you back with all the rest," he laughed, then pointed at Ben. "And Ben over there throws out one line, pretty much ignores it, and in comes a monster yellow tail." His tone was humorous, friendly.

"That's nothing," said Tony, puffing up. "I once brought in an 80 pounder." Everyone turned to look at him. "It was the biggest yellowtail caught that entire season."

Stuart shook his head in disbelief. "Fishing stories...man. Are you sure it wasn't 150 pounds, Tony?" Everyone laughed, and Tony turned red.

"What do you know? You weren't there," Tony challenged Stuart. "Man, you don't know nothing," he said, now beet red in the face, muscles tensing visibly.

"Don't need to be there to know you're making it up," Stuart said, taking another pull on his beer. "Jerk," he added, not quite under his breath.

Tony looked ready to explode. Jack shot him a warning look.

Paul intervened, asking if anyone wanted to play cards. The tension ratcheted down, and they sat and began dealing cards. The three guests began a game of poker.

Tony sat apart from them, sulking and drinking.

Paul was friendly, bantering about the game as they played. Stuart responded with more of the same. Ben was mostly quiet, playing relentlessly. He had by far the best poker face, and that provoked friendly ribbing from Stuart. They played for over an hour, but eventually, Stuart folded his latest hand, yielding again to Ben.

Later, as they sat and shared the last drink of the night, the mood in the room turned mellow, and Stuart broached the question.

"So, you're married?" He looked at Paul, who unconsciously twisted his wedding ring. Paul gazed off and said yes. "She's the best thing that's ever happened to me," he said softly, but there was no joy in his eyes. "We're separated now."

"That's too bad. How long were you married? Any kids?" Stuart asked.

"15 years, and no children," said Paul.

"So, what happened?" asked Stuart softly.

"Me. I'm what happened," said Paul, looking down. "I blew up my marriage over not much of anything."

Stuart whistled softly. "Sorry to hear that. Do you want to talk about it?"

Paul shook his head. "Not now, but thanks."

Stuart turned to Ben, "And what's your relationship status?"

Ben was silent at first.

"No comment," he said. But his tone wasn't harsh; it merely signaled that the sad, closed relationship chapter of his life was not available for inspection.

Stuart shrugged. "Whatever, man."

Paul asked Stuart, "What about you?"

Stuart offered a grin. "Single and happy, man! Best time of my life." The strain around his eyes, which he covered with another chug of beer, belied the statement.

Tony took up that refrain. "Me too. Shook off the last girlfriend six months ago after she gave me the old marriage ultimatum. Since then, it's been boats and banging. Chicks love the feel of the water rocking the boat," he held his hand out, mimicking the undulation, leering.

"Gets 'em real horny. All I have to do is hit the bars near the marina, drop a few hints about having a boat, and before I know it, someone's peeling off her panties."

"That's enough, Tony," said Jack, shooting him a look. But Tony was undeterred, emboldened by alcohol.

"And what about you, *Captain Jack*? You're unattached. I can just hear 'em now. *Oh, Captain Jack! Take me to your boat!*" Tony laughed, but it was twisted laughter. No one else laughed. Paul looked away, clearly uncomfortable.

Jack turned away, heading downstairs to bed. He stopped just before going below and turned. "Get some sleep, everyone. 4:00 a.m. comes real early." The others called it a night and headed down as well.

Day one of Ben's short vacation, and so far, he felt no relief from the pain he'd been carrying around for months. Maybe day two would make a difference.

CHAPTER TWO

Tony stood on the bridge deck, ordered to stay put by Jack while he went below. He was resentful, disliking the boredom of sitting at the helm with nothing to do. It was a shit job. Why did he have to stand here anyway?

His orders were to watch the water, a job that didn't make any sense. What was there to see? There was nothing but blue water and blue sky for as far as the eye could see. Their intel on weather showed nothing for hundreds of miles, and not much beyond that.

He wasn't an idiot. But Jack sure treated him like one. Keep an eye out for anything that looks out of place. There are floating containers in the ocean and other things. Our job is to keep ourselves and the passengers safe on this boat.

Duh.

In the few months Tony had worked as a fishing hand, he'd never seen an issue. Boats went out, people fished and drank, and boats came back. He got paid for doing a whole lot of not much. Sweet deal. Except when he had to do something stupid and boring like this.

Jack was different than some of the other Captains. He seemed overly cautious, the type to cross all the t's and dot the i's in everything he did. What a waste of time. No one really gave a shit on these small-time fishing boats.

All these guys like Jack were the same to Tony—full of themselves, acting like they commanded a Navy battleship or something. He snorted to himself, shaking his head. He needed a smoke, bad, but Jack said he couldn't smoke on board in case it bothered one of the paying passengers. To hell with that—he was going to sneak one later anyway.

Tony pulled his cellphone out of his pocket. Too bad there was no internet signal. But he had enough downloaded content to keep him busy. Girls, girls, and more girls, in all kinds of poses, dressed in nothing. He grinned, rubbing himself, his eyes glued to the phone.

Far away, on the horizon, a dark swell appeared. To the untrained eye, it appeared to stand still, but any sailor who'd spent time on the open water would have known better—if they'd been watching. As the swell grew larger, Tony eyes remained glued to the tiny screen.

Suddenly, Jack was back, standing behind Tony.

"Tony!" Jack was pointing to the horizon, jabbing his finger. "Do you see that? It's headed directly for this boat!"

Tony leaped up, dropping his phone, shocked at the size of the wave approaching the boat. He'd never seen anything like it before.

"Get down below and get the lifeboat ready!" ordered Jack. For once in his life, Tony didn't balk at being told what to do and scrambled below.

WEDNESDAY, 8:20 A.M.

Jack made a rapid sweep of the other guests on the boat to make sure they were all wearing life jackets. Thankfully, they had all heeded his advice and were. He got their attention by telling them to drop their lines.

"As fast and safely as you can, proceed to the lower deck and forward. There's a large wave headed for us. It's going to be a bumpy ride, so everyone needs to get in a spot to hold on. Be ready to board the lifeboat because we may need to abandon the boat."

At their blank stares, he yelled, "Now!" He literally pushed them down the stairs. They stumbled along, aimless but for Jack's rapid-fire directions.

Jack's heart rate accelerated, but he kept a cool head. Military training—there was no substitute for the skills of crisis management.

First, he put out an emergency call. He held down the distress button, then punched Channel 16 on the radio. "Mayday, mayday, mayday. This is the *Princess Rose.*" He gave the boat's MMSI (Maritime Mobile Search Identity). "We are in distress, possibly going down." He gave the boat's longitude and latitude. "Over." He threw down the mic, ran for the emergency ditch bag, grabbed it, and carried it with him. He rushed to the helm.

Tony struggled with the life raft, contained inside an enclosed, white plastic clamshell, clearly not sure what to do with it or how to release the straps that anchored it in place. The wave loomed at an impossible height—75 or 100 feet. Jack yelled down at the men, "Grab something and hold on!"

WEDNESDAY, 8:23 A.M.

With an almighty slam, the wave hit the boat, and everyone clung to whatever they could as the boat took an impossible ride almost 90 degrees up in the air for a few, heart-stopping seconds. The wave was so high Jack couldn't see the sky above as they ascended.

He gunned the engine and, at one point, believed they might actually make it. But about 10 meters from the top, disaster struck. The boat began to roll, and it was clear that they would not summit the wave and ride safely down the other side.

Shit, this was going to be much worse than he thought.

Everything slowed down for Jack as his heart rate accelerated, and his focus narrowed. He drew in a couple of slow, deep breaths, allowing his brain to re-engage. *Life raft, ditch bag, water.* Without those three things, their odds of survival would go dramatically down. One or more of the boat's 5-gallon water jugs might float loose from the boat, and they might find them later. Could he get to the rest of their lifelines in time?

"Hold on!" yelled Jack. "When we hit the water, let go and swim as fast as you can to the surface!" He abandoned the helm, then grabbed and threw the ditch bag overboard, activating the light beacon clipped to the side.

"Release the life raft!" he yelled at Tony, who was frozen, clinging to the railing in shock.

Jack pulled himself along the railing and grabbed the straps that held the lifeboat to the boat, quickly unbuckling the restraints. He couldn't do it fast enough. The boat pitched at an impossible angle, and the hard clamshell pressed into Jack, who tugged with all his strength on the last restraint. As the seawater rushed at him, he gave one last mighty tug and felt the life raft loosen. Just before he was pitched overboard, he hit the release button on the clamshell to open it and tossed it free of the boat.

Jack tumbled, free-falling briefly in mid-air. The ocean rushed toward him. This was it—he would either make it or he wouldn't. There was no time to reflect on his life, on how well he'd lived it, whether he'd made a positive difference to anyone. There was only this one moment, and after that, about three minutes to figure out how to survive, because that's about how long he could hold his breath underwater. That was assuming he wasn't knocked unconscious or killed in the fall.

Jack hit the water, slamming it from the side. Still conscious, although feeling pain in his ribs, he took one huge gulp of air before he went under. The boat, now completely capsized, wasted no time sinking.

Jack was underwater, disoriented, and in pain, not sure of the direction of the surface. He fought the instinct to expend energy flailing around and instead held still long enough to let his body settle. Now he could see the light above his head, so he kicked his legs strongly but surely and moved slowly upward.

Just before he broke the surface, he risked one last look down at his beautiful boat, slowly descending to the ocean bottom. His life's dream—gone in an instant. But now was not the time to reflect on that loss. He was almost out of air. He felt his vision narrow, and dark spots began to appear in front of him. With all his strength, he powered to the surface, fighting the urge to suck in, to expand his lungs.

Finally, Jack broke the surface. He gulped in air, struggling to maintain consciousness. *He must be alert, must be there to help everyone else.* He shook his head and scanned all around, sucking air in deeply. He didn't see any other heads above water, but the water continued to undulate from the residual power of the rogue wave and from the displaced energy of the boat going down, blocking his view. He shouted, "Anyone there?"

Someone shouted back. Jack swung his head around and saw Stuart nearby.

"Where are the others?" Jack shouted at Stuart. Stuart swung his head around frantically, searching nearby, treading water.

"I don't see them!" he yelled back at Jack, who began swimming in slow arcs.

Suddenly, Ben broke the surface nearby, and so did Tony. They both gasped for air and treaded water. Only Paul was missing.

"Stay together! Get to the lifeboat! I'll find Paul," yelled Jack. He took a deep breath and dove underwater, looking all around. Nothing. He broke the surface, took another deep breath, and went under again. Over and over, he dove. *Where was he?* There was little time to haul him to the surface, alive. Jack dove again.

He broke the surface and scanned the surface of the water. He saw Paul about 20 yards away, floating face down and not moving. He swam with all his might. Reaching Paul, he quickly flipped him over, so his face was out of the water. Even with the life jacket, it was a struggle to keep Paul's head above water. He felt himself weakening.

23

Jack rapidly clicked through the options for helping Paul. What could he do? They needed a place to lay him down, stabilize him, and do CPR.

"Tony, Stuart, Ben, get over here!" he yelled, but Stuart had already rapidly closed the gap between them, swimming powerfully. Ben quickly followed.

As they drew closer, Jack saw the fear and panic in their eyes. He fired commands.

"We have to help Paul. Tony, Ben, get the lifeboat while Stuart and I haul him over there. Stuart, help me get Paul to the lifeboat."

Stuart was strong. He used the strength he'd built up from countless workouts to take Paul into a rescue hold and pull toward the lifeboat. Paul's lifejacket kept his upper body afloat. Stuart placed himself underneath Paul, put one arm around his chest from behind, and began swimming, using his other arm and his legs.

Jack motioned to Ben and Tony. Tony was frozen, eyes wide, panicked. Tony had obviously never been in a crisis, never been called upon to think clearly, spring into action, and take commands while under stress.

Jack's command jarred Tony out of his passivity. "Over there, Tony! Get over there and grab the straps on the raft. Pull it over here."

Ben swam quickly, and Tony finally followed. The two of them quickly reached the lifeboat and began pushing and pulling it toward Stuart and Paul.

Jack commanded, "Stuart, get in the boat first, then help me get Paul into the boat." Stuart climbed in and hauled Paul in while Jack pushed from the water.

Once they had Paul in the boat, Jack climbed in and went to work. He swiftly opened Paul's mouth, stuck his finger in, and looked for an obstruction. Finding none, he began to compress Paul's chest rhythmically. Nothing happened at first.

Suddenly, Paul spasmed, making a choking sound, and they quickly rolled him on his side. Paul's lungs disgorged the water in them, and he began to cough. His eyes opened halfway and rolled around as he continued to cough.

Paul's head lolled, his eyes showing only the whites. But he was alive. His face was pale, and he struggled to breathe normally. "I'm okay," he said weakly, but couldn't sit up.

One by one, the other two guys climbed into the raft. It was a tight squeeze. The inflated raft was constructed to mimic a small tent, maybe four feet on each side, the top sitting about four feet high, forcing them to sit huddled under the top. The sides were large inflated rubber tubes, with ballast underneath.

At least they were sheltered from the sun.

"Shit, man, I thought he was dead," said Tony, peering at Paul, his eyes wide with fear.

Everyone was shell shocked, water dripping everywhere, eyes dilated, mouths slack. Except for Jack. He was all business.

Jack had been in crisis situations far worse than this. In his mind's eye, old movies from his stint in Afghanistan threatened to re-run themselves—the IED going off, the fire and panic, watching helplessly as his best buddy died. He jerked himself back to the present, banishing the images.

"Look for the ditch bag," instructed Jack. The men looked at him blankly. "It's bright yellow, about the size of a backpack. It has equipment in it we need to survive." He told them about the 5-gallon water bottle as well.

That seemed to spurn the others to life. They collectively scanned the seas around the life raft, but there was nothing in sight. They looked back at Jack. "Keep looking," he instructed.

While the men were busy scanning for the ditch bag and water bottles, Jack checked the life raft, making sure there were no punctures or tears. There were two roll-down flaps, one on each side—so he posted one guy per opening—Ben and Stuart—then had them rotate, so there was always someone on the lookout with fresh eyes.

Tony slumped against the sides of the raft.

They floated for what seemed like hours. Stuart and Ben scanned the horizon for any signs of another boat or land. Jack had asked them to continue to be on the lookout for their ditch bag, which contained provisions along with several life-saving pieces of equipment.

"It floats, so unless it got stuck in the boat, it's out there on the water," he told them.

"Shit, we're fucked," muttered Tony. "This stupid life raft is fucked, and we're fucked. I didn't sign up for this kind of bullshit. That stupid boat wasn't worth crap getting us outta there. As for the ditch bag, that's gone too."

Everyone avoided eye contact with Tony. He twitched nervously and couldn't stop talking.

"What was that, man? Was that, like, a tsunami or something? Why didn't we get a warning? I thought they had all kinds of early warning shit out there. Is there another big tsunami wave headed for us? Shit, we're going to get hit again, aren't we?" He sounded close to the panic zone.

Jack shot him a look. "What?" Tony said defiantly, his eyes wide. "It wasn't my fault! I was looking everywhere, and I swear I didn't see it coming!"

Tony was by far the weakest link in the chain. His presence jeopardized everyone's safety. Jack wished for the tenth time he'd looked around more for a backup Deckhand, gotten someone seasoned and competent.

Paul still looked weak, but he seemed to be breathing normally with only the occasional watery cough. Ben continued to gaze at the horizon, ignoring Tony. Stuart looked pissed.

"Hey, man, why don't you shut up?" Stuart told Tony, who bristled.

"What the fuck is wrong with you, man?" Tony looked scared despite his bravado. Stuart was probably 50 pounds heavier than Tony, and all muscle. He shook his head, not making eye contact with Stuart.

He continued to mutter under his breath. "What are you gonna do about it, huh? What difference does it make? We're all gonna be dead soon anyway." Tony looked like he might begin to cry.

Oh, Christ, please don't cry, thought Jack.

"We all need to stay calm," Jack told them. "We are not going to die, Tony. We are floating in an ocean current that will take us to land or put us in the path of a freighter. It's just a matter of time. We're going to find the ditch bag, and that will help. I sent out a mayday before the boat went over, so there are people looking for us now."

Jack continued.

"That was not a tsunami, which is a wave caused by an underwater earthquake at the bottom of the ocean. On the open ocean, a tsunami is a ripple. It only gets big as it approaches land, so we are fine. We got hit by a rogue wave—very unusual, but it happens. At this point, our biggest problem isn't another wave, it's dehydration, which is why we need to keep an eye out for the water bottle and the ditch bag."

He left out other information that would only panic the men. He'd never actually seen a rogue wave, nor had he known anyone else who had. They were the subject of mythology by seafaring men, only in recent history confirmed as real due to the use of technology.

He had no idea if one rogue wave might be followed by another. If another one hit, their odds of surviving that event were not good. Everyone was exhausted and dehydrated, and thus less able to withstand the trauma. Their tiny life raft wouldn't likely survive that kind of blow. They'd be left on the open ocean with no shelter—if they were still alive.

He didn't tell them that he'd lied about the currents, that their position in the ocean meant that the currents were gradually pulling them further out into the Pacific, far away from land. He didn't need them to panic right now, but he knew the longer they drifted, the further out they would go, and the lower their odds of being found. Their only hope was a rapid rescue, or to quickly encounter an island on which to shelter and wait for help.

The Pacific was vast, and the open water contained little sea life, which meant no food. There were few storms this time of year, and at their latitude, there would be few at any time of year, so being able to obtain additional drinking water was almost impossible.

In short, Tony was right about their fate, unless they got lucky.

"Thanks, Jack." Paul looked grateful. "Tony, thanks for helping with the life raft. We all want to pull together and help any way we can."

His calm voice and acknowledgment seemed to mollify Tony, who turned away but had nothing more to say.

They fell silent, and all they could hear was the sound of the waves gently lapping against the inflated sides of the life raft.

Dusk fell slowly but dramatically, the sky an ever-deepening shade of violet. The sun kissed the horizon, looking as if it could be doused by the ocean, but miraculously, it slowly sank as it turned a brilliant shade of orange, aflame the entire way.

Suddenly, Stuart pointed to the east, telling everyone to look. The remaining light seemed to reflect off of something. Everyone turned to look, but there was nothing apparent.

After the initial excitement, they gave up trying to spot whatever Stuart had seen, choosing to go back to gazing down or a few feet around the raft. Occasionally, tiny fish jumped at the surface, their silvery forms reflecting the moonlight. Overall, though, open water surrounded them, with little marine life.

There was nothing except deeply darkened water for as far as the eye could see. The sounds of marine life and the waves took on a menacing quality. Unable to see what might approach, their active minds envisioned another rogue wave or a huge sea monster overturning the raft, sending all of them deep into the ocean on a permanent journey to the bottom.

The men gradually dozed off, but sleep was difficult to impossible.

Jack was the last to fall asleep. He worried about being hit by a shipping container. There was nothing they could do to prevent it, so there was no point in having a lookout. Though the sky was filled with stars, the water was black as ink, inhibiting them from being able to spot any kind of floating object.

Jack gazed upward at the heavens, sending a silent prayer for their safety. He lowered his eyelids, forcing himself to breathe deeply. He focused on his breathing, gradually putting himself into a light sleep.

CHAPTER THREE

Jack squinted and scanned the water, slowly, utilizing a grid approach. The default for looking around the environment to identify an object was rapid eye scanning, but that was the least effective way. Jack took one section of water at a time and zeroed in, searching for any visual sign of something other than water. He was patient. Besides, there wasn't anything else to do to pass the time, and it was mission-critical that they find the ditch bag.

Time crawled by, and still, Jack scanned. There were no clouds, only blue sky, and the unrelenting tropical sun. Though they were sheltered, the water's reflection of the light and heat had begun to affect them. The atmosphere was crisp, providing an astonishingly clear visual field, but with nothing to focus on, it was difficult to maintain the effort. Eyestrain and fatigue set in. Jack shook his head to make himself more alert.

Tony lightly dozed, curled up on the bottom of the raft, oblivious to the small puddles of water that now soaked most of his tee-shirt and shorts. Ben and Stuart leaned back, eyes closed, but did not appear to be sleeping.

There! Jack saw something, and it appeared to float on top of the water. He sat up and squinted, confirming it wasn't just an illusion.

Jack handed the two paddles that had been tucked into the life raft to Ben and Stuart. "I see something over there," he told them, pointing. He gave instructions on how to paddle and steer the raft. Slowly they made their way in the direction of the object in the water. As they got closer, they saw it was one of the 5-gallon jugs of water from the boat.

Finally, they were close enough to reach the jug. Stuart reached out and grabbed the plastic handle, but before he could haul it in, Jack stopped him.

"We don't need the displacement of mass in the boat, plus it doesn't need to be in here anyway." He passed over a small line which Stuart threaded through the handle of the jug. They pulled it tight against the boat and tied it down. The top was upright now, and they took it off, awkwardly pulling the bottle upward for each to take a drink of water.

Jack told them to conserve, so they drank as little as possible. Tony defiantly took a long drink. No one said anything directly, but Stuart said, "asshole," only partly under his breath.

THURSDAY AFTERNOON

The sun had been up for some time, and it was getting harder to float along with nothing to do. They spent some time searching around visually, hoping to spot the ditch bag. They sipped the water carefully, everyone fearful of running out.

Who would have ever imagined that a simple fishing trip would take Ben to this place and circumstance? He thought about his children, wondering if he would ever see them again.

Ben's daughter, Katie, giggled, teasing her little brother Jordan as usual. Her golden curls bounced, and he ran his hand quickly through them as he picked her up. She loved going "Up high, Dad!"

so he hoisted her up, even though she was getting a little big to be carried.

Katie sat high on his shoulders, a pretend princess, as she commanded him to go first this way and then that, tugging his hair like the reins on a horse. He complied but complained loudly that she was too heavy, grimacing with each hair tug as if in intense pain, all of which caused her to grin and laugh. She kicked her heels into his chest, and he pretended to be severely injured. Finally, he pulled her off his shoulders, spun her around, and they fell to the floor, breathless. Katie giggled uncontrollably, and Ben had a smile that wouldn't stop.

Jordan ran over and threw himself across the two of them, laughing while Katie tried to shove him off.

Katie said, "Again, Daddy!" He rolled his eyes, turned to look at her, and said, "It's time for Dad to make dinner." She started to whine, and he said in a stage voice, "Get used to disappointment, kid." She repeated it after him, mimicking him. The words in her tiny girl voice sounded so silly that he laughed out loud. She said it again and again, following him into the kitchen.

Ben snapped back to the present, realizing that he'd flashed back to a time before the divorce. That was the way it had been, in happier times.

Lately, when he spent time with the kids, he was subdued, unable to connect with them the way he once had. He took them out for a Happy Meal and then home to his cramped and gloomy apartment. He turned on the television and parked them in front of it while he sipped from a glass of whiskey. And then another.

They, too, were subdued, uncomfortable in his apartment. It wasn't a home to them since he hadn't made it a home. He'd purchased a set of twin beds and put them in the second bedroom. But their toys and games were in the home that he'd once shared with his wife. Ex-wife now. He couldn't bring himself to make this apartment into a kid-friendly place, to stock up the toys and games, to put cartoon character themed sheets on their beds.

Deep down, he continued to fantasize that this was temporary, that Michelle would forgive him, and they would resume their life together. He would move home, never needing to make a home in his dingy apartment for the kids.

Stupid fantasy, never going to happen, he thought harshly. Michelle will never forgive me.

His children were not the same. The divorce had introduced them to the painful realities of an imperfect life at an early age. They had experienced betrayal, anger, sadness, and loneliness through the eyes of their parents. They were too young to understand any of it, unable to process the swirling sea of emotions in which they were forced to swim. They had no words for this experience.

Katie didn't laugh the way she used to. She no longer teased her little brother. They played together and seemed to converse in a secret childhood language that only they understood.

The one good thing was that they seemed closer as siblings.

Of course, they were, Ben thought. They shared two common enemies, their emotionally withdrawn Mom and Dad, neither of whom had the presence of mind as parents they once did. As much as Katie and Jordan were loved, they were no longer living in the same loving environment as before, and no one was doing anything to fix it.

Ben felt a deep sadness well up in his chest, threatening to spill over. A darkness and emptiness that felt as bottomless as the ocean on which he now floated aimlessly. He swallowed rapidly and breathed through his nose, willing it to go back down. Gradually, it did, but he was exhausted from the effort. He turned in on himself and withdrew from the others even more.

Stuart sat quietly, but the buzzing inside his head was almost deafening. He heard it in his ears, though the only real sound was that of the waves lapping against the sides of the life raft. Filled with adrenaline, his system was too much on high alert to doze off and take a nap like Tony, who couldn't seem to stay awake.

Stuart slid his eyes over and saw Tony's head tilted back against the side of the raft, mouth open, with a slight snore. Sheesh, what a pain in the ass that guy was. Awake, he drove them crazy with his senseless and never-ending complaints. Even asleep, he was irritating and annoying.

Stuart slid his eyes back to the unending monotony of the view of the water. What he wouldn't give for an ice-cold beer right now. Or two, or three.

He indulged in a little fantasy of life back on dry land. He was out cruising around on foot, looking for a great place to sit and drink, take in a game. That was his modus operandi—go out on foot. That way, he never needed to share a ride after thoroughly enjoying himself.

He saw himself arrive at his favorite spot—Touchdown—the sports bar just a few blocks from his condo. He pictured the dark leather booths, the embossed ceiling, the giant flat-screen HD TVs all around. The largest was a full 16 diagonal feet—perfect for watching the game. His mouth watered as he thought about his favorite—BBQ brisket sandwich and a giant margarita. Oh, man. He allowed himself to slide further into the memory of one of his evenings at his favorite watering hole.

Samantha, Stuart's favorite hostess, sashayed over and stood in front of him, putting one hand on her hip. "Well?"

He laughed. "Is that the way you greet all your customers?"

"Customer? Oh, right! I thought you were my permanent guest."
Her eyes sparkled as she raised one eyebrow. In her mid-twenties,

Samantha seemed way too smart to be working at a place like this but excused it with the story that she was in the "performing arts," taking local theater gigs and doing radio voice-over work, aspiring for more. She took classes in theater arts at a local college as well.

"The usual?" she asked, to which he nodded. He handed her a folded napkin. She unfolded it, gasped at what she saw, and wadded it up, throwing it on the table.

"I'm going to report you to management," she announced. He grinned, she sashayed away, and thus their ritual began. He looked forward to it, relishing the pinging of their sexual energy. Samantha was pretty in a girl-next-door kind of way, with streaked dark blond curls, full lips, wide eyes that made her appear a bit naïve. But she was smart and perceptive, and completely had his number.

Stuart figured he'd known Samantha for four or five years, and he'd been attracted to her the entire time. Oddly, he'd never once asked her out or pursued any kind of relationship outside of the bar. He'd listened as she occasionally complained about a current boyfriend. One of them had lasted for over three years. He'd complained about his baffling short-term relationships with various women.

But she remained single, and so did he. They talked and flirted, and that was it. It was a friendship without benefits, an emotionally intimate relationship that took place solely within the walls of a neighborhood sports bar. Instinctively, Stuart knew that if he tried to date Samantha, he'd likely blow it and lose his one sounding board, the one person with whom he could be candid.

Stuart took a deep breath, feeling better as he envisioned her the last time, just before going on the fishing trip.

It was the end of the evening, after almost everyone had gone when she crossed the room and flopped down across from him. She looked exhausted, her eyes slightly bloodshot with a smudge of darkness underneath, her shoulders a bit down. She took off one shoe, rubbed her foot, and stared at him. "Well? Have you thought about what I said last night?"

He sighed. "Nope." *Not looking at her.*

"Really? Why don't I think you're being straight with me?"

He didn't answer.

"It's time, Stuart. You've been sitting here feeling sorry for yourself for as long as I've worked here—what is it, like, five years now? Meanwhile, life is moving on, but you are not. Where is she now? How much longer do you have before it's too late? Before she finds someone else?"

He was silent, taking one last sip of his fourth giant margarita.

She reached across the table and placed her hand on his, and that sent a tingle up his spine. "Stuart."

"What?" *he said sarcastically.* "Isn't this the pot calling the kettle black? Your personal life isn't exactly going anywhere, is it?"

Stung, she pulled her hand away, put her shoe back on, and stood abruptly. She stalked away, but the great thing was, he knew he'd see her again tomorrow night at the beginning of her shift. And at the end of her shift, they'd have the same conversation, or rather, version three of the same conversation.

The conversation cycled between three: One, move on and find someone new. Two, find Jillian and try to make up, or three, go ahead and drown your sorrows, idiot.

It didn't matter which version because the bottom line was the same conversation—Stuart, you are a wreck, and you need to be fixed.

Samantha thought she could fix him. Good luck with that.

❦

Stuart relished the memory, most of it. But he kept his eyes closed and saw a scene he didn't want to revisit.

❦

Stuart climbed out of the car while the driver sped off, clearly glad to be rid of him. He walked unsteadily to the front door and fumbled with the keys, dropping them. A loud burp issued forth, and at that moment, he thought he was going to relieve his stomach of its contents right on the front lawn. He bent over to retrieve the keys, straightening abruptly, and hitting his head on the doorknob. "Shit!" he yelled. Why was it so hard to get into the house?

But he got in, somehow managed to lock the front door, and crept toward the guest bedroom. He pulled off his shoes and threw himself on the bed without getting undressed. If he got lucky, she wouldn't know he was there, and he could avoid a confrontation. But his hand flung itself outward clumsily, and the bedside lamp crashed to the floor. Oh, shit.

He heard her run to the front door, so he called out, "In here." She stood in the doorway, taking in the sorry sight of him.

"Where have you been?" her voice was soft and a bit sad.

"Out."

She breathed in deeply, exhaled. "Well, I'm glad you're okay." She turned, padding away to their bedroom. He tried to summon the energy to go after her, to explain his behavior, but he felt that energy drain quickly away. He rolled over. The next thing he knew, her hand gently shook his shoulder.

"Stuart, wake up. We need to talk."

He opened his eyes to a manageable slit and tried to sit up. His head fell off and rolled away somewhere under the bed in agony. He didn't care.

He cracked his bloodshot eyes open and got a glimpse of his beloved. She was fully dressed, all tumbled red curls, sad green eyes, and slender, straight back. Jillian was a former dancer, so one of the first things he'd fallen in love with was her beautiful posture. He wasn't sure it was the highest of compliments to a woman, but when he'd told her on their third date that her straight back turned him on, she'd seemed utterly smitten.

He rolled over the other way. "I'm tired, Jillian. Let's talk later."

Without touching him again, she softly said, "We have to talk now because I'm not sure there will be a later."

He rolled back over and sat up quickly, head throbbing.

"What are you talking about?"

Her eyes shimmered with the beginning of tears. "I'm leaving, Stuart."

He reached out to wrap his arms around her, but she gently pushed him away. "No, just listen to me for a few minutes."

"Look, I know you have every reason to be mad, and I'm sorry. I shouldn't have gone out last night like that." He couldn't keep the hollow sound of the partial truth out of his voice. He was not sorry. He felt justified.

"It wasn't just any night, Stuart. It was our engagement party, during which you made sure that you drank a full glass of champagne for every toast and for every pause in between toasts, and then more. Do you remember telling my family and our friends that you couldn't wait to donate the sperm that would enable your crappy family line to continue?"

Embarrassment washed over him. Sadly, he'd been unable to erase the memory of that unfortunate comment, despite the heavy libations he'd enjoyed later.

"And, while we're on the subject, do you remember telling Ashley's boyfriend—boyfriend to my best friend in the world—to make sure he puts it in their prenuptial how many babies he is willing or not willing to produce? Why on earth would you say something like that?"

She looked down, then held out her hand as he started to speak. "No, I don't really want to hear anything—it was a rhetorical question."

The conversation was surreal. Jillian was typically soft-spoken and leaned far away from confrontation. But he felt a surge of indignation.

"Okay, look. I know I was a jerk last night. But you're the one that has been pushing so hard about starting a family, and we're not even married yet! Do you know how that makes me feel, knowing that your biggest priority is making a baby—forget about all the things we used to say we would do. Whatever happened to traveling the world for a few years as happy-go-lucky DINKS?"

They used to brag about it—"Dual Income, No Kids"—how fun their married life was going to be and to heck with reproducing. That was something people mainly did to please their parents and to stave off the fear of loneliness in old age. They were contemptuous of their friends who married and couldn't seem to conceive fast enough.

Or were they contemptuous? Was it only him?

Hungover and pathetic, he found no need to filter his thoughts and feelings.

"I find it fascinating how all this talk about babies started the minute I put that engagement ring on your finger."

Her face turned white with shock.

He felt even shittier about himself, but he didn't stop. He was on a roll now. "I thought it was enough for you to marry me, but I guess not."

"It was," she whispered. "It always was way more than enough."

Tears rolled down her beautiful face, but he felt cold as ice inside.

"Really? Well, just tell me one thing, Jillian. If I said I didn't want kids, would you stay with me? Would I really be enough? Would you still want to get married to me?"

Now she openly sobbed, wiping away the tears. She slowly looked up at him as if he were a stranger. She stood shakily and turned to the dresser. She slowly slipped off her engagement ring and put it down carefully, then left the room.

"I guess I have my answer," he called out as harshly as he could, putting the last nail in the coffin of their misguided relationship. But there was no one to hear or validate the nastiness in which he'd been swimming for weeks. He heard the front door open and close gently. He picked up the broken lamp on the floor beside the bed and threw it as hard as he could, feeling satisfied at the loud shattering sounds. She was gone.

It had been years since he and Jillian had broken up, disappointing her parents and extended family members, not to mention friends. Everyone loved Jillian. Everyone saw a brilliant future for them.

Everyone but her, apparently.

One unfortunate night, and one fight, and she was out of there at the speed of light. So much for true love. So much for commitment. Good thing he'd found out about her before they got married.

"Women leave." His father said, repeatedly, after Stuart's Mom left when he was nine. She'd been gone for weeks before she called one day. He knew it was her because his father, after answering the phone, went red in the face and began shouting. "What the fuck do you want, Rebecca? You left, remember?" He paused, briefly listening. "So, fucking what? He doesn't want to talk to you. He doesn't have a Mom anymore!" He slammed down the phone, cursing out loud.

Stuart shook as he listened to his father's rage.

Stuart's father had never hit him before in his life, but something had changed since his Mom had left. He felt afraid of his father.

He had no idea what might happen, but it seemed like it could be something bad.

He ran to his room, grabbed his favorite stuffed toy, and clambered under his bed. He pushed himself as far underneath as he could get, with his back against the wall. He clutched Simon the giraffe and silently sobbed. He didn't mind the dust bunnies.

With his Mom gone, the house was falling apart.

Later, his father stumbled down the hallway calling his name. "Stu? Where are you, son?" His voice was weird and scary. Stuart stayed quiet as a mouse.

"Stuart, come out here, son." Then when he got no answer, he raised his voice. "Get out here, Stuart, now!" He slammed open the door to Stuart's room. He looked in the closet and yelled Stuart's name.

Stuart shrank against the wall as hard as he could.

His father stumbled back down the hall muttering to himself. "That little shit. I can't believe he's acting like this. I'm gonna tan his hide when I find him."

Stuart heard ice cubes plinking into a glass. He heard his father turn on the television and tune in to a loud sports channel.

Hours later, Stuart's stomach growled. But he stayed under the bed. No point in coming out anyway. They hadn't had real food in days. His father never seemed to need to eat, and when Stuart complained about being hungry, he pointed at the pantry and told him to get his own dinner. But there wasn't anything in the pantry except a stale half loaf of bread and a jar with some peanut butter in it. Stuart had managed to make a couple of sandwiches, but now that was gone.

Out of sheer exhaustion, Stuart's eyes gradually closed, and he fell asleep. The next morning, he crawled out from under the bed and crept into the living room.

His father slept in his easy chair, head lolling to the side, snoring. Empty glasses sat on the coffee table alongside tall bottles, which Stuart knew had contained booze, a substance that smelled awful. There was one shorter glass filled with cigarette ashes and butts, and the room reeked of stale smoke. His father had never smoked before.

He stirred, opened his eyes, and saw Stuart, who quickly shrank away.

"Hey buddy, what are you doing?" his father asked, in his normal voice, although a bit gravelly. Stuart was quiet. His father pulled the chair upright and looked around the room as if he didn't recognize the place. Stuart turned and ran back down the hall, but he was afraid to go under the bed again. That was now his secret place, and he didn't want to give it away. He crawled on top of the bed and put his back to the wall, shaking.

Stuart's father came down the hall and into his room. When he saw Stuart shrink away from him on the bed, he held up his hands and stepped back.

"Whoa, son, it's okay. Nothing's going to happen. I'm not mad at you."

Stuart burst into tears. His father approached slowly and sat on the bed, putting his head in his hands. Soon, they were both crying.

Later, they cleaned up the house together and went shopping. There was food in the house, and his father made a genuine effort at keeping things cleaner. But it didn't last.

Stuart learned to tread carefully on the weekends. That was when his father drank heavily and became dangerous. Stuart learned to find hiding places well in advance so that he could move from one to the other.

Sometimes his father found him, and those were the worst nights of all. He wasn't violent, not physically, but he had way with words, and tone of voice, so that Stuart felt targeted, trapped, and emotionally beaten.

Mostly, Stuart spent the night crouched, hidden, and hungry. Eventually, he learned how to go outside of the house and find peace and quiet in the yard, or even in a neighbor's yard. They lived in Houston, Texas, so the weather was mostly mild.

When it wasn't, he hid in the shed behind the lawnmower, making a bed of sorts out of an old blanket. Many years later, Stuart told Jillian in a dark moment that he would have never survived childhood had they lived in the snow belt. He would rather have frozen to death than stay in the house when his father drank.

Later, there was always remorse, but after a few times of that, Stuart didn't believe his father anymore.

At times, Stuart wondered where his Mom had gone. Where was she living? What was she doing? He wondered why she didn't call, why she didn't come back for him.

She never did come back, and she never called again, but after Stuart left home, he searched for her. He went to every one of his mother's relatives and asked for information. But no one knew, or maybe they didn't want to tell him. Most said that she had moved away and not stayed in touch, and he finally gave up the search after months of trying.

Then one day, he got an email out of the blue. The sender claimed to be a friend of his Mom's.

Dear Stuart: I am a friend of your mother's, and I heard from her family last week. They said you have been looking for her. Please contact me, I have information about her.

Ann Bushton

He emailed her immediately, she gave him a number, and he called and introduced himself.

"Thanks for emailing me. So, you knew my Mom?"

"Yes, I did. We were close friends for many years, but when she moved away, she chose not to tell me where she was. It wasn't until recently that I heard news about her. I'm so sorry to tell you this, Stuart, but your Mom died not long ago."

Stuart's heart dropped. He couldn't believe that after all those years, and all the efforts to find her, his Mom was gone. Tears welled up in his eyes, and he coughed to cover the grief.

"I'm sorry," said Ann softly.

Stuart cleared his throat and managed to croak out, "What happened?"

"It's a long story. Are you sure you want to talk about this over the phone?"

No, he wasn't sure at all. After finding out that Ann lived in the area, they made plans to meet over the weekend at her home.

He met her at her house—a small 1950s era ranch house. It was clean and neat, with a tidy living room that featured a small sofa with an old-fashioned coffee table and two overstuffed chairs. Next to the sofa was a basket with knitting materials and a couple of well-worn books. Ann brought him a glass of iced tea. There was a box sitting on the table, the cardboard worn and faded, packing tape barely holding the sides together.

After a little small talk, Stuart blurted, "Please, tell me about my Mom. What happened to her—how did she die?"

"She died of cancer, apparently after a long battle. It was originally breast cancer, after which she went into remission. But later, it came back, and it had metastasized. I went to see her a couple of

weeks before she died, and I spoke with her, um, partner, right after. She died peacefully in her home."

"Which was where? Where was her home?"

"She lived in Santa Fe, New Mexico."

Santa Fe? Why Santa Fe? Did he hear her right? Did she say "partner"?

"What can you tell me about her? Who is her husband? I want to know about my Mom, about her life."

Ann looked uncomfortable. She appeared to be weighing her options.

"Look, Ann, I don't care much about what you're thinking. I care about knowing about my Mom. There's nothing you can tell me that will hurt more than the fact that she left me when I was eight, and I never saw her again. Please, tell me."

She looked up and seemed to register the seriousness of his demand, along with the simmering anger under the surface.

"Of course. I'm sorry. It's just that it's a lot to cover, and it's not all good." But finally, she talked.

"Rebecca contacted me while she was dying of cancer. She wanted me to tell you this if you ever came around looking for her.

"Stuart, your mother had a hard life. She grew up in difficult circumstances and left home when she was too young to be on her own. She met your father immediately, and he was a lifeline to her. They got pregnant with you and married quickly." She paused.

"Your mother loved you, Stuart. You were everything to her, despite whatever you may have heard." She looked steadily at Stuart, who looked down, flooded with emotion.

"Rebecca left your father for many reasons, but the main one is that she was lesbian, and she couldn't continue to live a lie. She planned to come back for you, but when she contacted your father, he threatened her. He told her that he had hired an attorney who assured him that because of her sexual orientation, custody was out of the question. She could forget any kind of visitation—that if he had anything to do with it, she would never set eyes on you again. He also told her that you were refusing to see her, that you didn't want anything to do with her."

Stuart was shocked. None of this made sense. Why would his father do that to him? Sure, people were still prejudiced against gay people in the 1980s when Stuart was growing up, especially in the south. But that was no excuse for his Dad keeping him away from his Mom. Or for her staying away from him.

"Your mother was not an emotionally strong person. She didn't know how to combat the force of your father's strong will and anger. She was afraid of putting you through the stress of a contentious custody fight, and she was afraid of doing that only to find out that you didn't love her anymore. She was terrified that she had hurt you so deeply that you could never forgive her, that you wouldn't understand her lifestyle."

"Stuart, she never stopped loving you, despite how all of this sounds. She followed your life through the extended family, and she collected photographs of you. When social media came around, she followed you online as well. She loved you with all her heart."

She loved him. With all her heart? Stuart was stunned. What kind of love was that? What kind of woman abandons her only child and gives up on him?

Ann gazed at him sorrowfully.

"I'm sorry to have to say these things about your father, Stuart, but

I didn't know how to tell you about your mother without doing so. I hope you can try to understand who she was, and her love for you. I hope this somehow helps you with getting some closure."

She stopped talking and began putting photos in his hands. Pictures of his Mom, looking much older than the few photos he'd seen growing up, or his memories of her, standing with her arms around another woman. Photos of them on vacation, with swimming pools and oceans and exotic plants in the background. Smiling, relaxed, happy.

Whatever Stuart had thought about his Mom, this wasn't it.

She was dead. His Mom, whom he'd fantasized about seeing again someday, was dead. And she had been alive most of the time, could have found him, could have seen him before she died. But she hadn't.

She hadn't the entire time he was growing up with his alcoholic, abusive father. She'd preferred instead to live her own happy life, ignoring the fact that she'd had a child.

She hadn't contacted him after he left home, when clearly, he wasn't a child anymore, and there wasn't going to be a custody battle. She'd stayed away, preferring to leave him wondering for his whole life.

What kind of a woman does that? Who leaves their own child? Who stays away the rest of her life, and leaves only a message for him through a stranger?

After meeting with Ann, Stuart had stumbled out of her house in shock, still clutching the box of photos of his Mom. He'd driven home in a daze and set the box down just inside the door. Later, he'd taken everything out of the box, put all of it in the fireplace, and watched it go up in flames while the tears streaked down his face. After that, he never spoke of his mother again, except to cover up the pain with a lie.

He'd told Jillian that his mother had died when he was too young to remember her, that his father had raised him. His drunk, obnoxious, worthless father. He'd neglected to fill in the details about his mother, that she'd left him—and a permanent hole in his heart—in her wake. He'd neglected to tell Jillian a lot of things about himself. He'd never allowed himself to open up that much.

Stuart's insides recoiled with the memories of Jillian and his parents.

Elsewhere in the raft, Tony stirred, yawned, and looked at Paul, who was watching him. Belligerently, he said, "*What?*"

Paul looked away.

"Yeah, old man, quit staring at me. You're giving me the creeps," said Tony, spitting off the side of the raft contemptuously.

Stuart reached across, grabbed Tony by the shirt and yanked him forward until his face was inches away.

"If you say one more derogatory thing to anyone, I am going to put you in the deep waters of the ocean. Do you understand?"

Tony's eyes went wide, his face suddenly drained of color. He nodded.

Stuart shoved him roughly away. Jack and Ben looked at the water, avoiding eye contact with Tony.

Tony shrugged, acting like nothing had happened, but his face flushed crimson.

It was another long day on the water. The tension was palpable, but as time and the sun passed relentlessly, it dissipated, requiring too much energy. Exhausted, they took turns as lookout, or curled up with eyes closed in an attempt to rest.

That night, they all slept fitfully, though perhaps with a bit less anxiety than the previous night. After all, no other waves had appeared, and what were the odds of another when the first was such a rare phenomenon?

CHAPTER FOUR

FRIDAY AFTERNOON

The ocean gently rocked the tiny raft, water sloshing against the sides in an endless rhythm. Cotton ball clouds lingered, moving so slowly that it appeared they were painted in place against the deep blue backdrop of the sky. There were few of them, so that the sun's rays bore down on them. Despite the flap of shade above them, it was still uncomfortable.

They still had water, but they all wondered how much longer it would last.

Hunger had set in by now. There wasn't any point in complaining about it, so the men held their silence. Except for Tony.

"Shit, man. Why doesn't a life raft have stuff on it to keep you alive? Where are the energy bars? This totally sucks," he complained.

"Where the hell are we? And where are the rescue ships? I thought when you sent out a mayday signal—you did that, right, Jack? I thought that brought the U.S. Fucking Coast Guard to get you! So, where's the cavalry? Huh?" he continued railing.

No one responded, but they were all thinking the same thing.

Tony's obnoxious comments were adding an unnecessary layer of unpleasantness on top of their tenuous situation.

Jack scanned the horizon again, looking for more than one sign. They were drifting in a southwesterly direction, following the Pacific Ocean currents. That meant they were moving further and further away from the California coast. There was nothing west of them but open ocean, which would take weeks, months, to traverse as they drifted.

It was hot, much hotter than the day before. They were well past the cool, mild waters off Southern California and into the warmer waters further south.

The sun was unrelenting. They stayed well under the tent, but there was no way to avoid the sun. The space was so tight that, depending on the angle of the sun, someone was always exposed. They were all deep red.

Tony's intake of water had been restricted. Each time they took a turn, he would guzzle as fast as he could, taking more than his share. The second time he tried to take more than his share, Stuart pulled the water away roughly. Tony looked angry, like a petulant child, but didn't fight back. They rationed his water after that.

Paul looked red but also unwell. Jack had forced Paul to take in a couple more swallows of water than the rest of them, which earned him a contemptuous look from Tony.

Jack was concerned about the state of mind of the men. They couldn't afford to waste precious energy fighting, let alone endangering one another if things between Stuart and Tony took a bad turn.

If they didn't cross paths with a container ship soon, they faced far greater challenges. Eventually, their meager supply of water would run out. Food was already an issue, but they could survive a long time without food. Once the water ran out, their deaths would be agonizing but not swift enough. Dehydration and heat exhaustion were terrible ways to die.

He looked for any sign of a container ship. Wait a minute, what was that?

Jack sat up straighter and stared at the horizon. Was it a ship? Even if it was, what could he do? He had no flares—those were in the ditch bag. They did have paddles, but they would never be able to paddle fast enough to reach the faraway ship.

Still, they must try. He told Paul and Ben to begin paddling in the direction of whatever the object was on the horizon. Fortunately, it was in the same path that they were drifting, following the ocean current.

After what seemed like hours, the object on the horizon grew larger. It wasn't a container ship or any kind of ship. It was clearly an island. Disappointment surged in the men, followed by hope as Jack explained what that meant to their survival.

Stuart and Ben pulled as hard as they could, and when they approached exhaustion, Jack took over for Stuart while Ben surrendered an oar to Tony. They changed places periodically so that three men were always at rest. Paul offered to row, but Jack wouldn't let him. He looked embarrassed about not doing his part, but he was still obviously too weak.

The island grew larger, and as it did, the water grew choppier. Finally, they closed in on their target.

It was small, or so it appeared from the raft. It jutted up steeply, with low vegetation carpeting the peaks. There was almost no beach. Most of the island was surrounded by steep cliffs, the surf breaking directly against the base of them. There was a stretch of beach with a small cove, and they steered the raft in that direction, hoping to make landfall there.

The waves were higher now, and the raft rolled up one swell and down the other. They paddled furiously, trying to maintain control.

Tony looked frightened, and soon he was shouting. "We can't do it! The waves are going to knock us over! We have to go back out!"

"We have to get to the island, so we can shelter until rescue arrives," yelled Jack, trying to be heard over the sound of the crashing waves. "Just keep pulling for that beach!"

Tony threw down his paddle, and Stuart took it over, paddling alongside Jack.

If they didn't make it all the way to the beach, they stood a good chance of floundering at some point in the cove, possibly hitting rocks or razor-sharp coral and losing the raft. Jack urged them forward.

"We can do this—just keep aiming for that beach!"

Suddenly, they felt a bump under the raft. Rocks, or coral. Miraculously, the raft appeared to remain intact.

They slowed their paddling, conserving strength. They let the wave break carry them closer to shore. Clear blue water surrounded them, visibility far below the raft. They could see fish—lots of them—swimming far below. Paul pointed grinning.

Dolphins! Five bottlenose dolphins approached, swimming in circles around the raft, peering at them with curiosity. One of the dolphins blew water from its spout. Another leaped high in the air, splashing down playfully.

They picked up speed, paddling swiftly toward the island. The dolphins swam with them as if guiding them to shore.

As they approached, Jack noted the volcanic peak, the dominant feature of the island. High but relatively flat on top, the peak appeared to be covered with scrub.

The waves lifted higher, tossing them around like a toy boat in a child's bathtub. High waves appear beautiful and magical when viewed from the shore or in photos. Surfers glide up, hang at impossible positions in the air, then glide ferociously down the other side of the waves. It is all fun, all beautiful. But it is an illusion.

Waves gather energy and weight and turn monstrous in real life. The power of water in motion is far more dangerous than most people realize. Against such power, even the strongest of men are helpless.

The closer they got to the island, the higher and choppier the waves. It was touch and go. Jack didn't know if they would make it to the island all in one piece or be tossed about and forced to swim.

Jack's muscles strained with the effort to paddle and control the boat. He glanced at Stuart, his face tight with fierce determination. He was the kind of guy who never gave up.

Tony clutched the sides of the boat, shaking his head and muttering.

Paul looked green.

Ben alternately spelled Jack and Stuart with paddling. As hard as they worked, the island seemed to pull further away in a maddening illusion that it was in motion while their boat stood still.

"Listen up," yelled Jack. "As we get closer, we may need to get out of the boat at some point and pull it with us. We may have to swim in. Paul, you stay in the boat and we will pull it ashore." He started to protest, but Jack quickly silenced him.

"If you get in the water and start to have a problem, it will be much harder for us to help you. All of us will do better if you stay in the boat." Paul nodded unhappily.

It seemed to take forever, but finally, they made headway. Jack aimed for the small cove as they got closer to the island.

Another thump under the raft threatened to upend their precarious position. This time, they heard the clear sound of something ripping, of air escaping. One of the main sections of the raft began to rapidly deflate. Their journey to the island had just become far more dangerous. They couldn't afford to get another tear.

Without the raft, they would be forced to swim through the crashing waves that led to the cove. But if they could make it into the cove, they would be able to make it to the island.

But with another bump, and another section rapidly deflating, Jack knew their time in the raft was coming to an end. They had very little time to make a move, and no matter the move, it would be extremely dangerous.

"Everyone, it's time to abandon the raft," Jack told the men. "If we stay in, it will sink, and we could get tangled up in the tent and drown."

"Shit, shit!" yelled Tony. "We'll never make it!" He had a desperate look in his eyes as he clung to the sides of the disintegrating raft. Stuart shot him a contemptuous look. Paul looked resigned.

But even Tony saw the inevitability of their next steps.

The men clambered out of the openings of the tent and slid over the sides into the water. Everyone sat like bobbers, riding the dangerous waves up and down, up and down. The raft began slowly sinking, and they let go of the sides.

"Swim!" shouted Jack. "Watch out for the reef." He swam beside the men, encouraging each of them to keep going. Tony flailed, swimming too hard and getting out of breath. Stuart swam easily, his powerful arms making huge strokes. He'd done a fair amount of competitive swimming in his college days. Ben swam more slowly but steadily.

Paul looked strained, struggling to keep up. Stuart, seeing that Paul was quickly losing strength, circled back to him. At one point, he put Paul's arms around his neck and swam for the two of them. It was slower going, and they fell behind the others, but still made progress.

The water was rougher as they entered the outer edges of the island cove. They were further apart now, each man struggling to continue forward.

As they neared the shore, the ocean bottom suddenly rose to meet them. They encountered a shelf of some kind, sharp under their feet.

"Stay up high on the waves, away from the reef," Jack shouted at them. They all endeavored to swim over the reef that bordered the lagoon ahead. Dangerously sharp coral stretched upward, threatening severe injury. Finally, they were past the reef and in the lagoon.

They swam slowly, the waves more subdued here, with their feet tripping against the rough bottom. Their progress, though slow, took them gradually to the shore.

Now they were close enough to stand in the shallow surf. One by one, they clambered out of the surf and trudged slowly onto the beach. Unlike the tourist-friendly beaches of the Caribbean, this one was filled with rocks. The sand was coarse, embedded with millions of fragments of seashells pounded over tens of millions of years, but not enough to render them into the smooth, silken sand of the beaches in popular tourist areas.

Ben limped to shore behind Jack and Tony. Somehow, he'd lost his shoes, probably because they were slip-on, no ties. Looking down, he could see the trail of blood that he left behind, his feet scraped in multiple places.

Paul and Stuart were the last to make it onto land, Paul's arm draped over Stuart's neck, legs stumbling. Paul sat as soon as he could, breathing heavily with his head down.

The beach was small, maybe sixty yards wide and forty yards deep. Vegetation-covered cliffs thrust upward, so steep it would be almost impossible to scale them.

While the others rested, Jack took stock of their situation. As they'd approached the island, he'd tried to determine the size of the island, but the cliffs inhibited the view. From where he stood, the beach was visible for only a short distance, its curvature taking it quickly out of view. He stood and walked, following it as far as he could in each direction. It didn't take long to walk the small beach and find the end of it.

The volcanic mountain was fronted by a dense area of vegetation and palm trees, stretching in both directions to a point of connection with the small beach. Beyond the trees, the cliffs afforded no breaks, no diminishment, no opportunity to go over them. They were stuck in this cove—cerulean waters, rocky beach, tangled vegetation, and a few trees. There was some shade afforded by the mountain and small copse of trees, but little opportunity for shelter.

And that wasn't the worst of their problems. Without fresh water, and Jack could see no immediate source for that, they would not fare well.

They needed to search for sources for food. They also needed fire, both for cooking and to warm them on cool nights. But he made the decision to wait until the next morning before rallying the men to go to work on their survival issues. With night swiftly falling, it was too dangerous to explore, even for water. He hoped to solve that problem quickly the next morning before dehydration set in.

Tony surveyed their predicament. "Man, I knew we should have stayed out at sea. At least we had a raft and some water. We could have spotted a ship, gotten help. Now we're stuck on this godforsaken piece of shit island with nothing!" He shot a challenging look at Jack, who ignored him.

No one else bothered to reply either.

The sun dipped slowly toward the horizon, turning orange, then blood red, dropping into the water far away. They watched as it gradually disappeared until only a sliver remained. Then, that too, was gone. Deep blue twilight ensued.

The light abandoned the sky, and the stars began to appear. It was a breathtaking sight. Trillions of miles away, in the vast cosmos, billions of orbs cast out unbelievable amounts of brilliant energy eons ago, energy that only now reached this planet called Earth, in the form of vast numbers of twinkling lights that illuminated the beach where they lay.

Sea birds gradually ceased their calls, putting themselves to bed for the night. The ocean gently washed the shore, a repetitive sound that soothed them, despite their desperate circumstances.

One by one, the men fell asleep, cradling their heads on their arms, bodies curled against the cooler night air. Jack remained awake far into the night, thinking and wondering. At last, even he drifted off.

Soft light against his eyelids wakened Jack, and for a moment, he was disoriented. Then he realized where he was and opened his eyes. It was early morning, the sun not yet above the horizon, a few stars still visible. Warm pink near the horizon pushed slowly upward against the deep blue of the night sky. Stars slowly faded. It was deceptively beautiful and peaceful—a tropical island paradise at dawn's early light. He allowed himself a few moments to savor the exquisite view.

But they were not in some idyllic vacation spot, heading for a large breakfast buffet with the other tourists. They were marooned on an island with no immediately discernable food or water source.

Jack rolled his head toward a rustling sound. A sea bird standing oddly close by let out an undulating squawk, followed by a series of rapid clicks of its long beak. The bird shook its white feathers and eyed Jack. A large red circle surrounded the eye, giving it a manic look.

The bird seemed unconcerned about Jack's presence, or that of the other men. Jack eyed it back, thinking about the potential for breakfast. The bird slowly turned and waddled down the beach, pausing to pluck something from the sand, tossing it up in the air, then swallowing it.

Maybe breakfast lay on the beach.

Jack rolled over and saw the men sleeping nearby, arms underneath their heads, legs sprawled.

Raising his head, he inhaled deeply and drew in the familiar scent of the sea. He breathed out slowly, allowing his head to clear.

They were in a difficult situation, but he'd been in harsh environments in the past, with survival uncertain. He knew that staying calm was crucial, especially when others were anything but calm. Survival was rarely a matter of some sweeping Hollywood rescue scenario. Rather, it was the result of carefully thinking through the obstacles and solving the little puzzles along the way. Beginning with the most basic of problems to solve, and the most basic of all was a reliable, safe source of water.

Jack rose and quietly went over to check on Paul. His breathing was so shallow that for a moment, Jack wasn't sure he was still alive. He watched him carefully and saw that his chest slowly rose and fell, but barely.

There was something not right with Paul. Was it the after effect of nearly drowning? Or some other health issue? It was going to be difficult enough keeping them all alive without further complications but keeping someone alive whose health may be compromised—that could be almost impossible.

The men began to stir, rolling over, pushing themselves up to sitting positions, and looking around. Ben looked resigned, Tony looked pissed, but Jack knew it was a veneer to cover his fear. Stuart looked curious.

"Where are we?" asked Stuart, standing and looking around.

"We're on a fucking island—duh," muttered Tony. "We're screwed," he said, his face pinched, eyes narrowed.

Stuart ignored him, looking at Jack.

"I think we're a few hundred miles from the California coast, maybe closer to Mexico than the U.S., somewhere southwest of where we lost the boat," said Jack. "This island is volcanic, and the good news is there is significant vegetation, so that means it either gets a lot of rain, or there is a water source somewhere on the island. Our first mission is to find the source, or to prepare to capture any rain that falls."

"What about food?" Stuart asked Jack. "Seems like we might start with that."

"Actually, water is the most crucial. We can survive maybe three days without it, while we can go for weeks without food. Finding water is mission-critical, and we must do it today. After that, we can forage for food."

Jack continued. "But a word of caution. The vegetation may look edible, but it could be poisonous. A good place to start is to look for any marine life on the beach or in the shallow waters of this cove."

After a few minutes of stretching, the men stood and prepared for the day's activity. Jack sent them off to look for water but asked Paul to remain on the beach with the job of keeping an eye out for any boat detritus, including the remnants of their raft, the ditch bag, or the water jug. Tony grumbled loudly but departed with the other men, veering off by himself.

After everyone left, Jack queried Paul about his health. Paul shook his head. "I'm fine." His color was off, and he looked weak. He drew in a ragged breath but insisted that he was okay.

"Tell me if anything changes," Jack instructed him, but he knew it wasn't likely that he would. In Paul's shoes, he would probably do the same.

He left Paul on the beach with instructions to stay put and set about ensuring their survival.

CHAPTER FIVE

Billions of stars illuminated the beach as they slowly marched across the sky. The volcanic mountain cast dark, sharply irregular shapes against the western sky, blocking the stars and looming over them like a crumbling medieval castle. Something about it seemed eerie, and the men instinctively cast periodic glances toward it as if they expected otherworldly creatures to creep menacingly out of the vegetation.

It had been a long day, with some reward for their efforts. Coconut bearing trees provided some edible food and milk. Jack showed them how to obtain the green, young coconuts, the ones with the tastiest insides, and the ones filled with water, rich in electrolytes, which they sorely needed. It took time to reach the coconuts, to twist them off the tree, and to open them with sharp rocks.

The better water find was a small spring emerging from the side of a cliff, a trickle of freshwater that cascaded off the rocks into a tiny pool. There was no way to safely test it, but at this point, even contaminated water was better than none.

They used empty coconut shells to scoop the small quantities of water, greedily gulping what they could get. It took far too long for them to gain what amounted to a single glass of water per person.

From the palm trees, they harvested the edible hearts, taking them from the ends of the limbs, using sharp rocks to gradually peel away the outer layers. It was slow work that yielded little food, but still, it was better than nothing, plus it provided some hydration due to the water content of the fruit.

As the sun moved relentlessly overhead, they moved into the shade of the trees to rest and wait for dusk. Hours later, as the sun went behind the mountain, Stuart, Ben, and Jack went into action, gathering more coconuts for the next day's breakfast.

Later, they reclined on the beach, close to the trees where the sand was less rocky. They were far too exhausted to talk, and this Ben found comforting. Having to talk to others felt almost impossible. Confrontation made him uncomfortable, and with the tension between Tony and Stuart, Ben already found himself on edge. Their blatant animosity towards each other reminded him of his parents.

Ben's father sat in his easy chair, sipping Seagram's 7 on the rocks. He gestured toward Ben, who sat in front of the television, trying to ignore his parents' bickering. "Ben, your mother thinks I don't do enough around this house, that I'm lazy. She doesn't appreciate the fact that I work all day while she gets to spend the money that I make. She's tired at the end of the day, wants a break, even though she has a full-time housekeeper! When you grow up, son, puh-leeze, make sure you don't marry an entitled debutante!"

Ben's mother sat across from his father, legs tucked under her, sipping a martini. She was beautiful and slender, with long, straight dark hair that she wore draped over one shoulder. She turned to Ben and his sister, raising her perfectly shaped and tinted eyebrows incredulously.

"Do you kids believe this? All I ask is that we sit down and talk, so I have a chance to express myself. When I try to do that, I get berated for having feelings."

Turning her focus to their father, she continued. "Our therapist made it very clear in our last session that you have a problem with expressing emotions, Robert. In fact, she said that you are suppressing your feelings, and because you are so uncomfortable admitting that you have them, you can't stand it that I am willing to put mine out there."

She paused for dramatic effect, took a sip of her martini, set the glass down carefully, and tapped the side of it with her perfectly manicured nail. "Ben, Nicole, listen to me: it is normal, and natural, to express your feelings. I want you to grow up to be comfortable with your emotions, to express them fully, unlike your father."

Ben's father twirled his index finger in the air near his head, letting out a long whistle. "Fruit loops—you and that therapist are both completely nuts. You can't live your life vomiting your feelings everywhere—someone has to get real work done, and that won't happen sitting in the corner crying. I'm not going back there, never again. Nope!" He took a long drink and slammed his glass down on the table, shooting an I-dare-you-to-say-something look at his wife, who rolled her eyes and looked away in disgust.

Ben's sister, Nicole, sat reading a book, her face flushed with embarrassment and with the effort to remain outside of her parents' conflict. Ben's stomach clenched, witnessing the effect of their fighting on his sister. They could have gone to their rooms, closed the doors, and avoided it, but experience had taught them that the level of conflict would then escalate to an unbearable level, with screaming, shouting, and slamming doors.

Oddly, Ben and Nicole's parents contained the worst of their behavior when their children were in the room, moderating the level of their voices while they inflicted a thousand little emotional deaths on one another.

It was a hostage situation from which Ben and Nicole could not escape, not until they'd obtained drivers licenses and were able to go to their friends' homes and after school activities. At least, that's what Ben had done. Nicole, painfully shy and mostly friendless, remained trapped in the house until college.

The respite from the war between their parents was summer vacation.

Ben loved the summers at his grandparents' ranch. He and Nicole shared a bedroom with twin beds separated by a nightstand. At night, with the window raised high, the screen keeping out the insects, they lay whispering and giggling in the dark while cool breezes played with the white eyelet curtains. The chirping of crickets and the faraway sound of the occasional train passing through the small, nearby town, provided a gentle symphony that lulled them to sleep.

During the day, they "helped" with the chores, doing little things like sweeping a floor, or gathering eggs from the chicken coop. They explored the nearby creek, searching for exotic creatures from their imagination, but finding instead the occasional tadpoles, frogs, and once, a snapping turtle. Ben found a heavy stick and poked the turtle until it opened its mouth and latched tightly onto the end of the stick. He lifted the stick, and the turtle hung on, dangling above the water until Nicole began to cry because he was being "cruel." Ben lowered it and let go of the stick, teasing Nicole to stop being a baby. But she stopped crying, always his goal.

Dinner was so much better than at home—fried chicken, freshly cooked green beans floating in butter with pieces of bacon, corn on the cob slathered in more butter, huge fluffy biscuits, so hot the steam rose when broken open, and always dessert—chocolate layer cake baked that afternoon, filling the tiny farmhouse with heavenly scents. Sometimes dessert was lemon meringue pie, the white peaks six inches tall and lightly browned on the tips, the pie sugary sweet in defiance of the natural tart flavor of the lemon.

In the afternoons, they napped on top of their quilt-covered beds, waking later to the smells of dinner cooking. They ate watermelon sitting on the covered porch, listening to the cacophony of the cicadas in the trees, everyone utterly calm and content.

After dinner, they played cards with Mimi while Pops smoked his pipe, smiling at them and laughing when they "beat" their grandmother. Conversation flowed gently and naturally to offers of more food, practical matters about the running of the ranch, and little else.

No one talked about their feelings. Nor did anyone ever put anyone else down or criticize anyone else. The house was filled with kindness and love expressed through food, smiles, warmth, and the occasional hug. Nicole lost that painfully shy, frightened look that she wore at home. She smiled, laughed, and acted like a normal, happy little girl.

It was heaven. But heaven inevitably came to an end.

Nicole always cried the day they packed up to be driven home. Ben would never forget the summer Nicole turned ten, how she clung to Mimi, arms wrapped around her legs, begging to live there, the tears in Mimi's eyes as she tried to explain that their parents would be heartbroken without them and that they must return home.

Ben never cried, never spoke about the resentment he felt. Now his parents were getting older, and while they had managed to stay together and carve out a kind of détente, Ben couldn't bring himself to express much love toward them. He put up with them because it was the right thing to do, to let them know his children, their grandchildren.

Now, they rarely fought, and they treated Ben and Michelle's children with far more warmth and engagement than they had their own two children. Were they trying to make up for something? Or had time and aging mellowed them?

Nicole never married. She lived in a small town, taught art at a community college, and had a couple of cats whom she adored. She was content, preferring to shelter herself from life, from any kind of relationship that could prove emotionally dangerous.

Before the divorce, she had visited Ben and Michelle regularly, delighting in her niece and nephew. Now, she stayed away. Another casualty of Ben's ridiculously short, annihilating affair. They spoke on the phone periodically, but she never asked him the obvious— what did you do to drive away your wife? What, indeed?

Paul sat quietly, gazing into the fire, trying to ignore the wheezing each time he drew a breath. He was utterly exhausted, more so than he could ever recall except maybe for that time he'd had a severe case of the flu, not so long ago.

He'd lain in bed while Sara brought him aspirin and soup, wondering if this was how it felt to be elderly and feeble—completely drained of life, and unable to care for himself. He'd become depressed that winter, and the depression had lingered long after the virus was gone.

But the depression hadn't stemmed from the flu, from being too weak to take care of himself. It had been broiling for months, ever since the day he'd shut down his business. That had been the worst day of his life.

He recalled the day he'd broken the news to his remaining seven employees. He'd called them into their small conference room and told them it was their last day.

Donna, his bookkeeper for twenty-one years, stood with her chin wobbling, dabbing away the tears and sniffling, her blue eyes downcast. Gary, his number one project manager, tried to cheer everyone up. "Hey, at least now we can start happy hour at noon." But no one laughed.

Paul thanked them for their many years of service and tried to give them severance checks, but no one accepted, knowing that he was pulling the money from his personal bank account. He'd always been transparent with the books, so there were no secrets and no surprises.

They'd all seen it coming but had continued to come to work to take care of their few remaining clients when they could have been sending out their resumes and interviewing. They'd grown even tighter as a team, moving forward in a kind of collective denial, refusing to acknowledge the reality of their situation.

Paul turned out the lights after everyone left the office, insisting that it was his job to take that final step. They'd taken laptops and personal items. Paul had already copied all the client files and financial data, so there was nothing left to do. The furniture and remaining office equipment would go to the landlord as part of the settlement of his defaulted lease.

The sadness they'd expressed as they hugged each other and Paul before leaving, making promises to get together as frequently as possible, hung in the air, seemingly adding to the darkness in the corners as night fell. The drop ceiling tiles looked old and dirty, with water stains in several spots. The furniture looked scratched and worn out. What was once a cheerful space full of life and energy was now a cold, dreary shell.

He walked slowly through the offices, wanting to remember their collective experiences, hoping to sear them into his memory— hundreds of meetings, everyone working hard to solve problems but finding lots of humor along the way. The spitball fights, the silly "trust" exercises they'd hired consultants to take them through, the open boxes of pizza on those long evenings completing work just under the deadline.

The office was filled with so many happy memories, but with sad ones too. The worst being the day their largest client, and 85% of their revenue, walked away. That was seventeen months before they closed their doors permanently. The company—or rather, Paul—never recovered from the blow. He'd never wanted to look at the vulnerability and exposure of having one big client and only a handful of small ones.

Paul had loved nurturing that one relationship. He'd literally loved the client's CEO, Nathan, like a brother. They took vacation trips together with their wives, attended the same synagogue, celebrated Nathan's kid's mitzvahs together. But when Nathan sold his business to a private equity firm, Paul put on his blinders, refusing to see the oncoming risk to his own business.

He'd felt betrayed. Nathan had apologized numerous times, trying to explain his decision to sell. He swore that the private equity company had made promises to him, chief among them, to retain Paul's company as their vendor. But they had reneged shortly after closing, and Nathan couldn't stop them.

Paul had insisted they stop accepting social invitations from Nathan and his wife. Over time, estrangement set in.

Sarah had repeatedly begged Paul to reconcile with Nathan. "How can you walk away from so many years of friendship?" But he couldn't swallow his pride, couldn't let go of the resentment and envy, the anger.

How could she defend Nathan over him? He'd lashed out at Sarah, accusing her of not having his back, of taking other people's sides over his. She'd stood there, shaking her head. "There aren't any sides, Paul," she'd said, walking away.

The last time he'd heard from Nathan, it was a voice message.

"Paul, it's Nathan, just wondering if you have time for breakfast today, or dinner or drinks tonight. I'm in town for a couple of weeks. Let's get together and talk. I'm sure that we can work this out." He'd sighed and murmured something about how their wives missed each other. "Anyway, call me back, buddy. Any time."

Paul had played that voice message several times, alternately listening for any signs of deception, and fighting the urge to call back. But he walked away from the call, from his friend, and from his wife's pleading.

Over time, Nathan had quit trying, gave up. At first, Paul felt vindicated. Later, he felt even angrier. The only thing worse than a friend's betrayal was his subsequent abandonment because you couldn't forgive him.

Now, Paul felt empty of the resentment, drained of the anger he'd been hauling around. Looking at the stars overhead, listening to the endless susurration of the ocean waves, he couldn't remember what had angered him so much that he gave up a twenty-year-plus friendship.

Odd thoughts filtered his consciousness. Thoughts about the expanse of his life, his loves, his hatreds, and where his journey in life had taken him. The stars were not angry, nor was the ocean, although it could be argued that the ocean both gave and took life. But it did so without apparent emotion one way or the other.

Maybe the ocean didn't give and take life. Maybe life came and went, and the ocean was a carrier of life—the origins eons ago when the first single-cell creatures came into being. Paul tried to imagine millions of years passing and then seeing a small, unintelligent but hopeful creature crawling out of the ocean to sit on this beach before darting back into the waves. But later crawling out again, its descendants gradually adapting to life on land over millions of years.

Adaptation. Paul hadn't adapted to the sudden changes in his life. He'd fought them—the loss of his business, his "business family" dispersed, his wife endlessly disappointed in him, or so he thought.

He'd ignored the signs that his life could and would go on. They weren't in financial straits. They'd saved enough money over the years. Sarah still worked and enjoyed it, providing a more than adequate income stream as a bridge to retirement. They could easily afford a reasonable travel budget. Their home was paid for. They were both healthy.

What was missing? Absolutely nothing, yet he'd felt empty, hollowed out, lacking in purpose, and deeply resentful. Of what? His best friend's success?

In the back of Paul's mind, something crawled out of the muck and began to take shape, like the blob that had crawled out of this ocean millions of years ago. He'd suppressed it for years, but it was there.

Envy. He'd never been genuinely happy with others' success. He'd always compared himself and found himself lacking.

But rather than pull himself upward and onward, he'd told himself that he wasn't "money motivated." That he was a relationship guy, preferring to nurture a handful of business connections, focus on his work "family," and do good service work for his few customers.

It was comfortable, safe. It had worked for him.

In Paul's mind, the ugly truth crawled out into the open. As long as Nathan was about as relatively successful as Paul, they'd been fine. They were peers, neither significantly ahead of the other. That had felt good to Paul.

But Nathan was far more driven than Paul. While his business revenue was on par with Paul's for many years, his entrepreneurial skills and hunger had vastly outpaced Paul's.

While Paul stayed in his comfort zone, Nathan invested heavily in products that could go to market, products that would prove to be hugely valuable in the eyes of an investor. He took significant business risks, and as a result, his revenue skyrocketed in the last two or three years before he sold the business, resulting in the high valuation that yielded the large payday for him.

Nathan didn't significantly change his lifestyle until after the business sold, although he could have done so easily. Paul ignored the signs that Nathan was on a different path, that he was headed for a level of wealth far beyond Paul's.

It was too late for that for Paul. He'd deliberately chosen a service business that was only as valuable as this month's revenue, only insofar as his ability to give himself and his employees a paycheck. He'd always told himself that was enough.

After Nathan sold, Paul was consumed with envy. He felt the ugly resentment festering long before he lost the contract with Nathan's new business owners. He pretended to be happy for Nathan, toasting him and his wife, making promises that he and Sarah would travel with them and celebrate their success.

He feigned interest when Nathan talked about setting up a charitable foundation with a large portion of his wealth, concerned about how to choose the right one. He plastered on a smile and said that sure, of course, he would help vet them, even sit on a board or two alongside Nathan. Inside, he seethed, thinking how arrogant it was to talk about this like it was a real problem when there were far bigger problems in the world.

He'd felt less than Nathan, and it burned. Then the contract got canceled, and he had an excuse to allow his envy to turn into legitimate anger at being "betrayed."

If only he could talk to Sarah, tell her she'd been right, that the problem was him and that Nathan had done nothing wrong. She'd hold his hands, listen compassionately, and tell him it would be okay. She'd hold him close, whispering in his ear that she was proud of him for realizing that. She'd reassure him that they had everything, a good life together.

Then she'd pick up the phone, call Nathan's wife, and set up their next visit. They'd smile at each other and talk about how much fun they would have with their dear friends.

An ache in Paul's chest spread slowly, and the pain was such that he thought he wouldn't be able to survive it. Maybe he'd be lucky enough to have a heart attack take him out swiftly, sparing him the grief that he'd postponed for so long, the grief that now overwhelmed him.

A tear found enough moisture in his body to leave the corner of his eye and slowly descend, following the slight fissures of his face, dripping off his chin onto the sand. He felt the deep pressure in his chest break open like a fissure, felt his heart breaking.

Over the next few days, they spent most of their time searching for edible plants and sea life. The beach was a source of small sand crabs and other tiny creatures that washed up on shore in the early morning. But they had to be quick before the birds ate them. They tried catching small fish in the shallow waters, but that was an exercise in frustration. They had no equipment, no nets, nothing with which they might snare the rapidly darting fish, each of which if caught would only be one bite.

They discussed swimming further out to hunt larger sea creatures, but with no means of capturing them, it seemed futile. Stuart began working on a spear. He carefully searched for a branch just the right size and began carefully peeling the bark and plant matter from one of the ends. He used sharp volcanic rocks to whittle away the bark, gradually creating a sharp point. It was painstaking work, and the others doubted it would result in a working spear. He kept at it, figuring at least he was attempting a solution.

They captured small quantities of drinking water from the spring, but no one ever felt his thirst was fully quenched. At first, they used individual coconut shells, waiting patiently until filled, then sipping the few mouthfuls. Jack later cobbled together a number of the shells using palm leaves twisted together. That created a reservoir that would fill with water overnight. Still, it was never enough.

On the afternoon of the second day on the island, as the sun waned, Stuart was ravenous. He waited patiently until a large sea bird landed nearby, hunting for darting sand crabs. He walked up to the bird, which continued hunting, unconcerned, and grabbed it, quickly twisting its neck. The bird died instantly, but its large gaping eye continued to stare at Stuart. He felt a brief flush of guilt, then reminded himself he was no vegetarian, that he'd eaten thousands of birds in his lifetime with no guilt. This was no different.

Jack had started their first fire on the second day. He used sharp volcanic rock to carve two sticks. He patiently twirled the sharpened end of the first "fire stick" in a tiny hole in the second stick until it smoked, then gradually added the small bits of coconut fibers he'd gathered. Once the kindling began to smoke, he blew on it patiently until a flame appeared, then added dried palm leaves, and gradually built a roaring fire.

That night, they ate the roasted seabird. It tasted much like the sea creatures it ate every day, but they didn't care. It was by far the most food than they'd had in days. They tossed other small sea life edibles onto the fire and found those morsels were also much better cooked than raw.

They'd gathered a plant that day, similar to taro, which Jack explained wasn't edible until well cooked. Both the leaves and the underground tubers, which resembled small potatoes, were edible. With no cooking utensils, they couldn't manage cooking the leaves, but they were able to throw the potatoes into the embers of the fire and drag them out with a stick. Charred on the outside, they were still tasty.

It was their first time to feel satiated. Their stomachs had shrunk so much that it took about a quarter of their normal intake to fill them.

They were all losing weight and becoming leaner.

Especially Paul, who seemed to be shrinking and weakening at an alarming rate.

Enjoying their first real meal, Stuart offered up words of encouragement. "I think we did a fine job getting food today. We're going to be okay. I'm sure the rescue team is narrowing down our location, and before we know it, we'll be back home eating steak and potatoes again. Right, Jack?" he ended pointedly, giving the Captain a look.

"Reality is, as long as we manage to find food and water, we'll be okay. And yes, I'm sure they're still looking for us," Jack said. Stuart noted Jack's lack of solid eye contact as he spoke that last part. Still, it seemed to energize everyone. Except for Tony.

"That is bullshit," he declared in a voice laced with contempt. "We are stuck on this godforsaken island. You can fool yourselves all you want, but we're fucked, man!"

"Shut up," said Stuart with a hard stare at Tony, who flushed but didn't say anything more. "We're alive, we've got food and water, and we're going to be rescued."

It might be false hope, but it was better than no hope, and Stuart was determined to keep it alive.

CHAPTER SIX

Distant thunder crashed. The sky lit up as lightning flashed, rapidly followed by another boom. Clouds loomed, lightning lacing through them. The men, startled awake, sat up and peered at the horizon, each flash of lightning illuminating the distant but rapidly growing storm clouds.

"That storm is headed for us," Jack told them. "We need to find more shelter."

They scrambled to their feet, and Jack guided them toward the mountain. Wind whipped them, slowing their progress as they navigated into the trees toward the mountain.

"Wait a minute! Won't the lightning strike these trees? Isn't the beach better?" demanded Tony, darting his eyes back at the beach.

"Lightning seeks the quickest path to the ground, so the trees on the mountain top would be the ones to strike, not these," Jack said, continuing forward into the brush. Everyone followed while Tony hung back temporarily. Reluctantly, he followed as the rest of the men moved out of sight.

Jack had noticed a small cave earlier that day. It wasn't much, basically a dent in the side of the mountain, just large enough to crawl in and sit in a circle. But it would provide protection from the worst of the rapidly advancing storm.

Now, if he could just find that cave. Wind lashed as they moved quickly through the trees and low vegetation, following Jack. Branches whipped them with the fury of a scorned lover, scratching their faces and arms.

The rain began to fall, at first in a gentle shower, then suddenly, the skies opened up, and it poured. With the wind blowing it almost sideways, they were plunged into the equivalent of an outdoor car wash, minus the soap.

Visibility shrank to almost zero as Jack searched desperately for any sign of the cave. The men pushed forward, fighting the wind, already drenched by the rain.

Jack knew the cave was roughly at the end of a perpendicular line from the beach to the highest peak of the mountain, almost due east. But with no visibility, he had no idea if he was headed toward the highest peak.

A flash of lightning lit up the area, and Jack saw the base of the mountain. A remnant of an ancient volcano, the mountain rose abruptly and steeply. Most of the volcano lay below the sea, only the tip visible as a large, hilly, vegetation-covered geologic formation, with a small beach on the western slope.

The wind howled, increasing in strength. Jack feared a tropical storm, with dangerous winds that could cause serious injury. *Where was that damn cave?*

Jack took them around the base of the mountain, further to the northeast, but all they found was more vegetation and rocky slopes. Rain pelted their bodies. Palm tree fronds whipped them mercilessly. They leaned into the ferocity of the wind, progressing in slow, agonizing steps.

Lightning lit the sky once again, and Jack feverishly scanned the base, desperate for any signs of the cave. There, he saw a dark slash. He veered that way, and soon they were huddled inside the cave. They were soaked, but relatively safe.

Ben sat with his arms wrapped around his knees, listening to the howling wind, and wondered how he was going to keep from losing his mind. He might as well be on the other side of the moon, trapped on this island with so little chance of any possible rescue.

How many other people had found themselves in this kind of situation? How many people did you see on the news that were "saved" from certain death, rescued from islands like this one? He couldn't think of anyone, couldn't recall a single case. Either those stories didn't rate the national news, or they didn't exist.

Ben felt a searing hopelessness grip his heart.

He remembered reading a book many years ago as part of his college curriculum about finding the meaning in life, written by a holocaust death camp survivor. *Who was that? Viktor someone. Franks? No, Frankl, Victor Frankl.*

Frankl talked about hanging onto visions of his future life in his mind. He held conversations in his head with his wife, imagining himself, upon his return, helping hundreds—no, thousands of people, improve their lives. Holding those visions of joy, relationship, and love, of future contribution, enabled him to survive.

The author also wrote about the deaths of those with no vision, who had lost all hope. He noted how, even if everyone had the same amount of food and shelter, that the hopeless died first.

He couldn't afford to let himself become hopeless.

Ben visualized making a home for his children, buying sheets with princesses and action heroes on them, games, and toys. He imagined preparing home-cooked meals, like the ones he and Nicole had shared at their grandparents' home in the summers. He was fairly sure he could figure out how to cook like that. He'd never had any interest in cooking but imagining all that wonderful food inspired him. He began salivating.

Then he saw his children in his newly kid-zoned apartment, playing and laughing, chasing him and each other around the living room.

Tucking them into their beds after bath time, breathing in the indescribable scent of warm child skin. Kissing them good night, later checking on them and watching them sleep, arms and legs flung outward, soft curly locks splayed on their pillows.

Ben built that vision in his mind, filling in more and more detail, resolved to hold onto it.

Tony sat sullenly, averting his eyes from the others. He was soaked to the bone, cold and hungry. There was never enough food, no matter what anyone else said. Nasty sea birds tasted like saltwater and dead octopus, or at least, how he imagined that would taste.

Tony looked at Stuart from the corner of his eye, burning inside. While Tony shrank from lack of food, Stuart seemed to be gaining strength, increasing Tony's worry that he wouldn't be able to defend himself in a physical match.

He'd spent most of his life avoiding guys like Stuart, guys who were bigger and stronger, guys who had bullied him. He'd been forced to skulk around school until the bullies were gone for the day, pretending to have something to do so he could walk home safely, alone. Sometimes that worked, and other times it didn't.

If he rushed out the door first, inevitably, a small gang of guys followed him. They taunted him all the way to his neighborhood. Even if they never touched him, it was terrorizing as he imagined all the terrible things they might do to him if they caught him. Sometimes they caught him, and he took a beating.

At home, he'd have to put up with more abuse from his old man, who never lost the opportunity to tell him what a loser he was. Tony's old man was big, and when he got drunk, he used Tony as a punching bag. His only defense was to hang around outside until his old man fell into a stupor on the sofa, and he could sneak back into his room.

Tony's old man was a pitiful sight at those times, and that was when Tony fantasized about killing him—picking up a beer bottle and smashing it on his temple over and over until blood gushed, and he stopped breathing permanently.

Beer bottle, weapon. Rock, weapon. Something else, weapon. Tony began imagining getting the best of Stuart in ways that didn't involve overpowering him physically. Or in ways that involved sneakiness and stealth, two things at which Tony excelled.

Stuart stretched his legs as far as he could without impinging on the other men. He rolled and cracked his neck, using the opportunity to take a look at each of the men, focusing last on Tony. Tony sat as far as he could from Stuart, his eyes darting here and there, anxiety evident in his body language. He cleared his throat repeatedly and mumbled something about how fucked up this was, how screwed they were.

Tony, Stuart knew, was the most dangerous guy in their group, despite his small stature and obvious lack of character and fortitude. Tony was dangerous because he was the most frightened. He was the kind of guy who always looked for someone to blame. Guys like that were unstable, likely to act impulsively and compromise the safety of the rest of them.

Stuart made up his mind that if necessary, he would take care of Tony, whatever that took.

Paul sat with his head against the wall of the cave, trying to catch his breath. He was losing strength every day. His appetite was low, despite the lack of regular nutrition. The other men talked about needing more to eat, but he found that he didn't care that much.

With so much time, his thoughts spiraled into despair. He was consumed with shame. How could he have thrown away the joy and happiness in his life, the friendship, the treasure of his wife's love? How could he have been so filled with envy, so small and petty?

Paul felt worthless. Surely his wife was grateful he was gone. Most likely, she was going out and meeting new people, meeting new men. She was very attractive for her age, with skin that gave her the look of a woman ten or more years younger. He pictured her intelligent eyes, thick, silky hair, and slender, toned body. But what really set her apart was her heart.

How could he have been so stupid? He'd thrown away his marriage as he'd also thrown away his best friend.

He'd been so lucky to find Sarah 15 years ago, after so many single years, two long-term dating relationships that had failed, and almost giving up.

The night they met, he saw her across the crowded room. It was a charity event, one that he'd almost decided not to attend. But he went, and had a drink in his hand, when Nathan followed his line of sight to Sarah, standing across the room, laughing with the woman standing next to her. Nathan cut his eyes over to Paul and wiggled his eyebrows suggestively.

"Well? Are you going to go talk to her?" he asked. Paul wondered out loud if she was single.

"How about asking her?" Nathan said, rolling his eyes.

Nathan and his wife, Debra, married for six or so years, with one baby and a toddler at home, were enjoying a much-needed "date night." They were anxious to fix Paul up with someone great. Debra turned to Paul and said, "There's only one way to find out—go and ask her. Women like men with balls."

That was completely unlike Debra, normally demure, but she'd had a couple of drinks. Her eyes sparkled as Paul sauntered off to introduce himself to Sarah. He rehearsed several things to say, discarding each one as lame or snarky or sounding like a predatory bar shark.

Finally, as he stood in front of Sarah, taking in her smile, her beautiful, clear gray eyes with the slight crinkles at the edges, and, most of all, her warmth. All his opening lines fled his consciousness. He offered, "Hi, my name is Paul." So inadequate to the most significant moment of his life. Each time they celebrated an anniversary over the years, or told another couple their "story," they laughed about that line.

As Paul allowed memories of Sarah to crowd his mind, he felt a bit of the chill leave the hole that was his heart. Warmth spread, and, for the first time in days, he felt comforted. He heard her whispering to him. "It's okay, sweetheart. Go to sleep." As he drifted off, he wasn't sure if it was Sarah or the wind, but he'd have sworn he felt a soft kiss graze his cheek.

CHAPTER SEVEN

The sun peeking into the cave opening woke Jack. The first thing he noticed was the quiet. The storm had blown through and was over. He slowly moved into a sitting position, stretching and rolling his neck to relieve the cramps from sleeping on a rock. As he moved around, the other men woke. Gradually they crawled out of their cave and stood, stretching their bodies to relieve the cramps.

Large branches and huge fronds lay on the ground everywhere. Trees leaned tiredly, exhausted from hours of thrashing. They stepped carefully, watching out for branches and other tripping hazards, making their way slowly to the spring. Stuart reached it first and let out a loud whoop. The other men crowded forward and found their first gift from the storm.

The spring flowed, a gushing waterfall from the top of the cliff. Everyone crowded around it, cupping their hands, taking long drinks of water, and grinning at each other.

Jack sprang into action, barking instructions.

"Enough guys—here's our opportunity. We can build a pool and capture most of this water. We can't use it for too long because of stagnation, but it may be drinkable for a few days."

First, he had them use their hands to dig a shallow pool. It was hard and backbreaking, but they finally had an area about the size of a small baby pool.

Then, he led them back to the beach, where they stripped off their shirts and began loading them up with pebbles and coarse scree. Back at the pool, they lined all of it with gravel and built a reasonably clear landing point for the spring/waterfall. Slowly their hand-built pool began to fill. They drank deeply from the waterfall, leaving the water in the pool for later.

Exhausted at that point, they gradually made their way back to the beach. They waded into the ocean first and rinsed their shirts, laying them out on the beach to dry. They found spots at the edge of the sand and the trees to recline and rest.

Ben's eyelids felt heavy, and he dozed a bit but didn't sleep. Later, he woke to the sounds of waves slapping against something that sounded different. *What was that?* He wondered drowsily. He was closest to the water. He sat up and gazed at the shore, watching the waves gently roll in. There—what was that? Something was moving forward and back with the waves, reflecting sunlight. He got up and walked to the ocean's edge and found another gift from the storm. One of the 5-gallon water bottles had found its way to their island!

Ben waded out and grabbed the large bottle, hauling it onto the sand. It was one of the water bottles from the boat, and it was full—not the one they'd mostly drunk. Somehow, it had drifted here, or been propelled by the storm waters.

Later, the men inspected the lagoon and shore more closely, finding other items from the boat that had been washed in by the storm. A coil of rope that hadn't been untied. Two large metal buckets. A section of awning. Several cushions from the deck furniture.

And, amazingly, the ditch bag, which contained several useful items: a folding knife, flares, emergency medical supplies, a small spear gun, food bars and trail mix in small packets, a rope, and a flashlight.

One thing it did not contain, however, was an EPIRB [Emergency Position Indicating Radio Beacon], duly noted by Jack with great disappointment. Had the ditch bag contained one, they could have sent an emergency distress signal which would have been picked up by satellite and transmitted to the Coast Guard. Their rescue would have been virtually guaranteed at that point.

Once again, Jack noted the disastrous mistake he'd made hiring Tony. He'd given Tony the job of packing the ditch bag—a job he'd done as sloppily as everything else Jack had given him to do.

The rope was useful. They conserved it by pulling out smaller strands and cutting them off with the knife. They were able to tie the awning to a tree, and that became an additional sturdy shelter. The cushions became their pillows at night. One bucket was used to scoop up small fish or to store in seawater the creatures they planned to eat for dinner. The other bucket became a cooking pot.

Now that they had a spear gun, Stuart began hunting for larger fish. Since it was a small bay, the larger fish were only so large—mostly smaller varieties of jack, snapper, sturgeon, and the odd-looking grouper. After countless missed shots, he finally speared a jack, big enough for all to share. That night, they feasted on the jack plus the random food items of the day—sand dabs, a large crab, cooked hearts of palm and coconut flesh.

After they consumed the water in the 5-gallon water bottle, they rigged it to the place where the spring bubbled over so that it would refill each day. With a constant source of water and greater access to food, they all relaxed a bit. Even Paul gained strength from the water and regular food. His color and energy improved, he was less gaunt than before, and he participated in work almost to the level of the other guys.

The fire crackled, occasionally shooting vivid blue and orange sparks upward, like fireflies in the summer where Ben grew up. He picked up a piece of fish, pulled the meat off the bone, and chewed thoughtfully. Catch of the day—snapper.

Tony filled the air with his usual unbelievable stories, while everyone tried to ignore him. This time, he managed somehow to fight off a wolf while camping in West Texas.

"We're minding our own business around the campfire, and a wolf runs in, jumps on our pile of supplies, and starts dragging away our stuff. I managed to wrestle my backpack away from him, but the other guys were too scared to do anything." He swore in disgust. "Bunch of pussies."

Stuart rolled his eyes.

"Hey, Tony, you num-nuts. There aren't any wolves in Texas."

Tony puffed up indignantly. "Of course, there are. I saw it with my own eyes. He wasn't the only one—we saw a bunch of 'em out there that time and other times too!"

Stuart snorted. "You idiot. The last remaining wolves in Texas were killed decades ago after a bunch of them were removed for captive breeding. You saw some measly coyotes.

"Man, you don't know what the fuck you're talking about! We saw wolves! It was Big Bend, man, there are lots of wild animals around there!"

Tony was getting more and more agitated. Stuart laughed at him while he poked his stick at another juicy bite of fish. Enraged, Tony knocked the stick out of Stuart's hand. They all watched it land a few feet away in the sand, the fish ruined.

Stuart froze. Slowly he raised his gaze to Tony.

"If you ever do anything like that again, you will regret it." Stuart's voice dripped with repressed violence.

Tony, undeterred, poked at Stuart again.

"You'll do what? What are you going to do, huh? Listen man, I'm used to bullies and assholes, so go ahead!"

Tony sprang to his feet, pulling himself into an awkward fighting stance, holding his fists up in front of himself.

Ben sucked in his breath, waiting for Stuart to pound Tony into the sand, an event to which he was looking forward.

Jack gazed at Stuart with a look that said, *is it really worth it?* He raised his hands in a placating manner.

"Guys, let's all calm down."

Stuart shook his head, got up, and slowly walked away a few feet, stopping to look at the ocean. His muscles were bunched like he was ready to turn around and go after Tony.

"Like I said—bullies are always cowards!" Tony trumpeted to Stuart's retreating back. He picked up a handful of sand and threw it after Stuart in frustration, making himself look even more ridiculous. The sand fell a couple of feet away from Stuart.

"Asshole," he muttered. He stomped away quickly into the trees.

The other guys looked at each other in the ensuing silence as Stuart came back and sat down.

"Well, that was fun," said Ben, and Paul added, "Yeah, about as much fun as pimples are."

Jack smiled, Stuart laughed, and they all relaxed. The stars revolved slowly across the sky as always—a spectacular display that could only have been improved if observed from home.

Tony stalked into the trees, pent up rage making him see red. He stopped and kicked at a tree and was rewarded with a shot of pain that traveled rapidly from his toes to his knee.

"Fucking asshole! Look at what you made me do!" he yelled as he grabbed his injured foot with one hand and hopped around helplessly. Forced to sit down, he fumed as he examined his toes. The pain slowly lessened as he decided that nothing was broken.

The pain in his foot brought back terrible memories of trying to deal with the bullies in his past and always ending up injured far worse than them. He burned with shame as he recalled the fights, the running, the hiding, and the next day at school, kids pointing at his bruises, laughing at him.

Stuart grew large in Tony's mind—an image of a twisted face laughing at him, a fist landing a painful punch in his face. Standing over Tony as he lay helplessly on the ground, kicking him in his sides, walking away and leaving Tony bleeding.

That know-it-all cowboy is going to get it. There was no way Tony would let him continue to humiliate him. His bruised ego receded, and firm resolve took its place.

"We never did finish that conversation we had on the boat," Paul said after a period of silence.

The other guys looked at him curiously.

"You remember—we started to talk about the women in our lives, or maybe no longer in our lives." Paul cleared his throat and poked at the fire with a stick.

"I said I was married, but the truth is we're separated and probably headed to a divorce." He paused.

"It's all my fault. I was truly the biggest fool ever. I blew it," he rushed out the words, as though he'd held them inside for far too long. A tear tracked down his face, and he flicked it away, sighing.

"She was—is—the best thing that ever happened to me. But I lost my business, and then I managed to ruin things with my best friend, Nathan. After that, I treated her so badly that she finally asked me to move out, which was exactly what she should have done."

Ben felt uncomfortable, but at the same time, compelled to listen. Paul seemed like such a nice guy. It was difficult to imagine him being so offensive to his wife that she made him leave. Not everyone was stupid enough to have an affair, a surefire guarantee of divorce.

"Somehow, I can't picture you being the guy who gets kicked out for bad behavior," ventured Ben.

Paul shook his head.

"No. I was awful to her. She is so sweet, and she tried so hard to be supportive, but I pushed her away. After months of that, she tried to get me to go to counseling. I told her no way was I going to counseling.

"That's not all," he continued, staring at the ground. "I pushed away my best friend, after he sold his business, and I lost him as a customer. Not his fault, and he did his best, but I couldn't forgive him for having a huge success right at the time I was failing. So, suddenly, I had no business, no wife, and no best friend, yet still, I thought I was right." He looked up at the other guys.

"Have you ever been so incredibly *right* about something that you were *dead wrong about*?"

Jack and Ben looked at each other, then away. Stuart stared at Paul for a moment, then gazed into the distance, as if the question had triggered uncomfortable memories. The silence stretched.

Ben didn't want to answer the question. It was far too personal, hit far too close to home. Of course, he had been dead wrong. But then Michelle had refused to give him a chance to make it up to her, hadn't she? Was one night with another woman really enough for their entire family life to go up in flames?

He felt a surge of resentment. What about Michelle's sister, always interfering? If not for Liz, he'd have had a fighting chance at putting his family back together. But Liz had stood solidly in the way.

Ben stirred as he felt a surge of anger through his body. He picked up a shell and hurled it at the water. He looked up and saw both Paul and Jack staring at him. Stuart, sitting across from Ben, raised his eyebrows.

What the hell. No one else was here to listen to his sorry life accounting except these three guys, and the stars above. Since he would probably die an awful death on this lost island, why the hell not just tell his story. He'd never done that before—never unloaded about his emotions. He avoided counseling, and since he wasn't close to his parents, and his sister was too sensitive to handle it, that left no one.

"I was wrong about one thing, but not about a lot of the rest of it," Ben blurted. "I think one mistake, even when it's awful, shouldn't negate a million other good things. I mean, I was a great husband for eight years, and what about the kids? What kind of life will they have with us divorced? Doesn't that count for anything?" Now that he was finally talking, it was like he had diarrhea of the mouth. He couldn't stop.

The men looked at him, surprised.

"Uh, Ben. Why don't you start at the beginning?" Stuart asked.

A pregnant silence ensued. He cleared his throat, willing the lump in it to go away.

"I had an affair. But it was only one night!"

Heads nodded sympathetically.

"And was this other woman someone you loved?" asked Stuart.

"No. She was a co-worker, it was after a conference with too much drinking, we met in the hotel bar, and one thing led to another. Huge mistake, but...," he trailed off.

"But, what?" said Stuart.

"Okay, then I told my wife about it. Six months later."

Heads shook slowly side to side.

"So, let me get this straight. You had a one-night stand, your wife didn't know anything about it, and six months later, *you told her*? Wow, man. Why did you do that?" Stuart asked what they were all wondering.

"Seems like all that would do is hurt her. It's not like telling her would help either one of you, right?" said Stuart. "I mean, even if you're not Catholic, couldn't you just go to a priest and confess or something? If it was bothering you that much."

Ben sat back, shocked.

"But I never lied to her before that, not about anything that mattered. I couldn't live with the lie—it was eating me up inside. I couldn't look into her eyes anymore. It felt like this huge thing between us."

"Yeah, well, that's all about you, isn't it?" Stuart said, not unkindly.

"I'm putting myself in her shoes," ventured Paul. "No judgment against you, Ben, but it does seem like that would be devastating for her to hear. Plus, where do you go from there?"

"If I was married, and my wife cheated on me just one time, that's the last thing I would want to know about," said Stuart emphatically. "In fact, I would be pissed if she told me, like not only did she do something awful, the worst thing you can do to a guy, but now she's rubbing salt into the wound. No win, man."

Jack, silent until now, asked, "Just curious, but what did you expect her to do with that information?"

Ben was stunned. He'd expected to hear at least some recriminations about cheating on his wife, but maybe he shouldn't be surprised. Lots of guys cheated, and in his experience around the water cooler at work, it was often bragging rights, not a source of embarrassment or shame like he'd felt.

But these guys seemed like good guys—guys who would make sure to tell him what an idiot he was to cheat on his wife. Nothing new, only what he deserved to hear.

But the last thing he expected to hear was that the bigger crime was *telling his wife* about his one-night stand.

Images of his wife's devastation at the restaurant slid into his mind's eye. Her face turning white, her hands shaking as she stood up, her unsteady walk as she fled the restaurant. Later, at the house, her eyes searing him with pain and anguish, layered over with an angry defense. The way she'd gazed at him, stunned, as he left and looked back one last time. The sound of her sobs on the phone the handful of times they talked later.

Ben's chest caught. He looked down at the sand, his hands holding his head, elbows on his knees.

Now he saw himself in the weeks after the divorce, closed off, displaying no emotion when he picked up and dropped off the kids, making little eye contact with Michelle. Barricaded against the guilt and remorse, telling himself it was Liz's fault he was now a single Dad.

But he'd never told Michelle how he felt deep down—instead, holding onto resentment that she never gave him a second chance.

After the first couple of tries, while separated, he'd made no further efforts to reconcile with Michelle. He'd closed his heart like a steel trap, concluding that she and her sister were far more to blame than he. He'd shown little compassion toward Michelle—and forget about Liz. Never once had he considered how much it must have hurt Liz to see her sister so devastated.

Liz was right about one thing. He'd been extraordinarily selfish, placing his emotional needs ahead of everyone else's.

What good had it done to tell Michelle about his one-night stand? Zero. Yes, he'd cleared his conscience, but at what cost?

The catch in Ben's chest became a tsunami of pain. He choked and gasped, trying desperately to hold back tears, not wanting to do this in front of a bunch of guys he barely knew. But then, just when he thought he'd contained it, Paul reached over and gently placed his hand on Ben's shoulder. The flood broke, and Ben cried, like the sad and lonely boy who'd been forced to live with his parent's contempt for one another.

Slowly the flood subsided, and Ben sniffled, slinging snot into the sand.

"Thanks," he said to Paul, without looking at him, embarrassment flooding him.

"It's okay, man," said Paul. "We've all been there."

After a few more minutes, they all said good night and retired to their sleeping spots on the sand, including Tony, who'd crept back to his spot after the rest of them had settled.

Later, Ben lay awake, gazing up at the stars.

Not that it excused what he did, but he realized that one of his problems was the lack of a confidant. He'd spent so much of his life avoiding close relationships, except with Michelle, that he'd had no one to talk to, no one to advise him.

If he wasn't such a loner, maybe he'd have a good friend—a guy—who would have told him not to "confess" to Michelle, who might have told him to just go home, hold his wife as tightly as he could, and do everything in his power to make her happy for the rest of their lives.

Even better, maybe with a good friend or two, he would've had someone to tell him to be patient with Michelle's adjustment to parenting two small children all day long, to focus on supporting her instead of thinking so much about his own needs. Maybe a friend would have told him it was normal to feel attracted to someone else but to resist that temptation, to let his marriage normalize.

"If only," he murmured as if summarizing his tale of woe to the stars above.

The stars gazed back at him, blazing against the impossibly dark skies, saying nothing.

CHAPTER EIGHT

Tony crept through the scraggly forest, looking for the right vegetation. Jack had warned them about vegetation with a bad taste—extremely bitter or unpleasant. That usually meant it was poisonous to humans, an early warning sign from nature to man.

He pulled random leaves from plants, and gingerly tested them using the advice from Jack. First, he rubbed the leaves on his skin, then waited a few hours to see what would happen. Most of the time, nothing, but sometimes a light rash. Over time, he identified several leaves that caused a rash. He tested them further by licking them.

Finally, he found one that caused a rash, and caused his mouth to pucker when licked. The leaves of the plant were starfish-shaped, pointed on the ends with serrated edges. The color was reddish-purple. He plucked several of them and stuffed them in his pockets, being careful not to crush them and to touch them as little as possible. One of the leaves had a seed pod attached, which escaped Tony's notice.

"What are you doing?"

Tony jumped, hastily stuffing the leaves in his pockets as he turned.

Stuart walked closer, and Tony backed away.

"Nothing, man!"

"What do you have there?" Stuart asked.

"What are you doing sneaking up on me like that?" Tony asked belligerently, puffing up. "How about a little privacy for doing my business?" He pretended to zip up his pants.

Stuart stared at Tony silently, then turned and walked away.

Relieved, Tony set about his task again, this time keeping one ear tuned for any sounds that might indicate someone's approach.

Days and nights dragged. They occupied themselves by day with foraging for food. With the knife and small spear gun, they killed larger fish in the bay. Stuart became the master fisherman, along with Jack. Between the two of them, dinner regularly featured crab and fish he found in the lagoon, cooked over a crackling fire. They also found various fruits and berries to augment their meals. They discovered a type of nut that resembled the almond, and when roasted over the fire became savory and edible. They added a different kind of protein by cooking snails.

Jack worked on the problem of rescue. He figured there were only a couple of options. One, find some way to get out in the open water again, away from the island, and hope to stumble onto a shipping lane and a cargo vessel. Two, pray for the miracle of rescuers somehow finding them. Currently, they had no way of getting to the ocean, with no boat or raft. That left being spotted by rescue aircraft.

Right now, they were too small to be easily spotted from above. Once the island was identified as their location, oceangoing vessels could be used for their rescue. But first, they needed to be spotted by air.

Their fire wasn't big enough to attract attention. That meant they needed to increase their visibility. Jack put everyone to work on building a message on the beach: HELP in 20-foot-tall letters, spelled out with the largest rocks they could find, then augmented with gravel so that the letters were very wide and visible.

One of the advantages of countless hours spent at sea was the time to read and study things that interested Jack. He was drawn to information about the ocean, about navigation, and even astronomy, including how to survive on a deserted island. Now, that knowledge provided a huge resource for all of them.

With the aid of the rope as well as vines and other vegetation, they built rudimentary shelters—lean-tos, providing better protection from the elements. One of the shelters now hung over the opening to their small cave, for use in the event of another storm. Using bamboo, they made flooring for the largest of their shelters, which enabled them to avoid the pests that crawled on the beach at night.

Gradually, the freshwater stream shrank to a trickle, and again, they found themselves short on water. For several days, they watched thunderheads build in the distance, but they were miles away and never advanced to the island.

Jack told them that soon, they might have to resort to desalination of seawater for consumption, a time-consuming and laborious process that would only yield small quantities of drinkable water.

In the meantime, he rigged a way to capture water. Using a plastic covering from a deck cushion, he suspended it over a bucket, covering the surrounding area with lush leaves. He placed a sizeable rock in the center over the bucket to create an indentation. This method slowly created condensation, which dripped into the bucket. They made three of them, and this gave them a minimum quantity of water for survival.

But Jack knew they were not going to fare well if they didn't get another source of water. Paul started to go downhill again with the loss of abundant fresh water.

In the evenings, Tony stayed away from the other men. He ate with them, for the most part, silently, then slipped away to his spot under one of the trees. What he did with his time at that point was anyone's guess, but the relief of his absence was palpable. As a result, the other men slowly developed a warm comradery.

c%o

Stuart rose before sunrise, searching for and finding large coconut crabs in burrows. He managed to catch five of them, despite a wicked wound hand-delivered by the large pincer of one angry crab.

Hunting gave him satisfaction, the sense of accomplishing something. It was just challenging enough to give his mind a focus. It was physical enough to keep his body moving. Stuart needed movement, had always needed it. He wasn't the kind of guy to sit around and reflect on life. He was high energy with an active mind. He made life happen. And when it didn't go his way, he made other things happen.

Back home, he'd utilized his energy and focus to build a nice business. Except for the occasional evenings out at his neighborhood sports bar, and the rare short-term relationships that went nowhere, he poured his energies into his company, a boutique commercial real estate venture. It was enough to keep his mind off of the detritus of his personal life.

On the island, there was enough to do to keep him moving, enough focus for his active mind, but not enough to banish the past. As difficult memories surfaced, Stuart felt his ire building.

c%o

They were still feasting on the remnants of roasted crab when Tony left the campfire area. Stuart watched him leave, eyes filled with suspicion.

"That guy is up to something," he said.

Jack said nothing.

"What do you mean?" asked Paul.

"I don't know, but I've seen guys like him before, and he's trouble. We all need to keep our eyes and ears open."

Paul looked genuinely surprised.

"He's definitely a bit of a jerk, but I don't think he's that bad," he said hopefully.

"I think Stuart's right," said Jack.

"What do you mean?" asked Paul.

"Don't know," said Jack, "Just a feeling, but we need to pay attention to what he's doing."

They all went quiet on that note, and Stuart added more kindling to the fire.

"So, one of the little games I play in my head is *what is the first thing?*" Paul began and paused. No one spoke. "Meaning, what will I do first when we get home."

He launched in. "It's easy for me. The first thing I'll do is find Sarah and tell her how much I love her and how sorry I am for everything. I will do everything I can to make it right with her. Then, I'm going to jump on a plane and go see Nathan in Colorado and make amends with him as well."

Paul drew a long breath and let it out.

"If I can do those two things, I will be the happiest man alive." He smiled reflectively. "It's funny how different I see my life now. I thought the most important thing in the world was my business. I guess I had something to prove. And when I lost it, I didn't know how to handle it. But the only thing I really needed to prove was that I could be a good husband, be worthy of Sarah's love." His chin wobbled a bit, and he looked down.

"I pray every night for God to bring me back to Sarah, so I get another chance."

He looked up at the other guys.

"If anything happens to me and I don't make it back, but you do, promise me you'll tell Sarah how much I love her, how sorry I am," he asked solemnly.

"Hey, buddy, that's not going to happen," said Stuart adamantly. "When we get off this godawful island, you'll be there with Sarah in person, and you can tell her yourself."

"But if I don't, promise me." Paul looked at them steadily.

"Of course," said Ben, and Stuart nodded yes.

"Good," said Paul, relieved.

He then turned to Ben and raised his eyebrows expectantly. Ben sighed, then spoke.

"The first thing I'm going to do is go see my kids. I can't imagine anything better than holding them in my arms again, making sure they're okay," Ben stated with conviction. The men nodded.

"What about your wife?" asked Stuart.

Ben was silent at first.

"I'm not sure. I mean, I pretty much blew my marriage. I can't imagine she would be interested in anything I might say at this point." Ben's heart sank, hearing his own voice utter the words.

"So, you're just giving up, huh?" said Stuart. "That's probably what she's expecting you to do."

Stung, Ben asked, "What do you mean by that? You guys told me I did the wrong thing telling her about my one-night stand. What good would it do to open that wound again? She wouldn't want that, would she?"

"See, that's what I mean. You're looking at this all wrong, man. Don't re-open the old wound—nothing gained with that move," said Stuart. "But why don't you give her something else to think about?"

"Something else?"

"Yeah. See, she's had months to think about your little, uh, indiscretion. Problem is, that's the last note you rang on the relationship bell. What if you went back to her and started a new note?"

"A new note? Like what?"

"That's for you to figure out." Stuart stretched out his legs and said no more.

Ben went quiet as well, trying to puzzle out the meaning of Stuart's advice. A new note? What would that be? He couldn't imagine any kind of scenario with Michelle in which she would do anything other than slam the door in his face. Women were hard enough to figure out, but trying to figure out a new move with a woman who'd been cheated on? *Impossible.*

The one thing he had going for himself was the loads of time on his hands. Maybe, just maybe, he could figure something out.

He turned to Stuart and asked, "How about you, dude? You're single, so there's nobody waiting for you. What's the first thing you'll do when you get back?"

Stuart didn't answer. He rolled his neck, the cracking audible. He used a big green stick to stoke the fire. He fingered his scraggly beard. Finally, he looked up at Ben.

"Actually, there is a woman, but she's not exactly waiting for me."

They waited.

"*And?*" asked Ben after a lengthy silence.

"Her name is Jillian, we were engaged for a few months, and she broke it off a couple of weeks before the wedding. End of story."

Jack, Ben, and Paul looked at each other knowingly.

"So, what did you do to make her do that?" asked Paul curiously.

"I didn't do anything," said Stuart unconvincingly.

"Yeah, right," said Ben. It felt good to not be in the spotlight, to have another one of the guys under scrutiny.

"Wait—first, tell us about her. What is she like?" asked Paul.

"She's tall, beautiful, and has the most amazing posture," said Stuart, gazing in the distance as though he could see her standing there. "She has gorgeous, silky hair, red with these—sort of lighter streaks. When she stands in the sun, her hair looks like copper and gold." He paused, then said softly, "and she's smart and sweet."

The other guys stared at each other, astonished.

"And how long since you broke up with this goddess?" asked Jack.

"Over five years," said Stuart, his face darkening.

"*And?*" asked Ben again. "What's the real reason you broke up?"

Stuart was silent.

"Come on, man, you got us to spill our guts. It's your turn," said Ben.

"Actually, Paul spilled his with no help from us," said Stuart defensively.

The other three guys looked at each other again.

"Okay, okay. Give me a minute," said Stuart.

Stuart's gut twisted. He knew this was inevitable, that he was going to tell the story of his and Jillian's relationship, but that didn't mean he was comfortable with it.

What else was there to do on a freaking deserted island but tell their life stories? The other guys, except for Jack, had already done it, and now it was his turn. Might as well.

"It was a few weeks before the wedding, and I got a little drunk with my buddies." Wow, what a lame admission.

"Actually, it was the night of our engagement party, and that, it turned out, was a problem for Jillian."

They waited. Stuart cleared his throat.

"So, the background is that we'd argued about having kids, or rather, about the fact that she wanted them, and I didn't. The next morning, she woke me up for one final talk on the subject, and I was just sick of it."

"Wait," Paul said. "How did you get to the point of planning your wedding without working that out? That's a pretty big issue going into marriage to not have decided, isn't it?"

Stuart felt confused. They *had* worked it out. Jillian and Stuart—DINKs—Dual Income, No Kids. True, he never actually told her that kids were out of the question, but then again, she never told him how important it was to her to have kids, not until much later. She tricked him, didn't she?

"We never talked about kids as a part of our future. We always talked about traveling and spending our money on adventures."

The other guys were quiet. Then Paul spoke up and said what they were thinking.

"So, you thought you had it covered?"

"Well, yeah, we did," said Stuart defensively.

"I don't think so," said Ben, looking at Paul, who nodded in agreement.

"Women always want more," said Jack sagely, leaving Stuart shaking his head.

"Well, if she wanted more, why didn't she tell me?" he asked.

No one answered.

"Why didn't you tell her you didn't want kids?" asked Paul.

Stuart was stumped. He *did* tell her, didn't he? But had he made it clear? Or had he mentioned it in passing, glazed over it, hoping she wouldn't make an issue out of it? He'd wanted Jillian, wanted her in his life, had never wanted to let her go. If he thought she *had* to have kids, and he didn't... Well, it would have ruined everything.

Oh, wait. It ended up ruining everything anyway.

"Even more important, why *not* kids?" asked Ben. "I mean, it's a natural part of life, having children with the woman you love. Or didn't you love her?"

"I loved her," stated Stuart adamantly.

"So, why not kids?"

Why not kids? *Why not?* It hit Stuart that he had never really asked himself that question, never challenged his own point of view. It wasn't something he thought about or delved into. It was just his mantra, something he'd told himself for years—*"I don't want kids."*

But why not? He didn't know. He only knew that he felt an aversion to parenthood, going back as far back as he could remember.

"I don't know," he said lamely.

The guys didn't push, sensing that they'd gone far enough with him for the time being. They slowly banked the fire, stood, and made their way to their separate sleeping areas.

As Stuart lay awake, staring at the gathering clouds, slowly blacking out the stars, he rolled the question around in his head. Why not kids? *Why not?*

That night, Stuart dreamed about a little girl with golden-red hair and deep blue eyes. She ran toward him, and he reached out his arms to pick her up, but she disappeared just before she got to him. He felt a huge emptiness in his heart. A sob rose in his chest, and that sob became a rumble that ended in a crash.

Startled, he woke to the beginning of raindrops hitting him in the face, far away lightning illuminating the dense clouds at the horizon. He stood quickly, woke everyone up, and they made their way swiftly to their cave shelter to wait out the rainstorm.

Luckily, this one contained none of the violence of the last storm. Instead, it rained steadily, with occasional thunder. As dawn began to break, the clouds scuttled away. The island was refreshed, and their water source flowed, filling their pond.

Another long day stretched ahead of them. The men set about doing their chores and Stuart pushed the dream to the back of his mind.

CHAPTER NINE

Tony worked on his project. He figured he'd found the right leaves, so he tried different methods of disguising the bitter taste. He crushed them and put them in fruit, but it was too obvious. He made a paste and stuffed it inside of some crab meat, but he knew that wouldn't work.

He fantasized about Stuart falling ill, turning green and vomiting uncontrollably, unable to breathe, dying a slow, painful death. In his mind's eye, Stuart's face morphed into his father's face and back again. He felt confused, disoriented at that vision. Then he hardened his resolve.

It was Stuart he wanted to kill. His old man was out of his life long ago. He'd heard from a cousin that his father had died of something— liver problems? Who knew? There was no funeral, but maybe someday he'd find the grave so he could piss on it.

He re-focused on Stuart, the guy who would surely kill him if he didn't kill him first. He knew it, could see Stuart advancing on him, probably at night, choking him to death while he slept. He'd wake just long enough to see Stuart's face over his, laughing as the life slowly leaked out of his body. No way was he going to let that happen.

But how could he get Stuart to eat something with the poison? What if it wasn't poisonous enough? What if it only made him sick, but he survived? He pictured Stuart miraculously surviving the poison and killing Tony in retribution. He had to find a better solution, fast.

One day as Tony was wandering in the trees thinking about the problem, he tripped over a vine and landed flat on his back. Winded, he gasped and struggled to get air back into his lungs. He sat up and waited to breathe better before he stood. Then he looked around. A completely new plan began to form in his mind.

The men sat on the beach with the fire crackling, nibbling at the remnants of their catch—lobster, with a side of berries. Ben was tired of their diet but ate anyway. It wouldn't be good to lose any more weight.

As usual, Tony sat slightly away from the others, and as soon as he finished eating, he rose and departed quickly. They watched him go.

"What do you think he's up to?" Stuart wondered out loud.

"I don't think he likes you," said Ben.

"I think he's afraid of you," said Paul.

"Couldn't care less," said Stuart.

No one answered. They stared into the distance, listening to the susurration of the ocean's insatiable rhythmic pounding of the shore.

"How long have we been here?" Paul wondered. "It seems like weeks, but I don't think it's been that long."

"I count 47 days since we left San Diego," said Jack. "I started notching a stick the day we got here, including two notches for the days at sea."

Ben shook his head.

"I wonder what Michelle thinks happened, how the kids are doing," he said. He pictured his children—playing, laughing, eating dinner with their Mom. He felt that familiar ache in his chest, the constriction.

Paul looked up. "Knowing Sarah, she's worried sick." He slowly twisted his wedding ring, gazing into the fire.

"Hey, guys?" said Paul. They looked up.

"If I don't make it back, I need you to do something for me."

They protested.

"What are you talking about? We're all going back home together," insisted Ben.

Though he didn't really believe that. Truth be told, it was unlikely any of them would ever see home again. It had been so long, the odds of a search-and-rescue continuation of effort was almost nil. He diverted his mind, unwilling to be fatalistic. His children needed him to hold out hope. He deliberately pulled up a memory, one that made him smile.

It was Katie's first day of pre-school. She'd packed her backpack the night before, obsessing about what to take, and that morning she'd gotten up before anyone else and dressed herself. They found her sitting on the floor by the front door, munching on an energy bar. He and Michelle looked at her and then at each other, astonished. They asked her what she was doing.

"I'm ready for school," she announced. "And I don't want to be late."

"Katie, honey," Michelle said, kneeling in front of her. "It's six o'clock in the morning. We don't need to leave for another hour and a half."

Katie sighed but stayed in place. "That's okay, Mom. I'll just wait here." They held back laughter and nodded solemnly. But they allowed her to wait for school by the front door. Of course, she was utterly exhausted later that day, and after that, she'd allowed Mom

111

and Dad to get her up for school.

They'd smiled about her level of organization for one so young, called her a future CEO. What an amazing little girl.

❦

Ben's heart swelled with the memory and vision of his amazing, smart daughter, with the personality of a future titan of business. His attention came back to the campfire and Paul.

"I hope so, I really do. But just in case, there's something important I need you to do," said Paul intently.

"Sure."

"Of course."

"Please go and see her. Give her this ring." He pointed to his wedding band.

"And tell her that she was—is—the love of my life, that I never stopped loving her." Paul's voice cracked, and tears ran down his face.

"Tell her—tell her I'm sorry. I'm so sorry for ruining things between us, and not just us, but with Nathan as well. Please, promise me you'll do this," Paul finished, wiping away tears.

Ben and Stuart both nodded. Paul drew a ragged breath.

"Of course," said Ben, but now everyone felt the heaviness.

"What about you, Stuart? What do you think is going on with Jillian?" Ben asked, hoping to shift the conversation.

Stuart blew out a breath. "Man, I seriously don't know. I'm not sure if she even knows I'm lost at sea. She never liked watching the news, said it made her too sad, or anxious, or something."

"So, what would you do if you could go back? About Jillian," asked Paul.

Stuart stared at the sand, steadily poking a short branch into the ground, leaving holes in a pattern, not unlike the outline of a building foundation.

"First of all, I seriously doubt she's sitting around pining for me. It's been years, and she's bound to be in a new relationship." He frowned, stood, and threw the stick as far as he could toward the ocean, where it landed just short of the waves gently rolling in.

"I wouldn't be surprised to find out she's married," Stuart said, gazing out to sea, watching the sunset. "Maybe she's had a kid by now, the one I wouldn't have with her," he said with a false tone of humor. "Heck, maybe she named the kid after me if it's a boy," he chuckled.

But no one laughed with him.

Stuart turned to Ben. "What about your ex, man? Do you think she's dating?"

Ben was shocked. He'd never once thought of Michelle moving on, dating other men.

"I don't think so. She told me a long time ago dating wasn't something she would expose the kids to, that she didn't want them to go through all of the messiness of someone new coming into their lives and if it didn't work out, going away."

The other guys looked at each other.

"What?" Ben asked, looking at them.

"Is your ex-wife, uh, not that attractive?" asked Stuart.

"Are you kidding? She's *gorgeous*," said Ben hotly.

"Well, then?" said Stuart. "So, she's beautiful, and single, after you cheated on her and left her, and you think she's not going to date? Man, you really don't get it, do you?"

"Get what?" Ben asked defensively.

"There's nothing more attractive to a guy than a beautiful woman who is in sore need of having her ego restored. Flowers, a couple of romantic dinners out, and what follows is the great sex—just the ticket. She is ripe for that—don't kid yourself."

Stuart nodded his head, more to himself than to Ben.

"Yep, Jillian is probably married, and your ex-wife is out right now drinking wine with some other dude, headed for another night of hot sex," said Stuart flatly.

Ben's face tightened. No way. There was no way Michelle would be having sex with another man. She was a *Mom*, after all.

A single Mom. Ben flashed back to the school the kids attended, to the drive-up area where he dropped them off after spending the night with him. After the divorce, he'd found himself the object of attention from two or three single Moms.

He'd often driven up and had to roll down his window because of a manicured nail tapping on the glass. At which point Rachel or Amanda or some other divorced Mom would lean in, smelling of expensive soap or perfume, eyes carefully made up, blond or brunette hair over the shoulder, sleek body in tight yoga outfit, and ask him an innocuous question, or tell him how cute his kids were. He'd respond politely but couldn't wait to drive away. He'd never wanted to follow up.

The last thing in the world he wanted to do was date. He assumed that Michelle felt the same way.

"So, Ben, if your wife is so gorgeous, why exactly did you cheat on her?" asked Stuart. "Is there some kind of other problem? Alcohol? Crazy? I mean, you seem like a decent guy, not a player." He looked genuinely puzzled.

"Why does any guy cheat?" Ben asked. "It was a business trip. I was lonely, she was there, we drank way too much, and one thing led to another."

Shame washed over Ben again.

"There is no excuse," he said dejectedly. "I don't know how to explain it. I just know it was wrong, and the worst mistake of my life."

He looked up at the other guys intently. "It will always be the greatest regret of my life," he said.

"Well, that explains the jealousy," said Stuart.

"Jealousy?" Ben asked defensively.

"You should have seen your face when I said your ex is probably out with some other dude," said Stuart. "You haven't gotten over her, have you?" he added softly.

Ben said nothing. *Jealous?* Was that the horrible feeling in the pit of his stomach, at the thought of her with someone else? Had he really not "gotten over" Michelle? And what did that mean, anyway?

Everyone was quiet for a while. The sun sank completely below the horizon.

Paul turned to Jack.

"What about you, Captain? Whose heart have you broken? Is someone waiting for you?"

Jack gazed into the distance for a moment.

"I have someone waiting for me." He was silent again. "But I'm not sure if she's going to break my heart or vice versa. We haven't exactly talked about the future."

"And how have you managed to avoid that?" asked Stuart. "My experience—women always want to talk about the future. Can't get out of it if you're with someone for more than a few months."

The other men nodded.

"I agree," said Jack. "But I made it clear when we started out that I'm not the guy for her if she wants commitment and marriage. She agreed, and we have always said we were on the same page," he went on.

"And for how long have you been on this no-commitment same page?" asked Stuart.

"For about two years," said Jack.

"So, do you love her?" Ben asked.

Jack was quiet, not looking at them.

"Well, that clears that up," said Stuart. "Too long to answer, or no answer, means you don't love her."

Jack looked up. "It's complicated."

"Uh-huh," said Stuart.

But it was clear the conversation was over for Jack.

"Who really thinks we're going to get off this island?" asked Paul.

"I think we will," ventured Ben.

"What makes you think that?" asked Stuart.

"Just a feeling," said Ben. "I can't imagine never seeing my kids again. In fact, I can't stop hoping we get back, for their sake and mine."

"What do you think?" Stuart asked Captain Jack.

"I think it depends on a lot of things. If we're close to shipping lanes, at some point, someone could notice something. If they're still searching, there's a good chance they will spot our message on the beach. As long as we keep finding sources of water and food, we can wait a long time."

"But how long will we be here?" asked Paul.

"No way to tell," said Jack.

"One thing I know—the longer we're here, the more likely they will call off the search," said Stuart.

Jack didn't say anything. In his experience, 47 days was far past the "search-and-rescue" phase of any Coast Guard operation. They wouldn't get off the island due to some miraculous rescue mission. Their only real hope was pure luck—the luck of a container ship straying close enough to spot the island and see them. The luck of someone on the vessel knowing about them, being curious, calling in a report.

Bottom line: they were unlikely to ever get off this island, unlikely to ever return home. Like it or not, they were stuck here and stuck with each other.

They were silent, lost in their own thoughts.

Overhead, the stars splashed brilliantly across the vastness of the universe. The Milky Way showcased its billions of luminous bodies of light scattered within colorful gaseous bands of interstellar dust.

"Amazing how much you can see here," said Paul. "It's so beautiful. We're looking at the Milky Way, right? Our galaxy. I wonder how many stars are in our galaxy."

"No accurate count, but estimates are somewhere between one and four hundred billion," said Jack. Astonished noises emanated from the men.

Jack continued, "The Milky Way is a vast, relatively flat area of stars, with four enormous arms that swirl outwards from the center bar. Each arm has between 50 and 100 billion stars. Our solar system sits in one of the arms, about midway out from the center of the galaxy."

"I can't imagine the scale," said Stuart.

"It's almost impossible to imagine, but here's one way to try," said Jack. "If you picture one average household container of salt, and if you imagine us re-creating the shape of the Milky Way by shaking out the entire container on a dark floor, with the four large arms swirling outward, how many of those containers do you think it would take? How large would the room have to be so that each grain of salt represented one star in our galaxy?"

"I'm guessing the floor of a very large room, like a ballroom in one of those castles you see in Europe," said Ben.

"I think you'd have to use an entire gymnasium floor," said Stuart.

"Any other guesses?" asked Jack.

Paul appeared to be calculating heavily in his head, and finally held up a finger. "I think it would be more like a football field," he said.

"Not a bad guess. Each salt container has roughly five million grains of salt, so if you do the math—not precise, just approximate—it would take around 60,000 salt containers to create a representation of the Milky Way, each grain of salt representing one star."

Everyone stared at the sky in wonderment.

"Then, if you really want to imagine scale, consider this. Most scientists believe there are *at least* one hundred billion galaxies in the Universe, many of them the size and scale of the Milky Way," said Jack.

The men groaned out loud.

"No way."

"Too big to comprehend."

They were silent again, staring at the sky.

"What is that dark area in the middle?" asked Paul. "There are so many stars, so much mass, but then there's this big wide stripe of dark, no light, no stars. Or we can't see them. Do you guys see that?"

"Yep," they echoed each other.

"It's called the Dark Rift and is believed to be a vast area of molecular dust clouds. It keeps us from seeing the stars behind it, giving the impression that the Milky Way has a large dark center," said Jack. "A lot of old cultures saw shapes in the dark area and created legends about them. But scientists say it's the place where new stars are forming."

Stuart sighed loudly. "I never get to really see the stars like this at home, living in the city. The sky is so much brighter there, with all the billboards and streetlights, so few stars are visible. I don't think I've ever really seen the Milky Way before."

"That's right," said Jack. "With population explosion in the past few decades and the growth of large urban areas with all the lights, we've gradually lost most of the dark skies that once dominated our planet. It's why I love going out on the ocean."

The men were quiet for a moment, gazing at the stars.

"That huge, dark rift is kind of like us, isn't it?" said Paul, surprising himself. "I'm not exactly the philosophical type, but I see something there. Relationships with women—how do you get back across the rift? You have to cross it again to get home. Seems so unlikely, right? But you can't give up hope."

Ben thought about that, about this place, this island, in the middle of the vast Pacific Ocean, with nothing but dark skies above, lit by hundreds of billions of stars. There weren't any dark skies in the city, so you couldn't tap the perspective.

Where would he be in his life if he hadn't gotten on the boat, hadn't been flung to this distant island? He'd have his kids, his routine, his work. He wouldn't be wondering every day if his life was about to be cut short, or if he'd grow old, get sick, and die in this place.

He wouldn't feel the constant, dull ache of missing his children, of visualizing them, of longing to hold them. Knowing they would grow up without him, that he'd never see them graduate, get married, have their own children.

It would be far better if he'd stayed home, hadn't decided to go on this doomed fishing trip. Wouldn't it?

But he had gotten on the boat. And, now, looking at the sky, and the stars, and with no sound except the ocean nearby, he saw what he couldn't see before.

In the unlikeliest place on the planet, Ben felt a tiny surge of hope, hope that he might return to his life, make it right again.

If only they could get off this island, get back home, he knew he would be different. He would try again with Michelle. He would somehow find a way to get his family back.

Stuart closed his eyes, opened them again as he lay back on the sand with his arm under his head. He wondered if Jillian was looking at the same sky, also wondering about the stars. Did she ever think of him? Had she missed him since their breakup? Or had she moved on? Maybe met someone better than him. Someone who felt like he'd felt when he met her—that he'd died, gone to heaven, and met an angel.

But that someone would surely be smarter than Stuart. He'd do all the right things, make sure that Jillian was his, now and forever. He would be the kind of guy who'd love her completely, devote himself to her, never let her go. He would, of course, have a baby with her, more if she wanted them.

Stuart could no longer see why he'd been so opposed to having children. It had made sense back then, somehow, but here, it looked different. Confronted with the possibility of dying on this tiny island, or worse, growing old here, condemned to a life of scrounging for food and water, with only the company of other men, it made no sense at all. Now, it seemed limited and petty.

Why hadn't he seen this when he had Jillian in his life? A question he might never answer, but maybe it wasn't the right question anyway. Maybe a better question was whether or not he had the guts to do something about all of this if he ever got back home.

Huge "if."

The ocean lapped at the shore, taking itself further away with the tidal change, as though to distance itself from the men and their thoughts, their fears, their hopes, and their confusion.

A limb cracked distantly in the trees, causing everyone to look that direction. Another limb cracked.

Then it was silent. They stood and made their way to their sleeping areas.

CHAPTER TEN

Tony stooped and picked up another handful of small branches and leaves, carefully scattering them. He stood, took a step or two back, and surveyed his work. That should do it. He felt a surge of anticipation as he imagined the results.

This will stop that asshole. Images of all the times he'd felt bullied or bested flashed through his mind, and his cheeks burned. His fists tightened.

Now or never. He turned and made his way back to the camping area. As he got closer, he began to run.

"Paul!" he called out. "I think you'd better come see this," he said urgently. He turned back into the trees.

Paul hesitated, then rose from his spot on the beach and quickly followed. It was odd for Tony to have anything to do with the rest of them, but he seemed distressed, so maybe there was a problem. As he moved into the trees, he lost sight of Tony. He peered through the branches, then stopped to listen. Nothing. What was going on?

He moved more quickly now, peering in all directions. He continued, now taking time to glance around, periodically calling Tony's name. He followed the well-worn pathway they'd all been taking each day to get to the spring. Foliage slapped him in the face as he hurried along. He pushed his way through, looking.

Where was Tony? Then, he stopped. There were two pathways in front of him. Strange, he couldn't remember the path branching off like that.

Paul stood and thought about which way to go. Suddenly, he felt something heavy hit the back of his head. He swayed as the edges of his sight went dark, then crumpled to the ground.

Stuart made his way through the shallow water at the shoreline, waves lapping at his feet. He carried a large lobster on the end of the sharp stick he often used for fishing. He made his way to the cooking area and threw the lobster into the bucket in which they accumulated the catches of the day. He looked around, noticing that Paul was not around, and neither was Jack nor Tony. He shrugged and turned to head back into the surf.

Tony emerged from the trees, panting. He looked frightened.

"Stuart! Come quick—it's Paul. He's hurt!"

Stuart froze, staring at Tony, who gestured urgently.

"Hurry!" yelled Tony.

He turned and hurried back into the trees. Odd for Tony to ask Stuart for help. Stuart's stomach clenched. But Paul was hurt. He followed Tony, picked up the pace, then ran.

Moving into the trees, Stuart could just see Tony ahead, who motioned for him to follow. "This way—he's over here!"

The back of Stuart's neck crawled slightly, sending him warning signals that something was off. He followed, but more slowly now, looking around, covering himself.

"Hurry! I think he's seriously hurt," Tony urged, continuing to move deeper into the trees.

Tony stopped in his tracks in a slightly more cleared area. He looked down, then around, frowning, puzzled.

"Shit," he said, then turned toward Stuart as he slowly approached.

"He was right here," he said, indicating a spot in the pathway. Lots of small branches and leaves were piled across the spot in a way that didn't appear natural.

Stuart approached cautiously, then stopped a few yards away from Tony. He stared hard.

"What are you up to?"

"Man, what is your problem? I swear, Paul was hurt, lying here just a few minutes ago!" shouted Tony.

Just then, Paul came through the trees behind Tony, weaving unsteadily.

"Uh, guys, I'm not sure what happened, but something hit the back of my head," said Paul weakly. He held his hand to the back of his head, then moved it forward, peering at it. Blood dripped from Paul's fingers. He continued forward into the pathway between the two other men, stumbling.

"What's going on?" Paul asked, looking around in confusion.

Stuart's entire body vibrated with awareness.

"Paul! Stay where you are," called out Stuart. But Paul stumbled, and suddenly, the ground gave way underneath him. He fell into the pile of leaves and sticks, which dropped away, and he landed in a shallow pit with a loud thump. He groaned once, then fell silent. Stuart ran to the pit and began scrambling to get to Paul.

"What the hell? Goddamn it! " yelled Tony, glaring down at Paul. "You fucking idiot! You've ruined everything!"

Stuart frantically pulled leaves and branches off of Paul, and as he did, he saw a sharp, pointed branch piercing all the way through his shoulder. Blood flowed from the wound.

Stuart began pulling Paul out of the pit, who rolled his head and moaned. His eyes rolled back, whites showing. Stuart managed to get

Paul laid out on the ground near the pit. Paul's eyes were closed. Blood continued to pool under his upper body. He lay utterly still, and Stuart couldn't tell if he was still breathing.

Stuart stood, facing Tony, who looked apoplectic.

"You did this, didn't you?" Stuart asked, voice flat. "You killed him."

"Yeah, so what? That was supposed to be you!" shouted Tony, brandishing something back and forth, crouched as if he was about to make a run at Stuart. He waved Jack's knife, usually in Jack's possession, but somehow, in Tony's hand.

Stuart moved toward Tony to disarm him, but Tony stepped back, continuing to wave the knife around. Stuart stood still and focused. He allowed his senses to take in the environment—the trees, the vines, the strange pit, Paul's body nearby. He focused his attention on Tony—his frantic movements, the fear wafting from him with an odd odor.

Suddenly, Tony lunged forward with the knife. Stuart stepped back quickly, but Tony stepped forward faster and swiped. Stuart felt a searing pain across his abdomen, looked down at blood beginning to seep out of the shallow wound. He looked up at Tony, his eyes flat.

Tony lunged again, and this time, Stuart easily evaded him. He prepared for the next attack, planning his moves. He held his arms loosely at his sides but with tightly bunched muscles.

When someone attacks in a rage, they aren't focused. They are not cognizant of the environment or of the possibility of the other person's potential counterattack. Rage fuels adrenaline, and with adrenaline, oxygen flows to the body's extremities, away from the rational, thinking brain.

But a trained person knows to breathe deeply so that the brain can strategize, focus, and prepare. In the few seconds he had, Stuart drew a couple of deep, slow breaths. Simultaneously, he scanned Tony's body position, his shaking hands, his wild eyes and shallow breath. Perfect.

Maybe it was growing up in chaos and fear with his alcoholic father. Maybe it was his largely kinesthetic makeup, the demand for strenuous physical outlets for stress. Whatever the reason, Stuart had gotten training years ago in hand to hand combat. He never wanted to be in a position of vulnerability and fear. He liked knowing that he could defend himself when he went out at night, cruised the bars around downtown Austin, Texas, and walked home in the middle of the night, unconcerned for his safety.

It also meant he had no fear of Tony, even though the knife gave him the clear advantage. No fear meant no adrenaline surge. No fear didn't mean he was overly confident, only that he felt no sense of panic.

Tony let out a growl of rage and ran at Stuart with the knife in both hands. Dangerous if he made a hit, with so much force behind it. But rage pulled Tony off-center. He ran erratically, relying on nothing but sheer rabid force.

Stuart easily turned sideways as Tony lunged past him, stumbling from the sudden lack of a target. He reached out and took Tony's arm, pulling him forward, using his own momentum. Once Tony was past him, Stuart reached for his knife hand, intending to remove the weapon.

But Tony tripped, falling into the pit of his own making. He screamed as he fell, there was a muffled thump, and then silence.

Stuart walked to the edge of the pit and stared. Tony lay face down, the knife poking through the side of his neck. Bright red blood gushed from the wound, arterial blood, a severed carotid. There was nothing he could do for him. He would bleed out in seconds if he hadn't already. Stuart turned away and bent to examine Paul, who lay still and white.

Ben and Jack appeared, both out of breath. They looked in shock at the two men in the clearing, one on the ground and the other at the bottom of the shallow pit.

"What happened?" Ben asked Stuart, who stood and faced them.

Two men lay incapacitated, one clearly dead, the other all but dead. Stuart rapidly explained what had happened. Their doubtful rescue had now become a life and death issue.

PART TWO

THE WOMEN, THE MISSING

CHAPTER ELEVEN

SEVERAL MONTHS EARLIER

Michelle was distracted by a text, which now relentlessly played an abstract marimba. Why hadn't she downloaded something better? Katie and Jordan played nearby, or at least that was one way to look at it. He was trying desperately to develop his motor skills by carefully stacking blocks, only to be defeated by his older sister gleefully knocking them over and exploding with laughter. He'd had enough and yelled at her, "Stop it, Kay-ree!" to which she taunted him with, "make me, make me!" He toddled toward her, and she scooted away, staying just out of reach, giggling.

Jordan revered his sister, lived for the moments when she stopped teasing him and would instead open a picture storybook and read to him out loud. At those times, he would watch her face solemnly, adoration clear in his eyes.

Most of the time, however, she delighted in teasing him.

"Stop it, Kate," Michelle futilely ordered as she pulled out her phone and attempted to focus on the text. Kate continued to tease her brother, and he continued to whine. Mercy me.

It was Ben, her husband.

"Meet me at 6:00 at The Harvest." *What?*

It was the restaurant where they'd had their first date. But it wasn't their anniversary, and it wasn't her birthday or his. Ben never drew upon nostalgia unless there was a good reason. Not in the last couple of years, anyway.

"What for?" she typed, but then decided that sounded too harsh. She erased and typed, "Did I forget something, a special date or—?"

"No special occasion other than wanting to see you alone. Date night."

Odd, because they typically planned their date nights far in advance so they could secure childcare. At least, that was how it used to be when they had made time for date nights. Lately, though, they'd been few and far between. Their choices for childcare were limited on such short notice—either her sister or his parents.

"I asked Liz—eta 5:30."

That was it. No hearts, no smiley face, no terms of endearment. Well, alrighty, then.

Emotions tugged—pleasure at her husband wanting to see her and the thought of dressing up for once—followed by the strong desire to simply collapse into a hot tub of bubbles and stay there for hours. Maybe she could ask Liz to watch the kids while she did that. Such a simple pleasure, but impossible with two little ones.

The demands of motherhood had removed every inclination toward intimacy with Ben. She barely remembered what it was like when they made love slowly, lingering in each other's arms afterward, or lit candles, sipped wine and talked softly—foreplay to the foreplay.

Now, they rarely had sex, and when they did, it was a quickie after a shower, or fumbling with each other in the middle of the night—opportunistic sex, as she thought of it. Forget foreplay, after play, or romance. She got little out of it but realized she couldn't continually push Ben away until the kids went off to college, and she recovered her sexuality. If she ever did. Having kids had changed her.

She wondered for the thousandth time—is it me? Is it him? Did they ever have any real chemistry, or did they marry because she'd felt the ticking of the fertility clock so loudly that she'd been compelled to pounce on him? Had she pushed him into starting a family? They had loved each other deeply. Or so she'd felt years ago.

She'd been so busy with her career, founding a small law firm, struggling to get clients, working 70-hour weeks. Ben was a breath of fresh air in her workaholic life. He was so laid back, so unlike the driven, type-A attorneys she'd dated.

At first, she'd hesitated—he was nothing like the dating "list" she'd written down years before. *Tall, athletic, top tier school, driven, successful, on his way to his second million, sophisticated, well-traveled.* And, of course, things that were not typically found in that package: *Sweet, romantic, wants marriage and children, emotionally supportive, giving.*

After a couple of dates with Ben, she'd talked it over with her sister, Liz—her best friend and confidante. Liz, in her usual blunt fashion, scoffed.

"So, let me get this straight. You met this good looking, sweet guy, who is gainfully employed, crazy about you, as witnessed by the bouquet of flowers at your office after the second date, and the non-stop requests to spend more time with you. Maybe not exactly the Wall Street type, but—tell me again, what is his problem? Oh yeah—he's not burning up the career ladder and hasn't made his first million. Oh, and let's not forget—he's not a dickhead like the last two guys you dated, one of whom dumped you in the middle of a cruise because he ran into an ex-girlfriend on board and decided to hook up again with her!"

She shook her head mournfully, "Yeah, for sure, you should definitely get out of this one, Michelle. Run for the hills before he gets his hooks into you."

After that, she'd let herself go with the flow of the relationship, and within four months, she was marriage bound and knew it. It was a whirlwind courtship—they were married after only eleven months of dating, and she was pregnant by the time she'd finished decorating their apartment.

After the birth of their first child, she'd left the law firm, become a full-time Mom. She'd felt happier than ever before in her life.

That was real, wasn't it?

But lately, she found herself struggling so hard to feel anything for him other than irritation that she wondered.

She thought again about the first few months of dating—the spontaneous gestures of romance, the lovemaking. How much she'd fallen in love with him, and with the delicious feeling of being totally desired on every level by a wonderful man.

For the first time in her life, she hadn't felt insecure. She didn't have to wonder where it was going. They were going straight toward a wonderful future together—there were no doubts, no dramatic moments of one pulling away and the other having to fight to re-connect, followed by doubts, romantic reconciliations, but always cycling toward the inevitable breakup. No, with Ben, it had been a wonderful, perfect beginning.

It's me, she thought. She'd lost something inside. Or maybe she was just too messed up after years of dysfunctional dating. Maybe she'd brought too much baggage into the relationship to ever have a shot at anything good in the long run.

Then again, Ben hadn't exactly been the most attentive of husbands in the past few months. She'd felt his withdrawal and her own growing resentment.

It was him. It was her. It was the two of them. Her head ached from pondering their messed-up relationship once again, with no solutions in sight.

Date night. She was skeptical but also curious. This was not Ben's M.O., so something was up, of that she was sure. Maybe he was trying to revive their intimacy by surprising her. Maybe he was trying to be less predictable so that it might create a little zing in their relationship.

Ben? Not likely. He wasn't that spontaneous. He was a genuinely nice, safe guy, and she'd chosen him for those qualities, sick of the six to 18-month relationships with guys who were exciting but not marriage and family material.

She herded the kids into the master bedroom, popped in a movie, made sure they were enthralled, and then headed into the bathroom, leaving the door ajar as a just in case. She yearned for the old days of privacy as she quickly showered.

Later, she lingered over choosing what to wear. Sexy? Demure? Did anyone really care? Did she?

Before Mom-hood, she'd thoroughly enjoyed dressing up, both for herself and for her husband. She loved choosing something short and clingy, accentuating her slender figure. She always wore one sparkly thing—a long, slender necklace or big dangling earrings. Now, she couldn't seem to drum up any of the old pleasure of dressing up. She pushed clothes back and forth on the rack, her frustration growing.

Finally, she chose a knee-length black skirt, white blouse, and plain silver earrings. She slipped on flat black shoes, put on a minimal amount of makeup, pulled her long blond hair into a ponytail, and figured she was good to go.

She transferred the kids downstairs and started another movie on the screen in the family room.

Waiting for Liz, she poured a glass of wine and sat on the sofa. The kids watched Frozen for the umpteenth time, eyes glazed over in rapture, so she had a moment of peace.

But she wasn't peaceful inside. An unpleasant feeling nagged her, along with the thought that there was more to this than a simple date night.

Liz, her little sister with unfashionably short, auburn hair, freckles sprinkled lightly across her nose, blue eyes wide, breezed in the door. They looked like they had different parents. Michelle was tall and awkward, completely lacking in athleticism, far more comfortable curled up with a good book than out doing all those things that physical people do.

Liz was diminutive—short, toned, and lithe, always pushing up onto the balls of her feet like she was poised for a race. Liz moved rapidly through life, uncomfortable unless she was in motion. They were close in age, one year apart.

As little girls, Liz and Michelle were like ping pong balls, bouncing off each other—close one minute, fighting the next. Then, in high school, a tormenter targeted Michelle—Erin, the meanest Mean Girl you could imagine.

Erin was beautiful and popular, with long, thick, sun-streaked blond hair, perfect golden honey skin, and hazel eyes that sparkled when she was in "charming" mode, which was any time she wanted something. She spoke in a soft voice that dripped with sugar, often shortly before she stuck the social knife in someone's back. She had rich parents, which meant that she drove a brand-new BMW by her sophomore year.

Erin was head cheerleader, so all the boys wanted her. She had it all, but it wasn't enough. She craved the spotlight, and needed control over her click of friends, and sway over everyone else in the school.

One day, Michelle found herself in the uncomfortable position of being on the receiving end of high praise in senior English class. They'd been asked to write an essay on 9/11, and she'd chosen to write from the perspective of the towers that were destroyed, personifying them in their dying minutes.

Mr. Foster was the youngest teacher in the school, and by far the most good-looking, with sandy hair and stubble on his chiseled jawline. But that never mattered to Michelle.

That day, he gave Michelle high praise for her writing assignment and asked her to read it in front of the class. She squirmed in her seat, panicked, and shook her head, heart racing. He nodded encouragement as he walked to her desk and handed her the paper.

"Go ahead, Michelle. People, listen and tell me what Michelle did with her essay that makes it so compelling."

There were a couple of snickers, and that pissed her off. So, she stood and read her paper with pride. Mr. Foster beamed. A couple of brave kids raised their hands and offered praise, but that stopped when Erin shot a glare their way.

The punishment came later. What she didn't know was that Erin had set her sights on Mr. Foster, bored with the hordes of high school boys with whom she regularly toyed and discarded. Over the next two weeks, Michelle found herself the butt of cruel jokes at school, perpetrated by Erin and her small tribe of Mean Girls who did whatever Erin wanted, anything to stay in her good graces.

It all culminated in the incident that set off Liz. Michelle opened her locker one day and found syrup all over her books and things, including a paper that she'd spent days writing, due the next day. She burst into tears, and later at home, cried for hours. Mom and Dad comforted her and sagely advised her to not take it personally, that it really was all about Erin's immaturity and cruelty, and not about her at all. Liz protested that advice loudly, burning with anger.

Liz found out where Erin lived, and waited for the day she knew Erin would be home alone. She insisted that Michelle go with her to Erin's house, so she did, figuring they were going to talk it out. Maybe loudly, with Liz in charge.

Liz was fearless, and confrontation only energized her. Erin, despite being head cheerleader and supposedly athletic, feared physical confrontation, as they later discovered. She'd blithely inflicted a thousand little social deaths in and outside of her peer group, and she didn't care if others tried to do the same to her, but it had never occurred to her that someone might threaten her with physical violence as a result.

Liz confronted her, demanding an apology. When Erin boldly sneered at Michelle's pain, Liz shoved her, hard, so that she stumbled backward and fell on her butt. She looked up in shock and fear, and Liz told her in excruciating detail exactly what she would do to her if she ever caused Michelle a problem again in the future. Before leaving, Liz delivered one swift kick to Erin's side, causing her to curl up and cry out. They left her sobbing, mascara running.

Michelle knew Liz was fierce, but she'd never suspected that her sister could do something like this. Shocked, she stumbled out behind Liz as she stormed away, muttering something about how that little shit had gotten off far too easy.

After that, the Mean Girls backed off, cutting Michelle a wide berth at school for the rest of the year, which didn't bother her since she was such an introvert anyway. After that, Liz was her absolute hero, and they remained inseparable.

No one had ever loved Michelle so ferociously, not even Ben.

As Liz walked in, she scooped up the kids one by one, giving them huge smooches. She stood surveying them with hands on her hips, face serious.

"Now, listen up. Aunt Liz is here. There will be no more laughing or playing or anything fun at all." They burst into giggles and begin running around her in circles.

"Hey, you little munchkins, stop that! I mean it. Your Mom told me you need more discipline, so we are all going to sit quietly while she's away. That means no touching the toys, and certainly no throwing them around." This caused them to begin picking up toys and throwing them. Michelle dodged one of Kate's and it crashed into her wine glass, thankfully now empty, which smashed into pieces on the floor.

It was amazing how one small human could trigger so much chaos.

Michelle sighed. Liz laughed and went to the kitchen, coming back with a broom, dustpan, and bag for the broken glass. After she finished cleaning up, she looked at Michelle, taking in her attire head to toe.

"Uh, Michelle, aren't you going to get dressed?" she asked pointedly.

"Do you have a problem with what I'm wearing?"

"Aren't you meeting your husband for date night?"

Who was she, a relationship consultant?

"Yes, we are meeting. Whether or not it's a date night remains to be seen. Anyway, I'm late." She started to walk away.

Liz walked over and looked at Michelle up and down.

"Hey sis, don't get mad at me, but it seems like you're not putting much effort into this. I mean, Ben is a great guy, and he's trying."

"Hey, Liz?"

"Yeah?"

"I don't remember asking for marital advice. You have no clue what this is about—after all, you're single."

Stung, Liz drew back.

Michelle grabbed her purse and headed for the door, pausing with her back to Liz.

"Thanks for watching the kids, Liz, really." She softened her voice. "They love you, and so do I."

CHAPTER TWELVE

Arriving early, Michelle settled in at the table and ordered a glass of wine while she waited for Ben. The restaurant buzzed with the sounds of people enjoying alcohol and good food. It was one of those eclectic places with exposed brick walls, concrete floors, and random items like hubcaps and gears scattered around as decor. The food was a cross between comfort food and fast food, with a twist, so that there were things on the menu with names like "the green wedgie" for a wedge salad, and "crabbed out" for crab cakes.

It was one of their frequent haunts, but they hadn't been there in months, especially since she'd been trying to lose the baby weight—though without really putting much effort in, of course. She crossed her legs and tapped her foot against the table leg impatiently while glancing periodically at her phone for texts. Finally, he walked in the door and made his way to the table.

Ben leaned over for a quick, chaste kiss and slid into his seat. Their table was in the back, so it was a bit more private. After putting in his drink and their dinner orders, they sat back and regarded one another carefully, like prizefighters waiting for the bell to ring.

He reached across the table and took her hand in his, running his thumb over the top of her hand. His touch was warm, and she closed her eyes for a moment, remembering how it used to be. Even with their waning connection, his touch still gave her a zing.

She opened her eyes, pulled her hand away, and took the first shot.

"So, what is this about? Date night isn't really your style these days." She expected banter at the least, knowing they would probably escalate into a full-blown argument. Any time she confronted, he got defensive, and something in her wanted that to happen.

Pent up emotions yearned for release, and at this point, she didn't care if it was a healthy release or the opposite.

"Hey, Ben? I am talking to you. Do you realize how I felt after I got your text? Asking me out but with absolutely no signs of real affection? What's going on with you? I swear I don't get it. You're here, but you're really not." Her voice was laced with pain, despite the harshness of her words.

He was utterly quiet, eyes cast down.

Where was the fight in him? She'd pushed hard, and instead of meeting a nice, thick wall of emotional resistance against which she could flail around and wear herself out, she'd encountered air. It felt wildly uncomfortable.

When he looked up, his eyes were sad. Did she see a trace of moisture there?

"Michelle, I'm sorry. I don't know how to tell you this, but...,"

Her heart thumped, and her breath quickened.

"Do you remember that business trip I took to Atlanta a few months ago?"

She nodded, completely bewildered.

"Do you remember what it was like when I got back? Between us?"

Memories kicked in. The flowers, hand-delivered, the uncharacteristically helpful way he took over with the kids when he was home. The surprise gift of diamond earrings.

The way he'd made love, holding her so tightly, whispering over and over how much he loved her. The way she'd resisted at first, but then had allowed herself to relax again inside, allowed herself to fall in love all over again. Just a little.

But it hadn't lasted. After a few weeks, the distance grew once again between them, and they returned to their separate corners. He the stressed out, distant, always running-out-the-door breadwinner. She the exhausted, irritable, stay-at-home Mom. It stung, but she chalked it up to the demands of career and parenthood, imagining it would magically change someday.

Lately, though, she'd begun to seethe with resentment.

"Yes, I remember. What about it?"

He was quiet again, restless, tugging at his hair in the back. He couldn't seem to make eye contact.

He sighed heavily, then put on a determined look, raising his eyes to hers. He looked agonized. Realization dawned, and she felt her heart rate escalate. Suddenly, her hands were cold, and she began shivering, waiting for the blow.

"There's no easy way to say this, Michelle. I made a huge mistake on that trip."

"A mistake?" She asked in a dangerously even voice. "What do you mean, a *mistake*? Did you forget something in the hotel? Did you steal the bathrobe?" She welcomed the sarcasm—anything but the shocked helplessness she'd felt moments before.

"Oh. Wait, perhaps you forgot your vows. Is that it?"

She waited for him to scoff and retort angrily that she was being ridiculous. *Please*, she pleaded inside, *let me be wrong*.

Silence.

"Are you telling me you screwed some other woman? I don't believe this!" Her voice rose.

"Michelle, listen to me. It didn't mean anything."

"It? Don't you mean she? *Who is she?*"

He looked away. "It doesn't matter who she is. I couldn't go on with this lie between us." He started to cry. "I'm so sorry," he choked out.

"You're sorry? You are sorry! *Who are you?*"

She pulled her seat back and tried to stand, grabbing her purse.

"What are you doing?" Ben grabbed her hand and tried to tug her back down.

"Let go!" she yelled, jerking her hand away.

The restaurant buzz stopped momentarily. It was a small place, and they were visible to virtually every table. People stared.

Ben released her hand, stood, and told her it was okay. "We can leave and go somewhere else to talk." As if another location would change the way things were, would alter the breathtaking new trajectory of their lives.

She barely heard him, the buzzing in her ears was so loud. She swayed slightly, but then got her bearings and turned to leave as fast as she could.

He stayed behind to settle the check, calling after her. Everyone stared at their little drama. It was the best entertainment of the evening.

She ran for the door, flung it open, and raced for the car, hands shaking as she pulled open the door and slid in. As she pulled away, Ben ran after the car but gave up as she accelerated and left him behind. Tears ran down her face. She swiped at them, trying to see. She swerved suddenly, almost hitting a parked car on the street. That made her slow down and focus. She was upset but not suicidal.

It was indescribable—the way she felt when she let herself in the door of their home. She looked around the cozy living room with the gas log fireplace, glowing cheerily. She'd meticulously restored their craftsman style bungalow to its former vintage glory, decorating it with children and a long tenure in mind—warm, colorful prints and solids, fabrics that were designed to weather the test of time, easy to clean rugs, stylish yet durable furniture.

The house was quiet, Liz asleep on the sofa, the kids in bed. She went into the master bedroom and stood there, dazed. She saw her beautiful home but felt oddly disassociated from it like it was now a container for someone else's life.

All the little details that had given her so much delight—the tiffany lamps by the four-poster bed, the white comforter with the soft, gray plaid blanket over the foot of it, the tray ceiling painted creamy white, the tile fireplace with the wood surround and mantel—now produced a deep ache in her chest as she gazed around the room.

The tears stopped, and an unsettling numbness descended. She felt as though someone she loved had unexpectedly died. Heaviness pressed on her chest.

Her mind raced ahead—how fast could she sell the house? What would she get for it? What could she afford on her own? Who would take care of the kids while she went back to work?

Not one part of her envisioned a life going forward with Ben.

Ben, the alien she now found she'd married. Ben, no different than all the other jerks she'd dated, after all.

Her racing thoughts focused on the future, solo—how to get away as fast and as far as she could, and how to take care of herself and the kids. She turned in slow circles, unable to focus. Nausea rolled through her stomach.

The front door opened and closed. Ben. Now something else kicked in. Rage. She turned as he entered the bedroom and told him in a flat voice, "get out."

"Michelle, please...,"

"I said, get out!"

"We need to talk, Michelle. I am so sorry—we can work this out, baby. I love you! I'm not leaving you, I love you. Please, Michelle."

She had never seen her husband in so much emotional pain, and the old Michelle would have melted. But that person was dead, along with all her hopes and dreams, the ones she'd foolishly placed into the hands of the man before her.

143

He walked up to her, tried to put his arms around her. She shoved him away roughly, and he stumbled and tripped, falling and hitting his head on the edge of the dresser on the way down.

"Ben!" She was horrified. She had never assaulted another human being or any other being for that matter. He pulled himself into a sitting position, rubbing a spot on his head. "I guess I deserved that, huh?" he said grimly.

She stopped herself from going to him, frozen in place. After a moment, he took a deep breath and pulled himself into a standing position.

"I better leave before this gets worse. We can talk after things cool off." He went to the closet, pulled out his overnighter, and began to pack. She watched in disbelief.

"Are you kidding me? You hit me with this, with the biggest emotional bomb of all time, and now you're *leaving*?"

He quietly finished packing. Finally, he turned to her.

"Michelle, I've made a terrible mistake. I don't know how to make it up to you, but I will. I'm not giving up on us."

He paused, uncertain. "I'll call you tomorrow."

He turned and walked out while she stood in complete shock. She heard the front door open and gently close.

Liz came into the bedroom, eyes quizzical.

"What's going on?" she asked. Seeing her sister's face, she rushed over, put her arms around Michelle, who collapsed, wailing. After a few minutes, she gulped in air and began talking.

She told Liz every excruciating detail.

Liz's face turned to stone. She held Michelle closer.

"Don't worry, Michelle. We'll figure out what to do. That dirtball won't ever hurt you again, not if I have anything to say about it."

Her little sister had turned back into protector and tigress, just like in high school.

CHAPTER THIRTEEN

FIVE AND A HALF YEARS EARLIER

An only child conceived late in life by her parents, Jillian felt lonely growing up and fantasized about having a sister and a brother, like her friends' families. She'd always dreamed of a big family, but none of her relationships had worked out in the long run.

Then she met Stuart—handsome, smart, successful, fun-loving, and, in short, everything she'd ever dreamed of in a man. Even better—and to her surprise—he fell head over heels in love with her. Their courtship was perfect, filled with romantic adventure, passionate lovemaking, and more joy than she could ever have imagined.

Then the shoe dropped. A few months into their relationship, he casually disclosed that he wasn't interested in having children, and she swallowed her desires, wanting so much to be with him, already deeply in love. Surely, she rationalized, he will come around to the idea of children, especially when he sees how happy we are together.

But they moved on without that conversation, eventually got engaged, and began planning their wedding. It wasn't that Jillian never gave the conversation about children another thought. She did. As their wedding date grew closer, she thought about it more, even made a couple of cursory attempts to raise the subject. And then, everything changed.

Jillian arrived early and secured a table. Sighing, she sat back and smiled inwardly, but her reverie was broken by the waiter.

"What can I get for you—a cocktail, glass of wine?" The waiter was cute and friendly, and she ordered her usual, a Cosmopolitan. He turned to leave, and she grabbed his arm suddenly.

"Wait! Uh, forget that drink. I'll have sparkling water with a twist of lime."

He nodded. "Of course."

Jillian unconsciously placed her hand over her flat belly protectively. This was not going to be an easy conversation.

Ashley, an attractive brunette, breezed in, threw down her jacket and purse in the seat opposite Jillian, swished into place, and blew out her breath. She was Jillian's best friend and only real confidante.

"Sorry I'm late—traffic, assholes on the freeway, not to mention THE witch of compliance laid a new project on me right before I left, and, of COURSE, she needed to tell me every little detail about it, no matter how many times I looked at my watch. Did I tell you about that guy from accounting who's been creeping after me? He sneaks up to my office, with some ridiculous excuse about needing me to sign off on...,"

The waiter interrupted, took Ashley's order for a glass of wine, and she continued, hardly pausing for breath, not noticing the little smile playing on Jillian's lips. She rattled on for a while, rolling her eyes. She grabbed her wine glass from the waiter and took a long sip, then suddenly seemed to become aware of Jillian. She stopped, looked sideways, narrowed her eyes.

"Okay, what's up with you?"

Jillian's eyes went wide and innocent. "What?"

Ashley took another sip of her wine.

Jillian pointedly picked up her glass of sparkling water and took a long, languid drink, carefully watching Ashley's eyes, which suddenly flew open.

"Wait! Where's your Cosmo? Why are you drinking...you're having water, aren't you? Wait—You aren't...? What the...? Are you...?"

Jillian waited.

"Pregnant?"

Ashley's voice was a bit too loud. Jillian looked around quickly and shushed her.

"Yes, I am, and you're the first—and only person—to know."

"Oh, my God! Seriously? Oh, Jillian—that is so wonderful! Congratulations, Sweetie! When did this happen? How long have you known? What about your wedding dress? I mean, we're going to have to make some changes, right?"

Ashley dabbled at wedding planning outside of her day job, and of course, she was doing Jillian and Stuart's wedding.

Jillian laughed. "Whoa, hold on there. I just found out. In fact, I just came from the doctor. I'm at about eight weeks, and I don't want to make a big deal about it until I'm further along."

Then her face fell. She nervously tapped a nail on the side of her glass, not looking at Ashley.

"Wait, you don't look all that happy. Sure, your wedding dress may need a slight alteration, but we're so close to the wedding, you won't show much, if at all. Unless you're having twins!"

Jillian looked a little pale at that. She slowly let out her breath.

"Ashley, I'm not worried about how I will look in my dress, but I am worried about the wedding."

"What do you mean? Wait. What about Stuart? Have you told him? I guess not—I mean, you just got back from the doctor. I can't believe you told me first."

"No, I haven't told him. I could have. I've had time to call him, but it will be better in person."

"Of course."

"That is if I tell him."

"What do you mean? Of course, you're going to tell him!" Ashley was shocked. She waited, but Jillian said nothing.

"Jillian. What in the holy hell are you saying? You can't NOT tell Stuart."

Jillian looked away.

"Wait. Are you saying Stuart isn't going to be happy about this? Jillian, is there a problem with you guys? I thought you were blissful—you're the happiest couple I know."

Jillian looked up at Ashley, and this time her eyes were brimming with unshed tears.

"Oh, honey! What is it?" Ashley grabbed Jillian's hand, eyebrows scrunched in worry.

Jillian's tears spilled over as she struggled to speak. "I'm not sure I can tell him. He doesn't...he doesn't...really want children." She openly sobbed.

Ashley froze. "Jillian," she whispered.

How could this be? Stuart and Jillian were the perfect couple—totally in love—everyone could see that! Why wouldn't they have children? Jillian had always wanted kids—it was so much a part of who she was. How could they have gotten this far—weeks before their wedding—without knowing they were not on the same page about children?

Ashley's face morphed from shock to anger. What in the hell was wrong with him, anyway? What kind of a man was he? How could he not want to have children with beautiful, perfect Jillian? He didn't deserve her!

"Jillian, honey, that is awful. Why didn't you tell me he didn't want kids, and what are you doing with him anyway? How could this not have come out?"

"It did, early on. He told me, but I...I just thought he was being a typical guy, not really thinking of the future. We were still getting to know each other, and I figured if we fell in love, it would all naturally sort itself out. But it didn't take me long to fall in love with him, and at that point, I didn't want to rock the boat by bringing up children."

She took a deep, shaky breath. "I just thought it would all work out. It does for everyone else."

They sat quietly.

Suddenly, Jillian wiped away her tears and looked determined.

"So, listen Ashley, here's what I'm going to do. I'm going to bring it up again—not by telling him I'm pregnant, not yet—but just to get us talking about the topic of children. I think maybe I'm working myself up too much about nothing. He's crazy about me, don't you think?"

"Of course, he is!"

"So, this will work out then. He's going to be fine once we start talking about it. Most guys change their minds about kids once they meet 'the one,' don't they? How often have we seen that with our friends? Guys start out saying things like, 'I'm in no hurry about kids,' or 'let's see about kids later,' and the next thing you know, she's pregnant. Then the baby is born, someone puts that little tiny being into his arms, and he's over the moon. Doubts about having kids— gone. Hesitation about fatherhood—vanished. *Right?*"

Ashley slowly nodded. "I hope so, for your sake, honey."

They reached across the table and held hands. Jillian's face brightened, she took her purse, stood, and said good-bye.

She would do it tonight, talk to Stuart. He'd melt when he saw the sonogram. He'd put his hand on her belly and start talking to the little guy or girl in there. It would be as magical as the rest of their relationship.

But she couldn't do it, couldn't tell him the truth that night. Instead, she talked about having children in a generic sense. About how—at some point—it would be nice to be a Mom. Stuart looked at her as if she was crazy. She dropped the subject.

He never noticed that she wasn't drinking her usual red wine with dinner.

The second attempt at the conversation was even worse. This time, she told him he would be a great Dad, someday. He got angry and talked about his own worthless Dad.

"*Dad?* What are you talking about, Jillian? Are you trying to piss me off? You know I'm not even inviting my drunk father to the wedding, for obvious reasons."

That night he drank more than usual and withdrew from her in a way she'd never experienced with him. *How in the world would she ever tell him the truth now?*

Time flew as their wedding day approached. She found excuses to not have the conversation—*not today*. She paid off the dress and took it home, and they played the game of "you can't see it!" He mimed opening the closet door while she pushed it shut.

Not today. They did their food testing for the reception, sipping sparkling water, and taking small bites. Stuart told the caterer that the last thing he wanted was one of those events with giant plates occupied by three tiny bites that wouldn't fill up a mosquito. Jillian caught the caterer's eye and smiled. He winked back. Stuart sighed dramatically but with a smile. "I guess, as usual, it's not up to me. I'm just the groom."

They were having so much fun planning the wedding that she didn't want to risk provoking his anger. But tonight—this would be the night. Tonight, she'd tell him after the party, as they curled up together on the sofa in front of the fireplace. She'd find the right words, and his heart would open. He'd hold her tight and tell her everything would be okay, reassure her of his love.

As they drove to their engagement party, Jillian felt the tension building inside. Her heart rate rose, and she felt her cheeks flush. She struggled to find the right words, but something else took over. She blurted out, "Look Stuart, the truth is I want children!" She caught him so off-guard that he swerved the car. Getting it back under control, he pulled over to the curb, put the car in park and turned to her.

"What?" He did not look happy at hearing this announcement. He looked angry, and she felt herself shrinking, at a loss for words.

"What do you mean?" he asked slowly, now staring ahead.

It was time to tell him, but he looked so angry, his face tight and pinched.

"At some point," she said lamely, "when we're ready, I mean."

He stared at her and said, "I will never be ready." He was firm.

Shocked, she felt tears forming. He looked at her then and softened.

"It's okay, Jill," he said as he pulled her toward him for a hug. "We're going to be very happy, just the two of us, the way we always planned it."

That night, he drank almost non-stop. She drove home alone, leaving him to continue partying with his friends, wondering why he didn't seem to notice that she hadn't touched alcohol in weeks.

Ashley's cell phone jerked her out of a deep sleep. She reached over, pushed the "ignore" button, and rolled over to go back to sleep. The sound of an incoming text stirred her again. She picked up the phone, looked at the screen. It was from Jillian:

Ashley—please call me. I need to talk now. I am sorry—I know you like to sleep in—but this is urgent.

Jillian didn't believe in the use of abbreviations or emojis when she texted. She was a believer in the full use of language. She was an elementary education teacher, English, of course.

One thing Jillian didn't do was set off false alarms. If she said "now," then something important was going on. Was it the baby? Ashley picked up the phone and texted back:

Yes! —phone or in person? Are you okay?

In person. I'm okay. Let's meet for coffee, the usual place, in 10.

How about 15?

Done. I'll see you there.

When Ashley arrived, she found Jillian waiting, their coffee drinks already on the table. She slid in and grabbed her cup gratefully. It was so nice to have a friend who knew what to order for you. But the minute Ashley took a closer look at Jillian's face, her stomach dropped.

Jillian was all puffy eyes, dark circles underneath, no makeup, hair looking slept in without her usual regard for making it look perfect. Jillian loved to look her best. As college roommates, Ashley typically got ready in five minutes, while Jillian took well over an hour, as she tried on one outfit after the other and meticulously did her hair and applied makeup. *Where was that Jillian?*

This Jillian wore old sweats and a frumpy, large sweater, face pale, no makeup, and the look of someone who'd been out all night. But the most telltale sign was her bare left-hand ring finger. Ashely picked up her hand and rubbed the empty spot.

"What happened?" she whispered.

Jillian's half-dead eyes stared into the space behind Ashley's left shoulder. "We broke up, or, to be more accurate, I broke it off. He went out again last night, after the engagement party, and got even more drunk. It was after 3am when he got home. We had a terrible fight early this morning. I can't do it anymore. It's not working at all, and now I have a baby to think about."

Stunned, Ashley sat quietly.

"How could I bring a little person into this awful relationship?"

Jillian whispered. Her eyes leaked, and she fumbled in her pockets to draw out a single, crumpled tissue, which she used to blow her nose loudly. Ashley reached into her purse and handed Jillian a wad of fresh tissues, which she took with a small, grateful smile.

"Hey, Jill?"

Loud, long blow followed by nose wiping. "What?" in a watery voice.

"He's a loser and a drunk. He doesn't deserve you at all."

"Actually, I wish that were true. He's not an alcoholic. He didn't start drinking until I started pressuring him about having kids."

"That's ridiculous. You should be able to bring up conversations about having children, or anything else that concerns you. What kind of a guy folds up when you want to talk about...about things you have to talk about when you're getting married?"

Ashley shook her head, mouth in a tight line.

"I repeat—what a loser. You're better off without him. I mean, what kind of a guy starts binge drinking and messes up his relationship with his pregnant fiancée?"

Jillian burst into fresh tears. "You're talking about the only guy I've ever truly loved! I'm the one who screwed it all up."

Ashley bit her lip, wanting to scream. How could Jillian be such a victim over a guy? Ashley dated frequently, but Jillian was always the girl who caught the eye of almost every guy in whatever room they found themselves. She was stunning, with long, shimmering red hair in stylish, tumbled curls, almond-shaped deep blue eyes, and model-next-door good looks. But what really set her apart was her inner glow, fueled by her warm, loving heart.

Jillian radiated joy and friendliness, as well as curiosity about others. She was the quintessential "How to Win Friends and Influence People" girl—always the one to ask about others, always so happy to see her friends and family, always listening and asking, looking for ways to help. People were drawn to her, unconsciously seeking contact with her spirit.

Sure, Stuart was good-looking. He was smart and successful enough. But Jillian could have Brad-fucking-Pitt if she wanted. Why was she letting herself get so messed up over Stuart?

Ashley blew out a breath. "Look, I'm sorry for calling him a loser. I know you love him." She gritted her teeth and didn't say the rest of her thoughts.

Jillian blew her nose again, sniffling loudly.

"At least you'll have child support to help you get started, and you know I will do everything I can to help. What are you going to do about visitation rights? You know, I have this great attorney friend. Maybe you should go see him and start the process, you know, preemptively before he hires someone. You don't want to wait for him to start making your life miserable."

Jillian said nothing, not making eye contact.

Ashley cleared her throat. "Hey, um, sweetie?"

Nothing.

"Jill?"

She raised her eyes slowly to Ashley's.

"Tell me you told him. You did tell him about the baby?"

"No, I didn't."

"What?! That's crazy! How could you not tell him? Why not?"

"I didn't tell him because he wouldn't want to know. No, wait, hear me out. He's made it clear that he's not interested in having children. If I tell him, he will only want visitation out of a sense of obligation. Why would I want my baby to be subjected to that? You of all people should understand. We both know how it feels."

Ashley had no answer for that.

Ashley's own father had left when she was in grade school and had little contact with her over the years of her childhood.

Big-hearted, overly empathetic Jillian had heard countless stories about Ashley's childhood, including the latest chapters—her adult relationship with her father was anything but idyllic. He was only vaguely interested in Ashley's life, rarely contacted her, and was distant when they did get together. Ashley was mostly stoic about it, but Jillian saw through it, saw her wounded heart.

"Okay, Jillian, I can see why you're hesitating to tell him. But you have to do it. You can't just leave him out of the most important thing about his life so far. I could see it if he'd been abusive to you, but—yes, he's been a jerk lately. But—wait, has he hit you? Did he hurt you?"

"Of course not! Stuart would never harm me, not physically."

"Well, then, barring that, he deserves to know that he's got a child coming into this world. He might not turn out to be much of a parent, but he has to be given the opportunity, doesn't he?"

Jillian dug in. "No, he doesn't. Please try to understand. It's just easier this way."

Ashley couldn't let it go. "But why, Jill?"

Jillian sighed. "Look, every day, I work with these adorable, innocent children. And I do parent/teacher conferences. Half the time, only the moms show up, single moms, completely stressed out. And when I ask them about the child's father—his involvement—I get a blank stare. Sometimes I get tears. It kills me to see the impact of an absent father on a woman."

She paused. "The worst part is the family pictures the kids draw—the father looking like a stick figure standing way off to the side, the sadness in the child's eyes as he or she tries to explain the family, the lack of relationship with an absent father. I've thought many times that these children would be better off if they didn't even know about their Dads."

They sat quietly, sipping coffee.

"Ashley, with Mom not doing well, and Dad gone, I don't have anyone but you."

She waved her hand. "I don't mean there's no one else to hang out with, but I'm not that close to my other friends. You are my *best* friend, and I need you now more than ever. Please," she finished, and the sadness in Jillian's voice broke Ashley's heart.

Ashley moved quickly to the other side of the booth and hugged Jillian close for a moment, then pulled away and looked in her eyes.

"Of course, Jillian. You never have to wonder about that, you know that. I'm standing behind you all the way. Just try to think about it, okay? You still have plenty of time to tell him."

"Okay." Jillian nodded her head, but Ashley wasn't convinced. She'd never seen her best friend so adamant about something that didn't seem quite right.

CHAPTER FOURTEEN

18 MONTHS EARLIER

Sarah stood still, not moving because she wasn't sure which direction to go. Paul was underneath the car—his prized 1970 Big Block Corvette, the one he'd been lovingly restoring for the past 14 years. He dropped something.

"Shit." He sounded angry. Nothing new.

He rolled out from underneath the car and looked surprised to see her standing there.

"Hey." He wiped his hands on a shop towel, sat up.

She took a deep breath. "Paul, we need to talk about what happened."

His face deepened in color, and his jawline tightened. "Nothing happened."

"Yes, it did. You're mad at me—again—and now you're working on the car as if nothing happened."

"I'm not mad."

"Look, Sarah, I'm just trying to have a good day, but maybe that's not okay with you." He turned away, walked to one of his tool chests, pulled out a drawer and began searching for something.

Sarah felt that familiar feeling of dread building inside. He was emotionally shut down and cold as ice, unreachable. She had been trying for the past three days to penetrate his emotional armor. She'd tried to let it go, to wait it out, but there was no shift. He appeared to have an endless capacity to disconnect.

But the waiting was draining. She was not okay with the cold war.

"You can't keep shutting me out."

"I'm not shutting you out."

"You are. We have to talk about what to do now that you're not getting any income from the business."

He turned to her again, furious. "Well, thanks so much for your loving support. I guess you're sick of being married to a loser like me."

"Those are not my words."

"That's what you're saying!" His voice rose, the hostility playing out on his features, once so loving, now so distorted.

"Paul, please quit shouting at me. I'm trying to get through to you, so we can deal with the issues in our marriage and make some decisions regarding money." Her voice was calm, but she might as well be shouting, his reaction was so intense.

He threw down the wrench in his hand, and it hit the concrete floor so hard it chipped a piece of it, which went flying.

She began to shake inside. There was no way he would physically hurt her, but she was still afraid.

"Great—see what you made me do?"

"Did you just accuse me of making you throw down a wrench? Seriously? Paul, you are turning things back on me that have to do with you. You are the one who is angry and who is throwing things. Not me. Can't you see that?" she pleaded.

"I am not angry! And I'm not throwing things! It slipped."

"Please, honey, just come in and talk. I can't keep doing this with you."

"So, don't." He turned away again and dug around in his toolbox.

She stood there another minute, hoping he would respond. But instead, he went back to work on his car, refusing to make eye contact, saying nothing. Slowly, she turned around and went back into the house.

She was packed but couldn't bring herself to leave. The door from the garage opened, closed, and she heard Paul's footsteps as he made his way into the living room. He walked in, looked at her bags by the door, then looked at her.

"What the hell is going on?"

She pointed to the sofa, to the spot nearby. "Please, just sit down and talk."

He stalked over and sat on the edge of the sofa, vibrating. "What?"

"I have to go for a while, and I'm hoping it's temporary. I am having a hard time with the lack of communication, the constant anger." She tried her best to use her therapist voice, honed through years of use with clients.

"Oh, great! Would you tell me something, Sarah?"

She raised her eyebrows.

"Why is it that whenever we have a problem, you feel the need to put our entire relationship on the table?"

She blew out a breath.

"I'm not trying to do that, Paul. I feel hurt because when I try to talk to you about the things we need to work out, you blow up at me. Then you stop talking to me, and while that used to be your way of coping for a couple of hours, now you don't speak to me for days! I don't know how to describe to you how much that hurts."

She paused, her breathing shallow, her chest tight.

"You are the guy who told me when we were dating, that if one of us has a problem, then both of us have a problem. You told me that we would always talk about whatever is bothering either of us. What happened to that guy?" Her voice was soft, pleading.

"Well, I feel hurt too, Sarah. I don't feel safe with you." He crossed his arms defensively. "I feel like you are so disappointed in me that you can hardly stand me. I failed, all right? I screwed up the business! We lost a lot of money! I'm a loser—I got that. You have made that abundantly clear."

He took rapid breaths, his face red.

Stunned and afraid he was about to have a cardiac event, she tried to soothe him.

"What are you talking about? I've never called you a loser or anything remotely like that. I would never say that to you. It's just that we need to talk about our plans going forward, how we're going to deal with this financially. We need to work through the anger and get back to us. Look, maybe we should get a good counselor, talk this out with a third party—"

"Well, that's just great. You *are* a therapist. We don't need another shrink in our lives. Besides, that doesn't work for me."

The creeping sense of hopelessness that had invaded her spirit now threatened to crush. She felt impending doom, the loss, once again, of her most treasured relationship. Denial stepped in protectively— *surely, he can't be serious. He's just angry right now. He will come around, and we will talk like we used to.*

But it had been months since they'd last talked without arguing, without inflicting multiple little emotional deaths. Couples who know each other well can kill each other slowly with a thousand tiny cuts until they finally bleed out.

But the truth broke through her attempts at denial—he wasn't listening, not anymore. He wasn't responding to her distress, not anymore. He did not see the damage he was inflicting.

Her breath tightened—the stress of this moment, and so many others, pressing in. She felt trapped, caught in a nightmare scenario from which she could not escape. Her rational brain was in a coma—all she felt was the urge to leave, to find some way to escape and calm down.

"Okay, Paul. No therapy. At this point, I'm not sure what to do. I need some time, some space, and I'm hoping that by giving both of us some time and space, it will somehow help. I'm sorry."

She stood, took her bags, and left. The last time she saw his face, he was genuinely astonished. But he did nothing to stop her, nothing to fix this. And she desperately needed him to fix it.

Sarah took another sip of wine, picked up her cell phone, and stared at the screen for the thousandth time. Nothing.

She opened the text function and stabbed at the messages from Paul, scrolling through them, going back for days. Words and phrases jumped out at her, each one causing another pang.

Where are you?

I'm at the hotel. I'm fine.

When are you coming home?

I'm not coming home right now. We need to talk with someone else in the room. I'm afraid we will just fight again.

Like I said, you ARE the therapist. This is bullshit!

I'm sorry you feel that way. Can't you see how angry you are?

I'm not the one who left!

I didn't want to leave; I just didn't want to fight anymore.

Seems like you just DON'T want any more of this marriage. Why don't you just go ahead and say so?

That's putting words in my mouth. Look, texting isn't the way to do this. Let's make an appointment and go talk. I have a wonderful referral, someone neither one of us knows. Will you go?

"..."

And the dots lingered, then disappeared. He didn't bother to try after that.

Later, she'd called, but when he answered, he had little to say. She begged again for him to go to counseling with her, but he refused.

Sarah picked up the remote and turned on the television, seeking oblivion through mindless content. It worked, a little. Later, she crawled into bed and cried herself to sleep.

CHAPTER FIFTEEN

PRESENT DAY

Michelle tapped another text message. *Where are you? You're two hours late!* Irritated, she flipped the television channel again, swinging her leg against the living room table. Finally, she called Liz, who snorted after she heard the report on Ben's no-show.

"I'm sure he's rolling in the sack with some hottie. What a worthless piece of scum."

Michelle was silent briefly. "Actually, he's never been even so much as five minutes late to pick up the kids. This is out of character."

"Character?" Liz laughed out loud.

"No, wait, Liz. Think about it. Yes, he ruined our marriage, and yes, it turns out he's a liar and a cheat. But he's always been a devoted father. He's never once let the kids down, no matter what."

A small ball of tension coiled in Michelle's gut. Something was wrong, and the more she explained it to Liz, the more certain she was.

Katie and Jordan thundered into the living room, bright faces full of smiles.

"Mom! When's Dad coming?" asked Katie for the third time.

"I don't know, sweetie. I think he got hung up at work, but he'll be here soon. Did you pack your toothbrush?" At her daughter's guilty expression, she continued. "Of course not. Go get it and put it in your backpack. You, too, Jordan."

They ran off to get their toothbrushes, and Michelle spoke to Liz quietly.

"I'm going to make some calls, Liz. Something is definitely wrong, and I need to find out what it is." She hung up after promising to call Liz back.

Michelle called Ben's parents, who reported that they had no idea where he was today. They'd seen him two weekends ago along with the kids but hadn't spoken with him since.

Ben's Mom, Diane, sounded anxious. Michelle reassured her that something had probably happened at work, and Ben had most likely forgotten to tell her he would be late.

"Don't worry, I'll let you know as soon as I hear something," she said.

Michelle adored Ben's parents, who'd miraculously stuck by her through the nastiness of the divorce. She had to give full credit to Diane, one of the most charitable human beings she'd ever known. Diane had pulled her aside as soon as she'd heard about the affair and divorce.

"Michelle, I want you to know that I love my son and will continue to do so despite his horrendous mistakes. As a mother yourself, I'm sure you can understand that. But I will always have a huge space in my heart for you. I want our relationship to continue, even though I know it will be awkward at times for us both. I am there for you, as odd as that sounds. I seriously hit the lottery with you as a daughter-in-law, and as far as I'm concerned, that's who you will always be to me."

Michelle had teared up in relief that day, but not really expected it to be true. Months later, Diane had been abundantly true to her word. They were, if anything, closer than ever.

After ending that call, Michelle began calling Ben's contacts. First, his boss. Alarmingly, he reported that he hadn't seen Ben at all that day. He hadn't responded to texts, calls, or emails, which was very unusual for Ben. He was about to contact Michelle to see if everything was okay.

"He took a few days off, but he was supposed to be back today," he said.

With a sinking heart, Michelle called a few of their friends, but they hadn't heard from him either. She called Liz, then waited impatiently for her to arrive to take care of the kids. Liz drove up a few minutes later, and Michelle grabbed her keys and ran to her car. Ten agonizing minutes later, she arrived at Ben's apartment.

One of the things they'd been able to do despite their personal bitterness was to make certain arrangements for the sake of their children. One of those was giving each other full access to one another's homes, for use only in emergencies. Oddly, they trusted each other to honor that boundary.

The first thing she noticed was that Ben's car was parked in his reserved spot. That caused her heart rate to kick up.

Michelle rushed up the stairs to Ben's apartment and, first, rang the bell. Waited. No answer. She rang it again. Still, no answer. With shaking hands, she unlocked the door. She walked in slowly, calling Ben's name. She envisioned Ben lying on the floor, dead of a heart attack, or something else. Her heart thudded in her chest as she slowly walked through the apartment, checking each room carefully.

The apartment was eerily still.

In the master bedroom, she saw evidence of packing—closet door open, a few hangars askew, a sock lying on the floor, and the bed hastily made. She inspected the bathroom, where she noticed there was no toothbrush or razor.

It hit her with a jolt—of course! She recalled that Ben had told her weeks ago that he was going on a fishing trip. He hadn't mentioned it again, but, clearly, he'd left for that reason. But he'd also assured her that he would be back the day before and was planning on having the kids for the weekend as usual. Obviously, his boss had expected his return that day as well.

Where did he go? She thought about it as she wandered back into the living room, now feeling guilty about the invasion of his space. She saw a brochure on the dinette table and went over to pick it up. *San Diego Sportfishing*. The brochure showed a fishing boat loaded with gear, and a photo of a guy holding up a huge sailfish for the shot, grinning. She put it down and turned to leave.

Perhaps the boat returned late, and he missed his flight back to Sacramento. But why wouldn't he have notified his boss, not to mention the mother of his children? Ben was the kind of guy who did what he said he was going to do, and if not, he let people know. *Dependable*—that was his modus operandi, with the tiny exception of his infidelity.

No, it didn't make sense. His vehicle was here, but he wasn't, and now he was missing. Something was clearly wrong.

Now, what? She went back in and grabbed the brochure again, looking for a contact number. She quickly dialed the number and listened as it rang and rang. She clicked off and left the apartment, taking the brochure. She would do an online search and try to find out more information.

Back at the house, Michelle booted her laptop and pulled up a search screen while Liz hovered in the background. She searched for the name of the fishing company and found a website. Searching through the website, she discovered the name of the marina out of which it was based and called the main number.

The woman who answered sounded young.

"I'm trying to find out information about San Diego Sportfishing. My...husband went out on one of their boats a few days ago and hasn't returned," Michelle told her.

"This is the marina," the girl explained. "People keep their boats here, and many of them run sportfishing businesses out of them. But we, like, don't have anything to do with that."

"I realize that," Michelle countered impatiently. "But someone may have heard something." She looked at the brochure in her hand again. "The boat appears to be named *Princess Rose*. Can you please check on that?"

"I don't know. I'm, like, supposed to answer the phone, not go around asking questions. Um, let me go find my boss and ask him."

Before Michelle could protest, the line went silent. After what seemed like an eternity, a male voice answered.

"Hello? I understand you're trying to find out information about San Diego Sportfishing."

"Who is this?" asked Michelle.

"I'm Skip Dugan, and I manage the marina. Normally, we don't keep up with the owners of these boats and their schedules, but I happen to know this guy personally. His name is Jack Heard, and his boat is the *Princess Rose*. I'm going to do some checking and try to find out his schedule. I'm not certain, but I think he was supposed to be back yesterday. The weather being what it is...," He stopped.

"What?" asked Michelle frantically.

"Well, if there was bad weather, I'd say not to expect him back on time, but it's been perfect. There's no reason for him to be delayed, unless...,"

"Unless, what?"

He ignored her question. "Look, give me your name and number, and I'll call you back when I know more."

She did and hung up, her hands shaking.

Melanie let herself into the house, carefully placed her handbag and keys on the small table in the entryway and sighed. Then she brightened, remembering what day it was. Jack would be back today. He'd come over later to say hello. Maybe he'd stay for a glass of wine.

She smiled and poured a glass of wine, taking small sips as she set the mood while she waited for him.

An hour later, she thought about texting him, but that would make her look like a girlfriend waiting for her man to return from the sea. No good. She poured herself a glass of wine.

Another hour later, Melanie blew out the candles, which now looked ridiculous, and poured another glass of wine, fuming. What the heck was wrong with her, anyway? Why on earth did she waste her time like this? Why did she think this amazing, great-looking, much younger guy would ever be interested in her?

Melanie, 58 years old and widowed, had done the stupidest of things. She'd allowed herself to fall in love with a completely unavailable man. Hadn't she learned that lesson decades ago?

Yes, she'd made wrong choices when she was young, but then she'd met her husband, Lyle, and they'd had 24 wonderful years together. She'd lost him to cancer four years ago. Now, she was back to making the mistakes that typically, only young girls make. *Wow, way to go, Melanie*, she said to herself.

But Jack was special, so hard to resist. He was in his late 40s, a great-looking guy—medium height, muscular, mocha skin, chiseled features, and intelligent, hazel eyes that gazed at her—really *looked* at her—in a way that made her feel stirrings she hadn't felt since the early years with her husband.

When she spoke, he really listened. She tried not to overdo that—sometimes, the strong, silent types were used by a world full of people who were starving to be heard. She was careful to make attempts to turn the conversation to him, but her efforts were met by evasion most of the time.

All she knew about him was that he had a girlfriend—Amanda—in her early 30s, hormones raging, clearly, the girl who would be a tigress in bed. But that wasn't really fair, was it? She didn't know anything about Amanda. Truth be told, the couple of times she'd met her, she seemed nice enough, and obviously crazy about Jack. And much younger.

Proving how unavailable Jack really was. Experience had taught her that men who pursued much younger women typically had that emotional bent that said, "I don't want a commitment, but I do want a great romp in the hay now and then. And I want to do it with someone who won't make any big demands on me."

Again, putting words in his mouth. Melanie chastised herself for being so judgmental. Jack didn't seem like a player. He seemed serious, someone who cared. He did things for her that he didn't have to do—small repairs around the house, little maintenance chores—and she let him, not because she couldn't hire a handyman to do it, but because doing those things for her seemed to give Jack pleasure. And it gave her an excuse to offer a meal afterward, gain some time with him.

Pitiful. She was acting like a lovesick teenager with a man who was never going to be interested in her. Who would want her at this stage of life, anyway? Some old, desperate guy with papery skin and bad teeth? The guys her age wanted much younger women. Jack included.

Jeez, her mind was headed into a dark place. But where else could it go?

The reality was that she *was* an older woman, lonely because her husband had died, fantasizing about a younger guy because he was the only guy she saw on a regular basis.

Here she was sitting around waiting for the Captain-at-sea to return "home" to her when the reality was that he had probably gotten off his ship and gone straight to Amanda's house.

Melanie sighed. She ate all of the appetizers, even though it was far too much. She finished her glass of wine. Finally, she went to bed, sad and tired.

Melanie woke to the sound of her cell phone ringing. She picked it up drowsily and peered at the tiny screen.

"Hello?"

"Melanie? This is Amanda. I'm sorry to bother you, but Jack was supposed to be back yesterday from his latest gig. Not only is he not back, but when I called the marina, they told me that his boat was reported to have sent out a mayday Wednesday morning and since then, nothing."

Melanie's heart lurched. She sat up swiftly in bed.

"Oh my God!"

She heard Amanda sniffling.

"I know! I'm beside myself, so worried I can't think straight. I had to call in sick to work. I just thought you would want to know." She was openly sobbing now.

"Amanda, please. What else do you know?" Melanie begged.

"I don't know anything! They won't tell me anything else, but they said they would call back."

"Call me as soon as you hear something. Please," said Melanie, heart sinking.

"Okay. I'll let you know as soon as I hear something from the marina."

With a heavy heart, Melanie hung up and lay back on the pillow in shock. This couldn't be happening. Jack was extremely safety conscious. He'd been going out to sea for literally decades. He would never make the kind of amateur mistakes that other boaters made. What could have happened?

Michelle's phone rang, pulling her out of a deep sleep. She was stretched out on the sofa, still wearing her clothes. Her sister Liz was curled up on the love seat, snoring softly. Liz jerked awake, muttering, "What, what?"

Michelle jumped up, grabbed the phone, looked at the caller i.d. and saw "Seaside Marina, San Diego." She punched the button and answered, slightly out of breath.

"Hello? This is Michelle."

"Yes, ma'am, this is Skip Dugan. I'm sorry to have to tell you this. I found out that the *Princess Rose* sent out a mayday call on Wednesday, and after that went out of contact. The Coast Guard is sending out a search today. I've given them your name and information, and they will keep you informed."

Michelle's heart sank. Feeling light-headed, she dropped onto the sofa, buried her head in her hands, and let the tears pour. Liz rushed over and sat by her, wrapping her arms around her sister, and holding on tight. Just then, Katie wandered into the living room, took one look at her Mom, and immediately began to wail. Once again, Liz seethed as Ben-the-jerk set off another round of pain and anguish for the people she loved most.

That evening, Michelle and Liz watched as news anchor Alicia Morrison, from a top San Diego station, relayed the day's top news stories.

"This morning, Seaside Marina's general manager Skip Dugan confirmed that a fishing vessel, the *Princess Rose*, failed to return to the marina after a three-day excursion. Field reporter Heather Steel is on-site and has the details. Heather?"

On the screen, Heather, dressed in a blue-and-white striped top with white pants, dark hair pulled up in a ponytail, stood holding a mic. In the background, yachts and sailing boats floated serenely beneath a calm blue sky.

"Yes, Alicia. This morning, Mr. Skip Dugan, the marina's manager, contacted the U.S. Coast Guard regarding the *Princess Rose*, owned by Captain Jack Heard. That is when he was informed that the *Princess Rose* issued a mayday call in the early morning hours of Wednesday. No further communication from the vessel has been received. I've been told that the Coast Guard began a search of the bay, but so far, there have been no sightings of the boat or any of the passengers. According to Mr. Dugan, there were a total of five men on board the *Princess Rose*—three clients and one crew member in addition to the Captain. Five people are now missing while the search continues. Their names are being withheld pending notification of family. Back to you, Alicia."

"Thank you, Heather," said Alicia, looking into the camera intently. "And in other news," she continued.

Michelle put her head in her hands and groaned softly.

CHAPTER SIXTEEN

"And, we're off," said Alan, the cameraman, and her unofficial assistant. Heather Steel stood thoughtfully for a moment.

"Hey, Alan. What do you think about this story?" she asked him.

"What do you mean?" he mumbled as he packed up his equipment. She was silent, so he stopped and turned to her.

"I want to find out who the people were on the boat. I'm sure they have families, loved ones. They're probably on social media, maybe visible in the business community since they obviously have money to spend."

"You may be onto something," said Alan.

"Yeah, I think so. But we won't be the only ones to connect those dots. Let's get back to the office," Heather said, anxious to get started and turning to go.

She stopped. "Wait. I have an idea," she told Alan. She outlined her plan, then went to the marina main office while Alan waited. Just before she opened the door to the office, she moved her ring from right hand to left. She took a deep breath and did a silent prayer to recall those method acting classes she'd taken years ago.

"Excuse me," Heather said breathlessly to the girl at the front desk, who looked up blankly. "I just heard that there's a lost boat, and I think my husband is on it!"

The receptionist's eyes widened. Heather didn't give her a chance to respond.

"I have to know if he's on that boat!" she exclaimed, willing a small tear to appear. "Please, tell me the names of the men on the boat," she begged, her eyes shimmering.

"I—I'm not supposed to tell," said the girl, clearly inexperienced and out of her depth. She looked around as if she expected the marina police to arrest her.

"Look, what is your name?" Heather asked, slowing down a bit, but maintaining her flustered demeanor.

"Jessica," she said hesitantly.

"Jessica, please, I can't wait for the Coast Guard to tell me later that something happened to my husband. Can you imagine what that would be like? And what if I see something on television first? I can't handle that, I just can't! I promise you. I will make sure that no one ever knows you told me. Please, Jessica."

The tears, thankfully, increased in volume. Jessica looked pale and swallowed.

"Okay, okay, just give me a minute," she said, hastily shuffling papers on her desk. Finally, she picked up a slip of paper which appeared to have been scribbled on hastily. She hesitated.

"Um, here are the names." She looked up at Heather fearfully. "You swear you won't tell?"

"I swear!" Heather vowed, wiping away tears.

Jessica gave her the names. Heather gasped, "Thank God—none of them is my husband!" She thanked Jessica profusely, turned around, and hurried out to meet Alan. They raced back to the office, where they rushed to put together the results of their research.

❧

Hours later, they sat down breathlessly at the daily newsroom meeting.

Dave, one of the editors, turned to Heather, finally. "What have you got? You look like the cat that ate the canary," he said.

Heather turned on her smart tablet and pulled up a series of photos. Here goes, she thought.

"Here's the story. Three men go out on a pleasure fishing cruise and now they're missing. I found out about their lives, their businesses, and their families. I think it's important to tell their stories," and she pulled up the photos, swiping after each one until done.

One her screen appeared a guy who could have been a movie star—tall, lean, muscular, chiseled features, dark blond hair, and gray eyes. Intense gray eyes, his face with a dusting of beard. One of the women gasped.

"This guy is a real estate developer in Austin, Texas. He's well known there, but it's easy enough to play off that here. I can't find evidence of a wife or even a girlfriend, but that's perfect. *Drop-dead gorgeous single guy gets lost at sea*. If he makes it back, he'll probably be the next star of The Bachelor," she said. "Or maybe even Dancing with the Stars!"

Next, she showed a guy who wasn't movie-star quality but close— well built, slightly curly brown hair, a smile to melt your heart with a cleft in the chin. Whew.

"This guy isn't well known from a business perspective but check out his family. They're divorced."

On the screen were photos she'd pulled from Facebook—a beautiful blond with two little children in various scenarios of play. She was stunning, and her kids were just like her—gorgeous, adorable.

"I can't imagine the heartache of having two small children ask about their Dad and not having any idea what to tell them."

Heads nodded around the room.

The third guy was nice looking, older, smiling for the camera at what appeared to be a conference of some kind.

"This guy owned and ran a business in Sacramento for many years," she said, flashing a company logo on the screen. "His business folded, and so did his marriage shortly after that, so isn't that a tragedy? First, you lose the business, and your wife, then you get lost at sea." She showed them a photo of his wife—attractive, early 50s, with intelligent eyes. "They're separated now, but not divorced. I found her business online—get this—she's a licensed psychologist. Marriage and family specialist."

Now the questions. "Do you know where these people live? What else do you know about them? Can you get them on camera?"

"Whoa, everyone, slow down," said Heather. "I know where the ex-wife and kids of the second guy are, and the wife of the older guy, but I don't know enough yet about the gorgeous real estate developer. His personal life is a bit absent online, but I think I can get more."

"Run with it, then," said Mike, the News Director. The entire team brainstormed for a couple of minutes, giving Heather even more ideas for how to further develop the story. She walked out of the meeting, mind whirling with ideas, already envisioning where this could take her career.

It was day one of the story.

The next day, Heather provided an update on the morning news, standing outside at the marina. She looked very serious.

"Thanks, Alicia. Our research has uncovered more about the missing passengers of the *Princess Rose*. That's the fishing yacht that departed three days ago and hasn't been heard from since. In addition to the Captain and one crew member, three men boarded the boat for a two-day fishing excursion. They are…" and on the screen flashed the photos of the men, along with their names.

"We've been able to contact the father of one of the men," she continued. While Stuart's photo stayed on the screen, a voice came over audio.

"My son is missing, and I just pray for his return. I'm very grateful for the Coast Guard's efforts, and I want to ask for everyone else to pray for these men," said the voice.

"That was one father's anguish. Another passenger's children wait anxiously for his return."

The next clip showed a beautiful blond walking with two small children who looked frightened. She waved the camera away as she rushed to the front door of a house, ushering the children inside. A second woman—petite with curly hair—appeared to be shouting at the cameraman. She shoved the camera, which almost went to the ground, but swung back up in time to catch her slamming the door of the house.

"We can only imagine the anxiety of these families, waiting to hear the news," intoned Heather gravely. "Finally, this passenger's wife waits to hear the news about her husband, yearns for his return. She is a psychologist in private practice in the Sacramento area."

On the screen flashed a photo of Paul, followed by one of him and Sarah together at some kind of charity event.

The camera returned to a live shot of Heather.

"Now, at this point, the Coast Guard isn't providing a lot of information, but here's what we know. The *Princess Rose* set out on Tuesday for a two and a half-day fishing excursion, and on Wednesday sent out a mayday call. We don't know the nature of the call at this point, but we're told that it may have indicated the boat itself was in distress.

"With me now is the marina manager, Mr. Skip Dugan, with more details. Mr. Dugan, when did the Coast Guard begin its search-and-rescue operation?"

"They started early this morning," said Skip Dugan, peering uneasily into the camera.

"What else can you tell us about the operation?"

"Well, if it's a typical search-and-rescue, they will cover the area within a few miles of here, using a grid pattern. They will probably use a combination of air and water vessels."

The camera turned back to Heather.

"That's all we have for now, but we will continue to report. Later this morning, there will be a press conference with the Coast Guard.

"We are all pulling for the five passengers of the *Princess Rose*. Back to you, Alicia."

On the screen, scrolling at the bottom was the headline, "Coast Guard searches for the *Princess Rose Five*."

Back at the station, Heather and Alan worked tirelessly, posting feeds of the story all over social media. They tweeted headlines and links to every national reporter they could find. They posted on Facebook, again targeting every national news outlet they could find.

A little after 6:00 p.m., they sat back, exhausted, slowly chewing pizza, feet thrown up on the conference room table.

"Well? How do you think it's going?" Alan asked.

"Swimmingly," said Heather sarcastically. "I thought this was a slow news day, but no one seems to be catching on." She shook her head, pulling her silky hair from one shoulder to the other.

The door of the small conference room swung open, and Dave poked his head in.

"How's it going?" he asked, eyebrows raised.

"Progress has been made," said Alan, wiggling his own brows.

"Really," said Dave skeptically. "Any reaction from the national guys?"

"Yes, Dave, and in fact, Anderson Cooper called and wants me on as a guest correspondent," said Heather, rolling her eyes.

Dave looked like he almost believed her.

"Right," he said finally. "You do realize we can't go much further with this story unless we get some national play."

"Yes, we know that, *Dave*," said Heather, drawing out his name.

"Well, get after it. And text me when you get a bite," he said, closing the door.

They looked at each other and rolled their eyes. Heather threw her crust into the pizza box, wadded her napkin, and sat up, opening her laptop.

"Okay, I'm on CNN; how about you?"

"I'm on Fox News," he answered, flipping open his own laptop. They both pounded the keys.

Heather's cell phone rang, and she snatched it up.

"Heather Steel here," she snapped. She jerked upright suddenly.

"Yes? Yes! Yes, that's me, and yes, that's my story." She grabbed paper and pen and began scribbling rapidly. After a minute or so, she said, "Thanks! Thank you so much." She punched the off button and sat back, grinning.

"Guess," she said to Alan, smiling.

"Uh, Anderson Cooper?" he said teasingly.

"Nope. Guess again," she said.

"Let's see—uh, Robin Roberts? Wait—THE Robin Roberts?" he gaped.

"None other! Well, close enough, anyway," she said gleefully. "That was an editor, and she says Robin wants me to be a correspondent for tomorrow's GMA newscast. They're going to air the story!"

"Wow, congratulations!" Alan exclaimed. He jumped up and high-fived her, and she got up and did a little happy dance.

Breathless, she sat down and grinned.

"Okay, now we get ready because this is just the beginning," she said.

CHAPTER SEVENTEEN

Jillian aimed carefully and swung the hammer, smashing her thumb. She swore, which caused Sophie to look up from her coloring book.

"It's okay, honey. Mommy, uh—well, I hit my thumb, but it's fine."

Sophie went back to her project, wrinkling her forehead as she concentrated on trying to color inside the lines.

Jillian looked at the cabinet door she was attempting to hang. It was not the first repair project she'd tackled in this fixer-upper house. It was a never-ending battle to stay ahead of all the home improvement projects. She sighed as she rooted around in the toolbox for another screw that might approximate the size she needed. No dice.

"Sophie, Mommy has to go to the hardware store again. Let's go."

She looked up at Jillian seriously and put down her crayon. "Okay, Mommy."

Sophie was a remarkably compliant child, in fact so much so that Jillian worried she wasn't developing normally. She was serious, rarely laughed or smiled, and tended to play like it was a project to complete, rather than something fun. Jillian had to invent fun for the two of them, often dragging Sophie into activities that were more child-like and playful.

They bundled up in their coats—the Pacific northwest weather swung cold to cool, but rarely was it warm. Today, it was overcast with drizzle off and on, and the air was chilled. They drove into the charming little downtown area, and Jillian pulled up in front of Young's Hardware store. It was a throwback establishment, complete with small checkout counter and rows of shelves filled with household improvement items.

"Hello, Sophie!" beamed Dan. He was in his late sixties, with a white mustache, and twinkling eyes. He always seemed happy to see Jillian and Sophie. Still holding her mother's hand, Sophie gazed solemnly up at him and said, "Hello, Mr. Young."

"Jillian," he said, turning to her. "How can I help you today?"

After she explained her project, he took her to the hardware section and helped her choose the things she needed.

Sophie stood quietly nearby regarding Mr. Young carefully. He turned to her and smiled.

"Sophie, would you like one of those cookies like the last time? Mrs. Young just made a fresh batch."

She looked up at Jillian inquiringly, who nodded.

"Yes, sir." The corners of her mouth turned up a bit.

Dan returned to the front of the store and brought out the cookie box, normally hidden behind the counter and reserved only for special people. He opened it and showed Sophie. Heavenly scents wafted upward.

"There's chocolate chip, and chocolate-chocolate chip. Which one would you like?" he asked her, smiling mischievously.

Sophie stared into the box and carefully considered her options.

"Or," he said, "maybe you'd like one of each?"

Sophie's eyes went wide, and she looked questioningly at her mother, who nodded again, smiling.

"Well, you can have one of each, but we'll save one of them for dessert after dinner tonight."

Sophie grinned and pointed at two of the cookies. Dan wrapped one of them in paper and put it in a small bag. The other he put in tissue paper and handed it to Sophie, who took a small bite and chewed happily.

Jillian looked gratefully at Dan, but he waved away her offer of money for the cookies.

"Mrs. Young—Karen—would flat out kill me if she thought I was taking payment for giving Sophie a couple of cookies!" he chuckled.

Just then, Jillian's eye was drawn to the television above the counter. It was tuned to CNN, and the banner "Breaking Story" scrolled across the bottom of the screen. The sound was off, but she quickly got the gist of the story.

"Mr. Young, could you turn up the sound?" she asked frantically.

He turned to the television and picked up the remote to turn on the sound.

The story featured a fishing vessel that had apparently vanished off the coast of California. In shock, Jillian stared slack jawed as a photo of her ex-fiancé, Stuart, flashed on the screen. There were photos of other men as well.

"… and the Coast Guard has expanded the search today, hoping to find the boat or evidence of its sinking," intoned the beautiful brunette with the microphone who stood on a pier at a marina. "With us now is the father of one of the missing men." Jillian felt another jolt as the camera focused on Stuart's father. He looked remarkably well and fit as he spoke soberly about his son. "… and I'm praying every day that he will be found and returned safely," he said, as he wiped away a small tear.

What? Where was the "drunk Dad" that Stuart abhorred? This guy looked a lot like Stuart—tall, fit, healthy-looking, although 25+ years older.

Jillian might not be the best judge of character in the world—Lord knew she'd picked some peculiar guys before Stuart—but she thought she could tell that this guy wasn't the falling-down-drunk loser that Stuart had told her about so many times.

183

Now Stuart's photo appeared again on the screen, this time one that showed him standing, his lean, muscular physique on display, flashing his smile. Jillian's heart skipped a beat. He was so damn good-looking.

Mr. Young stared at Jillian, puzzled. "That story has been playing for the last couple of days," he said. "What is it? You look like you've seen a ghost."

"I think I have," she said weakly, feeling slightly light-headed. She took Sophie's hand and turned to leave.

"Wait—are you okay, dear? Maybe you should sit down for a few minutes," he told her, pointing to the chair he kept behind the counter.

"No, thanks, Mr. Young, I'm fine," Jillian said. Sophie looked up at her, slightly alarmed.

"What's wrong, Mommy?" she asked as Jillian tugged her arm a bit too hard.

"Ouch," she said, and that jolted Jillian out of her shock. She quickly knelt next to Sophie, pulling her into her arms. "I'm so sorry, baby!"

Sophie wriggled away after a moment.

Jillian stood, sighed, and turned to Mr. Young.

"I'm sorry about that. I'm fine, really. Thank you so much for the cookies and for the help."

She paused, then asked, "Did you say that story has been playing for a couple of days?"

"Yes, it has—it's been all over the media," said Mr. Young, still looking at her, puzzled.

"I, it's just that I don't have a television at the house," she said lamely. He nodded his head. She paid for the supplies, and they left, Sophie still clutching her cookie but not eating it.

Jillian made dinner for Sophie, bathed her, and tucked her into bed. Spent, she threw herself on the sofa. She didn't have a television, preferring to read in her off-hours, or play with Sophie, or work on home improvement projects. She'd never been an avid TV watcher, so why start now?

Her laptop sat on the coffee table. She opened it up, powered it on, and brought up a browser. She queried "lost San Diego fishing vessel" and quickly found a chain of articles going back for the past few days. She clicked on each one and read it thoroughly, and after she'd devoured every bit of news on the story, she closed the laptop and sank back against the cushions.

Stuart—lost at sea. Her daughter's father, whom she'd left years ago, was somewhere either on a boat, or dead. The thought made her heart pound. She felt light-headed again, shocked at the depth of her emotions. It had been so long, years, in fact, since she'd made the decision that would impact hers and her daughter's lives forever. It had seemed like the right decision at the time. Now, she wasn't so sure.

Stuart had made it clear that he didn't want to be a father, not then, not ever. She'd believed him—had taken in that message and believed it completely. She'd allowed that belief to guide her thoughts, feelings, and decisions.

After leaving Stuart that day, she'd been firm in her resolve. When she'd told Ashley, and seen her response, even then, she'd remained firm. There wasn't any way that she would expose her future child to the heartbreak of a detached, completely disinterested father.

Even though that father was Stuart, who wasn't really a bad guy. He just wasn't father material, something she'd discovered very late in their relationship.

Never once had she considered the option of telling Stuart and letting things play out. But what if she had?

How many times had she seen other women go through pregnancy, husband or fiancée or boyfriend standing by their sides? Always supportive, always excited about impending fatherhood.

She even knew examples of women whose men weren't excited about fatherhood, not at first. But then, when presented with that little life, that tiny bundle in their arms, they were transformed into devoted fathers.

What if she had waited, maybe postponed the wedding to give Stuart time to adjust? What if she'd given him the chance to react one way or the other?

She visualized him reacting with anger, leaving her, wanting nothing more to do with her, let alone their future child. Or, participating half-heartedly, resigned to the chores of fatherhood, but with no heart in it. She shuddered.

It was too horrible to risk. While it had been painful to leave him and have the baby on her own, it would have been devastating to have Stuart abandon her in an act of contempt. He'd made it so clear, after all. *Completely and utterly clear*.

No, she'd done the right thing. It was safer this way.

Jillian went to Sophie's room and knelt by the bed. Her daughter lay sleeping, strawberry blonde curls softly tangling around her head. She lay on her back, her tiny hands open, breathing softly. Jillian gently pulled up the covers, and as she did, a tear slid down her cheek.

I did the right thing, she told herself again.

CHAPTER EIGHTEEN

"We've covered a lot of ground today, Eric. What would you like to do at this point?" Sarah asked her client.

"Well, I moved out last week," he said, looking down.

"You did. Why didn't you tell me at the beginning of the session?" she asked, both curious and surprised.

"I didn't think you would think it was a good idea," he said, looking up. "I never thought I would give up like this. We've been together for so many years, I thought we'd always be together." Tears began to well up in his eyes.

"I'm sure you did," she said softly, handing him the tissue box.

"I feel like I'm just giving up," he said, now crying openly and unashamedly.

"It can feel that way, at the end of a relationship," she said.

"At the end—is that what this is?" he asked desperately.

"I don't know," she said honestly. "But I do know you're grieving."

He sat for a few minutes, crying openly and unashamedly.

"You're not going to give me false reassurance, are you?" he asked with a slight smile, blowing his nose.

She was silent, raising her eyebrows.

"I know, I know. You forgot your crystal ball today."

She nodded.

They scheduled their next appointment for the following week, and he left, closing her office door behind him. Sarah took a minute to update her client notes, then put his file in her file cabinet and locked it. She sat quietly for a moment.

Giving up. Is that what I did?

Sarah felt the familiar ache in her heart. It had been months, but she still missed Paul. She still reached for him at night, woke in the mornings, and forgot he wasn't there until she saw the empty side of the bed. She managed to get herself through her days but with the sensation of a light blanket over her entire being, obscuring the light and joy.

Sarah's cell phone buzzed softly, in vibrate mode. She glanced at the screen but didn't recognize the number, so she didn't answer. It buzzed again a few seconds later, again with an unknown caller. Then again, just a few seconds later. Odd.

The phone buzzed again, and she almost ignored it. She looked at the screen and this time saw her best friend Vivian's name and photo flash. Quickly she swiped right, answering the call.

"Hello?"

"Sarah? I hope you're not in session," Vivian said.

"No, just finished. Is everything okay?" Sarah asked, anxious. Vivian never called her in the middle of the day.

"You are not going to believe what I just saw on the news. It's Paul."

"What?" Sarah's heart began thumping rapidly, her breathing shallow.

"Did something happen? Is he okay?" she asked urgently, standing and pacing in her office. "Tell me!"

"It's okay, at least there's no news—sorry, I'm not trying to be mysterious. It seems that he went out on a small fishing boat from San Diego a few days ago, and the boat didn't return. The media is covering it non-stop now, and the latest report is that the Coast Guard is out looking for them. I'm so sorry, Sarah."

Sarah burst into tears. Oh, dear God! *What was happening to Paul?* Was he still alive? Or was he in the ocean, at the bottom now. The horrifying images flipped through her mind even as she tried to push them aside.

"Look, I'm coming over there now," said Vivian urgently.

"No, don't do that," gasped Sarah. "I'll come to your place."

"You can't drive like this—I'll come pick you up," Vivian said firmly, disconnecting the call.

Sarah sat on the sofa in her office, trying to catch her breath. The unknown calls kept rolling in, and now she knew it was likely media people trying to get a response from her.

Paul! He was in trouble—she could feel it deeply, like a part of herself was tearing away, a part that she'd been denying mattered.

What had she done? She'd left the love of her life, so sure that it was necessary, so convinced that it would wake him up, pull him out of the hostile emotional in-house separation that had driven them apart. Surely, she'd thought, he would see what was happening, return to his old self, rush to her arms, and they'd make up.

But he'd not done any of that. Instead, the days had turned into weeks, the weeks into months, until they had finally occupied separate homes. They'd spoken cordially about how to separate their financial affairs. There'd been no acrimony, just a terrible distance, and coldness, that tore at her heart each time she'd spoken with Paul.

She spent time with their best friends—Nathan and Debra—and they were kind enough to let her pour out her heart. But the shelf life for listening to another's personal misery is short, and she'd known after a couple of visits to their vacation home in Colorado that she couldn't prevail upon them any further, not until she was in a better place.

Each day, she woke up and was reminded again that she and her husband were separated, that there was little hope of reconciliation. She'd sink back into the pillows and prepare herself for another gray day.

A thought struck her.

Wait, what had Vivian told her? That Paul went out on a fishing boat? Paul didn't fish! He'd never done anything remotely like that his entire adult life, as far as she knew.

Maybe it was a mistake. Maybe it wasn't Paul, but some other guy with the same first name. Maybe Vivian had jumped to conclusions.

Sarah went into the waiting room and clicked on the small flat-screen TV on the wall, scrolling through the channels to a local news station. Nothing, just regular programming. She scrolled to CNN.

On the screen, a pretty brunette faced the camera, mic in hand, talking while a banner played at the bottom: "Coast Guard searches for missing boat with five passengers ..." Sarah turned up the muted volume.

"...confirmation that five men left San Diego on the *Princess Rose* and have not been seen or heard from since their second day at sea. That morning, a mayday call was received by the Coast Guard, indicating that the boat was in distress, possibly going down. That was the last anyone heard from the *Princess Rose*, over four days ago."

A middle-aged guy with weather-beaten skin looked nervously into the camera.

The reporter—Heather Steel, according to the banner—began interviewing the man.

"With me is marina manager, Skip Dugan. Mr. Dugan, what have you heard from the Coast Guard about the *Princess Rose*?"

"The Coast Guard informed me that they are doing a very diligent search-and-rescue operation, focusing mainly on the area of the distress call."

"How long has that operation been going on?" she asked.

"Since yesterday."

"What have they found so far?" she asked.

"The Coast Guard isn't saying much at this point." He glanced at her disappointed face and hurried on, "but one thing I got out of them was that they had no indications that there was a weather event on the day of the mayday call."

At that, Heather looked interested.

"In fact, they believe at this point the boat was disabled some other way, and that there's a good chance they will find it."

"And what is the timeframe for finding the men?" she asked.

"Well, typically, if you don't find a lost boat within about a week, the chances of recovery are very slim. That's been my experience over the past twenty-five years running this place."

"And how often do boats go missing?" she asked.

"It's pretty rare these days. Almost all boats are equipped with an EPIRB. That's an Emergency Position Indicating Radio Beacon," he added.

"And did the *Princess Rose* have one?"

He looked hesitant to answer. "I'm not sure. The Coast Guard hasn't mentioned finding any EPIRB signal from them."

"So then will the Coast Guard even be able to find them?" asked Heather, a hungry gleam in her eye.

"Um...well, that's hard to tell. The biggest problem would be if they lost the ability to power the boat, setting them adrift. The ocean currents off of California mostly flow toward the southwest, and if nothing gets in the way, they could drift a long way. Of course," he began, then stopped.

The camera went back to Heather, who began to speak again.

"Mr. Skip Dugan, marina manager, is here explaining what may have happened to the *Princess Rose* after the mayday signal that was sent five days ago. I'm Heather Steel reporting. What else can you tell us, Mr. Dugan?"

"Well, one other thing that could have happened is the boat may have sunk. If that happened, there's little chance of recovery. Unless," he said, and stopped.

"It sounds like there could be another problem," the reporter said.

"Yes, there could be. If the boat sank, their only hope would be if they managed somehow to deploy the life raft and got everyone into it. But," he said, and stopped again, forehead wrinkling in concentration.

"Clearly, this is not easy to talk about," said Heather Steel. "The scenarios for recovery are difficult, and it has already been a week. So, if they got everyone into the life raft, wouldn't that mean a good outcome, Mr. Dugan?"

"Not necessarily. If they had no water in the life raft, they wouldn't last long, especially with the heat and sun exposure."

"And how long are we talking?" she urged.

"With that heat? I'd give them no more than about three days without water on a life raft in the middle of the Pacific." Immediately, he looked chagrined.

"But the families should know that it's very unlikely the boat sank; much more likely is that they are adrift and not far from here. The Coast Guard is good at these kinds of operations. I'm sure the boat and the men will be found," he finished encouragingly.

Heather spoke gravely as the camera focused her way.

"Thank you, Mr. Dugan. That's the latest report on the *Princess Rose Five*. They are the ship's Captain, a Deckhand, and these three passengers." Across the screen flashed photos of three men: two strangers to Sarah; the third one was Paul.

"Oh God, *Paul*," breathed Sarah, sitting down shakily.

"We all hope for the safe return of these people. The search continues, and we will be back with more details as the situation unfolds," Heather finished as the screen went to commercials."

Sarah put her head in her hands and began sobbing. The door to the hallway opened, and Vivian rushed in, putting her arms around her.

PART THREE

THE RETURN

CHAPTER NINETEEN

The story took on a life of its own. Every major national news station covered it, on the morning shows, on the evening news, and Fox and CNN offered hours of coverage during the day. What were they covering? The men were still gone, but their business associates, friends, and family could be interviewed. Their photos—from Facebook, from websites and social media, and from family—could be flashed endlessly onscreen.

With visibility on the internet, there was plenty of content for television, especially because the people involved were so attractive.

Random people showed up at the marina, set up a vigil, brought bouquets of flowers and lit candles. A couple of religious groups conducted prayer vigils at night, holding up votives, chanting.

The reporter who'd launched the story, Heather Steel, was so charismatic that everyone wanted her in front of the camera. She had a gift for talking endlessly about the tiniest snippet of actual news.

The Coast Guard found pieces of the boat, floating in the Pacific Ocean. It was an encouraging find. Because there was no life raft floating at the wreckage site, it boded well for the narrative of the passengers having escaped the sinking of the *Princess Rose*. That enabled the Coast Guard to continue the operation and extend the search area.

This development took hours upon hours to explain, featuring multiple interviews with members of the Coast Guard, asking them to talk about it in minute detail, all covered by the charismatic Heather Steel.

But after ten days of nothing more, the Coast Guard told the media they couldn't continue the effort. The search area was too far away, and it took far too many resources. They promised to alert all seagoing vessels for hundreds of miles out to be on the lookout for the survivors of the *Princess Rose*. Container ships, naval vessels, fishing yachts—all were issued detailed information about the *Princess Rose* and its passengers.

It was a feeble effort, and one that meant the story was drawing to a close. Whatever might happen to the passengers of the *Princess Rose*, and their return would be up to fate or the chance sighting of another seagoing vessel. As it would, fate had her last say.

ॐ

Following the latest broadcast, Heather Steel sat in the conference room with Alan, feet up on the table. She twisted a pen in her hand, rocking it between her fingers, brow furrowed in thought.

"You were great, Heather," he said encouragingly.

"That's great, Alan," she said impatiently, "but that's not what I need to know. We need more story. This thing's going to peter out if we don't do something to keep it alive."

"This story may be pretty much over," said Alan. He shrugged and peered at his computer screen.

"What do you mean?"

"I mean, the Coast Guard has pretty much called off the search-and-rescue. Without that, people are going to lose interest."

Was it over? It certainly looked that way.

How sad for the families, she thought. It was one of the hazards of the news business. You got exposure to people's most difficult life chapters—crime and punishment, near-death experiences that rarely resulted in rescue. Death and dying. Horrific losses.

She hated that expression, *if it bleeds, it leads*. But it was true.

She blew out a breath.

"I guess you're right."

But it still didn't feel right to her.

She threw her legs to the floor, stood, and grabbed her bag.

"I'm going out for coffee. Want some?"

"Sure," said Alan, barely looking up.

"Excuse me," said the woman who'd appeared out of nowhere at the coffee shop. Heather started and looked up. Her blond hair was pulled up into a ponytail that threaded through the loop on the back of a baseball cap. Large, round sunglasses perched on her nose. She was tall and slender. She looked familiar.

"Do I know you?" asked Heather, peering up at the woman—very attractive, as far as she could tell with the lame attempt at a disguise.

"No," said the woman. "I saw you leave the station. I was on my way in to find you. Can I talk to you? It's about the people who are lost at sea." She sounded a bit desperate.

"Look, we're not interested in the psychic angle, but thanks anyway," said Heather, turning back to her phone and scrolling, hoping the blond would leave.

"No, it's not that," said the woman. She pulled a business card out of her bag and placed it in front of Heather. "I'm the...the ex-wife of one of the men."

Heather grabbed the card and peered up at the woman.

Excited, she invited the woman to sit.

"Heather Steel," she said, holding out her hand. "How can I help you?"

"I know who you are. I'm Michelle. And I'm not sure."

"I'm listening," Heather said.

"I've been watching how you've reported on the story so far. I've been told that the Coast Guard has decided to call off the search-and-rescue. I've talked to them, but I can't seem to get anywhere."

Michelle bit her lip and frowned.

"It seems like...if the media continued to run the story, maybe it would put pressure on the Coast Guard to keep the search going. Can you do that?" she asked, looking at Heather imploringly.

Heather shook her head.

"I have an editorial team, and it's not up to me. Right now, the decision is to move on to—this sounds so heartless. But there's a cycle for news, for certain stories, and setting priorities. This one is moving to a lower priority."

Heather dropped her eyes.

"Look, I'm so sorry about what happened to your hus..., uh, ex-husband. With two little ones...I can't imagine how you deal with them losing their Dad," she said softly.

"Right," said Michelle. She looked so disappointed. They both stood and said awkward good-byes.

Making her way back to the office, juggling Alan's coffee, Heather felt like crap. Michelle had looked so sad, so distraught. It wasn't her business or her job—not really—to care about this woman who happened to be one of the people affected by the three men lost at sea.

And she did have a job to focus on, one that demanded a constant new set of compelling stories. She'd been so laser-focused on the *Princess Rose* passengers that she hadn't developed anything new. It was time—to move on from this story and on to others. There was nothing more to be done.

After all, what could she do to help Michelle? She didn't have any sway with the U.S. Coast Guard. She couldn't order them back out to sea, tell them to keep up the search. And she had no story if they weren't searching.

Still, it was hard to let go. This story was more than a story now. She couldn't shake off the idea that there might be some way she could help.

Back at the office, she briefed Alan on her encounter with Michelle.

"Too bad we can't do anything else with the story," he said. "I'm sorry, Heather. I know you liked this one. But without the Coast Guard...and there's no one else who can take up the search, is there? It's too big of an operation to do it privately, plus, who would pay for that?"

"You're right," said Heather. Suddenly, she sat up straight. "Wait. You've given me a brilliant idea!"

"I have?" he said.

"Yeah! Hold on while I make a call." She found the number she needed, pressed the button. A mature female voice answered.

"Aunt Janet? This is Heather."

"Heather! I'm so glad you called. I've been watching your interviews on air. Your career seems to be really taking off," said the woman on the line, pride in her voice. "Well done."

"Thanks, Aunt Janet. Actually, I'm calling about the story—the lost passengers of the *Princess Rose*. I need your help."

"I can't imagine what kind of help I could give," said her aunt, sounding puzzled.

"I don't know how it works, but I was wondering if you could get the Coast Guard or someone else, to extend the search for the passengers."

Hearing silence, Heather rushed to explain. "Aunt Janet, they've found the wreckage, or some of it anyway, and there's good reason to believe they escaped in a lifeboat and are now stranded either on the water or on a small island. These men all have families waiting for them—children, wives." Okay, so maybe she stretched that one a little.

"I'm not in a position to do anything with regard to the Coast Guard," she explained to her niece. "I'm not sure...,"

NINA ATWOOD

Heather reigned in her frustration. "Please, Aunt Janet, can't you do something? It is the U.S. Navy, after all."

Admiral Janet Steel paused, sighed, then spoke.

"There might be something, but it's a long shot, and I can't promise anything."

"That's great! Anything you can do would be wonderful, and I know the families of these men will be so grateful."

"That may be, but we can't give them false hope. Rescue missions at sea are almost always doomed after five or more days have passed. Currents carry them too far away, and it's easy to dehydrate and die from that, or from sharks."

"I know that, Aunt Janet. But we can't give up yet, can we?"

"I suppose not. Let me make a few calls and I'll let you know."

They hung up. Two hours later, Heather got the call she'd waited anxiously for.

"I pulled some strings with a few people I know and succeeded in getting someone to take this on. Remember, though," she continued as Heather whooped, "They can call it off at any point." Heather thanked her profusely.

❧

The next day, Heather stood in front of the cameras and reported. "My sources in the United States Navy have confirmed that they will take up the search-and-rescue operation for the lost passengers of the *Princess Rose*. Training exercises will be conducted in the area of the Pacific Ocean that is believed to be the likeliest location. They may be stranded in their life raft, or more likely, they are on a small island waiting for rescue. The Navy will utilize one of their longest-range aircraft, the C-130, flying in training and search patterns over the area. Additionally, they will do training operations with naval frigates in the area, each of which is equipped to do rescue missions."

Heather was a national media sensation, the darling of all the major news outlets, conducting interviews, facing the cameras with her drop-dead looks but very serious demeanor. As the search continued, she interviewed retired Naval commanders, airmen, and those who had done hundreds of search-and-rescue missions in the past. She queried them about the technical details and perils of those missions, always managing to steer them to acknowledge the possibility of a rescue, even though it had now been almost three weeks since the sinking of the Princess Rose.

She took her crew to Camp Pendleton to film the massive C-130 planes taking off. Bull-nosed, stocky, and low to the ground, with a flight range of well over 1,000 miles, the C-130 could cruise for hours over the ocean at 500 feet.

She skillfully filled in the many hours of waiting time with informative and titillating interviews, keeping her audience on the edge of their seats. Hundreds of thousands of Facebook, Twitter, and Instagram accounts posted updates throughout the day and night. It seemed that almost no one had anything better to do than follow the story of the *Princess Rose Five*.

Vigils at the marina increased in number and frequency.

Later, after she'd landed an anchor spot with the largest television station in Los Angeles, and after she became a frequent correspondent for Good Morning America, people would say that the story made her the success that she is today. They would say that she'd exploited the men and their families for her own personal gain.

Of course, most of the people who said that were her colleagues in the media, envious of her success.

But the families of the lost men would later say that she saved the lives of their loved ones. Because of Heather's relentless pursuit of every minute of airtime conceivable, because she never let go of the story, not until long after the men returned—there were the "return" interviews with the men, after all—the search-and-rescue operation never stopped.

Heather Steel single-handedly kept the pressure on so that the search continued for the men, day after day, far beyond the normal timeframe for an operation that was so costly, that looked so pointless.

❧

It was forty-nine days since the *Princess Rose* sank, except for a few random pieces that floated on the ocean—cushions, a cooler, some of the fishing equipment—when the crew of a Navy C-130 spotted a small island with something strewn across the beach, something that looked man-made. It was late in the day and too late to do more. The crew quickly located a Navy frigate with a helicopter on deck, a few hours away.

By the time the frigate anchored far outside the cove of the island, it was well into the next day. Late that afternoon, a helicopter approached the island, and that's when they spotted the large letters on the beach spelling "HELP."

The helicopter approached the island, the crew spotting smoke snaking upward from a large fire. Landing on the beach, they found the lost men on the island, one of them critically injured. Later, the men were transferred to a much smaller vessel, a U.S. Coast Guard cutter, for the remainder of the journey into San Diego.

❧

The cutter pulled in slowly, aligning the stern side against the dock. The U.S. flag flew bravely from the flagpole affixed to the stern. Media swarmed the marina, pointing large video cameras.

Reporter Heather Steel faced the camera, with her back to the cutter as it approached the marina and spoke gravely.

"51 days ago, five men embarked on the final voyage of the *Princess Rose*. Today, we know that only four men will return. The U.S. Navy, on a routine exercise, located the men on a small island in the Pacific, where they were apparently marooned since shortly after their disappearance. So far, there has been no confirmation of the condition of the men. Nor have we been able to obtain information about what happened to the fifth man."

Sarah waited anxiously at the marina. She stood, she sat, she drank from endless plastic cups of iced tea. Finally, far in the distance, a speck appeared on the horizon. Media people scurried, turned on cameras, all trying to get a shot of the rescue boat. The hotshot reporter who'd become the media sensation, Heather Steel, faced the camera, and talked, and talked.

The speck took forever to approach, gradually growing larger. The crowd on the dock grew in size too, and the media ran endless coverage. After the cutter pulled into the marina and finally docked, a roar went up from the crowd. Cameras flashed from every direction.

Sarah waited, her heart beating wildly. Coast Guard crew stepped onto the dock, securing lines swiftly and carefully. After what seemed an eternity, three men—in civilian clothing—climbed off of the cutter and stepped onto the dock. They looked a bit on the slender side, and two of them were deeply tanned with scraggly hair and beards.

Sarah scanned them desperately, looking for Paul, but there was no evidence of him. She began to feel light-headed. She made her way to the side of one of the buildings and leaned heavily against it.

Two crew members appeared, a stretcher between them. A body lay still on the stretcher. Sarah saw small black dots at the edge of her vision as she sank slowly to the ground. Just before she passed out, she heard someone say, "Wow, that dude is dead."

"Ma'am? Are you okay?"

Sarah blinked and looked up into a concerned face. She was lying uncomfortably on the ground, next to one of the buildings in the marina.

A young guy knelt by her side, peering anxiously into her eyes. "Do I need to call for a medic?"

She pulled herself into a sitting position, still feeling light-headed. *Where was she? What was she doing here?*

Then it all came flooding back.

Paul! They'd carried his body off the boat on a gurney. She looked frantically at the pier, where media still surrounded the three men she'd seen earlier, filming them, asking questions.

"I'm okay," she said, not really feeling okay, but the last thing she needed was a well-meaning person trying to help her. There wouldn't be any help for her today. Her husband was dead. She saw them carry off his body.

His body! She had to find out where they were taking him. Tears flooded her eyes as she struggled to hold back the sobs. No time for that right now. She had to find Paul—Paul's body—and find out what had happened to him.

She looked up at the guy. "What is your name?"

"I'm Seth. Can I, uh, get someone to help you?"

"I don't need help, I'm fine," she said, struggling to stand. She swayed a bit, and Seth took her arm.

"Why don't we go inside?" he said, looking concerned.

"No. Thank you, but I need to know—did you see where they took the—the person on the stretcher? Please, I need to know. Is there someone else I can talk to?" She felt desperate for answers.

"Uh, yeah. They put him into an ambulance and left."

An ambulance? She didn't dare hope too much, but if he was put into an ambulance and taken to a hospital, didn't that mean he was still alive?

A surge of hope coursed through Sarah's body.

Where could they have taken him? She pulled out her phone and opened a search screen, typed in *hospitals near me*. Her hands were shaking so badly it was difficult to press the right letters.

UC San Diego Medical Center was closest to the marina, and they had a trauma center. She quickly called the main number.

"Yes, I'm looking for information about my husband. I think he may have been taken there."

She was in luck—they were able to confirm that Paul had indeed gone there.

"What is his condition? Please—I'm on my way there," she said frantically as she walked as swiftly as she could toward her car. "But I need to know—is he, *is he all right?*"

"I'm sorry, ma'am. I'm afraid you'll have to talk to a doctor once you get here." She gave Sarah directions.

Shaky, she opened her car door, slid in, and started the car.

Sarah, she admonished herself, *get your act together!* She drew several deep breaths, felt her head clear enough to drive.

Sarah felt like she'd been waiting forever, although it was probably no more than two or three minutes. Finally, a dark-haired woman, wearing surgical scrubs, called her name from the doorway leading to the emergency area.

"This way, please. He's in one of the emergency rooms."

"What is his condition? Please tell me," Sarah demanded as she rushed to follow.

"I'm afraid you'll have to talk to one of the doctors," she said apologetically. "I'm sure it won't be long."

She showed Sarah into a small room with a hospital bed and lots of monitors nearby, most of which were hooked up to Paul. He was unconscious.

She rushed to his side, reached down, and touched his cheek. He mumbled something and stirred but didn't wake. She could see his eyes rolling underneath his lids. He moaned once, stirred again.

"Shh, honey. I'm here with you. You're going to be fine—everything's okay now," she whispered in her most soothing voice.

He stilled then, sighed once, and fell into a deep sleep.

Sarah looked at the monitors. While she wasn't a doctor, she'd had some training in hospital psychiatric corridors and knew a few things. She saw that Paul's heart rate was stable, not racing. His blood oxygen levels were normal. A saline bag snaked down to a taped catheter on Paul's arm.

Then she noticed the huge bandage on Paul's shoulder. *Oh, God, what happened to you?* She thought, panicked.

The door to the room opened and in walked a tall, pleasant-looking guy.

"Hi, I'm Dr. Watson," he said, holding out his hand for Sarah to shake. She offered her hand, and they shook briefly.

"I'm Sarah, Paul's wife," she said. "Tell me, how is he?"

He pulled the bandage away from Paul's shoulder, prodded something, and replaced it.

"What's wrong with his shoulder?" she demanded.

"Why don't you sit down. I'll explain everything."

"No," she declared, beginning to shake. But she sat anyway, on the edge of the chair. She listened to the doctor's explanation of Paul's condition, wiping away tears quietly as he spoke.

"Apparently, he was wounded on the island. Puncture wound in the shoulder with a stick of some kind. High risk of infection. If he hadn't been picked up shortly after the injury, he'd have probably gone septic within hours. But he and the other men were picked up and there was a medic onboard the ship. They removed the stick, gave him strong anti-biotics, and kept him stable."

"Why won't he wake up? I spoke to him, and he didn't seem to respond much."

"He's pretty heavily sedated. He came in complaining of severe pain, so we dosed him quite a bit so he could calm down and relax prior to surgery. He was also asking for you."

He was asking for her. Sarah's eyes welled with tears again. She lifted his hand and pressed it to her lips, wiping away tears.

"Is he going to be okay?"

"There are...complications. He's not out of the woods yet. We need to go ahead and get him into surgery," he said, rising.

"Try to stay positive," the doctor finished, moving toward the door.

She sobbed but choked it back. Paul would need all of her strength with his condition and uncertain outcome.

CHAPTER TWENTY

Ben pulled up in front of the house, killed the engine, and sat. He drew a deep breath, wiped his sweaty palms on his jeans, and opened the door. Before he could climb all the way out of the car, the front door of the house flew open, and the two most beautiful children in the world ran down the sidewalk.

"Daddy, Daddy!" screamed Katie and Jordan. He ran to meet them halfway and scooped them up in his arms. He held them tightly while tears coursed down his cheeks, and he kissed them repeatedly. After a minute of that, they squirmed, giggling, so he gently set them down.

"Daddy, what took you so long?" asked Katie, peering up at him, brows creased.

"I got here as fast as I could, munchkin," he told her seriously, kneeling down to look at her eye level. "I want you to know something. Daddy will always be here. I wasn't staying away from you. I just couldn't get here for a while. But I will always show up, I promise you."

Katie nodded in a matter-of-fact way and grabbed his hand.

"Let's go play a game!" she said as she tugged him toward the house.

"Yeah, wet's pway a game!" said Jordan, tugging his other hand.

He allowed himself to be pulled toward the front door. He could see Michelle standing just inside the doorway, eyes open wide, a slight smile playing on her lips. She was dressed in tight jeans and a form-fitting black t-shirt. She looked incredible.

"Ben," she said. Her tone was different—not filled with the heaviness to which he'd grown so accustomed. "It's good to see you," she said, and it sounded like she actually meant it.

"I wasn't expecting you today," she said. Her deep blue eyes searched his briefly as he approached.

"I know. I just couldn't wait another minute to see you and the kids."

"Of course," she said. Then she turned away as they went in.

"Michelle," Ben said as they walked into the living room. She stopped. "I'm sure you have lots of questions, and I have a lot to tell you, but right now, is it okay if I spend some time with the kids? I just...need a moment with them." He stared intently into her eyes, imploring her to understand his need to be with his kids right then.

He saw a complex mix, a wave of emotions shifting across her face—something warm but tentative, something else guarded and inaccessible.

"Sure," she said. "Have fun." And she turned and made her way to the kitchen.

Ben thought about going after her. But nothing—no power on earth—could have kept him from spending the next hour with his children. He resolved not to cry the whole time, but instead, to be lighthearted and fun so they could be completely reassured that things were back to normal. He kept that resolve.

An hour later, Ben made his way back to the living room, even though the kids begged him for another round of Super Mario Odyssey. Feeling slightly guilty, he set them up with a movie in the family room. In no time, their attention was glued to the television, and they barely noticed when he slipped out of the room.

In the living room, Ben sat on the sofa and waited for Michelle, taking in the surroundings. This was his home, the place he'd returned to every day for so many years. It felt so familiar, yet so not familiar. It wasn't his home, not really, but traces of himself lingered, almost as though he were the returning ghost from an afterlife.

She'd re-arranged a few things. The photos of the kids were still there, scattered around the room, and a couple of professional photos framed on the wall—the kids dressed in blue jeans and white shirts, romping in a field, holding wildflowers, smiling—he remembered that day clearly.

Michelle had wanted them dressed alike, had obsessed about the details. Ben didn't understand what the big deal was. Their phones could snap photos so easily—why not take the pictures themselves, get them framed? But she was adamant that this was special, and she was right. When they got the prints back, he was astonished at the result— the beauty of his children, eyes sparkling, lightly tanned skin glowing, their perfect smiles. He and Michelle would never have gotten those shots.

He could hear her in the kitchen doing something, a few plates clattering, the sounds of running water, her footsteps lightly moving across the floor. He'd paid so little attention before, taken so much for granted, spent far too many hours checking email or watching sports, oblivious to the homey sounds of his wife doing something for him, for the kids.

How many hours had he spent checked out, paying little attention to his home life, to the most cherished people in his life, silently resenting the amazing gift that they were? Far too many.

How often had he offered to help, gone into the kitchen and puttered by Michelle's side, cutting up vegetables, pouring their glasses of wine? Not many.

What was she doing? Was she making dinner? Would she invite him to stay?

Ben stood to go and offer to help in the kitchen, strangely excited, wanting to do it. But he was too late—that moment was lost.

Michelle walked into the living room, carrying a tray with cheese, crackers, and a little bowl of nuts. She set them down carefully on the coffee table and sat. Two wine glasses and ice-cold chardonnay sat on the table near the tray, an enticing, light condensation on the outside of the bottle. Ben noticed that she was as far away from him as she could get while still being on the same sofa.

He sighed, reaching for a cracker.

"Um, Ben, this is actually for a, um, friend. I'm sorry, but I already had plans made for tonight," said Michelle.

He drew back his hand, embarrassed and apologizing.

"No, it's okay, you didn't know," she said.

"Michelle, I want you to know something," he began. "Um, I know I've...,"

But she interrupted and held up her hand.

"Ben, my friend will be here any minute, and Liz is on her way to take care of the kids," she said. "I do want to talk, but let's do it tomorrow, okay?"

Just then, the front door opened, and in walked Liz. She stopped in her tracks when she saw Ben.

Ben froze. Crap. The last thing he wanted was a showdown with Liz.

"Well, look who's back," said Liz sarcastically, folding her arms.

Michelle stood and pushed her hands in the air toward her sister.

"Liz, Ben was just leaving. Please, don't start anything," she pleaded. "The kids are in the next room."

Liz, looking disgusted, turned and went into the family room. Ben and Michelle heard the kids squealing in delight. Discomfort coiled in Ben's stomach.

"Look, I'm going to take off," said Ben, standing awkwardly. But before he could leave, the doorbell rang. Michelle's face flushed.

She ran to the door and opened it, speaking quietly to someone who continued to stand on the porch. The door suddenly swung open, and Ben heard a man's voice say, "What's the problem? We can at least say hello. Don't worry, sweetie, it will be okay."

Sweetie?

Ben stood with his mouth slightly open as a good-looking guy

212

advanced confidently toward him, holding out his hand to shake. Lamely, he took the guy's hand and shook it. At the last moment, remembering to give it pressure.

"Hi, I'm Joe," said the guy, smiling widely, super white teeth gleaming. Joe had dark, thick, curly hair, sheared on the sides, and short on top. He was dressed in a long-sleeved shirt, open at the neck, untucked over nice jeans. He was clearly a guy who worked out.

"I'm Ben," he said, heart sinking.

"Yeah, I know. Hey, dude, sorry about what happened to you, but it's good that you're back okay, right?" said Joe. He sounded genuinely pleased.

They all stood awkwardly.

"Well, I have to go," said Ben. "I'll just go say good-bye to the kids."

He braved the icy wilderness of Liz's stare long enough to hug his kids one more time and tell them he loved them. Then another awkward good-bye to Michelle while Joe stood there looking far too comfortable with his arm protectively around her waist.

Shit. Why couldn't he be a jerk?

Outside in the car, Ben sat for a moment. Tension built in his stomach. Twice he started to open the car door to go back to the house, and twice he stopped himself.

He started the car, anger building. He slammed his fists on the steering wheel, breath short, heart pounding. He slumped, sat longer. He put the car in gear and slowly drove away.

That evening, Ben knocked on the door of a small, refurbished bungalow in a quiet neighborhood. The door flew open, and a slender figure wearing a sundress launched herself at him.

"Ben! Oh, Ben, I'm so glad to see you!" Nicole said as she wrapped her arms tightly around him. Finally letting go, she ushered Ben into the house, where she motioned for him to sit on the sofa. The fireplace glowed, and the small living room exuded warmth and comfort. Small, artsy pieces sat on tables with mosaic tops.

One large, scented candle sat on the coffee table alongside a full wine glass, an empty one, and a chilled bottle of rose´. She poured the wine into the empty glass and handed it to Ben.

Just then, a beautiful caramel-colored cat with long fur jumped into Ben's lap. He petted the cat who turned around twice and curled up, looking up at him adoringly and purring loudly.

Ben smiled at his sister, who had begun to look slightly weepy.

"Don't start the waterfall. I'm okay, really," he assured her.

Her eyes filled with tears, and she took a gulp of her wine.

"Nicole, it's okay. I'm okay," Ben said reassuringly, patting her hand.

"I know, it's just that...I could have lost you. And I'm so sorry I wasn't there for you during the divorce. I...I was selfish. It was all so uncomfortable for me, and I'm afraid I did what I do. I just pulled away. Oh, Ben, please forgive me," Nicole begged. Tears welled in her eyes.

"Hey, stop that. Really, you don't owe me an apology, not at all. I'm the one who messed up. I'm the one who blew up his entire family. Hey, hey, stop that. There's no need to cry. Besides, I really need to ask your advice," he finished.

He handed her the box of tissues sitting nearby, and she blew her nose loudly.

"Of course," she said, sounding better. "What's going on? Are the kids okay?"

"Yeah, they're good. I saw them today, and, well, they're great. I'm so lucky that they're too young to realize what's happened. I think everything is situation normal from their perspective," Ben said.

"And?" Nicole asked, eyebrows raised expectantly.

"Well, here's the thing. I want to make it up to Michelle, all the pain I've put her through. I don't know if there's any chance to ever get back together or not, but I don't want the cold war to continue. It's bad for the kids."

"Um-hum," said Nicole, listening intently.

"So, I went over there first of all to see the kids but also to talk to Michelle," he began. "But it didn't go at all like I thought it would," he said.

"Oh, no. Was she really angry?" Nicole asked, looking worried and backing away slightly.

"No, not really," he said. "In fact, I thought for a few minutes there that she was actually glad to see me. But just when we started to talk, Liz showed up."

Nicole stood and motioned Ben to follow her to the kitchen, where she seated him at the island and topped off his wine. She had some crackers and cheese on the table for them to munch on.

"So, there we are, just about to talk, and Liz blew in looking, as usual, totally pissed. That's when Michelle told me," he said, picking up another cracker.

"Told you what?" Nicole asked.

"Told me she had a 'friend' coming over and that the snacks and wine were for her 'friend,'" Ben said, making air quotes.

"Her friend?" Nicole asked, puzzled.

"Yeah, don't you get it? She's dating some dude, and right after that, he showed up."

Nicole nodded her head absently as she took a sip of her wine.

"Wait, you don't exactly look surprised," said Ben suspiciously. "Did you know about this guy Joe?"

"Don't get mad," she said, looking worried again. "I only know because she called me when you went missing, and we talked a few times. She told me she'd started dating and that there was someone else. But she was completely freaked out by your disappearance," she added hastily.

"Sure," said Ben sarcastically. "I guess she was worried about the alimony payments." He took a large gulp of wine and stuffed another flatbread into his mouth.

Nicole stared at Ben.

"You know that's not fair," she said gently.

"You're right, it's not," he said grimly.

His sister was right. He had no reason to be angry with Michelle. If he hadn't cheated on her, he would have had a wonderful homecoming that morning. In fact, he wouldn't have been on that stupid boat in the first place, wouldn't have had to go through what they all did on the island.

Which also meant that he wouldn't have yet another secret to walk around with in life. But this time, he recognized that telling this secret would only do harm and absolutely no good.

What about Michelle, though?

"So, what can I do? Should I try at this point with Michelle? To get past what I did to her. I mean, she's got another guy now. Maybe it doesn't even matter to her anymore," he said dejectedly.

Nicole sipped her wine thoughtfully.

"You know, Ben, I'm not any kind of an expert on relationships. I don't date, and I'm happy that way," she said. "This is why I don't. It's so scary to me, even the thought that I could love someone who someday wouldn't love me back. The idea that someone might love me, and I wouldn't be able to give him what he needs."

She shuddered and took a gulp of wine.

"But one thing I wonder is, what do you want, Ben? Do you want Michelle back, your family back together? Or do you want to move on? Because it seems like you need to know that first."

What did he want? Ben thought.

"Great question."

He stood, kissed his sister's cheek, and told her good night. As he lay in bed in Nicole's guest room later, one cat sprawled out on his left and the other curled up on his right, he asked himself the question again.

Maybe it was the wine, the food, the cats, or the comfort of his sister's home. Maybe it was just time. But for the first time in far longer than he could remember, Ben's stomach unclenched. He began drifting toward sleep and allowed himself to fantasize.

In his fantasy, he and Michelle were back together, the kids were happy, and there was no more guilt, remorse, anger, retaliation, or any of the rest of the pain. He saw them on a picnic blanket with wine and cheese and crackers, talking softly. He saw them making love again the way they did in the beginning, before his colossal mistake.

Imagining this scene, he felt warmth spread throughout his body. His mind stilled, and a sense of euphoria engulfed him. He heard his own voice whisper, *"God, please, if you're there, please."*

What he wanted was his wife back. He gasped out loud, and tears coursed down his cheeks. *What he wanted more than anything in the world was Michelle, his wife, the love of his life.*

But she was out of reach, involved with another guy. What chance did he have? The new guy didn't have the baggage that Ben had. He'd never cheated on her. He was all fun and romance and new. He was the golden future.

Ben was yesterday. He was pain, devastation, and the never-ending stink of the guy who was unfaithful to her.

Ben tossed and turned, sleeping fitfully. Finally, he got up at 5:00 a.m. and went for a run. Exhausted, he took a shower and dressed, packed to leave.

Over breakfast, Nicole peered at Ben's exhausted expression, the dark circles under his eyes. She asked him a simple question—*are you okay?* The dam broke, and everything poured out again. All the pain and sorrow, the unbelievable guilt and remorse, and what he wanted more than anything.

Then he talked about his plan, and Nicole slowly nodded her head.

"It might work, Ben, but what if it doesn't?" she asked.

"If it doesn't, at least I'll know I tried. I've never worked hard at anything before. I've never taken any big risks in anything. I think it's time I did."

They finished breakfast, and he hugged his sister good-bye.

"Call me," she whispered into his shoulder. "I want to know how things go with you and Michelle." He promised her he would, squeezing her once more before leaving.

CHAPTER TWENTY-ONE

Stuart entered the downtown Austin coffee shop, walked up to the attractive brunette, and placed his hand gently on her shoulder. She spun around in surprise.

"Stuart!"

"Hi, Ashley," he said.

"You scared me to death," she said, looking relieved.

"Sorry about that. Look, do you have a few minutes?" he asked, to which she nodded. They threaded their way through the crowds and found a small table in the back. Stuart asked what she wanted, left to put in their orders, and returned with two overpriced coffees. Ashley sipped hers as she sat back, eyeing Stuart carefully.

"How did you find me?" she asked suspiciously.

"I wasn't sure I would," he said. "But you and Jillian used to meet here almost every Saturday morning, so I thought I'd take a chance you might be here."

"So, how are you? I've been following the story in the news," she said.

"I'm fine. It's been a little crazy with the media and all."

"I can imagine. What was it like to be on the cover of People Magazine?" she asked, although not so much out of curiosity than out of diversion.

"It was a madhouse. Sometimes I wish I hadn't done it, but I had a motive."

"And what was that?"

"I was hoping Jillian would see it and contact me."

She was quiet.

"Ashley, how is she? Jillian?"

"She's fine, Stuart," Ashley said curtly, not making eye contact.

"And?"

"And what? She got on with her life, and she's fine," she said, eyes looking everywhere but at him.

He rolled his eyes.

"I got that, but I'm not really here for the headline. Look, you don't owe me anything, but I'm here talking to you because I want to see her. I don't care what's going on in her life now, and you don't have to tell me anything. I'm asking you to tell me where she is."

Stuart had spent the last few days doing his own research and had come up empty-handed. Jillian wasn't on social media, and her landlord from when they'd dated said she'd moved out shortly after their breakup with no forwarding address. He'd known Jillian's Dad was deceased but had just found out that her Mom had passed away a couple of years ago, leaving no one for Stuart to contact except Ashley.

"I don't know, Stuart," said Ashley guardedly.

He waited. She sighed.

"She asked me to keep her information confidential. She is very private, you know that. Besides, you have the media buzzing around you. I'm sure People Magazine paid you a pretty penny for that story."

He ignored the jab.

"This isn't about the media. This is about us. It's been years, and I've had a lot of time to think lately."

"Good for you," said Ashley unkindly.

He sat back. She rolled her eyes.

"Okay, maybe that wasn't completely fair. But I have to tell you, Stuart, I'm not sure about you, and I'm especially not sure about this."

But something in the way she said it didn't ring true. It was as though she was trying hard to be mad at him and not quite succeeding. Strange.

Stuart leaned forward, gazing at her. "Look, one thing you know about me is I'm a straight shooter."

She grudgingly agreed.

"The only reason I want to see her is to apologize for how I treated her, for how we broke up."

He raked his fingers through his hair, eyes looking down and moving back and forth rapidly.

"I feel responsible for our breakup. I...look, some of it is very private, and I don't feel comfortable talking about it right now. But just so you know, my intentions are to do my best to make amends. I'm not trying to get anything from her, although I admit it would be great if there might be a chance to get back together."

She started to speak, and he held up a hand.

"I'd rather find out for myself if you don't mind," he said adamantly.

She closed her mouth.

He waited.

She pulled out her smartphone and began scrolling, and while she did, she said, "Do not hurt her, Stuart. She's been through enough."

"I'm not going to hurt her," he said.

"And, Stuart? She's not the same girl you knew before."

Five minutes later, Stuart walked out of the coffee shop with Jillian's phone number and address safely recorded in his own smartphone.

Stuart sat at the bar, sipping a glass of seltzer and lime. Finally, she walked in through the staff entrance, laughing with a co-worker. Her eyes moved to Stuart, and she froze. Then, her face lit up, and she raced to him. He stood, wrapped his arms around her, and lifted her in a huge bear hug.

"Shit, Stuart! It's about time you got here," Samantha grinned up at him.

"Yeah, well, I got a little held up," he said, grinning back.

"I want to hear everything, but you'll have to wait until the end of my shift," she told him.

"I know. I just wanted to come by first to say hi. What time do you get off?"

They made plans for much later, including dinner. Stuart turned around to go, but she stopped him.

"Wait. Where are you going? What about your usual, uh, drinks and snacks?" she asked, looking surprised.

"I'm not in the mood for drinks, and I'd rather wait until dinner with you later," he said. "Besides, I've got some other things to handle before we get together."

"Okay," she said puzzled.

Stuart pulled up in front of the house, killed the engine, and got out. It was time to confront some old ghosts. He went to the front door and rang the bell. His father opened the door, looking shocked, and gestured for Stuart to come in.

They sat in the living room, his father, Bob, gazing serenely at him. Bob looked amazing, especially considering how he'd been when Stuart had last seen him over eight years ago. Then, he'd looked puffy and red-faced, his eyes bloodshot and his attitude worse. Stuart had told him then not to expect him back for a visit.

"I'm so glad you're here, Stuart. I wasn't sure if you'd want to see me at all," he said. "I was ready to get in touch with you right before your boat got lost at sea. I couldn't believe it—finally, I had a chance to maybe get my son back, and you were gone." His eyes began to water.

Stuart sat in silence, not feeling at all sorry for the guy who had cost him so much.

"Look, the first thing you need to know is that I'm not here for you. I'm here because there are things I need to get straight about my life."

"Of course," Bob said, pulling himself together. "I want you to feel like you can tell me everything, son. I mean everything—about growing up, all the drinking, all of it."

Shit thought Stuart. This was not going at all the way he'd thought it would. Where was the belligerent, drunk father, the one he'd dreaded confronting? Where was the guy he'd hated for so long?

"I have some things to tell you, so let me talk," said Stuart harshly.

"I know you do, but first, I want you to go somewhere with me," Bob said.

"What? No way I'm going anywhere with you," Stuart said angrily, standing up. "As usual, this is going to end up being all about you. Typical," he said in disgust.

"Stuart, please," Bob begged. "It will all make sense if you just give me a chance. I won't ask anything else of you, just this one thing. It won't take long, I promise you."

Stuart stopped at the door, heart beating fast. He wanted to take the guy's head off. But he didn't. He took a deep breath and slowly turned.

"This better not take long, and it better not be a bar."

"It's not a bar, and it won't take long. Let's go," Bob said, grabbing the car keys.

A few minutes later, they pulled up in front of what looked like a community center of some kind. They parked on the street and headed into the building. They walked down a hallway with tile floors and bare walls. *What the hell is this?*

They entered a room that looked like Stuart's first-grade classroom, except that instead of tiny desks, there were mismatched chairs arranged in a circle large enough for about ten people. Eight people sat in the chairs talking quietly, some of them sipping coffee.

"Hello, Bob," said the guy at the front of the room, also sitting in a chair. He stood, walked over, and introduced himself as Steve. "You must be Stuart," he said, smiling.

Surprised, Stuart shook his hand, nodding. They sat down, but before Stuart could ask any questions, Steve called the meeting to order. He spoke quietly to a hushed audience.

"Alcoholics Anonymous is a fellowship of men and women who share their experience, strength, and hope with each other that they may solve their common problem and help others to recover from alcoholism.

"The only requirement for membership is a desire to stop drinking. There are no dues or fees for A.A. membership; we are self-supporting through our own contributions. A.A. is not allied with any sect, denomination, politics, organization, or institution. A.A. does not wish to engage in any controversy, neither endorses nor opposes any causes. Our primary purpose is to stay sober and help other alcoholics to achieve sobriety."

He paused, and everyone bowed their heads as he continued.

"God, grant me the serenity to accept the things I cannot change; courage to change the things I can; and wisdom to know the difference. Amen."

Stuart sat in shock. A.A.? *His Dad was going to A.A.?*

Steve looked directly at Bob, who rose and went to the front. He pulled a folded sheet of paper out of his pocket, glanced at it as he held it with shaky hands, then folded it again and put it in his pocket. He looked up and began speaking in a quiet but steady voice, hands placed on the back of a chair behind which he stood.

"Hi, I'm Bob, and I'm an alcoholic," he said firmly.

"Hi, Bob," everyone else said in chorus.

Stuart rolled his eyes internally but didn't say anything.

"Four and a half years ago, I came here, to my first meeting. I sat in that chair," he said, pointing at the chair in which Stuart sat. "That is my son." His eyes filled with tears.

"Twenty-four years ago, my wife, Rebecca, my son's mother, left us." He took a deep, shaky breath.

"I'd always been a drinker, but after Rebecca left, I upped my game. I started drinking every evening after work. My main drink of choice was scotch, but later I switched to vodka because it was cheaper.

"Weekends, I drank almost non-stop from Friday after work until Sunday night, late. It's a miracle I kept my job, but I learned to manage it well enough so that no one noticed, or at least if they did, it wasn't enough to get me fired.

"I drank because I was angry and because I felt sorry for myself. You see, I'd thought that my wife, Rebecca, loved me, and I couldn't imagine her ever leaving. But then again, I didn't really know my wife. You see, I was self-righteous and demanding. I wanted her to take care of my needs, but I wasn't as interested in hers."

He stopped and looked down for a moment as if searching his memory.

"Honestly, it's been so long ago that I can't tell you exactly where we went wrong, but I knew something was wrong, and I ignored it. I never asked her what was going on, what was bothering her. Not once. Not ever.

"One day, she just walked out. After that, I drank like it was my own personal religion. I felt *entitled* to alcohol. It was my friend, my only friend. It was my reward for having been hurt so deeply. Gradually, I lost any sense of who I was, of what mattered in my life. I didn't care, not about myself, and not about anyone else."

Bob stopped talking as the tears ran down his face. Someone handed him a tissue, and he blew his nose.

"Not even my son."

Stuart felt a wave begin somewhere deep in his body. It was an unfamiliar sensation, and it frightened him.

"You see, the real casualty of my drinking back then was my son. He was only eight years old when his mother left, and he had only me to take care of him."

Bob's voice began to choke, but he forged on.

"I can't even tell you what was going on with my son at that time. Was he sad, hurt, upset? Did he feel abandoned by his mother? Was he afraid I would leave him, too? Did he have a hard time at school? Was he afraid?"

Stuart's body began to flush with heat. He sat up straight and rigid, clasping his hands as tightly as he could, trying to control whatever it was that was happening. He began to sweat.

"The reason that I can't answer those questions is because I don't know the answers. I was too busy drinking and blacking out to pay attention to my son. *My son*," he sobbed.

Stuart was sure that someone would put a halt to this emotional outpouring. It was way too much. They didn't.

No one moved, not even a muscle. No one looked put off, or shocked, or as if they pitied his Dad. No one looked disgusted or contemptuous. No one got up and walked out.

"So, while I drowned my sorrows and wallowed in self-pity, my son was forced to live in whatever emotional state he suffered from, and, even worse, he had to deal with me. Because I know I was angry. A lot.

"Anger was my defense. It was a way that I could still feel alive, still feel something through all the numbness.

"I don't recall the things I said to my son in those angry states, which I'm sure lasted for hours at a time. You see, I was a mean drunk. Some people are funny and charming. Other people are just sad. I was sad at first, then angry.

"I don't remember what I said, but I do remember trying to find my son. I went looking for him because I needed someone to yell at, someone to take out my anger on. I guess he learned how to hide from me, and for that, I'm grateful, because I don't think I ever hit him." He looked directly at Stuart with a question in his eyes.

Stuart's body went from hot to cold, and he began to shake. *What was happening to him?*

"What I did was drive him away. As soon as he got old enough, he began staying away from the house, going to friends' homes, and not coming home. After he learned to drive, I rarely saw him, and he couldn't wait to move out after high school graduation. Still, even then, I kept drinking, in fact, even more.

"I had relationships with women, but I succeeded in driving them off almost as soon as I met them. But one night, I took my girlfriend at the time out to dinner. Dinner!" he laughed raggedly.

"Truth was, I didn't even eat. Oh, I ordered food, but it just sat there because my focus was on the liquid nourishment in my glass. My girlfriend asked me to slow down, but I didn't listen. She finally told me she was going to take a taxi home, and that was fine with me.

"She left, and I left and got in the car to drive home. Most of the time, I drank at home because I could do it without worrying about anyone noticing how much I drank. But that night, I got in the car in a highly intoxicated state, and I pulled out of the restaurant parking lot—

"—right into the taxi in which my girlfriend sat."

Bob stopped again, tears streaming down his face, and blew his nose.

"I didn't even feel the impact. I was barely aware that I'd caused a horrific accident. I tried to put the car in reverse and back up so I could keep going. But the car was stuck, and I couldn't move. I got out, falling-down drunk, and the cops showed up and arrested me.

"The taxi driver was injured, although not badly, but my girlfriend was severely injured because my car hit her side of the car—T-boned it. She almost died of her injuries."

The room was utterly silent.

"I was charged with vehicular assault, but because it was my first offense, my attorney was able to get me the minimum sentence. I served two years in prison, and it wasn't enough. I deserved far more.

"Being in prison helped me. Since I couldn't drink, and alcohol was my drug of choice, I was forced into sobriety. I had a hell of a time with it, too—DTs, the works. But I got there, and then when I could think straight, I had to really look at my life. I couldn't escape into an alcoholic fog. There wasn't much else to do in prison. So, I sat there, and I reflected on my life.

"What I saw was terrible. I saw someone who'd been selfish most of his adult life. I saw someone who had hurt other people, especially the people he loved most. I saw someone who, because of his selfishness and drinking, severely impacted the life of another person. It took her many months to recover, and some of her injuries are permanent. I saw someone who'd driven off his own wife and son.

"One day, this guy showed up who was doing prison ministry. He went around to the prisons and offered to spend time with people like me. If I'd wanted it, he would have prayed with me, read the Bible. But I didn't want that.

"I had only one question—Is there any way that God could ever love someone like me?

"He told me that God loves everyone."

Bob choked up. Heads nodded in the room, and someone called out, "Amen."

"This was a foreign concept to me. God, loving people like me. But I decided not to figure it out at the time. Instead, I started asking myself another question. *What would I do with my life when I got out of prison?* I found out about A.A. and decided I would go when I got out. And I did."

He paused again and took a breath.

"That was the real turning point because the fact that I was sober wasn't enough. I had to confront all the damage that I'd done to others, confront how I'd wasted my life for so long, and what was I going to do with the time I had left."

He looked at Stuart.

"And today, my son came to see me. I don't deserve his

forgiveness. I don't deserve to be alive today, not after what I've done. Every day, I ask again what I'm supposed to be doing with my life.

"One thing I'm going to do is be there for my son. Whether he wants me to or not."

Again, Bob looked directly at Stuart. "I'm so sorry, son. I'm so terribly sorry," he whispered.

Stuart's body shook as he stood to leave. He stumbled out of the room, down the hallway, and out of the building. He reached the sidewalk and began walking fast as the tears poured down his face. He began to run haphazardly, not knowing where he was or where he was going. He ran until he could barely breathe, finally stopping, bent over with hands on his knees, struggling to get air in his lungs.

He cried like a little boy, the sad and lonely little boy he'd been after his parent's divorce. The sad little boy who had hidden in his room, and later outside, while his father drank away his own pain.

Stuart pulled out his phone and summoned an Uber driver, who took him to the restaurant where Samantha worked.

CHAPTER TWENTY-TWO

Stuart banged on the door of the restaurant, ignoring the "CLOSED" sign. A guy appeared on the other side of the glass and pointed angrily at the sign. Stuart shouted, "Is Samantha still here?" to which the guy shook his head and walked away. Stuart began banging again.

Samantha finally arrived at the door and unlocked it, opening it to talk to Stuart.

"Stuart! Be quiet, please. Where have you been? I thought you'd be back hours ago. I'm not supposed to let people in. Wait here, and we can leave together."

She turned, grabbed her bag from a nearby table, slipped out the door, and locked it behind her. She began walking quickly down the sidewalk. Stuart rushed to keep up.

"Honestly, Stuart. You are taking a lot for granted, you know." She sounded irritated, something Stuart wasn't used to hearing in her voice. He grabbed her shoulder and stopped her, turning her around. She peered at him, frustration evident on her face.

"What?"

Then she got a good look at him.

"Stuart, what's wrong? You look like someone died."

He looked down, shaking his head as tears dripped off the end of his nose, hands in his pockets.

Samantha walked up, put her arms around him, and held him. After a few seconds, he sniffled and stepped gently out of her arms.

She looped her arm through his and pulled him along the sidewalk.

"Come on. Let's get something to drink—and I'm starving—then we can talk."

⁂

At a nearby coffee house, they bought coffee and scones, and settled in on an overstuffed sofa in the corner.

Stuart told her everything—about the island, about coming back, trying to find out about Jillian, and going to see his Dad. He told her about the A.A. meeting. She listened intently, nodding her head now and then.

"What about hitting someone with his car, hurting that woman? Who does that? And prison? And who would have ever thought my Dad would get sober? I'm not even sure I can believe all of this." He shook his head again as if doing so would ward off what he'd discovered. He wanted to return to the familiar cocoon of who he'd thought his father to be, who he'd pushed away for so many years.

"I don't know what he wants from me at this point. I guess he needed to confess, to get everything off his chest, but what am I supposed to do with it?"

"Well?" Samantha asked.

"Well, what?" he said belligerently.

"What do you want to do with it?" Samantha asked.

"Nothing! I don't want to do anything with it," he said unconvincingly.

"You mean, him."

"Right."

"It is a lot to take in," Samantha said. She waited, eyebrows raised,

232

but he remained silent.

"Why did you go see him in the first place?" she asked.

"I wanted to tell him how much he'd hurt me, finally confront the guy who'd done so much damage to me and to my Mom. I've always told myself I didn't need to do that, that it wouldn't do any good, and so why bother. But after the island, I felt ready. And I wanted to do it before I saw Jillian."

He stopped and grimaced. "That's if I do go and see her."

"Why wouldn't you?"

"What if she's moved on? What if she's married? Maybe it's better I just get on with my life, start dating again."

"Yeah, right," she said sarcastically.

Stuart looked up at Samantha—so fresh-faced, so compassionate, her lovely blue eyes gazing at him. Her full lips looked so enticing. He took one of her hands and began lightly stroking it with his thumb. She began turning a light shade of pink and tried to withdraw her hand.

Stuart leaned in and kissed her, and for a moment, she kissed him back, slowly. They pulled apart slightly, and she sighed, eyes half-closed.

"You have no idea how much I've wanted to do that," she whispered.

"Me, too," he breathed. He leaned in for another kiss, pulling her close, but she stopped him.

"What's wrong?" he asked, surprised.

"Nothing's wrong," she said. "Oh, hell, everything's wrong." She took a breath.

"What?"

"Stuart, you're not the only one who has been thinking about things since you've been gone. Wait, let me talk for a minute," she said as he began protesting.

"You've been coming here for years, and I've become a friend, I think."

"Of course, and I'm so thankful," he began.

"But then I started to feel more than that for you."

Stuart sat back.

"I started falling in love with you, Stuart, and I wanted more. A lot more."

He felt his heart knocking and waited for the rest.

"I thought maybe we could have more, be a real couple, not just two people sitting in the restaurant late at night talking. So, I was planning on asking you over for dinner one night. And I don't mean just dinner," she said, staring intently into his eyes. His heart skipped a beat. *Oh, man.*

"But then you went missing, and I wasn't sure if I would ever see you again. That gave me a chance to sit back and really think."

Crap. Women thinking—never leads to anything good. He felt his chance with Samantha slipping away.

"And here's what I thought about. I thought about all the times we talked about Jillian, and how your face lit up every time you said her name. I thought about the time you left to go to the men's room, and I picked up your cell phone to keep it safe, since you'd stupidly left it on the bar, and I couldn't help myself. I saw your screen saver, and there was the most gorgeous red-head I've ever seen. In a shot in some vacation spot with you looking at her, and her looking into the camera.

"I wanted to hate her, but I saw the kindness in her eyes, the way she beamed. How you gazed at her, and how freaking happy you looked.

"I've only known the sarcastic guy, Stuart. The guy with the bleeding heart, the guy filled with fake bitterness who was clearly broken up over a relationship. The guy who came on to me, but who *never once asked me for a date.*"

She stopped, eyes looking into the distance.

"In that one photo, I saw the happy guy, the guy who was madly in love, and who, no matter what you say, will *never* look at me that way."

She stopped and blew out a breath. Taking a sip of coffee, she stared at him, resigned. Stuart felt like shit.

"Samantha, look, I'm sorry for coming on to you. You deserve way more than that from a guy. You deserve roses and candles and all the rest of it."

She lifted her chin and said, "Yes, I do!"

He touched her chin and planted a kiss on her cheek.

"Yes, you do," he said softly.

They sat quietly.

"So, look Stuart, I'm going to make this easy for you. You need to go and find Jillian, and you need to try to make things right with her. I am going to go on with my job at the restaurant and keep looking on the dating apps."

"You're right. I do need to find Jillian. She may not be available at this point, but I have to try."

He smiled. "And the dating apps are for shit. Watch out for those guys; some of them are real creeps."

They stood and made their way out of the coffee bar. Standing outside, Samantha shivered, and Stuart drew her in for a hug. But it was a friendship hug, no question about it. She pulled back and looked up at him.

"One thing, Stuart. If things don't work out with Jillian, don't come back here for me. I could never be happy as your Plan B."

Stuart's shoulders sank. "Of course not. You are going to be some lucky guy's Plan A, the only plan."

Stuart rang the doorbell. A dog barked in the distance for a moment. He knocked on the door, then knocked louder. The porch light came on, the locks were pulled back, and the door swung open.

Bob stood there looking rumpled in his house robe, his hair sticking up, and his mouth slightly open in surprise.

Stuart stepped into the house, turned, and looked at his father, who began to cry.

"If you don't stop that, I'm going to leave," Stuart said, but jokingly, causing Bob to smile through his tears.

"Let me make some tea for us," said Bob, padding into the kitchen. A few minutes later, they sat in the small living room, awkwardly holding their tea. Bob looked at Stuart like he might be a mirage, like he might disappear any minute.

"I'm so glad you came back," he said. "I didn't think you would. But I was going to wait a couple of days and call you," he said. "Wasn't sure you'd like that either, but still—"

Stuart looked up. "Look, I still have some things to say, and I think I have the right to say them, don't you?"

"Of course," said Bob, although he looked taken aback.

"Here's the thing. You got your say today, but I've never had mine. I don't want you falling apart just because of what I have to say. For once, I need you to just sit there, be quiet, don't get upset, and listen. For as long as it takes."

Bob sat up straight, folded his hands, took a deep breath, and nodded.

"You're right. It's okay, I'm ready for whatever you need to say. And take your time, as long as it takes."

Stuart took a deep breath and let him have it. Everything. From the way he'd spoken to Stuart's mom the one time he'd overheard her call, to the way he'd been drunk so many times. The neglect of their house, not buying food, making Stuart forage in the pantry when he was still too little to have to figure out his own dinner.

He told Bob about having to hide from him, how he'd learned to find new places to go to keep from his father's wrath. How he'd spent so many nights on the sofa at friends' houses, enduring the pity of their parents.

How he'd had to figure out how to get into college on his own. How Bob had been checked out from the process of determining his education, too drunk to read the information, too out of it to give him advice.

Stuart coming back after college, his father barely acknowledging his presence, and trying to get through to him. Finally, after trying to have a relationship with a drunk, giving up eight years ago and deciding not to come back.

Feeling the hole in his heart where a father's love should be.

Bob listened intently, never once interrupting until Stuart ran out of things to say.

Stuart waited for his heart rate to come down, completely wrung out.

They sat quietly for a time. Finally, Stuart looked up.

"What do you know about what happened to Mom?" he asked.

Bob shook his head sadly. "I'm sorry, son, I don't know anything."

"Well, I do. She left us because she was lesbian. She didn't want to be married to a man, but I think she might have stayed anyway if you'd been kinder to her. She apparently felt terribly guilty about leaving me, at least, according to her friend.

"But once she left and you refused to let her come see me, she gave up. After that, she met a woman, and they lived together for the rest of her life."

Bob looked shaken. "The rest of her life? Are you saying she's dead?"

"Yes, she is. She died of cancer years ago."

"Oh, God, I'm so sorry, Stuart." He put his head in his hands.

"Yeah, well, that's another thing. You need to know that I never saw her again after she left us. By the time I found out about her, it was too late."

They sat there, emotional burdens weighing on them heavily, no relief in sight.

Time passed, and neither said anything more. Finally, Stuart stood up to leave. "It's getting late—"

"Wait. I have a guest room upstairs," said Bob, standing. "I hope you'll stay over."

Stuart thought about it for a moment, then accepted the offer. "Okay."

They made their way upstairs, and Stuart settled in the guest room.

He lay in bed.

He'd never felt so raw and vulnerable. He felt like his insides had been turned outside—like sandpaper had been rubbed on his emotions until there was little left.

His father, the 12-step meeting, *Samantha*. She'd been right, of course. He wasn't in love with her. She'd have been short-changed in that relationship.

His Mom—lost so long ago.

Jillian. Was she lost to him as well?

He turned over, punched the pillow, and out of sheer exhaustion, dropped into sleep.

CHAPTER TWENTY-THREE

In the waiting room, thumbing through a magazine, seeing none of the words, Ben felt like his pulse might accelerate to the point of a heart attack. He wiped his sweaty hands on his jeans, stood up, and was about to walk out when the inner door to the office opened.

In the doorway stood a slender, fifty-something woman with short, wavy hair. She was dressed in black pants and a soft sweater. Blue stones dangled from her ears.

"Ben?"

"Yes," he said hesitantly, still thinking of bolting.

"I'm Suzanne," she said, holding out her right hand. He shook it, feeling embarrassed about the transfer of sweat.

"Please, come in." She led him to a nicely furnished office with large windows overlooking a landscaped courtyard filled with flowering plants. She indicated the sofa, and he sat down. She sat opposite him in a large, upholstered chair. She picked up a legal pad and pen and set them in her lap, smiling softly at him.

"You must be finding re-entry into your life challenging," she said gently.

He sighed and nodded.

"Where would you like to begin?" she asked.

"I'm not sure," he said. But unaccountably, he felt his chest tightening.

She said nothing. Calm exuded from her. She maintained eye contact with Ben, but strangely, he didn't feel stared at like he sometimes did in the stores and restaurants. *Thank you, People Magazine.*

"Is this your first time?" she asked. "In therapy?"

"Yes," he said, relieved. "I don't know what to do here."

"Most people like to start with what they want to accomplish in the session. What about that?" she said. "But it can really be anywhere you want to start," she added.

What would he like to accomplish here? He'd made the appointment with something in mind, and it had seemed like a great idea at the time, but now he was having a hard time remembering what it was.

"Look, maybe this isn't for me. I've never done this before, and now I'm thinking it's a bad idea." He pushed to the edge of the sofa, preparing to stand.

"So, it's something new, and you don't know what's going to happen," she said calmly, as if what he'd said was something her patients said all the time. Maybe it was.

"I'm curious, though. I wonder what it is that you're afraid of?" she asked.

"Afraid?" he said, feeling a bit defensive. "I'm not afraid," he said. He laughed hollowly. "You're not exactly a scary person," he added lamely.

She laughed softly. "You're right, I'm not. Most people feel pretty safe around me. But I've found that when people come here for the first time, they often have doubts."

"Yeah, I do," he admitted.

She waited. No rushing from this lady. The silence got to him, and the words began to leak out.

"My parents went to therapy," he said. "A lot. It seemed like my

240

mother dragged my father to therapy every single week, and he hated it."

"What do you think they were going to therapy about?" she asked.

"About them. To hear my mother talk about it—and she talked about it all the time—you would think their marriage was in dire straits. Yet they are still married decades later, although I'm not sure they're happy together. I don't think they're any happier now than they were when I was growing up."

She looked down at the note pad and made a short note.

"They talked about it openly?" she asked. "Therapy?"

"Yes. All the time, in front of me and my sister, Nicole. My mother would go on and on about the importance of her feelings and how vital it was for her to express them. My father just sat there and sulked, arguing with her about how worthless it all was, going to therapy, having to listen to her. How spoiled she was because she had nothing better to do than go to see her shrink while he worked all the time to pay for our big house and all her nice clothes."

"And you and your sister? How was it for you?"

Ben's chest tightened. He felt tears in his eyes. *What was going on?* He couldn't seem to stop crying these days. He *never* cried.

She waited.

"It was awful," he whispered. The tears streamed down his face.

"What was awful?" she asked gently.

"The look on my sister's face," he said, voice now raspy. "She looked like the life was being sucked out of her. She *hates* conflict. She's quiet and shy, very introverted. Them having feelings all over the place stressed her out. But that wasn't the worst of it," he said. He grabbed a handful of tissues out of the box sitting on the table next to the sofa and blew loudly.

"What was the worst of it?" she asked, even more gently.

"The worst part was that we couldn't escape it. We learned early on that if we tried to escape to our rooms, it got worse, much worse.

Without us there, they screamed at each other. Once, when we were out of the room, we heard loud crashing and rushed in to find my Dad smashing my Mom's favorite wine glasses, one by one, on the fireplace. Somehow, having us in the room, they controlled themselves better. In fact, they talked *through* us."

"Talked through you?" she asked.

"Yeah as in, 'Ben, your father thinks I'm crazy because I shared my feelings this morning about the last session I had with my therapist,' and 'Ben, your mother is a fucking lunatic, although a well-dressed one, I'll give her that.'"

"Oh, I see," said Suzanne, making another note.

She looked up at him. "So, you grew up in a house where you couldn't escape from your parents' angry relationship," she said. "And where the adults had no emotional boundaries." She let that sit there. "I would imagine you didn't feel very safe around them."

"Safe?" he asked.

"Yes," she said. "You see, when people around you express strong emotions, you feel the impact in your body. There are times in life when you need to sit with someone who is going through something, who needs a shoulder to cry on. But when people are angry and throw those kinds of emotions around, on a regular basis and with no real purpose, it can be very toxic to anyone else around them.

"Not that you can't sometimes come home in a bad mood, throw your keys down, and raise your voice to the first person you encounter. That's normal. Most people self-correct in those situations. They go to cool off, or quickly apologize."

Ben nodded.

"Your parents, for reasons I can't explore because they are not here, vocalized their negative emotions, it sounds like, on a regular and frequent basis. Because anger sets off adrenaline in others, you and your sister were sitting there and experiencing your hearts race, your own bodies going into 'fight or flight' mode. That is the stress reaction in the body. Does that make sense?"

"Yes, it does," said Ben. "That's exactly how it felt—as if I was on fire with their feelings, with no escape." For the first time in his life, someone understood what home life was like for him.

"So, you didn't feel emotionally safe in that situation, and of course, you might relate that to being here, in a therapy situation."

"Yes!" he said, letting out a deep breath. His chest finally relaxed.

"I'm wondering how you coped," she said.

"Coped?" Ben asked, puzzled.

"Yes, coped. You see, when children find themselves in very uncomfortable circumstances that are outside of their control, they develop coping mechanisms to get them through it. For example, some kids shut down emotionally in difficult circumstances, others 'act out' their reactions to the circumstances at school—bullying or fighting with other kids, getting into trouble."

Ben nodded.

"The problem is that the things we do to cope as children are often not very good strategies as adults. But by then, we've formed these habits of relating, habits of dealing with difficult feelings, and we tend to drag those into adulthood."

Ben let that sink in.

"My sister coped by completely shutting down. Even now, she lives alone, and she doesn't date. She has a quiet job teaching school in a small town, and generally avoids life so that she won't get stressed."

"Makes total sense," said Suzanne.

"It does?" he asked, surprised.

"Yes, of course. One coping strategy is to shut down feelings and withdraw, lowering the fight or flight response and enabling you to get through the situation. As an adult, that could result in avoidance of people and relationships, because, let's face it—that's where most of life's stressful situations take place, especially between couples."

Ben went quiet and sat back. After a moment or so, he raised his eyes to Suzanne's.

"As for me, I coped by—I don't know what this is—but I got to the point that I just didn't let my parents' arguments get to me. I pretty much ignored them. As I got older, I left the house, went over to friends' homes. I got a job as soon as I turned 15. I didn't care how low the pay was. It was a huge relief to go somewhere and do something productive instead of sitting in that house."

Ben was quiet, reflective.

"I think it affected my sister way more than me. I just moved on," he said.

"Did you?" she asked.

"Did I?" he asked.

"It's interesting how you sometimes refer to yourself as if you are talking about someone else, as if you don't know your own feelings," she suggested.

"I do?" he asked, shocked.

She was silent.

"I guess I do," he admitted. "Most of the time, I feel like I'm a stranger to myself. I felt that way with Michelle, my ex-wife. That wasn't her fault," he added quickly.

"No, it wasn't," Suzanne said. After a pause, she said, "Tell me about you and your wife."

Ben talked for a long time, trying to describe their life together, getting married, having children so quickly. How he'd withdrawn emotionally.

"So, let me see if I understand this," Suzanne ventured. "You had strong feelings about the loss of intimacy with your wife, but instead of talking about it or trying to suggest ways to keep your relationship alive, you withdrew. And you felt sorry for yourself," she added softly.

Ben nodded, feeling shame surge again.

"Your coping mechanism," said Suzanne compassionately. "And how did that affect your marriage?"

"I had a one-night stand," Ben blurted out.

"Okay," said Suzanne, totally nonplussed.

Probably hears confessions like that all day long, thought Ben, from cheaters like me.

He was quiet. Softly, she asked, "How did Michelle find out?"

"I told her," he said. "I tried to make it up to her, but she wouldn't give me a chance," he finished bitterly.

"And you're surprised by that?"

"We had years of great married life and two children. How could one mistake erase all that? I don't get it. She didn't even give me a chance!"

Even to Ben's own ears, he sounded childish. He dipped his head and looked away. Suzanne was quiet, letting those last words float in the air, increasing Ben's discomfort. When he looked up, finally, she was gazing at him.

"Ben," she said. "I understand you're hurt that Michelle didn't give you a chance to make up to her for the affair, but was that a realistic expectation?"

He knew it wasn't, but the urge to defend himself prevented him from saying so. He sat silently, arms crossed, looking away.

"Let's put a bookmark in that one for now," she said, "and talk about your one-night stand.

"Frankly, I'm not terribly surprised you did it, and believe me, I'm not condoning it, but it does make sense given your background. And I'm not saying it's anyone else's responsibility either. Your parents did what they did, possibly coping with something from their backgrounds. That's them. You did what you did, and that was your choice as an adult, your mistake."

She paused. "But when you grow up having to cope with that much emotional stress, and your way of doing so means that you compartmentalize feelings, you don't have the practice at dealing with the emotions generated by these kinds of life transitions. Having children changes couples, mostly in positive ways, but also, there are sacrifices until the kids get older, and intimacy is one of them if you're not careful."

"I don't want to make any excuses for myself," Ben said adamantly. "And I do still resent my parents sometimes, but I don't blame them for what I did."

"Of course not," she said. "Let me ask you something. Would you describe yourself as more of a giver in your marriage, or would you say that you were more of a taker, maybe even selfish?"

"I gave Michelle everything I could think of," Ben said defensively. He stood up, began pacing. Finally, he stopped at the window, turning to glare at Suzanne. "I worked 60-hour weeks so we could have a nice home, so she could stay home with the kids!"

"Of course, you did," she said, "but tell me something. Were you happy to give your wife a nice home and the freedom to take care of the kids all day, or were you resentful?"

Bang. She'd found his weak spot.

Stricken, Ben sat back down and put his head in his hands. Finally, he looked up.

"I was resentful," he admitted. "Very resentful."

She let that sit there for a moment.

"Ben, we're not trying to add to the guilt you already feel. What we're going for, ultimately, is to find a pathway that gives you the emotional freedom to choose a new way of being in your life. So, with that goal in mind, I have another question."

Ben looked up guardedly. He sighed. "Okay, fire away."

"What did Michelle want? Was the nice house, the cars, and clothes, or whatever the money you made bought, and staying at home with the kids—was that her dream? Since you gave her all that and resented it, did you at least succeed in making her happy? And I don't mean momentarily gratified as in that whoosh you get when you buy something new or receive a gift. I mean *happy*, as in content, joyful about life, fulfilled overall, day to day."

Stunned, Ben sat back.

What did Michelle want?

He'd operated for so long out of the belief that he'd given her everything she'd wanted—fulfilled her dreams—that he'd never questioned it. He'd assumed for years that she was happy, that his *sacrifices* were worthwhile because they made her happy. But had they really, or was that his perception of what he thought she wanted?

When was the last time he'd sat down and asked her, and really wanted to hear what she was feeling about their life, the choices they'd made?

What did Michelle really want?

"I don't know," he said dejectedly.

She was quiet. "Well, that sounds like a fine place to start," she said, and he looked up quickly, thinking she was making fun or being sarcastic.

"Huh?"

"Not knowing. It's a great place to begin learning and finding out something new. Your old strategy is understandable, but how has that been working for you?"

"Not too great," he said.

"Right. So, let's begin with something new," she said.

They extended the session for another hour. At one point, he looked up at Suzanne in despair. "I made a huge mistake telling her, didn't I?" he pleaded. "I should have kept my mouth shut!"

Suzanne gazed at him with compassion. "I can't say one way or the other on the topic of telling versus not telling your partner about an affair. But I don't believe it's realistic to expect it to automatically blow over, or to resolve itself magically. People are far too complex for that. Pain and hurt need time to heal, and it's different for everyone."

Ben rang the doorbell and waited patiently. He heard someone approaching on the other side. There was a long pause, and finally, the door opened. Liz stood there, hair tousled from sleep, wearing sweats, with her head tilted to one side and a hand on her other hip.

"What. Do. You. Want." She spoke in a monotone.

"I want to talk. May I come in?"

She stared at him for a moment, then turned around and walked away, leaving the door open. She stopped at the living room sofa and waved a hand signal exaggeratedly for him to have a seat. He sat.

She perched on a chair opposite the sofa and crossed her arms and legs, glaring at him. She was silent, except for the sound of her foot tapping on the hardwood floor.

Ben took a deep breath and ran his hand through his hair.

"Thanks for letting me in, Liz. I don't know a good way to say all this, but what I want to say to you first is I'm sorry."

Silence. More foot tapping.

"For what, exactly? I'm not the one whose life you wrecked by fucking another woman, Ben."

She leaned forward then and said, "Do you realize what you've done? Do you have any clue how much destruction you wrecked on this family just because you wanted to get off with another woman? I mean, it's not even like you had a love affair where you met someone new you couldn't live without. This was a one-night stand, for Christ's sakes!"

Red splotches bloomed on her cheeks. Her eyes blazed, and her fists clenched.

"Please, give me a chance to explain," Ben began.

"Explain? What is there to *explain*?" she said, raising her voice.

"You're right, there's no explanation that makes any sense. I was stupid. It was crazy. It was wrong in every way. There's no way I can or would justify what I did. I know how much you love Michelle, and therefore I know that what I did hurt you, too," Ben spoke in a rush.

"*I'm so sorry*," he whispered, tears forming in his eyes. He drew a ragged breath but maintained eye contact.

An uncomfortable silence grew. Liz looked away, and Ben sniffled.

Finally, Liz said, "And what do you want me to do with this information, Ben?" Her tone was flat. "If you're looking for any kind of sympathy or forgiveness, you have come to the wrong girl."

Ben took another deep breath.

"I'm not telling you this expecting redemption. I'm not trying to get you to accept my apology or to forgive me. I don't deserve that.

"While I was on the island, I had a lot of time to think, Liz. I realized some things about myself, things I want to change. I was a selfish man. I thought about myself way too much of the time. Oh, I looked like the loving, self-sacrificing husband, going off to work every day to take care of my wife and children. But inside, I was resentful."

"Yeah, you had us all fooled," interrupted Liz. "Do you know I was your biggest fan? Do you know I defended you when Michelle started talking about something being wrong between you? Man, I can't believe I let you fool me!"

Ben sat still until Liz looked at him again, then continued.

"We had two beautiful children together, and that should have been enough, along with my wife's love, to build a great life, to be grateful. But instead, I resented how tired she was, how different our life was after kids. I *resented* her because she didn't have a lot left over to give to *me* when I got home."

"And that's why I had the one-night stand. It wasn't so much about the sex as it was about pretending, for one night, that I didn't have to sacrifice. That I could, for one night, be entirely selfish. As if the rest of the time, I was being a *stand-up guy*."

He looked deeply embarrassed.

"But the truth is, I was rotting on the inside. I wasn't being the good guy. I was thinking about only myself, about only my needs, completely neglecting Michelle's."

He raised his eyes to hers. She looked shell-shocked.

"Do you know I realized something else today? It hit me like a ton of bricks. I don't even know if all my so-called sacrifice was giving Michelle what she wanted. I never even bothered to ask if she was happy!"

Liz opened her mouth to speak, shut it.

"What kind of a guy does that?" he queried the air, looking past Liz.

Liz's eyes narrowed again.

"If you think I'm going to go all soft just because you're confessing your sins, Ben, you've got—"

"I'm not," he interrupted. "That's not what this is about."

He drew a breath. "I'm not used to this stuff, Liz, and I've been a shitty husband. But we have two great children together, and they deserve our best. *My* best."

"And what does that mean?" she asked.

"That means that I'm going to do my best to find some way to make up to Michelle for what I did to her, to our family. I know she's found someone new, and if he makes her happy, then I will find a way to be okay with it, for her sake and for the sake of the kids. Still, though, I'm going to work on making it up to her, even if only as her children's father and, maybe, if I'm lucky, as a friend."

Liz was silent for a moment. She looked up at Ben intently.

"What are you getting at?"

"I'm trying to say that I want to have another chance with Michelle. Even if that doesn't work, I want a...a real friendship again."

"Why are you telling me all this, Ben?" Liz asked.

"Because you're the person who loves her the most in this world, besides me. Because I want you to agree not to interfere, to give me a chance to do this with Michelle. She trusts you more than anyone, and if you tell her to show me the door, chances are she will, and we won't have a shot."

"You mean *you* won't have a shot," she said.

"That's right," he agreed, saying no more.

She tapped her foot while he waited. Finally, she spoke again.

"Ben, here's the thing. If you are bullshitting me, if you don't really mean this, you'd better get up and walk out that door right now. Because it will not go well for you if I find out later that this was just a game to you."

"It's not," he started to say, but she interrupted.

"The other thing is this. You can't do this halfway. If you give this a half-hearted effort, if you stick a toe in and just because she doesn't fall all over you right away, you bail again—"

"No, Liz," Ben said adamantly. "I'm in this for the long haul. I know there's no way I'm going to make it up to her if I don't give it my all. Look, I've lived a lot of my life taking the easy way out of difficult situations, but on the island, I got a big dose of things that have opened my eyes. I'm not going to stop until I have shown her that I've changed, that she can count on me. And even though I don't deserve her, I'm going to try to get her back."

Liz sat and stared at Ben as if she were trying to read his mind, trying to determine whether or not he was being for real. She drew a deep breath and let it out, but her arms and legs remained crossed.

They sat quietly; she glared at him; he met her stare.

"I don't know, Ben," she said, but was no longer red-faced furious.

"Please, Liz. Just don't interfere, that's all I'm asking. Let this play out. Give us a chance to find our way back to each other if it's meant to be. If it's not, I promise to bow out gracefully and always be a great friend and co-parent."

He waited. Finally, she looked at him again.

"Okay, for now, I won't interfere. I will give you exactly one opportunity, Ben, but if you do *anything* to hurt her, I won't even bother telling her to close the door. I will hurt you—I'll find some way to make you pay for this and everything before."

She stared at him, hard.

"Liz?" he said, after a minute.

"What?"

"You are one scary lady," he said.

She cracked the tiniest of smiles.

CHAPTER TWENTY-FOUR

Windshield wipers pulsed continuously, carrying away the constant, cold drizzle. The streets were narrow, the stoplights long, and the traffic heavy for such a small town.

The real estate developer in him saw all the signs, the reasons for the heavy traffic—quaint, charming downtown, filled with new or recently-renovated boutiques, restaurants, and coffee shops. Gently rolling hills gave way to mountains nearby, fog hanging over the tops, evergreen trees reaching upward into the haze.

It was a stunning display of natural beauty, with a small town nestled cozily inside the embrace of the mountains. A place where people who loved the cold, rainy climate—punctuated by stunning, crystal blue-sky days suitable for every kind of outdoor activity—bought second homes. Or bought homes in which to retire. Or opened a charming boutique for the tax benefits in retirement, not to mention the opportunity to socialize with the community, if you didn't mind the hard work of retail.

Why Jillian would choose such a place to live was beyond Stuart. He'd always thought of her as a moderately big-city girl. Austin was young, bustling, supercharged with the endless energy of people their age. Jobs were abundant, with opportunities in everything from finance to high tech. Masses of young couples with school-age children meant that Jillian had her choice for teaching positions. They'd always loved the nightlife, the endless array of cuisines. With her dance background, Jillian was a terrific partner for going out dancing in the clubs that ranged from disco to Latin to country western.

This Washington State small town wouldn't know a dance club from a coffee shop. Not that it was all that important to anyone's life; it was just that he was having a very hard time picturing the life that Jillian must be living.

Maybe she was married after all, and her husband grew up somewhere nearby, so he brought her here. Maybe she had more than one kid, maybe two, and small towns were, after all, great places to raise children. Or so he'd heard.

Maybe she'd wanted to put as much geographical distance between herself and him as possible. Well, this was a long way from Austin, Texas, that was for sure. Stuart's heart sank as he pondered the options for where Jillian's life may have taken her and why.

He spied an open spot along the main street and swerved into it as quickly as possible. He got out, pulling up the hood of his sweatshirt to keep off some of the rain. It was the kind of light yet constant rain that swirled lazily in the air, defying gravity, and ensuring that everyone and everything outdoors got thoroughly soaked. And cold.

He made his way into the nearest shop, a small hardware store. The shopkeeper, an older guy with a white mustache, greeted him, smiling in that friendly way that small-town people can afford to display.

"Hello. How can I help you?" he asked.

Stuart dug in his pocket, pulled out his cell phone, and scrolled, finding the address Ashley had given him. He showed it to the shopkeeper, who frowned slightly.

"Can you tell me how to get there?" Stuart said. "I've driven around here for the past hour, but I can't seem to find how to get to this road."

The guy paused, looked concerned, and shook his head.

"Not sure. There's lots of roads that lead away from town. Some people like to live kind of out in the woods. They like their privacy," he said cryptically.

Stuart waited, but the man said nothing more.

"So, can you tell me how to find *this* road?" he asked, getting impatient.

The guy looked at Stuart, seeming to take him in.

"Well, like I said, there's lots of those little roads, and they're not on the internet. I can tell you that for sure."

Stuart waited for him to finish, but he was quiet again. He began fiddling with something behind the check-out counter. Stuart shifted his feet.

"Are you ignoring me, or are you just rude?" Stuart said, steel in his eyes.

The older guy stopped fiddling, looked up, and fixed Stuart with a cold look.

"You have two choices. You can either leave now, or I can make you leave."

Stuart deflated. This was no way to get the information he needed. He backed up a little and hung his head, then looked up at the guy.

"Look, I'm sorry to come off that way. It's just that I've traveled a long way, and not just distance, but time, and I'm a little tired."

The guy looked slightly mollified but still guarded.

"Where are you from?" he asked. "You don't sound like you're from around here."

"I'm sorry, let's start over," Stuart said. He held out his hand to shake.

"I'm Stuart, and I've come all the way from Austin, Texas."

"Dan Young." He shook Stuart's hand. His eyes were sharp and piercing. He seemed to be checking Stuart out, but now with less hostility.

Odd way for a shopkeeper to act.

255

"What are you doing all the way up here in Washington State?" Dan asked.

"I'm looking for someone. Her name's Jillian. I'm not sure what her last name is now—she may be married."

Dan didn't look surprised, but he nodded.

"And why are you trying to find her? As I said, people around here really value their privacy. Not saying that I know her or that she's around here, just pointing out the problem you may have with finding her."

Stuart tried not to look too excited. Clearly, this guy knew Jillian, but for some reason, he was reluctant to tell Stuart. What that was about, he didn't know and didn't care. He only cared about finding a way to break down the guy's defenses so he would tell Stuart how to get to Jillian's house.

Stuart leaned casually against the counter and began talking.

"Jillian is my ex-fiancé. We broke up a long time ago, and it was pretty much my fault. Frankly, I screwed up, big-time. She's the one that got away, you know?"

He stared at Dan.

"Have you ever really messed up with the woman you've loved for years? Do you have any idea what I'm talking about?"

Dan shook his head slowly. "Not exactly. I've been with my wife for over 35 years, and I've made mistakes, but I've never done anything that would make her want to leave me, at least I don't think I have." He chuckled a bit.

"But if I did, and if she left, I'd be one miserable son of a bitch, that's for sure." He cleared his throat.

"What exactly did you do to drive this—Jillian?—away?" he asked. But when he said her name, it sounded like he was faking not knowing her. Stuart's hopes rose.

"I told her I didn't want kids, and I realized—too late—that she did. It wasn't so much that I didn't want kids, it was more that I wasn't sure. I had doubts. Most of it had to do with my family growing up, or maybe

I should say, the lack of any kind of family life. I just didn't want to bring a kid into the world and risk giving them the kind of childhood I had."

This opening up stuff was still hard. Stuart felt uncomfortable, tugging at his sweatshirt collar, and shifting his feet.

Dan nodded, this time with a compassionate look on his face.

"Tell you what. It's time for my lunch break. What do you say we go down the street and have a cup of coffee?" Dan said.

"I'm fine with that, but tell me—do you know Jillian? Can you tell me where she is?" Stuart was starting to feel anxious. This might be a huge waste of time. This dude could just be a lonely older guy who saw the chance to jaw with someone from out of town, fuel a little gossip.

Dan hesitated. "I won't say yes or no at this point. If you can take that hint, let's go down the street for a few minutes. I need to be sure who I'm dealing with."

Dan turned around the sign in the glass front door of the shop from OPEN to CLOSED and locked it behind them. They strolled half a block and entered a coffee shop. It was warm and cozy, with overstuffed, leather sofas and chairs, antique wooden tables arranged here and there. They ordered coffee from the pimply-faced gangly teenager at the bar, nothing fancy for either of them, then found a place to sit.

Dan stirred his coffee for a minute, staring into the cup, then put aside the wooden stirrer and looked at Stuart.

"So, what's your story?" he said.

Stuart figured he had nothing to lose at this point and everything to gain. This guy seemed okay, so he told him. Everything.

At one point, Dan interrupted him.

"I thought I recognized you back there in the store, but I couldn't place you. So, you're one of the guys that got lost at sea, spent a few weeks on a desert island, and got rescued."

Stuart nodded and said, "Please don't hold the People Magazine story against me. They offered a lot of money for that, too much to refuse."

Dan smiled. "Well, it wasn't that bad. Just struck me as one of those fluff stories that doesn't tell the real story but makes people buy magazines. I wouldn't even have known about it, but my wife loves that magazine, and when she read it, she told me all about it, showed me the photos of you guys." He looked slightly embarrassed.

"Hey, I have no problem with anyone reading that magazine, and let me take the opportunity to thank you for that since you helped line my pockets," Stuart said, smiling.

Dan visibly relaxed after that. "Go on," he said.

Stuart didn't get the feeling that Dan was interested in the details of how they survived on the island. So, he focused on his and Jillian's story—how he'd pushed her away, how they ultimately broke up.

As his story wound down, Stuart fell into silence. They both stared out the window at the people passing by.

Not looking at Stuart, continuing to look out the window, Dan asked softly, "So, what do you plan to do when you find her? And why now, after all these years?"

Stuart hadn't mentioned how many years it had been, so the comment gave him more reason to hope that his time wasn't wasted. He knew in his heart that Dan knew Jillian, knew where she lived.

"You care about her, don't you?" Stuart said gently.

"I do," said Dan. "She reminds me of my daughter. My wife and I had two children, a son who lives in Seattle, and a daughter. But our daughter was killed in a skiing accident when she was 19." His eyes filled with the kind of pained look that someone carries for the rest of their lives—old, irreconcilable.

"Jillian is her own person—she's not my daughter—but I can't help it, I do feel protective of her."

Stuart felt confused. His working assumption was that Jillian was married, and if that was the case, she wasn't exactly on her own, didn't need to be watched over. But this guy was acting like she was someone to feel concerned about, someone to protect.

Before he could ask about that, Dan asked him again about what he planned to do when he found Jillian.

"I'm not sure. I haven't exactly moved on with my life since we broke up," Stuart said slowly. "I still love her, and if there's any chance we could get back together, that's what I want. But if she's moved on, if she's married, or engaged, or serious about someone, then I just want to know that door is closed, so I can move on."

He paused, eyes searching the ground as if to find the answers to the mystery of Jillian's life there. He raised his eyes and spoke quickly, reassuringly.

"Hey, I'm not a stalker here. I just want you to know I'm not going to follow her around if she doesn't want me back in her life. I mean, if she's still single, I'm going to make a good effort, but if she tells me she's not interested, then I'm out of there. Of here."

Dan stared at Stuart again, then slowly nodded his head.

"Okay. But just so you know, I will be watching to see what happens, and if you give us any reason to think you're trouble for her in any way, I have friends in the Sheriff's department. You don't want to get in trouble with those guys, out here away from the big city."

Having fired that last warning shot, Dan smiled.

Stuart smiled back uneasily.

They finished their coffee, and Dan gave Stuart detailed directions to Jillian's cabin in the woods as they stood on the sidewalk together.

Dan turned to go, then stopped and looked back at Stuart. "One more thing," said Dan. "She may not be the same person you knew years ago." With that, he walked away.

Strange. That was the second person to say something like that to Stuart. First, Ashley, and now this guy.

CHAPTER TWENTY-FIVE

The rain had stopped, but water dripped off the trees, hitting the windshield with large spatters as Stuart made his way up the mountain. The blacktop road was so narrow he wondered what would happen if he encountered another vehicle going the opposite direction. Huge conifers soared overhead, their tops obscured by the fog. The trees crowded the road, spreading their heavy, dripping branches over the narrow lane, creating a false sense of dusk, even though it was early afternoon.

Stuart almost missed the sign. It was weathered wood, on a large stake, and it displayed the address of Jillian's cabin, carved there many years ago by some previous homeowner. The pathway that it indicated was even narrower than the blacktop and was covered in pine needles. Hardly a road at all. Perhaps it was a long driveway because he couldn't see the house from the road.

He turned in and slowly made his way through the trees, tires crunching slightly on the wet pine needles. The cabin came into view, and he stopped for a moment to stare.

It was small but well-maintained. The tiny front yard featured a small patch of green grass with flowers along the border of the pathway to the door. Several large pots overflowing with more flowers and ferns were scattered around the covered porch, which also featured a wooden swing suspended from overhead.

Stuart killed the engine and swung open the car door. He exited, closed the door as quietly as he could, and began walking up the pathway to the door. His heart thumped wildly, and his ears began a slight buzz. He forced in a deep breath to clear his head, shaking out his hands by his side. This wouldn't do. He couldn't knock on the door and pass out right in front of Jillian and possibly her husband, looking like a complete fool.

He stopped on the pathway, halfway turned to leave. But when he heard the door open, he turned back.

She stood framed by the doorway, still with that incredibly elegant posture, red hair tumbling over one shoulder. She gazed at him quietly, as though she'd been expecting him for a long time, wondering what took him so long.

Of course—Dan probably called her as soon as Stuart left to give her a heads up.

"Stuart," she breathed.

"Jillian," he said at the same time.

Little hands reached around Jillian to clutch her legs, and a tiny face peered around to stare wide-eyed at Stuart.

"Mommy, who is it?" the little one asked.

"It's okay, Sophie. It's a friend of Mommy's," said Jillian. She stroked her daughter's hair absently.

Stuart's heart fell so hard he thought he would drop down with the weight of it. Though he'd told himself that, logically, of course, Jillian would have moved on. That some guy would have snatched her up, and she would have those kids she wanted. Still, nothing could have prepared him for the reality.

He tried to leave, but his feet felt anchored in concrete, stiff and unable to move.

"Stuart, are you okay?" Jillian asked. "Why don't you come in and sit down?"

Come in and sit down? And shake hands with the lucky son-of-a-bitch who now slept with Jillian every night? Sit in their sweet little home, assaulted with the hominess, the domesticity of a life he passed up years ago?

No, thanks.

"This was a huge mistake," he hurled at Jillian.

He turned around and walked toward the car. He yanked open the car door, got in the car, and slammed the door shut.

Jillian stood on the porch, frozen, looking shocked.

He grabbed the steering wheel as hard as he could, and it vibrated under the weight of all his emotions.

He didn't start the car. He sat, looked down, took deep breaths.

What a loser; what a jerk; here you are, once again, running away as fast as you can...pissed off, with nothing good to say. When are you going to grow up and take responsibility for your actions? You are the cause of this...this situation. Get it together, man! Face the music so you can get on with your life.

Stuart flashed to his Dad at the A.A. meeting, standing firm, openly putting the sordid truth out there for everyone to hear, for his son to hear. No hesitation, no fudging, no defenses.

He felt the emotions rise again, of the pain and loneliness of his childhood, and of something else hard to put a finger on. Of being deeply touched, deeply moved by his father's transformational journey, by his father's willingness to stand there with him, be there for him, at last. He still wasn't sure he trusted it, trusted this new father, but still. He held a grudging admiration for how far he'd come.

Well, if dear old Dad could do it, so could he. He blew out a huge breath and opened the car door again. He got out, walked up the pathway to the door, which was now closed, and knocked.

There was no sound, no approaching footsteps. He knocked again, very gently, as though he feared he might frighten away a small animal.

More waiting, then the door opened slowly.

Jillian's daughter stood there, looking up at him, blue eyes enormous. She was dressed in tiny blue jeans, a pink sweater with the hood hanging down, and tennis shoes. Her wavy hair tumbled down her back, the same reddish color as Jillian's but even lighter, a waterfall of strawberry blond.

"Hi there," he said gently.

"Hi," she said shyly. "Mommy said I could let you in."

But she stood there in the way, hand clutching the doorknob, not seeming to know how to admit someone into the house. Stuart reached out and gently pushed the door an inch or so. She dropped her hand from the doorknob, turned away and ran to her mother, hiding behind her once again.

Stuart pushed the door open the rest of the way, stepped in, and closed it behind him. The inside of the cabin was one cozy great room—small sitting area with a loveseat, small antique coffee table, and two low chairs. There was a tiny dining area off the kitchen with a four-seat wooden table. He could see a small hallway from the front door, leading to one or two bedrooms and a bathroom.

The cabin had the air of a "fixer-upper," but was tidy and clean.

Stuart took in the details that made it Jillian—soft throws and pillows scattered about, lamps that added a warm glow, a couple of vases with fresh flowers. The fireplace crackled with real firewood. When they'd lived together, Jillian had made sure their home was warm, cozy, and filled with small touches that added an extra layer of beauty.

Like so much else, he hadn't appreciated that, not enough, anyway. He moved his gaze to Jillian, still so breathtakingly beautiful.

"I'm sorry to intrude on your life like this," he said to Jillian, who perched on the edge of the sofa, Sophie standing by her, clutching her arm. Sophie seemed to be torn between watching Stuart guardedly and trying to hide behind her mother's shoulder.

"It's okay, Stuart. I guess I've always known this day would come," she said quietly. "Why don't you sit down?" She pointed to one of the chairs. He came into the room and sat uneasily.

"How are you?" she asked. "After everything that happened with the boat, I mean," she said. Her hands were folded in her lap, and she seemed pale, an air of fear wafting about her. Made sense. She probably didn't want her husband walking into an emotional scene with her ex. He would try to keep it short and sweet. But if the guy walked in, that was okay too. Might as well get all the pain over with at once.

"I'm okay. It wasn't really that bad, but being stuck on a desert island gives a guy plenty of time to think."

She looked down, quiet.

"I thought a lot about you and me, Jillian, about how badly I messed things up with us."

She looked up.

"It's okay, Stuart. I've had a lot of time to get over it. Really, if that's why you're here, don't worry about me. I'm fine. I'm happy. I have a good life. I've moved on," she finished, giving Sophie's hair an absent stroke.

Sophie leaned in and whispered in her mother's ear. Jillian whispered back. Sophie nodded, face serious.

"I'm sorry for not being more polite. I'm a little thrown off. Sophie," she said, turning to her daughter, "this is Stuart. He's a friend of mine from before you were born."

Sophie looked solemnly at Stuart.

"Stuart, this is Sophie, my daughter."

Stuart nodded at Sophie and said, "Pleased to meet you," smiling warmly.

Sophie gave him a shy smile, picked up a stuffed toy nearby, a white bear, and hugged it close to her chest. She seemed to relax a bit.

"Sophie, why don't you go finish the drawing you were working on so you can show it to Stuart before he leaves?" Jillian said. Sophie nodded vigorously, padded over to the table, pulled out a chair, climbed onto it, and picked up her coloring pencil. She leaned over the drawing spread out in front of her and began laboriously coloring.

His dismissal imminent, Stuart plunged in.

"Uh, it's hard to know where to start, but I'll start with our breakup. There's no excuse for it, Jill, so I just want to say that I'm so sorry for all of it. For drinking too much, for being so awful to you, for pushing you away."

"It's okay, Stuart," she said softly, guardedly.

"No, it's really not," he said firmly. "It must have looked like I didn't really love you. Like, I just wanted to break up with you, but nothing could be further from the truth. I loved you, Jillian. I wanted to spend the rest of my life with you."

She was quiet.

"Here's the thing. Where I got stuck was about having kids," he began.

Jillian's face changed. Two small spots of rose pink bloomed on her cheeks, and her jaw set tight.

"Believe me, I am well aware of your aversion to children," she said. She crossed her arms and held them tightly against her body.

Crap. He'd hardly said two words, and already she was defensive.

"I'm so sorry, Jillian, for that. I know I said I was against having children, but it wasn't...it wasn't real. It was because of my crappy experience growing up. It wasn't that I didn't want to have children with you, it was that I didn't want to bring kids into the world and screw them up like my parents did. I know that sounds stupid."

He stopped, rubbed the stubble on his face for a moment.

Jillian was quiet, her mouth slightly open. Surprised, maybe? Or maybe she didn't give a damn at this point. After all, she had her husband and her beautiful daughter, her home. Her dreams fulfilled.

"Jillian, before I get too far into this, I'm sorry about your Mom. I just found out when I started looking for you."

She turned away, face dropping a bit, then looked back.

Taking a risk, he said softly, "I'm sorry I wasn't there for you."

She fixed her clear, blue eyes on him and nodded once.

"Thanks."

Part of him wished she would be furious, yell at him, throw something. Give him some indication she still cared.

Instead, she gave off a deeply wounded air and something else. What was it? Fear? What was she afraid of—her husband walking in? Was he a bad guy, abusive in some way? Was she afraid he'd have a jealous explosion, try to beat up Stuart, hurt her later?

But she didn't seem to be abused or living in fear. In fact, looking around the room again, Stuart couldn't see any signs of a male presence at all. There was a coat rack by the door, and on it hung exactly two coats—one for an adult, feminine in style, and one for a little girl. Doubt crept in. Maybe she wasn't married, after all.

Maybe she was a single Mom, knocked up by another guy who'd abandoned her. Or maybe she'd done the artificial insemination thing. Lots of single women were doing that these days.

He sneaked a peek at her left hand and—sure enough—saw no wedding band. Why hadn't he noticed that sooner? Maybe he had a real chance after all.

Feeling emboldened, Stuart continued with more urgency.

"Listen, Jillian, I came here because I haven't moved on. I've never forgotten you, never really stopped loving you. I came to see you because I want to find out if there's any chance—any chance at all— that I could try to make it up to you. I'm not trying to get something back right now, I just want to spend a little time with you, that's all. Maybe see if...see what develops."

He wound down, feeling stupid.

She was totally quiet.

He gazed at her, trying to read her, but her face was closed off.

"That's quite a story, Stuart. Look, I'm sorry you haven't gotten on with your life, but as I said, I have. You don't want children, and I have a daughter. I'm now a package deal, and I just don't think you're the right guy for that kind of deal."

He stared at her stonily.

She softened her voice. "Look, I appreciate what you're trying to do, really I do, and I'm flattered that you still have feelings for me, but...,"

"Jillian."

"What?"

"Sophie is not a deal-breaker. I mean, I just met her, but she's obviously a lot like her Mom. She's...well, she's adorable. Look, I'm a different man now. All I'm asking for is a chance."

"I don't know, Stuart, so much time has gone by. I had to shut those doors a long time ago. It was so hard, but I did what I had to do."

Tears welled up, glistened in her lashes. Her face flushed again.

Stuart stood, but he didn't go to her.

"Please, don't decide anything right now, Jillian. I'm staying in town for a few days, and all I want is to get together again and talk a little. I promise you, if there's nothing there and that's the answer, I won't bug you anymore. But let's give it a couple of days, okay?"

She looked doubtful, torn, and terrified.

"Please don't be afraid of me, Jillian," he whispered. "I'm not here to hurt you all over again."

"I'm not afraid of you," she said, "I'm afraid...never mind."

He waited.

"Okay, maybe we can talk again."

He sighed with relief.

"Okay, that's great. Thank you. How can I get ahold of you?" he asked.

"Um, here's my cell number," she said reluctantly. But she gave it to him.

"Stuart. One more thing," she said. "I don't have anyone to look after Sophie, so she might be with us if she's not in school."

He nodded. "I understand."

He waved at Sophie, who looked up from her drawing.

"Um, Sophie, I have to go now, but I'll be back tomorrow."

"But I'm not finished yet," she said doubtfully, looking at her mother and then back at Stuart.

"That's okay. Why don't you work on it today and have it ready by tomorrow when I come back?" he said.

She brightened and said, "Okay!" Bent her head again over her work.

As Stuart drove away, his heart lifted. She wasn't married. She didn't have a boyfriend. There was no man in the picture, at least not that he could see.

There was the matter of Sophie's father, whoever he was, but Stuart had experience with parental abandonment, so he brushed away thoughts of the guy, whoever he was. Whatever the reason, he was no longer in the picture. That much was clear. His loss.

He grinned to himself, head full of plans.

CHAPTER TWENTY-SIX

Ben lugged the final packages into the apartment. Lots of work ahead, but first, he had a call to make. He picked up his cell phone and pushed the button.

"Hello?"

"Hi Michelle, it's me."

"Ben. What's going on?" Terse.

"Um, well, I called because I wanted to know if you have plans for tonight."

"Yes, I do."

"With Joe?" Might as well put it right out there.

"Yes." Hesitant, suspicious.

"Okay. Well, since you do have plans, how about the kids come stay with me? I mean, spend the night, the whole nine yards. I'm getting everything set up in my apartment for them, and, well, I've missed them so much, and I want some time with them."

"Oh. Of course, you do, but I've already asked Liz to take care of them."

"I have a feeling she'll understand if you ask her," he said, having already called Liz to find out all the intel and give her the heads up.

She'd acquiesced to his request to stand aside so he could have the kids that night. Still wary of him but following through on her promise to not interfere with his plans. So far.

"Well, don't hold your breath. She adores her niece and nephew and looks forward to her time with them." She paused. "But I'll ask. Let me call you back."

A minute later, his cell phone rang.

"Well, that was strange. She said it was fine with her." Michelle sounded puzzled.

"Great! Okay, well, I'll be there to pick them up at 4:00, so you have time to get ready for your date."

Before she could answer, he hung up and said to himself out loud, "Step one, mission accomplished." He surveyed all the scattered packages and boxes, and thought, okay, time to get busy.

Ben was positively giddy about his plans. He'd gone to Michelle's to pick up the kids, who were over the moon with excitement. She looked puzzled again when she opened the door, frowning at Ben's smiling face.

"What's up with you? You look, I don't know…different," she said suspiciously.

"What? Can't a guy be happy about spending the evening and overnight with his two children he hasn't seen but once in almost two months?"

She ushered him in, and the kids ran toward him, backpacks in tow.

"Let's go, Dad!" shouted Katie. She never could seem to do anything quietly.

"Yeah, let's go!" shouted Jordan, as always, mimicking his big sister, who rolled her eyes at him.

Situation normal.

They tumbled out of the house, running for Ben's car, flung open the doors, and jumped in. He strapped them into their car seats and got behind the driver's wheel. Michelle came to the car and signaled for him to roll down the window, which he did.

She leaned in a bit and told the kids to be good. "I love you," she said, blowing kisses at them. They giggled and pretended to catch her kisses in the air.

She leaned back out and stared at Ben.

"Are you sure you're okay with all this? I mean, you babysitting for me while I go out on a date."

"First of all, I'm not babysitting," he said. "They're my kids, and I would be having them over anyway as part of my visitation schedule. Second, no, I'm not exactly thrilled about you dating Joe or any other guy, but since it's my fault this is happening, I'm trying to make the best of the situation." He paused, then added, "For the sake of the children, of course."

Then he winked at her.

She stepped back from the car, looking more puzzled than ever. He gave her a little wave, grinning at her as he backed away. She shrugged, turned, and walked back to the house, hips swaying. He stopped for a minute so he could admire her perfect backside. He sighed, put the car in gear, and drove away.

"Daddy, you were staring at Mom's butt," said Katie.

Jordan started giggling and said, "Mom's butt! Mom's butt!"

"I was not," said Ben, shocked.

"Were too!" shouted Katie.

"Were too! Were too!" shouted Jordan.

"Really?" said Ben. "Where do you kids get this kind of stuff, anyway?"

"From YouTube!" said Katie.

"Yeah, I guess so," said Ben. "Everything you're learning about life, you're getting off of YouTube," he said, resigned.

After going out for pizza, they drove to Ben's apartment. He opened the door, letting the kids in for the first time in weeks, and basked in their surprised expressions.

Two new bookshelves from Ikea, assembled that day, stood one on each side of the flat-screen television, previously the only thing on the long living room wall. The bookshelf was stocked with everything for kids—lots of board games, numerous Lego sets, card games, and lots of children's books.

Katie ran to the bookshelf and pulled out a game.

"Wow! Daddy, let's play *Exploding Kittens!*"

Jordan ran over, wide-eyed.

"Are there really exploding kittens?" he asked, worry crinkling his forehead, trying to get a look at the box Katie held just out of his reach.

"No, Jordan, there are no real exploding kittens—it's just a card game with a silly name," said Ben. "But before we do that, why don't you put your stuff in your room first."

They ran into their room, and he smiled at their exclamations. He followed them and got even more delight as they took in the Superman sheets on Jordan's bed, the Frozen sheets on Katie's, and the stuffed animals everywhere. There were night lights, and the lamp by Katie's bed had a princess theme, complete with pink lampshade. She ran to the bed, flopped on it, spreading her arms wide, looking up at him with shining eyes and a huge grin, and said, "Wow, Daddy! This is so cool!"

"Cool!" echoed Jordan, also grinning. He ran to his bed, grabbed the fuzzy, plush baby sloth, and hugged it tightly. "I love you!" he declared to the sloth.

"You're such a baby," said Katie, but she was smiling.

Later, as Ben lay in bed smiling, his heart full, he replayed all the fun of the evening. Cards, games, popcorn (which necessitated getting out the hand vac to remove the remnants from the sofa cushions), and a movie. The kids had been utterly exhausted, as had he when bedtime arrived, but everyone was happy and smiling. Even bath time went well, with everyone cooperating. There were plenty of hugs, kisses, and, of course, the requisite bedtime story.

Just before drifting off, her eyes half-closed, Katie sleepily asked, "Daddy, when are you going to move back?"

He smoothed her hair and pulled the covers up, whispering, "Soon, sweetheart, soon."

But she didn't hear him. She'd already fallen asleep.

Now, as he thought about the day, he didn't feel so confident. He tried not to think about it, but he imagined Michelle and Joe in their former marital bed, holding each other, kissing, making...*STOP IT!* He turned over, punched his pillow, and did his best to go to sleep. Thankfully, his body took over out of sheer exhaustion.

The next morning, after pancakes and waffles, and one more card game, Ben packed the kids into the car and drove them to Michelle's. They were quiet, as was he. It was too soon to say good-bye for all of them, after being apart for so long. But Michelle had insisted they come home for Sunday with her before going back to school on Monday.

He figured they would get back to a regular routine, and it wouldn't be so hard after each visitation. Wait, strike that. It was *always* hard, would never be easy.

They parked in front of the house, got out, and went to the door. Ben waited with the kids until Michelle opened the door, letting them in. The kids ran to their rooms to put away their things, and Michelle eyed them as they ran past. They'd clearly come home with more than they took with them the day before.

"Get a few toys for the kids, Ben?" she asked.

"Just a few things," he said. "Uh, Michelle, do you have a few minutes to talk?" he asked.

"Not really," she said. "I have some things to get ready before work tomorrow."

Since Ben's massive screw up, Michelle had taken a job at her old law firm, and that often meant working long hours.

"Look, I know you're busy, but this will seriously only take a couple of minutes."

After a pause, "All right, but make it fast." She led the way into the living room.

"Thanks," he said, sitting down across from her. She held herself upright a bit rigidly, her body language indicating reticence. Not completely cold, but definitely guarded.

"Here's the thing," he began. "I know you have no reason to trust me, and that's my fault. But while I was on the island—and I won't get deep into this, not yet—but while I was there, I had a lot of time to think, about you, about us, about all the damage I did. I don't want to rehash all the painful events, but I do want you to know one thing. And you can carve this in stone, Michelle, for the rest of our lives."

She'd raised her eyebrows.

"Oh...kay," she dragged out slowly.

His intensity was at its peak. Without thinking first, he moved over to Michelle, picked up both of her hands, which were limp with shock, and held them tightly.

"Losing you, no—driving you away after cheating on you—was the biggest mistake of my life. It is my biggest regret, and always will be." He stared into her eyes for a minute, not caring what he saw reflected there. If she hated him, she hated him. If she found him disgusting, so be it. If she didn't believe him, again, that was out of his control.

"I still love you," he said urgently, staring into her eyes. Her eyes fluttered downward. He could see her chest rising and falling rapidly, a tiny vein pulsing in her forehead. But she didn't remove her hands from his.

He massaged the tops of her hands slowly with his thumbs once, twice, feeling the silkiness of her skin, longing to...but now was not the time. Maybe not ever. He slowly placed her hands back in her lap and moved back, drew in a slow, deep breath. She smelled lightly of vanilla, her favorite scent, and his.

Finally, Michelle broke the silence.

"Ben, I—I don't know what to say." Looking at him now, sorrow in her eyes.

"You don't have to say anything. I wanted you to know that, and I thought I should say it, even though you have no reason to believe me."

"I wish you'd said this sooner," she whispered.

Ben's heart leaped into his throat. Did she just say she wished she'd known sooner that he still loved her?

"Michelle, baby...," he said, but she stopped him.

"No, Ben, don't say anymore. It's enough, for now."

She stood, and walked to the door, his signal to go. He followed her, turned around to face her, standing close. She didn't back up. He reached for her, to kiss her, but she turned her cheek into the kiss, still leaning into him slightly. He lingered there, brushing his lips across her cheek, breathing in her scent again, then slowly drew back and looked in her eyes, searching.

"Ben," she said. "I'm with someone else, and I'm not going to, you know...,"

"It's okay," he said softly. "I understand."

He took her hand, massaged it again, slowly let it drop.

"But I'm not giving up, either."

After he left the house and got into his car, he thought about Joe. *Dude had better mess up*, and soon. But, he thought, step two, mission accomplished.

After that night, Michelle seemed to take a step back. He didn't get another opportunity to be intimate in any kind of way. They exchanged the kids with one another, made small talk, and arranged things pertaining to Katie and Jordan.

But she was different, compared to before the boat and the island. The anger and coldness seemed to have vanished. She was warmer, friendlier. But never the slightest bit flirty, never anything that would have indicated she was available to him. Not exactly uncomfortable around him, either.

They'd achieved a friendly, easy relationship. But sometimes, he'd catch her looking at him out of the corner of his eye. A look that held something unexpressed, and at those times, he walked away feeling hopeful.

Then she'd open the door for him, dressed to kill in tight jeans, or a short skirt, blouse fitting her curves, sparkly necklace and earrings, blond hair loosely curled over one shoulder, and his heart would stop.

But the guy into whose arms she was headed was not him. It was Joe—friendly Joe with the chicklet teeth and the nice demeanor. Joe, who may or may not be sleeping with his ex-wife. Wait—of course, he was sleeping with her.

Whatever was going on between them, she wasn't about to kiss and tell. He never saw signs of a sleep-over with Joe—no masculine clothing around the house, no razor or extra toothbrush in the master bathroom (he'd gone there on a pretense of using it, and snooped around, looking).

Michelle was innately conservative—it would be just like her to make sure those details were never visible to their children. The fact that he didn't see the evidence didn't mean anything.

Once, in desperation, he'd called Liz and point-blank asked her if Joe and Michelle were sleeping together. "Really, Ben?" she'd said in disgust. He'd quickly apologized and hung up.

Ben went back to work at his old company long enough to put in his resignation and hand off his accounts to an associate. He could afford some time off with the payday from the People Magazine interview. The next step was to figure out the next phase of his work life, and there was no better time than now. He'd always wanted to start his own business, to do something with a serious stake in the game.

When he didn't have the kids, he used the time for research and drives along the coast. He relaxed inside for the first time in his life.

He continued his sessions with Suzanne. Some of them were painful, as he re-lived the grief and loss of his marriage. Others were more hopeful, as he spoke of his children and his hopes of getting back together with Michelle.

Suzanne was neutral, not advocating one way or the other. Instead, she listened and helped him understand his feelings, how his childhood connected to his motivations for cheating on his wife. She asked a few questions out of curiosity and let him fill in most of his own blanks.

She told him what she was hearing from him, the between-the-lines stuff that he'd not actually said out loud. But was still true. Gradually, he began to loosen up over the intense guilt and remorse he felt.

Ben felt refreshed, new. He'd landed on a business idea, and he was excited about getting it started. Before the boat and the island, he'd done sales for a large wine and spirits distribution company, and he'd worked in spirits. It wasn't truly his passion, and he'd walked around with so much emotional baggage that he'd never really performed at a high level. He'd been good enough to keep his job and earn a decent paycheck, but that was about it.

Ben had always wanted to be on the wine side of the business, but not for a mammoth distributor. They did a great job with the very large, very well-known wineries throughout Napa, Sonoma, and the California Central Valley.

Ben thought he saw a niche—small, independent wineries that were desperate to get the energy and focus of a large distributor, desperate for distribution, period.

What if he acted as an independent distributor to those guys, mostly family-owned businesses that struggled for distribution in a space dominated by the big guys? What if he found sales channels for them, helped them grow their brands? What if he carefully selected the wineries he would represent and built his own brand around them while building theirs? Staying out of the way of the big distributors, taking up space in that smaller channel.

He quickly discovered he wasn't the first guy with the idea, but that most independent wine distributors were solo guys working out of their homes, usually representing only one winery. He wanted to do something different, something on a larger scale.

Energized, Ben began talking to the owners of the small wineries, tasting their wines, and visiting small retail outlets for selling opportunities. Meanwhile, he found someone to create a website and a brand. Gradually, the business began to take shape, and Ben's days were full.

But he hadn't given up on Michelle. He tried not to, but occasionally he obsessed about where she was in her relationship with Joe.

One day, he noticed flowers—clearly delivered from a florist—on the entryway table, with the little envelope still attached, Michelle's name typed on the front. He wanted to order flowers for her as well, some innate masculine competitive thing jumping up inside. But he didn't. Instead, he racked his brains for ideas of things to give her or do for her, that wouldn't smack of overt romance or competition with Joe. Gradually, he landed on a few ideas.

Once, he gave her tickets to a concert, making it clear they were for her, counting himself out. Another time, he took the kids out shopping for clothes, brought everything back to Michelle's, and organized all of it for her. She was grateful for that move, so much so that she said "Thank you" more than once.

One Sunday morning, returning with the kids, he showed up with a small gift bag. Inside, two large, hand-painted ceramic coffee mugs and a freshly ground bag of coffee from a store in Seattle—not the typical Starbucks, but an expensive boutique brand they'd stumbled across once on a trip. He'd deliberately gotten the kids up early and ready to go, then texted Michelle that he was on his way, so she had time to kick Joe out if needed.

When they arrived 30 minutes later, she was dressed in sweats, hair up in a ponytail, with no makeup. She still looked ravishing. Without asking, he went into the kitchen, brewed coffee, and brought her a steaming serving in one of the two new mugs, just the right amount of creamer and sweetener already added. She smiled gratefully, and they sat comfortably together in the living room. He grabbed that opportunity to talk.

"You know, there's something I've wanted to ask you for a long time," he said. "It's about working again. I know you're back at your old law firm. How is it going?"

She sipped her coffee and answered thoughtfully. "It's actually going really well. I love case law, and they've got me doing some interesting research for a personal liability case. I feel like my brain is back in gear again. And, they really seem to appreciate having me there," she added, looking pleased.

"I'm so glad for you. I've worried that having to go back to work wasn't what you wanted. And that's what I wanted to ask you—one of the things I never did, or I sucked at it, was asking you what you wanted. I'm sorry to say that as much as I loved you, love you still, I don't know a lot about what's inside. That's my fault because I was, well, we can call it self-absorbed, can't we?"

He stopped and tried to gauge her reaction, but she was sitting with her face neutral. What the heck, he thought. Might as well go for it.

"So, I'd like to ask now. How *do* you feel about being a Mom *and* having a career? I mean, you didn't have to work before, and now...,"

She was quiet for a long time, looking into her coffee cup as though to find the answers there, like trying to read tea leaves. She looked up and out the front window.

"That's a big question, Ben, and you're right—you never took the time to ask me. But I never took the time to ask you about your job, either. Somehow, I have a strong feeling you weren't happy with it."

He didn't take that bait.

"You're right about that, but I don't want to talk about me right now. I'm doing great. In fact, at some point, I'll share a little with you about what I'm up to. But back to you."

"Okay," she sighed, seeming uncomfortable about opening up. He stayed quiet, still sipping his coffee and looking out the window.

Suzanne had told Ben recently that, although there was no upside in constant verbal vomiting about painful or uncomfortable subjects—a la his misguided parents—there was tremendous value in creating what she called an "emotionally safe space" for someone you love to share what they are really thinking and feeling. The key was making it safe for them, not prying them open with a crowbar, invading them for your own purposes. Not judging what they shared or trying to fix things for them.

When you love someone, she said, you pay attention, and choose a good time to ask an open-ended question, out of genuine curiosity and desire to know the person better. The idea is to foster intimacy—"into me see," and bring the two of you closer. But when you do that, she cautioned, you must "let the silence do the heavy lifting," i.e., don't rescue the other person with a comment or a diversion or—worst of all—humor.

He was trying. He waited.

"Okay, I'm not exactly sure what the answer is, but I'm just going to throw stuff out there," she said, standing up and walking over to the window, back turned to him.

"When we found out we were pregnant with Katie, I was, of course, thrilled. I wanted children, but I never thought we'd have them so fast. And then Jordan, so soon after Katie. My life was consumed with having babies and taking care of them, and I quit the firm because it was too much.

"I didn't want to drop my babies off at day-care, and your mother wasn't the right person to ask—no comments about her right now, please. I like Diane, and I know that pains you because of your experience with her growing up. But I don't have that experience. She's always been good to me, and with the kids, especially since the divorce."

She tugged her ponytail, pulling it over one shoulder, and walked back to set down her coffee cup. Ben stayed quiet, though his insides were screaming to say something, do something.

She looked at him piercingly.

"Are you uncomfortable with this? Because I can stop." Almost like a threat—the clamshell had opened and now wanted to slam shut.

"No, of course not. I'm listening," Ben said.

"But once both babies were off breast milk and potty trained, everything changed for me. I adore my—our—children, Ben, but if I'm being totally honest, it's not enough for me. I want—I *need*—intellectual stimulation. I need the challenge of work with a purpose. I meet other Moms with kids the same age, and I can't understand how they can be so content, so satisfied with, with that, and nothing more. Not that being a Mom isn't a lot, that it isn't important—it is! But, still.

"The other thing is this. I am not stupid. I look around me at women who are 10, 15, 20 years older, and I see that half of them are divorced. Some of them are lucky enough to have their own wealth or a successful career, or to have divorced a guy after he I.P.O.'d his business and made a gazillion dollars, so she gets half of a gazillion.

"But lots of them are living on the edge of mild poverty—scraping by, wearing the same old designer labels they've owned for decades, working at some low-level job because no one will hire a 'displaced homemaker,' no matter how intelligent or skilled she is. There are too many younger, more aggressive people to hire.

"So, they get passed over and take positions for which they are vastly over-qualified because they have to get a paycheck, somehow. Because with the advent of 'no-fault' divorce, women who get divorced later in life—when he takes off with the younger, newer version—get screwed."

Michelle stopped then and visibly shuddered, taking a calming breath. "I've seen it too many times," she said. Looked up at him intently again, "and, of course, now I'm divorced, a single Mom, and thank God I have a great job, and I'm still young enough to go somewhere with it."

"I feel lucky because I *want* to work, I want to have a successful career. But I would work anyway, even if we were still married, and even if I didn't love the work, because I never, *ever* want to be in the position of financial dependency on a man. No matter how good the marriage. But especially when things go—when they go terribly wrong."

She came back to the sofa, sat down.

"So, what do you think of that? Really." Again, the piercing look.

Ben was astonished. He'd never heard Michelle open up like that before. It was exhilarating. He felt like he was looking at someone new, someone who looked like his wife, his ex-wife, but who was entirely new at the same time.

"Wow," he said. He stood up and walked over to her, sat down by her, and said, "Thank you."

"What?"

"I really am glad you shared that with me. That's what."

"Well, good, I guess," she said lamely.

"Anything else?" he asked.

"Uh, no, I think that about covers it," she said, looking slightly lost.

Ben smiled.

"Well, okay then. I'm glad we had this talk, and I hope we can do it again soon," he said, standing up.

As he left, Ben could have sworn that Michelle looked like she regretted him leaving. She followed him slowly to the door, stood there looking at him curiously, but not opening the door. Instead, she asked if he'd forgotten anything—his keys, his phone? Asked one more question about arrangements for the kids, like they hadn't already covered it several times.

And, wasn't it odd that she'd talked about marriage, career, and kids, almost as if she was talking about their marriage? Like it was *their* conversation, a private and personal continuation of a longstanding conversation? Odd, maybe, but wonderful, nevertheless. Or maybe he was reading too much into it.

Ben drove away slowly, feeling satisfied. He grinned stupidly, ignoring the hostile looks of other drivers.

CHAPTER TWENTY-SEVEN

After spending time early in the day with Dan and Karen Young, pulling together supplies and setting plans, Stuart made his way to Jillian's cabin. This time, when he knocked on the door, he heard little feet pattering quickly, then the door swung open. Sophie was dressed in jeans, hoodie, and a small backpack slung over one shoulder. She looked up at him solemnly but with a sparkle in her eyes.

"Hi," she said.

"Hi, yourself," he said, crouching down to look at her eye level. She smiled shyly.

Jillian grabbed her coat, and Sophie's, and they made their way out. Jillian buckled Sophie into her car seat, then drove while Stuart gave directions. Soon they found a gravel lot next to the head of a hiking trail, parked, and started out.

It was a perfect Pacific Northwest day—deep blue sky, a slight breeze. Today, the conifers pointed gaily at the sky, no longer weighed down by a waterfall of rain. Up the mountain, a small haze of clouds hung around near the top. Everywhere else, blue skies dominated.

The trail was an easy one. Stuart didn't want to risk tiring Sophie out too quickly. He was sure Jillian could have handled a more demanding trail—she still looked in terrific shape, and she moved along easily, never out of breath. But Sophie, with her tiny tread, had to rush to keep up with the two adults.

A ground squirrel darted across the trail, and Sophie squealed in delight.

"Let's get him and take him home," she said, looking first at her mother, who shook her head, then at Stuart.

"Well, we could do that, Sophie," Stuart said thoughtfully, which caused Jillian to frown at him. "Just one problem, though." He waited.

"What," Sophie said.

"Actually, two problems," he said. "One, I dare you to catch the little guy. He's built for speed because he has to run away from other, much bigger, animals all the time—so he doesn't become their lunch."

Sophie nodded her head at that.

"Two, his family would really miss him because we don't know where they are, and even if we did, we couldn't take them all."

Sophie looked thoughtful at that, frowning slightly.

"But we could go ahead and try," said Stuart, looking at Sophie, waiting.

She sighed. "No, I don't think we should. He needs his Mom."

She turned around and walked up the trail. Stuart looked at Jillian, eyebrows raised like, *okay with you?* She smiled gratefully and whispered, "Thanks—you handled that really well."

They made their way slowly uphill, in the foothills of the mountain, trees beginning to thin out a bit. After almost an hour, they found a trail that veered off of the main trail. Following the sound of running water, they made their way to a clearing that featured a small runoff stream that filled a tiny pool of water before continuing downhill. Around the clearing were several very large boulders, and one of them was ideal—big and flat enough for all three of them to sit.

Stuart spread out the large, thick blanket he'd brought, and began setting out the picnic supplies—thick-sliced crusty bread, a large chunk of gouda cheese, a small tub of tuna salad and one of potato salad. For Sophie, he offered a small tub of macaroni and cheese. He pulled out water bottles for all of them, opened his, and drank deeply. Sophie took a sip of hers, and Jillian set hers aside.

"I would have brought a bottle of wine, but I figured it's a little too soon for that," he said. Jillian nodded her approval.

Stuart dug in and watched Jillian and Sophie.

Jillian made a small paper plate of food for Sophie, who ate slowly, taking little bites. She made one for herself, but like her daughter, only nibbled. She gazed around at the clearing, and after she finished eating, stretched out on the blanket with her hands under her head, staring at the small birds and squirrels that occasionally passed by in the trees overhead. Sophie snuggled next to her, pointing at the animals and asking questions which Jillian softly answered.

They were in their own little world, but Stuart didn't mind. It was truly a feast for his eyes to observe Jillian and her daughter. The clearing was utterly quiet except for the occasional chirp from a passing bird and the babbling of the water as it flowed over pebbles and rocks.

Stuart began to appreciate the beauty of the Pacific Northwest. Austin was outdoorsy in the sense that almost everyone either walked, ran, or bicycled for exercise. There were numerous paved trails around the city, and the Texas hill country was close by—ideal for outdoor activities.

But Austin was primarily hustle and bustle, a smaller version of a large metropolitan area, getting larger by the week with so many people moving there to take advantage of some new start-up or to escape the much higher cost of living in California or New York. It was high energy, noisy, absolutely crammed with traffic at all hours of the day or night, never quiet.

He could appreciate, for the first time, why Jillian might want to raise her daughter here. It was quiet, slow-paced, and with her job as a teacher, afforded the time to focus on her daughter—her life, her needs, her everything. Because Sophie was everything to Jillian.

And it was beautiful. You'd never find trees this tall in Texas, never be able to drive five minutes and find yourself in this kind of breathtaking natural beauty, just hop out of the car and hike up a hill in less than an hour to a spot like this. He sighed deeply, began to feel slightly drowsy.

He was on the island, making his way through the trees. He had blood on his hands, and he was trying desperately to get somewhere. He felt lost, disoriented. There were other people here, weren't there? But he had the strong sense that it was a completely deserted island, that he was all alone, forever stranded somewhere in the middle of nowhere. It was pitch black all around, no stars or moon to light the way.

He stood on the edge of a cliff, hearing the sound of the ocean far below, not knowing why he was there, what he was supposed to do. Suddenly, he felt the ground give way beneath him, and he fell, kept falling, hitched his breath desperately, anticipating sudden death.

He was shaking. No, someone was shaking him. He jerked awake, saw Jillian bending over him, hand gently shaking his shoulder.

"Stuart, wake up. You're having a bad dream."

He sat up slowly, saw Sophie staring at him, fear in her eyes.

"It's okay, Sophie. I'm sorry. Did I make any noise?" he asked Jillian, worried.

"Yes, a little, but it's okay. Are you okay?"

He drew in a deep breath, shook off the vapors of the dream, and forced himself to look natural, to smile a bit, for Sophie's sake.

"Well, I didn't think I was going to just fall asleep with you girls here," he said with an exaggerated, clown-like chagrin. "How embarrassing. Sophie, was I drooling?"

Sophie smiled a little, shaking her head.

"Want to know what I dreamed?" he asked Sophie.

She nodded.

"I dreamed that the little ground squirrel was following us home, and all of a sudden, he stopped and asked us a question."

Sophie giggled.

"Squirrels can't talk," she said.

"Well, this one did. And he asked me what the square root of pi is."

Stuart sat there, nodding sagely.

Sophie giggled again.

"Pie? Like chocolate or lemon?"

"Right," said Stuart. "Chocolate, of course!"

And they carried on this silly conversation for a few minutes until Jillian called a halt and suggested they pack up and head back. But she was smiling, and so was Sophie. Stuart was glad that the mood had passed, that Sophie was relaxed. Man, watching out for a little girl was a lot of work, but he thought he was doing great.

Back at Jillian's, Stuart offered to set out the picnic supplies again for early dinner, but she declined. So, he unloaded the food, put all of it in Jillian's refrigerator, and prepared to leave. She walked him to the door. Sophie was in her room after Jillian had tucked her in for a much-needed nap.

"Thanks for the hike, and the picnic," she said.

"Thanks for going," he said.

It was still so awkward between them. He stood in front of her, not knowing what to say, at a loss for words, uncertain. She stood in front of him, what? Angry, hurt, disgusted? He couldn't read her, but that wasn't anything new. Jillian had always been somewhat aloof, miserly with her deepest feelings.

He closed his eyes, opened them, and acted on instinct. He pressed in close, she backed up against the wall next to the door, looking up at him, startled. He stepped closer. He twirled a strand of her hair, and her breath hitched. He pressed the full length of his body against hers, leaned down, and kissed her.

She kissed him back—tasting like peppermint—a long, deep kiss that aroused every bit of the spark, the chemistry they'd shared so many years ago. He pressed her closer, and she leaned into him. He picked her up, she wrapped her legs around him, and he moved in a slow grind against her, her back pressed to the wall. He pushed one hand into her hair, feeling the silky strands, holding her head as their kiss deepened, the other arm holding her up.

He moved his hand from her hair slowly down her neck, then over her breast, massaging slowly, causing her to tremble. He slipped his hand under her sweater and underneath her bra, brushing her nipple, which stood at attention. She moaned softly. He gasped, kissed her harder.

Little footsteps padded noisily in the hallway coming from the bedroom.

"Mommy?"

Jillian's eyes flew open, she pushed her way out of Stuart's arms, dropped her feet on the ground, quickly adjusting her clothes, and turned toward Sophie as she came into the room. Face flushed pink, hair slightly out of place, she smiled at her daughter.

"What is it, honey? You're supposed to be taking a nap, remember?"

Did he hear regret in her voice? That Sophie wasn't fast asleep? He certainly felt it, standing there feeling all worked up with nowhere to go. He discreetly adjusted his pants in an attempt to hide the visual of his arousal.

"I know, Mommy, but I forgot to show Stuart my drawing from

yesterday, remember?" She looked at them both, holding a sheet of paper in her hands.

Jillian threw Stuart a helpless look and followed her daughter into the living room. They sat down and took turns looking at her artwork, then chose a new place to hang it. After that, Sophie asked Stuart when he was coming back. He looked at Jillian, who nodded carefully.

"I think we'll get together again tomorrow, if that's okay with you," said Stuart.

Sophie nodded her head solemnly.

"Yes," she said firmly.

After a chaste good-bye, with Sophie giving him a little wave, Stuart left and drove around for a while, wanting to be alone with his thoughts. He found a small out of the way diner and ordered a beer and a burger. He ate quickly, then made his way back to the motel.

A good start, he thought. But what had really happened back there? Did he seduce that response out of Jillian, or was it mutual? The chemistry, the spark? Was she just lonely after being a single Mom for so long? At least, it appeared she'd been alone for a while, but what did he know? Maybe some woodsy guy around here had romanced her. Maybe he was still in the picture. He sighed.

He thought of Sophie, her big blue eyes, her spun gold hair, the adorable way she had of cracking just a tiny smile when he found her funny button. He thought of the two of them, snuggled together on the blanket, looking up at the trees. Their sweet connection, the quiet conversations they had. His heart swelled.

Dear God, was he falling in love all over again with Jillian? Even more scary, was he falling in love with her adorable little girl? Was he getting attached to her in a way that would be devastating if things didn't work out with him and Jillian? His breath hitched in his chest. Damned if he knew, but he knew one thing. He wasn't going to stop.

The next day, Stuart showed up at Jillian's after school let out, and they spent the evening cooking dinner together and playing games until it was Sophie's bedtime. Stuart offered to help with that, but Jillian yawned, said she was super tired after work, and maybe they could get together again the next day.

It was clear that she didn't want another back-against-the-wall session that night. He'd hoped to pick up where they left off on that, but maybe she was being smarter than he was. They still needed to talk, really talk, about where their lives had been, had gone since they'd last seen each other. He knew the chemistry was still there, but was the heart?

Jillian showed him to the door, and he left.

As Stuart was settling in for the night in his motel room, his cell phone rang, surprising him.

"Hello?"

"Stuart? It's me," said Jillian, her voice low.

"Hi, Jill. Is Sophie, okay?"

"Yes, of course, she is. I just wanted a chance to talk without...you know," she said.

"I know," he said. "Look, I'm sorry if I was too, uh, forward the other night."

"No, you weren't. It's okay, really," She paused.

"I enjoyed it," she said softly. Seductively?

"Me too," he breathed. He felt his body responding to her voice. Were they about to have phone sex? His heart rate accelerated.

"Anyway, I thought it was best if we spent some time talking, without little ears listening, you know?" She sounded more matter of fact now. Too bad.

He sat up in bed to distract himself.

"Of course. I'm here, I want to talk to you, too. Jill, I've missed you so much," he said, surprising himself with the moisture forming in his eyes as he said it.

She was quiet. Too much?

"I've missed you too, Stuart. But I'm not the same girl who broke up with you years ago. A lot has changed. The obvious—Sophie. Stuart, she's my life, my heart. I would die for her. That's what parenthood does for you, does to you. It's...indescribable, the love that I feel for her."

"You're an amazing Mom," he said.

"She comes first, for me, now and forever. All my decisions, everything I've done in my life, or chosen to give up, is because of her— because I want the best for her."

"Of course. I understand," said Stuart, wondering where this was going, dreading where it was going.

"I won't do anything that compromises her happiness, no matter how much I might want it."

He was quiet.

"That includes you, Stuart. Look, you and I gave it our best effort years ago, and yes, I still have feelings, but—" she trailed off.

"But what? I told you, Sophie is not a deal-breaker for me. I've changed, too. I'm not the same bull-headed guy I was, the guy who made you feel like wanting kids was a bad thing. Jillian—"

He felt a sense of desperation. She was pushing him away again, giving up far too easily.

"Sophie deserves far more than *not being a deal-breaker* for someone. She deserves to have people in her life who are 100% there for her, who are completely devoted to her."

"That's not fair, Jill. I just met her two days ago! Give me a chance, would you?"

"It's just that it's too scary, Stuart. I'm too scared, and that's no way to start a new relationship. That's what it is for us, after so many years. But with lots of emotional baggage."

"Jill, don't do this, please." He was begging now.

"I'm sorry," she said, starting to cry. "I'm so sorry, Stuart."

And she hung up.

He sat there, stunned. From the clouds of romantic fantasy to this. His heart literally hurt in his chest. He stood up, paced around the room, tears streaming down his face.

After what seemed like hours of that, but was only minutes, he stopped, then quickly dressed, slammed his way out of the motel room, not stopping to lock the door, but who cared anyway? He was out in the boonies—let someone take his few shirts and his dirty socks if they needed them that badly.

He drove to Jillian's in a haze, parked, got out of the car, went to her door and stood there, afraid to knock, not wanting to scare Sophie. He pulled out his cell phone and texted, "*Come to your front door, please.*"

She texted back, "*What?*"

"Please."

Long pause.

"Okay, let me get dressed first."

She finally pulled open the door holding her index finger to her mouth, shushing him. She stepped outside, pulled the door after herself, wrapping her arms around herself against the chill night air.

"What are you doing here?"

Stuart picked her up and carried her to his car. She didn't fight him. He set her down, opened the door, and motioned for her to get in.

"I can't leave, Stuart. Sophie...,"

"I know that. We're not going anywhere. It's just for a few minutes."

She got in. He got in, started the car, and turned on the heater. He turned to her, pulled her into his arms, wrapped them around her, and whispered into her hair.

"You can't leave me again, Jillian. I just got here, and I'm not leaving," he said softly. He moved his face around and kissed her. She kissed him back, and it was an old-fashioned make-out session for a minute or two.

She pulled away a little, breathless, looking up at him.

"Stuart, what am I going to do with you?"

"Nothing, baby. Just don't leave, okay? Not until we've had a fair chance. I already adore Sophie, who wouldn't? But it takes a little time to become a family, don't you think? Don't we deserve the chance for that?"

She sighed heavily.

"Okay, you win for now. But there are still things you don't know, Stuart, and I'm not sure...,"

"I realize that, and the same goes for me. Now shut up and let's get back to the kissing part."

CHAPTER TWENTY-EIGHT

Ben slammed the car in park, barreled out, and raced into the emergency room. He hustled up to the waiting area and ran to the reception window.

"I'm looking for my wife—is she here? Please, my kid is hurt," he said, slightly out of breath.

"Well, you'll have to tell me her name, sir, and show me some i.d.," the twenty-something girl said. She flipped her hair back, turned to a keyboard, and began tapping, chewing gum. Ben told her Michelle's name, she continued to tap, then slowly turned back.

"They're in the back, in an exam room."

"Where? I need to see them. Now," said Ben. Wasn't this an Emergency Room? No one seemed to be acting like there were any emergencies. He could see medical personnel loitering in the background, chatting each other up, smiling, cracking jokes.

"The doctor's with them now. He'll come out and get you as soon as he knows something," hair flip said, turning back to her keyboard.

"Look, lady, *that's my son back there*, and I'm going back there and find him if you don't tell me where he is." Ben's face was red with anger.

She looked startled, then shrugged.

"Okay, let me find out which room."

After what seemed like forever, she gave him a room number and directions, then pointed at the door leading back to the exam rooms.

Ben hustled back as fast as he could go, knocking over a tray with medical supplies on a gurney as he passed it. A nurse standing nearby waved him on, going over to pick up the scissors, bandages, and other things. He kept going.

Finally, he found the room, opened the door carefully, and went in. Jordan was sitting up on a hospital bed, Toy Story character in one hand, the other hand lying limply by his side swathed in bandages. A television on the wall played a Disney movie, volume low. Jordan's gaze was fixed on the screen. Michelle looked up, motioned to Ben.

"Mommy and Daddy will be outside for a moment," she told Jordan, who nodded vaguely. Ben noticed Joe sitting nearby in the room. Heat rose in his face.

Outside the room, Ben asked Michelle loudly, "What is that guy doing here? I'm his Dad!"

"Shhh, Ben—don't make a scene. It's been stressful enough," she said, tucking her slightly disarrayed hair behind one ear.

"What the hell happened?" Ben asked, still steaming, but speaking in a lower tone of voice.

"He and Katie were playing a game, running in and out of the back door. Jordan grabbed the door, put his hand on the door jam, apparently, got distracted, and slammed it on his own hand."

"How bad is he hurt?"

"He's going to be fine. Cut the end of his finger, and it went to the bone, so there was a lot of blood and pain. Lots of nerve endings in the finger pad, the doctors tell me. He'll get a few stitches and some pain medication, and then we can go home."

That was way better than Ben had hoped.

"Thank God for that," he said.

"Yeah, it's not that bad. You know the Henderson's little boy broke his arm, and that was a much bigger deal. And the Tate's little girl? She got a huge cut on her head when she fell off her bicycle—they thought at first she had a bad concussion."

"Where's Katie?" he interrupted.

"With Liz."

"What is Joe doing here?" Ben said, less hostile, but still insistent.

"He was there when it happened. I think he's kind of rattled. He's not used to kids and the scrapes they can get into. Jordan screamed at the top of his lungs all the way to the hospital."

Good, thought Ben. Let him get a taste of real life with kids and see how long he sticks around.

They went back into the room. Joe stood up, looking a bit sheepish.

"Um...this room really isn't big enough for all of us, and it looks like things are under control, so I'll take off."

He turned to Jordan, patted his shoulder. "Hey, buddy, I'll see you later, okay?"

Jordan nodded sleepily. They'd apparently given him something to calm him down.

Joe hugged Michelle, kissed her on the cheek, whispered something to her, and slipped out of the room, leaving Michelle and Ben with their son. After that, the name of the game was diversion—from the doctor's exam of Jordan's finger, eliciting tears and protestations, to the ordeal of stitches, for which they had to further sedate him. Then, waiting to get discharged from the clinic. Finally, driving home, Jordan asleep in his car seat.

Back at their—Michelle's—house, they settled Jordan in bed. Katie was spending the night with Liz, so it was unnaturally quiet. Ben found an open bottle of chardonnay in the refrigerator, brought two glasses to Michelle, and poured. They clinked half-heartedly.

"To surviving another kid crisis," he said, giving her a lopsided smile.

"To surviving, " said Michelle, taking a sip.

"Remember when...?"

"Remember that time...?"

Spoken at the same time. Then both laughed softly, looked away from each other.

"Thanks for getting there so fast, and for helping out so much," she said.

"You don't have to thank me for showing up for my own children," he said.

Michelle's eyes welled up. Ben jumped up, sat beside her, but she looked away.

"Ben, I...I'm sorry—it's just been a day of it, you know?"

She sniffed, wiped her eyes, turned to him, took a breath, mouth slightly open as if about to speak.

"What can I do—how about some dinner? How about I order take-out? Unless there's something here to cook. Do you need an aspirin? Why don't you take a nap while I keep an eye on Jordan? In case he wakes up," Ben rattled off.

"Ben, I'm fine, really." Her face closed.

Ben did a stop-action mentally. Okay, this could be one of those times I need to just listen. Stop trying to fix it, he told himself. Crap, this was hard.

He forced himself to sit back on the sofa, gripped his legs to keep his hands still. Took a deep breath.

"A real day of it, huh?" he said slowly.

Long pause, agonizing wait.

She slid her gaze away from him, closed her eyes for a moment. It felt like forever before she turned back at last.

"Yeah. I was going to call you anyway. Then this happened." She stopped, seemed uncertain.

"Call me?" he said.

"Wait here." She got up, went away. It looked like she went into the master bedroom, but he wasn't sure. She came back after a few minutes.

Michelle placed a small box on the coffee table—a box that looked like a jeweler's box. Ben's heart stopped.

"Open it," she said.

Ben stared at her. Gingerly, he picked it up, as if it were a rattlesnake about to bite.

Slowly, he opened the small hinged lid. And gasped.

Inside sat an enormous diamond engagement ring—one huge center stone, surrounded by a dazzling array of smaller stones. He looked up at Michelle blankly.

"Joe proposed to me last night," she said.

Ben set the box down, stunned.

What the hell was wrong with him? Of course, Joe proposed! Why wouldn't some great guy want to seal up the option with a woman like Michelle?

Why hadn't he seen this coming? Why hadn't he *done* something—anything—to divert this train headed downhill?

All those lame, little efforts. Giving her concert tickets—please! Buying clothes for the kids and putting them away—so lame, so lacking in romantic effort. Sending her bottles of wine from the first winery he'd gained as a client. Anyone can give a bottle or two of wine.

Ben searched his memory for some evidence that he'd done something right but couldn't think of anything. Certainly, nothing that even came close to Joe's enormous diamond ring or his proposal. No doubt delivered in a fabulous restaurant overlooking the Pacific Ocean, complete with candles, flowers, and maybe even a singing waiter or two.

He sat back, defeated.

"Congratulations, Michelle."

"Thanks."

"I mean it," he said, raising his eyes to hers with his best game face. "I want you to be happy, and if Joe makes you happy, then this is what I want for you."

She gazed at him steadily.

"Do you mean that, Ben? Because it's my decision, you know, but we have two children together, and I would never marry anyone that you or anyone else I'm close to thought would be bad for them."

Ben said nothing for a moment, then spoke reluctantly.

"I don't know Joe, but he seems like a nice guy. What does your gut tell you about him, Michelle? I mean—I think you're a good judge of character."

"He's a good man," she said. And after a pause. "I—I had one of my colleagues at the law firm check him out when we first met, you know, legal history, all of that. You cannot be too careful—the kids, you know. Nothing came up, but that doesn't mean someone is a good person. But since then, in the time we've spent together, meeting his friends, his family. He really is a good guy. And he loves me."

Ben's heart sank. Why couldn't there be something wrong with Joe, some dark secret in his past? Why couldn't he be a jerk? But of course, he'd never want Michelle to be treated badly by a guy, even if it meant she'd dump him later, so she'd be available again.

Wouldn't want someone to treat her like I treated her, he thought grimly.

"Ben, I—I mean, I'm sorry to surprise you like this right after Jordan's accident. But I told Joe I wouldn't wear the ring until I told you. I didn't want you to see it on my finger and feel blindsided."

He didn't know what to say. *Thank you?*

But she didn't put it on her finger. It just sat there on the table like a giant, neon beacon, a sparkling, glorious signpost, stunning evidence of his epic stupidity. Every time he'd see it on Michelle's finger, for decades to come, he'd have to re-live the worst mistake of his life.

Of course, seeing her wear that ring would be nothing compared to seeing Joe by her side, day in and day out. Every birthday party, every school graduation, weddings, grandchildren. All of it played out in his mind.

The tightness in Ben's chest was almost unbearable. His teeth ground.

"Ben?"

Ben slammed back into the present.

"You took that rather well," said Michelle. "I'm glad you're okay, and that I can actually talk to you about this," she said, clearly relieved.

"Uh, yeah."

"Anyway, would you bring Katie back tomorrow? I'll let Liz know you're picking her up, and maybe by then, Jordan will be feeling better. But remember, he still needs the pain medication for a couple of more days. We don't want to get behind on that, right?"

"Right. Listen, Michelle, I've got to run. I'll see you tomorrow when I bring Katie back," he said, getting up quickly, making his way to the door. Getting out fast, practically running to his car.

In the car, he punched in his therapist's number, requested an urgent visit, and got a time set for the following day.

"That is news," said Suzanne.

"Yeah. I can't believe it!" Ben sat forward on the sofa in Suzanne's office, forehead in his hands, shaking his head.

"Of course, you can. You saw this coming, Ben."

He looked up, stricken.

"I guess I did. I mean, why wouldn't I see this coming? I feel like I've been a day late, my whole life—I mean, it's like I just can't learn—there's always something important, it's just out of my reach—and, I've always felt this way. It's like I'm always trying to catch up. I'm so sick of it," he finished angrily.

"Don't you mean, you're sick of yourself, your own mistakes?" she asked softly.

"Yes," he said flatly. "You got it."

Suzanne was quiet for a moment.

"Ben, you're awfully hard on yourself. Yes, you screwed up your marriage," she said. He looked up in shock.

"Yes, you've made a mess of that. You are human, and therefore deeply flawed, as are we all. But, tell me something," she said.

"Tell me—I wonder, that is, how it will look to your children? What will they learn from you about how to handle making big mistakes? How to deal with royally screwing up?"

She paused.

"How, I wonder, do you want your children to deal with themselves when they mess up, and I mean later in life when their mistakes are bigger?"

Ben felt rocked by the question. He'd been so busy over the last 48 hours obsessing about himself, about his own personal devastation. He hadn't really thought about how all of this might affect the kids.

Once again, Mr. Self-Absorbed.

"I didn't think of it that way," he said. "It's not like I'm showing something in front of them. I don't act jealous, I'm not being nasty to their Mom, in fact, to the contrary. I don't think they have any idea how I'm feeling inside."

"Okay, maybe not. But you don't want your kids to be well-adjusted in spite of you or whatever you are dealing with. Wouldn't it be even better if they grew up well-adjusted *because* of you?"

"Because of me," he said blankly.

"Because of you," she said.

"And how do I make sure they grow up well-adjusted? What exactly does that look like?" he said.

"Not to be too terribly clinical, but research shows that issues with children following divorce have less to do with the event itself and more to do with how the parents handle themselves.

"When divorced parents make it a point to let their grievances go, when they cooperate and align on what's in the kids' best interest, it tends to go well for them, or, at least, not much different than growing up in an intact family. And those can be messy—the ideal family life is pretty much a myth. But well-adjusted, as in staying away from drugs and alcohol—not turning into addicts or delinquents. Productive—school, career, starting their own family down the line, if that's what they want. In short, self-expressed and living their lives contentedly."

Ben nodded.

"But when people divorce in hostility, unable to let go of their personal grievances; when they use the kids to get back at one another, things tend to go very badly for the children. Or, when they follow the divorce with an unstable lifestyle—dating lots of different people, a revolving door of lovers, and so on, that also creates problems. It's much harder for them to stabilize, to get through the turbulent teens without too much damage."

"So, what does all this have to do with Michelle getting engaged?" Ben interrupted. "I think we're doing a really good job so far on the co-parenting thing. We get along great, we never fight," he said.

"So far, so good, right?" she said.

"Yeah."

"But...," she said.

"But I have to say I feel differently now that she and Joe are engaged. I mean, I'm just not feeling the motivation to keep doing those little things I was doing for her. I feel like giving up, sliding back into the single Dad thing. Pick up the kids, and drop them off, talk about crucial kid stuff with Michelle, nothing more."

"Right," she said.

"You're not surprised," he said.

"No," she said. "After all, it's easy to give when you think you might, at some point, get something back. As long as Michelle and Joe were just dating, you could convince yourself he was impermanent, something that would soon blow away. You could pretend that your mistakes were all in the past. Now that they're engaged...,"

"Yeah—now that they're engaged—I mean, I've made fun of him in my mind, seen him as just some good-looking dude, but not much more. No real competition. But now, he's obviously not going away. Goddammit!" he finished, raising his voice.

"Right. You're angry, now that you're seeing Joe as a real person in Michelle's life, and now that you can't deny how badly you messed up and where your mistake led the two of you. And now is when you have the tough choice."

"The tough choice?"

"Yes—how are you going to treat Michelle now that she's engaged to Joe, planning her wedding?"

"*Right*," he said in despair.

They sat silently.

"Part of me wants to bail completely where Michelle is concerned, but then again, I don't want to give up," Ben ventured.

"You're thinking about continuing to give of yourself to her."

"Yup. Dumb, right? I mean, at some point, I have to get on with my life."

"Maybe this is your life, for now," she said.

Baffling. What did that mean?

"So, Ben, what are your choices at this point—with regard to Michelle?"

"My choices?"

"For how to respond to this situation, to Michelle's engagement and re-marriage. And, maybe the unfair question is, what response do you want your children to see?"

Ben felt a twinge. That last question made it so much more difficult.

He thought about it. Maybe he had a couple of choices in the way he might respond, neither of which was very appealing.

One, he could go back to acting like a shithead, be distant and resentful toward Michelle, emotionally cut off, the way he was before the island.

Two, he could suck it up and be neutral—not resentful, but maybe no longer so open and warm. No longer so giving.

But there was another choice.

Three, and most difficult of all, he could continue to act the way he'd acted since he'd gotten back from the island—warm, sweet and kind, doing things for her, listening to her at those rare moments when she chose to open up.

Impossible choice.

His thoughts drifted to the island, the galaxy, the stars. That some things are immutable, just the way they are, for eons instead of the fleeting moments, days, and even years, of the life of an ordinary person.

On the island, they'd gazed at the stars overhead, wondering how long it took for that light to reach them, wondering for how many millions, billions of years they had burned. How unchanged they'd been for more human lifetimes than could ever be calculated.

Sometimes, love was like that. You couldn't change it. No matter what happened. It blazed away, in the heavens above, and in your heart.

Ben's eyes filled with tears as he broke down.

CHAPTER TWENTY-NINE

After that night in the car, they didn't talk about "us" again. Instead, they spent time together with everyday activities, always with Sophie. Stuart worked on his laptop and made phone calls during the day, watching the clock, waiting for Jillian to leave work. Then he picked up Sophie and Jillian for their evenings together.

They cooked dinner, played games with Sophie, and listened to music together while Sophie drew and colored. She was already an amazing, budding artist, producing drawings that Stuart thought were sophisticated for her age. Evenings were cozy in Jillian's house with the fireplace crackling and dusk settling around them like a soft, purple blanket.

On the weekends, they hiked and picnicked, boated, and even fished. Stuart didn't know how to fly fish, but since they were in the ideal place for that, he studied YouTube videos and asked Dan Young to fill in the details. He bought the equipment, and they went together, although Jillian didn't get much fishing done. Worried about Sophie falling in the river, she obsessed over the safety of her daughter.

As the days passed, Sophie and Stuart grew closer. At night, she began asking for Stuart to read her a bedtime story, to tuck her in. He loved those moments, watching her grow drowsy, trying to keep herself awake, begging for one more chapter. She'd drop off suddenly, in the middle of the first time Charlotte the spider met Wilbur, the pig in *Charlotte's Web*. He would stop reading, waiting to see if she woke again, begging for another chapter. He'd listen to her breathing, tuck the covers up around her, and tiptoe out of her room.

Each evening, he and Jillian sat in the living room, in front of the fireplace, sipping wine and talking. He told her all about the boat, the island, and getting back. There were some things he didn't share about the island, things that he'd sworn never to reveal. But he told her everything else.

He told her about his Dad, how they'd reconnected, his jail stint, and recovery with the help of A.A. He asked her if she thought it was real. She asked him what he believed, and he said he was skeptical, but wanted to wait and see.

"I don't understand it myself, but for some reason, I guess I'm willing to give him one more chance. But if I see any sign, he's falling off the wagon, I'm done with him for good."

Jillian nodded.

He told her the real story of his Mom and apologized for lying to her about it, years ago. He vowed to always be truthful with her.

She dropped her eyes and went quiet. He figured it was because she wasn't sure if she could trust him, maybe not because of that lie, but because of so many other mistakes he'd made with her.

He hoped she'd tell him all about Sophie—who her real father was, what kind of relationship she'd had with him. But she didn't. She talked about her Mom, how hard it was losing her.

She cried then, and Stuart wrapped her in his big embrace and held her until the sniffles died down. She looked up at him then and said, "I didn't realize I was still so sad. I've felt so alone in the world since she passed."

"Well, you're not alone now, Jill."

She looked away like she didn't fully believe that.

The day came for Stuart to leave to go back to Austin. He'd neglected his real estate business for far too long, letting it languish since coming back from the island. His flight was for the next day, and he and Jillian sat quietly in her living room after putting Sophie to bed.

"I'll be back soon," he told her.

"I know," she said, looking away, doubtful.

He reached over, pulled her face gently in his direction so that she had to look into his eyes.

"You have to believe me, Jill. I'm just going to check on my business, figure out how to get some things wrapped up so I can work better remotely."

She looked so sad.

"Jillian, I love you. And I love Sophie. I'm coming back in a couple of weeks, and we are going to start figuring things out together—our future, okay?"

"Stuart, I...I still need to tell you some things...,"

"It can wait, okay? It's not important anyway. Whatever happened while we were apart is water under the bridge. All that matters is now —we're together, and that's the way it's going to be."

He had enough love and confidence for the two of them. He felt strong, of heart and mind.

She stood, pulled him up by the hand, and led him to her bedroom. He stopped her, asked, "Are you sure?" and she whispered, yes.

Their reunion was wonderful, marred only by the fact that they had to be quiet so that they didn't wake Sophie. And the fact that he had to get up super early and get out before she found him in bed with her Mom. Cautious Jillian— "I'm not going to have my daughter going to kindergarten talking about the guy sleeping in her Mom's bed. And she will talk! Kids do that, even when they don't understand what's happening."

They said their good-byes in the bedroom, agreeing that Stuart would not come back to say good-bye to Sophie since she was too young to understand. Jillian would tell her later. They walked to the door quietly, kissed quickly, and shared one last hug. Stuart left her house happier than he'd been, well, pretty much ever.

Back in Austin, Stuart got busy. There was a lot to wrap up—a couple of closings that had languished while he was on the island but were ready now to complete. He had no new deals in the pipeline since there'd been no one to source a deal. He was pretty much a one-man show, utilizing the occasional intern to help out and to whom he would teach the ropes. But he hadn't had an intern in over a year.

He had one income-producing commercial property. He'd hired a manager two years earlier, and, thankfully, she was really good. She kept everything running smoothly in his absence. He sat down with her and worked out a deal giving her a small equity stake in the property, gaining her commitment to continue indefinitely. Good managers like Joanna were hard to find, and he didn't want to lose her.

He closed on the two deals and pocketed a nice payday, enough cash to fund a modest lifestyle for years to come. He packed up his condo, put his furniture and most of the household items in storage, had the place painted, staged, and put online for rent. It was a premium property, so he wasn't worried about finding a tenant who could afford the high rate. He put everything into Joanna's capable hands, entrusting her with the job of maintenance and handling renters.

Every night, he called Jillian. Sometimes he called early enough so that he could face-time with Sophie. Once, he face-timed while she was in the bathtub, giggling and splashing soap suds, talking to him about the boy in kindergarten who'd brought a fat toad to school that day.

After tucking Sophie in, Jillian called him back, and they chatted about their day. It was easygoing, lighthearted, and sometimes a bit sultry. She put on her bedroom voice and teased him, but Jillian refused to have phone sex, though he tried a couple of times.

"I want romance," she said. "You know that. And there's nothing romantic about—well, you know—over the phone."

So, he kept it romantic. And he was deliriously happy. As swiftly as a passing storm, the month away flew by. He bought a ticket to Seattle.

The drive from Seattle to the small town where Jillian lived was beautiful, but Stuart could barely appreciate it. Impatient, he pushed the speed limit one time too many, got pulled over, and ground his teeth while the highway patrol cop wrote a ticket.

"Watch it, buddy," the cop admonished him before he pulled out. He drove more carefully after that, but it chafed.

He hadn't talked to Jillian in two days. Mysteriously, his calls to her cell phone went to voice mail. He left multiple messages and texts, but she didn't respond. In desperation, he'd called Dan Young at his store, and Dan reassured him that he'd seen Jillian not two hours earlier and that she was fine. Stuart made some excuse, thanked him, and hung up.

That was early this morning, before his flight.

Stuart's face burned with embarrassment and anger. She was fine? Well, then, why wasn't she calling him back?

Finally, he pulled in front of Jillian's cabin. Impatiently, he hurried to the front door. He tried the door handle, intending to walk in, but it was locked. He knocked. Waited.

Nothing.

He moved over to one of the windows. Everything was dark, no signs that Jillian and Sophie were home. What gives?

Stuart paced up and down Jillian's front walkway, thinking. Something was wrong, he could feel that. But what? Everything had been fine, been wonderful, in fact, the last time they talked two days ago. He'd told her about his flight, and she'd said she couldn't wait to see him, that Sophie was excited.

He got in the car, drove away, and headed back into town. He pulled in front of Young's Hardware. Dan was busy with a customer but noticed Stuart and nodded. Stuart beckoned to him, but Dan gave him a "wait" signal. Finally, he was done with the customer and came over.

"Stuart, good to see you. Did you just get into town?" he asked.

"Yes, but I'm really worried about Jillian. She's not answering my calls or texts. I went to her house, and it's dark. Do you know where she is?"

"Come over here, Stuart, have a seat," Dan said, indicating a couple of chairs together behind the counter.

"I don't feel like sitting. Just tell me—*do you know where she is*?"

"Yes, I do. Have a seat, and we'll talk about it," Dan said firmly, pointing at the chair.

Impatiently, Stuart rounded the corner, and sat on the edge, knee popping up and down. He felt like he was going to hit the guy if he didn't tell him where Jillian was, STAT.

"She's in Seattle. She had to go for a medical appointment. It came up rather quickly, and she had to take off fast."

Seattle? *Medical?* Stuart's head spun.

"What kind of medical appointment?"

"That's for her to tell you, Stuart. Not my place to do it. But she asked me to let you know her friend Ashley is with her, and Sophie is fine—she's with them."

"So, they're both in Seattle? Sophie and Jillian?"

"Yes, they are, but they're driving back tomorrow, so there's no point in you going there. She asked me to ask you to settle in here, and when she gets back, she'll be in touch."

"She'll be in touch."

"Yes." Dan was firm, but he looked like he truly felt sorry for Stuart.

Well, that's just great, he thought. Why couldn't she have called and told him any of this, herself? Why all the mystery, the unanswered calls, and texts?

"Look, I know this is hard," said Dan, "but if you could just give her a little time...she'll be back tomorrow, and she'll explain everything."

He didn't have any choice, really. So, he got a motel room and made a trip to the convenience store. He didn't feel like eating, but instead, chugged six beers before falling into an uncomfortable sleep. He'd forgotten to take off his clothes, so he woke sweating and with cotton in his mouth. He ripped everything off and slept fitfully until dawn.

He woke with a pounding headache, remembered hangover repair 101 from his stint as an emergency responder, and drank about a gallon of water, taking three aspirin. He showered, and by the time he got dressed, he felt much better. He went down the street to the local diner and had breakfast, checking his cell phone every ten minutes.

She walked in the door of the diner. Her face was pale, her eyes too large, with dark circles underneath. She looked exhausted. She scanned the room, spotted Stuart, and made her way to the table, sitting down carefully, prolonging the placement of her coat, her bag. Finally, she looked up at him.

"Stuart. I'm glad you're here. I—I know you must be furious."

He reached out and took her hands, grateful for the contact. Her hands were ice cold, so he wrapped his around them, transferring heat.

"I'm not mad, Jillian. I was really worried. But I don't understand why you didn't call me, tell me you had to go to Seattle."

"You're right, of course, I should have."

But she was silent, no explanation.

"And?" he asked, trying to not sound pissed.

Slowly, she pulled her hands away, looked down, and he thought for a minute she might bolt again.

"I'm a little scared," she said, voice shaky.

Alarmed, he moved to her side of the table, put his arms around her.

"Don't be scared, baby. I'm not mad," he whispered, holding her closer. "Well, nothing that a few hugs and kisses won't fix," he attempted with levity.

"No, it's not that. It's just—I don't deserve this much love. I...I have so much to tell you...,"

"It's okay."

After a couple of minutes, she stopped shaking.

"Better?"

"Yes, I'm fine. It's okay," she said, but clearly, she was still shaken.

"I went to Seattle because the doctors are better there," she said. "I had an annual checkup, and I wasn't feeling quite right, so they did a full work-up. I thought I'd be there for a couple of hours, and I took Sophie with me. But after they did the scans, they pulled me in and told me I needed a closer work-up, that there was something on my breast sonogram that looked troubling.

"I called Ashley, and she flew up immediately to take care of Sophie. I stayed the whole day, going from one doctor to another, and the answer is," she stopped, her breathing getting erratic. "The answer is that I have Stage Two breast cancer, and it's a fairly aggressive type."

She began to talk about her treatment options, but Stuart could barely comprehend what she was saying. His ears buzzed, his head felt light. He pulled back a bit, dazed.

"Stuart?"

"What?" he was unfocused.

"Look, it's okay, we don't have to talk about this right now," said Jillian, concerned.

"Huh?" he said, shaking his head.

"Let's get out of here," said Jillian, gathering up her things. "Ashley has Sophie for the day. Let's go to the house."

They left, taking Jillian's car. Stuart was silent the entire drive, feeling like he'd been hit in the head. Why couldn't he understand what was happening? He felt odd, out of balance.

"Let's go in, Stuart," said Jillian. He looked up and saw they were parked outside her cabin. How had they gotten there? He felt like he had cotton in his ears, like sounds were far away, muffled.

He got out of the car, followed Jillian in the cabin, where she bustled around, lit a fire, put on water for hot tea. She walked over to him, where he was standing stock still in the living room, and gently pushed him down onto the sofa. He sat, but slumped, feeling like someone had let the air out of a balloon. And the balloon was him.

She brought steaming hot tea for them both, set the cups on the table, sat down next to Stuart. After a minute or so, Stuart shook his head.

Snap out of it, he told himself. This dazed, out of it guy didn't feel like him. He was the strong guy, the guy everyone else leaned on, wasn't he?

Or maybe not. After all, he'd never been in a position like this before, loving someone with a very difficult health crisis. He'd failed Jillian long ago, hadn't he? And he'd been hiding out from any kind of serious relationship for years. His only immediate family member was his alcoholic father from whom he'd been estranged until recently. So, there'd been no one to lean on him. Perfect arrangement.

Now it was time to step up for Jillian, and how was he doing? Shitty.

Stuart got up, went into the restroom, closed the door, turned on ice-cold water, and splashed it in his face. That woke him up. He raised his dripping face, looked at himself in the mirror, and shook his head. *You gotta do better than this*, he told himself. He rolled his neck and shoulders, hearing and feeling the slight cracking, which brought him back to full alert.

Back in the living room, Stuart sat next to Jillian, put his arms around her, pulled her close, and kissed the top of her head.

"I'm sorry, baby. I kind of lost it there for a few minutes, but I'm back, and I'm here for you. Forgive me?"

Her head was turned into his shoulder, and she mumbled something.

He pulled away a bit, tilted her face up and kissed her gently.

She kissed him back, eyes closed, and when the kiss ended, dreamily opened them. She sighed.

"Stuart, I think it's time to talk about some things. I—"

But she never finished. The front door flew open, Sophie danced in, stopped for a second, then ran toward Stuart, who stood and swooped her up in his arms as she giggled.

She wriggled down, then ran to her Mom for a hug. She ran back to Stuart, who sat back down. She climbed into his lap, faced him, and said, "Hi."

"Hi, yourself, bird."

"Bird?" she asked, clearly delighted.

"Yes, bird. You're like a little bird, flying here and there, eating a crumb or two now and then, perching on your bed for me to read a story."

"Why not a ground squirrel?" she inquired, tilting her head, grinning.

"Dunno. Maybe that's too long to say. 'Hi, ground squirrel,'" he mimicked.

She giggled hysterically.

"You're silly," she said to him, reaching up to touch his face. His heart melted into a huge puddle from which he knew he'd never recover.

"What kind of bird am I?" she asked.

"Not sure. We'll have to figure that out. Let's see, parrot? Too ordinary. Canary? Weird. Sparrow? Sounds bleak. Um, did you know there is a small parrot called a parrotlet?"

"Parrotlet! That's what I am!" she exclaimed gleefully.

"Then, there's finch, that's a type of small, cute bird. And, of course, we could go with crow...no?" at her look of dismay.

"Finch!" she shouted.

Jillian looked amazed, shaking her head, smiling.

"I've never seen her so animated," she said. "She's normally so quiet, you can hardly tell she's there."

Just then, the door opened again, and Ashley came in, carrying two small overnight bags, hers and Sophie's. She set them down and looked at Stuart, surprised.

"Hey, Ashley," he said to her, dodging Sophie's attempts to force him to look at her again.

"Hey, Stuart," she said.

"Hey," said Sophie, both hands on the sides of his face, looking into his eyes.

"Hey," he said.

"Guess what?" she said.

"Um, pumpkins?" he replied.

"Huh?"

"You said guess, so I'm guessing."

"No, not that! I say, 'Guess what,' and you're supposed to say, 'What'?" she explained carefully.

"Oh. Okay, let's try again."

"Guess what?" she said patiently.

"Um, monkeys?" he replied.

"No! I told you, you're supposed to say, 'What'?"

"Oh, yeah." He cleared his throat, looked like he was about to say something terribly important, opened his mouth. Sophie's mouth fell open, and her eyes widened in anticipation. She craned her neck toward him, waiting.

"Wha...wha..." he teased her. "Um, let's see, *what* was that word? *What* was it? Oh, yeah, WHAT!"

She clapped her hands and high-fived him.

"Guess what?" she said again, to which he snapped off, "What?"

"I'm going to be five tomorrow," and she held up all five fingers on her right hand, right in front of Stuart's face.

"Wow!" he said. "You're sure about that?" teasing her.

"Yes! Mommy's going to have a cake and presents, and you're invited," she said firmly, nodding her head once up and down.

"You, too, Aunt Ashley," she said to Ashley, who smiled.

"Wow, five. How about that?" Stuart said. He had no way to gauge the age of a small child. He'd thought she was younger somehow.

"You're a bigger girl than I thought you were, and now you're going to be...,"

Something tickled at the back of his mind, something bothersome.

"Five," he finished slowly, looking at Jillian with a blank expression.

Her face was white, her mouth slightly open.

Stuart looked at Ashley, who looked like a bomb had gone off.

"Um, I'm going to go unpack our stuff. Hey, Sophie, come help me put your things away, okay?"

Sophie climbed off of Stuart's lap and followed Ashley into the bedroom, leaving the two of them alone in a charged silence.

Stuart stared at Jillian, daring her to speak. She dropped her eyes, tears forming in her eyelashes.

"Stuart," she whispered. "I'm so sorry. I tried to tell you. I didn't want it coming out like this."

"Let me get this straight, Jill. Doing the math, Sophie turning five tomorrow, means you got pregnant while we were together. So, who's the father?" he asked in a deadly tone of voice.

Shocked, she looked up quickly, "What do you mean, who's the father? You are, of course!"

He stared at her.

"Stuart, I'm so sorry you found out like this—I was trying to tell you, I tried more than once, but," she began.

He stood up, glaring down at her. "You tried? You mean when we broke up, right? Right before you put that ring on the dresser, you *tried*," air quotes here, "to tell me you were pregnant? Funny, I can't seem to recall any of those words coming out of your mouth."

"No, I didn't try *then*, but I've been trying to tell you since you got here...,"

He let the ridiculousness of that comment linger in the air, like something insubstantial, a featherweight thing, not at all representative of the heaviness, the seriousness, of the information that he should have been given years ago. Years that he could have been with Sophie, maybe even with Jillian.

As the family, they never got the chance to be.

"All this time," he whispered, "I've blamed myself for our breakup. Why, Jillian? Did you hate me that much? I know I was a jerk at the end, but what about all the time before that? Didn't I mean any more to you than that? Dear God, was I nothing more to you than a...a *sperm donor?*"

Jillian sat with her head bowed, sobbing, tears running down her cheeks. She made no attempt to wipe them away.

He stared at her, but she was mute. There was no more to say to him, and he couldn't think of anything to say to her. He turned around and left. He found the nearest pub and ordered whiskey, neat.

CHAPTER THIRTY

Nursing his third drink, slowly munching on peanuts from the bar, Stuart vaguely registered Dan Young sliding into the other side of his booth. Dan ordered a scotch for himself. They sat in silence, sipping, Dan glancing now and then at Stuart, he childishly pretending Dan wasn't there.

Dan spoke first. "I guess you know everything now."

Stuart slid his eyes to Dan's. "So, you know, too? Am I the last guy to know about my own daughter?"

Dan sighed. "Actually, we just found out about that. Jillian's always been quiet about her background, and we didn't want to pry. But when your face started showing up in the national news...at first, she acted like something was up with that, and then she told us that you were her ex-fiancé, that you'd broken up a long time ago. It wasn't until this week that she told us you're Sophie's father."

"That's messed up. You know that, right?" Stuart said, glaring at Dan.

Dan was quiet for a while, looked out the window.

"Yes, it is. Look, this is none of my business— " Dan said.

"You're right—it isn't," said Stuart angrily, setting down his whiskey glass too hard, sloshing some on the tabletop.

Dan stood, waved to the waiter for the check.

"I'll pay and leave you to it, then," he said painfully.

"It's none of your business, that's true, but I don't exactly have a lot of people to talk to about this," Stuart said, not looking up. "You can go, or you can stay."

Dan slowly sat down, waved away the waiter, who took one look at their faces and made himself scarce.

"Actually, I have this one girl back in Austin. Her name's Samantha, and she works at a restaurant that I, uh, frequent. She's been the one to listen to me for a long time, and she's damn cute, you know what I mean? Freckles, girl next door type, and her lips, man. And she's a good kisser."

He looked up at Dan quickly.

"That's all it ever was, though. We mostly talked about Jillian. We're just friends, but what I'm trying to say is she's been just about my only real friend, until now."

He sighed, whispered, "What the hell am I going to do? This is a righteous mess. Jillian has cancer, I just found out Sophie is my daughter."

He took another sip, looked at Dan, shaking his head.

"I can't believe she didn't tell me all those years ago. What kind of a woman does that? Gets pregnant by her fiancé—*her fiancé*, for Christ's sakes—and then takes off without a word about it?"

Dan was silent, regarding Stuart carefully.

"Huh? Got any ideas about that, Dan?" he said softly, sadly.

"You would have to ask her about that," Dan said.

"Yeah, I guess I would," said Stuart, "But I don't know if I want to know the answer. It's not good, no matter what it is. *You were an asshole, so I didn't tell you*, or, maybe, *I wanted a baby, so I got pregnant without your consent* or something else I can't even think of."

"Last I checked, it takes two to make a baby," said Dan matter-of-factly.

"Huh?" said Stuart.

"Well, the way I figure it," said Dan, holding up his glass and twirling the whiskey, staring at the amber liquid in the glint of the light, "there's only one way to make sure you don't have a kid, and that's to not have sex with the opposite sex.

"Do you know how many children are conceived while their parents are supposedly using birth control, supposedly don't want to make a baby? My brother, who lives in Seattle, is an Ob/Gyn, and he assures me that it's most of the babies he delivers."

Dan chuckled. Stuart stared at him.

"So, I'm responsible for Sophie?"

"Do you doubt that you're her father?"

Stuart thought about Sophie. In many ways, she was the image of her mother, but in other ways, there were strong inklings that she was his daughter. The shape of her nose, the spacing of her eyes, her coloring. She reminded Stuart of someone else—*his mother*. Yes, she bore a striking resemblance to her grandmother. That thought gave him an unexpectedly warm feeling.

"No, I don't doubt she's mine."

"Well, then, you helped make her," said Dan.

"I guess I did, but that still doesn't excuse Jillian for not telling me."

"Nope, it doesn't."

Stuart gulped the last of his whiskey.

"So, how do I get past this?"

Dan was silent.

"I mean, part of me just wants to get back to Austin, forget I ever came here, get on with the life I had there."

But as soon as he said those words, he knew. There was no way he'd leave Sophie like that, no way he could pass another day without seeing her.

"But, there's Sophie." He looked up at Dan. "Have you ever seen a more adorable little girl?" Stuart asked. "I mean, look at her!"

He pulled out his cell phone and started scrolling through photos of Sophie as if Dan didn't live right there with them, see them every day. Feeling stupid, he stopped, put the phone away.

He blew out a breath.

"What am I going to do about her mother? I've had time to think since I found out, and I think the first thing I have to do is hire an attorney. I want my parental rights established as soon as possible. I want court-ordered visitation, and not this every other weekend bullshit. I want half of her time. I don't care about the child support—I'm more than willing to pay. Jill could use it, and I can afford it. But I want my visitation time." He was angry, adamant.

"And Jillian?" asked Dan, face looking tight.

"What about her?" said Stuart harshly.

Dan sat stone-faced, staring at Stuart.

"Okay, maybe I haven't thought this all the way through," admitted Stuart. "I guess it might be a little upsetting if I take that approach."

"A little upsetting?" Dan said.

Stuart sighed. "Okay, a lot upsetting. Doesn't mean I won't do it, though," said Stuart. "I have rights."

They were quiet for a time, sipping, staring out the window at the waning light of the day.

"Look, I think you'd better think this through before you do anything," Dan said. "Jillian has cancer. She's going to need every bit of her will and strength to get through it. She's going to need lots of emotional support. Now, you've been running around here telling her how much you love her for weeks—yes, I know about that—she confided in me and Karen. She was happy knowing you still loved her, although scared about how it might change when she told you about Sophie. And, now you've had a shock finding out Sophie is yours. But think about Sophie—how much she needs her Mom."

Dan fiddled with his drink some more.

"If you run out on Jillian now, you'd best keep on running, because I don't think it would be good for Sophie to have you in and out of her life. And it certainly won't be good for Jillian to have that kind of uncertainty while she's fighting cancer. Better to get it over with, go back to Austin. Better for both of them."

Stuart couldn't believe what he was hearing. *Run out on Sophie? Leave her forever, go back to Austin?* Not have his newly found daughter in his life. No way! No fucking way would he do that.

But Dan was right about Jillian. While it was totally unfair that she'd kept Sophie a secret from him, it would also be stressful for Jillian to put her through a custody fight.

But that wasn't his fault, was it? He wasn't the one who'd held back on the most important information of his life.

They sat in silence again. Stuart motioned for the waiter, who approached tentatively. He paid the entire bill, though Dan protested. They stood and walked out of the restaurant.

It was a beautiful evening—clear skies, stars beginning to pop out. They stood looking up at the sky for a minute or two. Stuart felt a tightness in his chest. He should be with Jillian right now, enjoying the beauty of this evening. Tucking Sophie in bed, reading her a story.

Damn her.

They shook hands good night and went their separate ways.

The next morning, Stuart called an attorney friend in Austin, described the situation, and got some advice. He hung up, knowing what he intended to do. To hell with how Jill felt about it. She'd thought nothing of depriving him of his daughter for five years.

⁂

Stuart showed up at Jillian's cabin late that afternoon. She'd called, asked for a meeting. She answered his knock immediately as if she were standing nervously on the other side of the door, waiting.

They sat in the living room, Stuart feeling restless. Sophie wasn't there; she was with Ashley, who'd extended her trip another day.

Jillian looked composed and serious, hands folded in her lap. Back straight—that beautiful posture.

"Thanks for being here, Stuart."

He nodded, said nothing, distant. She'd find out later when the papers were served.

She sighed. "First of all, I want to tell you how deeply sorry I am for holding back about Sophie, for not telling you at the time I was pregnant. I want to say more about that, not to excuse it, but to explain it a little. But first, I want you to know that I want you to be Sophie's Dad in every way that you're interested in being her Dad, with one request." She stopped, chewed her lip a bit, worry lines creasing her forehead.

He waited.

"As I told you before, I don't want her hurt from the experience of a part-time father who comes and goes. I can't keep you from doing whatever you choose to do—I guess now that you know, she's yours, too. But I'm asking you, please, be all in with her. She deserves that."

"I can't believe you even think you have to say this," said Stuart. "Of course, I want to be a full-time Dad. I have no intention of being halfway with her."

Jillian nodded, looking relieved.

"Okay, that's good. Now, I want you to know that I'm willing to sign whatever papers we need to sign so that you are legally her father. I— I'm sorry—but I didn't put you on her birth certificate. But I understand, from some internet research, it's not hard to get that done. Meanwhile, I want to draw up all the papers immediately and get them signed, given what's happening with my health."

She stopped, paused like she was mentally reviewing a checklist.

"We can establish paternity in one of two ways. One, we can do a genetic test. I totally understand if you want to do that to be sure. Two, we can do an Affidavit of Paternity—the forms are on the internet, and we can do them ourselves. Once we get that done, we do the custody papers."

She paused again.

Stuart was shocked. She'd been thinking all of this through while he was busy planning his legal attack, which now appeared to be entirely unnecessary. The wind went out of his sails.

"Oh—and one more thing. I'm not interested at all in child support. We are doing fine financially, so I don't want to hear anything about that. You can set up a college fund for Sophie if you wish, but even if you don't, that's okay too. I can handle it."

"Of course, I'm going to pay child support," said Stuart adamantly. "That's what any good father would do. I'm not going to shirk that duty, no matter what you say."

He puffed up again. It felt good to assert his rights, rights that had been usurped for years.

"I'm not trying to get money out of you, Stuart," Jillian said quietly. "I don't want you to think that's what these past few weeks have been about."

"And what exactly were these past few weeks about?" he said, hostility sparking off of him. He couldn't help himself.

She looked down, her cheeks turning pink.

"Uh-huh. I guess you were just a little bit horny, huh?"

She looked up at him, tears glistening.

Jesus, God, could he never filter his anger?

"I'm sorry, Jill. That was uncalled for," he said, ashamed. He raked his hand through his hair.

"I—I'm sorry," he said. "I'm not good at this stuff. It's a lot to process, and I need time."

Meaning, I'll try not to take your head off every chance I get, he thought.

But not meaning, *I've forgiven you, and let's cozy up again.* Not ready for that, maybe never will be.

Still, he reflected. Over the past few weeks, he'd told Jillian how much he loved her. She'd never said it back, not once. He'd managed to be okay with that by telling himself that, of course, she felt that way, she just wasn't ready to say it.

He'd never felt so confused and conflicted about a woman. It was as if he'd lived three different chapters with Jillian.

Chapter one, happily dating, falling in love, getting engaged, almost getting married.

Chapter two, breaking up, separated unhappily, nothing resolved, just pulled apart by his cruddy behavior and her bad decisions.

Chapter three, reunited, falling back in love again.

And now? What was Chapter Four? Now, they were estranged again. Familiar territory, only now, there was his daughter, Sophie. Now, he'd see Jillian every time he picked up and returned Sophie. Totally different scenario, one that would be massively uncomfortable.

Because as angry as he was, he was still in love with her. Couldn't expect those kinds of feelings to die instantly. Not at all hopeful it could be worked out, but, still, in love. With someone who'd lied to him, by omission, about one of the most important things in life, someone who had yet to indicate she still loved him.

"Stuart?"

He looked up at her.

"It's Sophie's birthday today. I sent Ashley out with her to get ice cream, but I promised her that when she got back, we would have her birthday party. There's going to be another party on Saturday with her friends, but I told her tonight was family time. She's so excited, and I want it to be fun for her."

She paused.

"I—I want you here for her party, today, and Saturday if you can. It's important to her. She has a bond with you now. I don't know how to handle telling her that you're—you're her Dad. Maybe we can get some advice about that from someone, a professional. But today, can we set aside things between us enough to make this special for her?"

She was tentative, clearly afraid of his response.

"Of course," said Stuart softly. "I want to do whatever it takes to make that little girl happy."

Jillian looked sad.

"I wish...I wish I'd realized all those years ago. But I should have known. I was so stupid."

Stuart didn't say anything. Yes, she had been stupid.

"What can I do to help get things ready?" he asked.

She seemed to brush away her sadness and get in gear.

They took things out of the trunk of her car that she'd hidden earlier—birthday cake, a couple of balloons, wrapped gifts. They set up the cabin with everything and sat back to survey their work.

Sophie and Ashley arrived just after that, and the party went perfectly. Sophie unwrapped her gifts, squealed in delight, and ran to her mother to kiss her. Stuart gave her the stuffed penguin he'd brought back from Austin. She held it close, regarded Stuart solemnly, and said, "Thank you."

By the time they'd had dinner, cake, and opened gifts, it was past Sophie's bedtime. Stuart tucked a happy but exhausted Sophie in bed while Ashley and Jillian talked quietly in the living room in front of the fire. After making sure Sophie was asleep, he went into the living room, said good-bye a bit stiffly and formally, and left. Jillian walked him to his car.

"We can get started on the legal work as soon as you want," she said.

"Okay. I'll call you," he said, climbing into his car. He drove away, leaving her standing there, watching him go.

After Sophie's birthday, over the next few days, Stuart and Jillian conducted the necessary conversations to handle the legal details. They were both distant and polite, but not warm. Whatever relationship they'd sparked up again had withered as if someone had come upon a tiny fire and thrown water on it.

They quickly came to a shared custody arrangement. Stuart would find a place to lease in the area, flying back to Austin when needed for business. It was too soon to figure out the long-term picture. Plus, they still had the hurdle of explaining things to Sophie. So, they created a visitation/custody agreement that covered the next year, with the understanding that they would take stock after Jillian finished her cancer treatments.

Stuart insisted on establishing regular child support payments as part of their agreement. Jillian said she would accept the money, but that she would put it into a college fund. Stuart told her that the money was to be used to buy things for Sophie, ensuring her comfort. Surely there were times when Jillian's budget precluded getting things for Sophie, maybe an extra winter coat, a toy she wanted but couldn't afford? Jillian agreed that yes, that was true, and yes, she would do those things when appropriate without spoiling Sophie.

The unspoken was Jillian's uncertain future. Although her doctors assured her that her prognosis was excellent with radiation and chemotherapy, still, there was no guarantee that she would go into remission. And, if she did go into remission, that the cancer wouldn't return.

It was deeply uncomfortable for Stuart to have these conversations, and he felt worn out after each one.

The ray of sunshine was time with Sophie. The difficulty was trying to explain why he picked her up to go hang out with him, without her mother. Jillian told her that she needed to take care of some work things, and would she please go hang out with Stuart for a while.

At first, Sophie balked, not wanting to go anywhere without her mother, so Stuart hung out with her at the cabin. But after a couple of days of that, he was able to persuade her to go out for a meal with him, keeping the time short. Gradually, he increased his time with her away from her mother, and she seemed to get more comfortable.

It was time for Jillian to go for her first round of treatments. Stuart insisted on getting rooms for them—separate, of course, so they could take Sophie, and he could look out for her while Jillian was at the clinic. They talked about having Stuart stay at the cabin with Sophie, but both felt it was too soon for an extended period of time without her mother.

Stuart drove them to Seattle, only a couple of hours away. They checked into their hotel first, then headed for the clinic. Luckily, the clinic featured a family waiting room, with books and toys for children. It was warm, brightly colored, and didn't look at all like a medical facility. Stuart was relieved. He'd dreaded having Sophie sit in a cold waiting room, that it would be too sterile and frightening.

They'd told her in advance that her Mom needed to see a doctor to help her get well. They'd agreed that talking about cancer would be okay, but in simple terms. They explained that no one knew why she had it and that it wasn't anyone's fault. It wasn't Sophie's fault, they stressed. They reassured her that everything would be normal except for these occasional trips to Seattle.

Before the nurse called her in, Jillian spoke to Sophie softly.

"Remember when I told you about how I have to go to the doctor, and it means I have to go to a different room for a while? And Stuart is going to take care of you?"

"Yes, Mommy," Sophie said solemnly.

"I want you to be good—don't make any trouble for Stuart, okay?"

Not that Sophie ever made trouble for anyone. She was the most well-behaved five-year-old Stuart had ever seen.

"Yes, Mommy," she said seriously.

"Okay. Give me a big hug and a kiss," said Jillian. And she did.

The nurse ushered Jillian to the back, and Stuart got out the deck of cards he'd brought.

"Ever play Go Fish, Sophie?" he said, shuffling the cards.

"No. What's that?" she asked.

"I'll teach you," he told her, passing out the cards.

They played for a few minutes. Sophie asked where her mother was.

"She's still with the doctor, bird," he said.

"When's she coming back out?"

"Soon," he said.

Next diversion thought Stuart. He pulled out Charlotte's Web to read, but Sophie pushed it closed.

"I want to save it for bed," she said.

"Okay. Let's go get something to eat. Are you hungry?" he said.

She shook her head.

"Well, I am. Let's check out the cafeteria downstairs."

They went, he ordered a turkey sandwich and French fries. Sophie refused to order anything. But when his food came out, he put a few fries on a napkin in front of her with some catsup and soon, she ate one, then another, and before long, she'd eaten all the fries on her napkin.

After that, Sophie's eyes began to look heavy, and Stuart wondered what to do. They hadn't discussed Sophie taking a nap at the clinic, and there wasn't any place for that, anyway. Not unless he took her back to the hotel.

They went back up the elevator to the waiting room. Stuart asked about Jillian's progress. The girl at the desk said she would check. The answer—she was almost done.

Stuart and Sophie sat in the waiting area, but it was obvious that Sophie was having a hard time. She looked tired and restless, but none of the ideas Stuart presented for things to do worked. She shook her head, rubbed her eyes, turned down the corners of her mouth.

"I want Mommy," she said, tears forming in her beautiful blue eyes, huge round tears that rolled over her ivory and pink cheeks, spilling off her wobbly chin.

Oh crap, thought Stuart. *This is terrible!* He felt his heart cracking, seeing Sophie cry.

He pulled her onto his lap, wrapped his arms around her, tried to distract her, but to no avail. She pushed Stuart away, broke into full-on crying, asking for her mother.

"Mommy! I want my Mommy," she wailed. The nurse at the front desk stared at them with pity.

Stuart stood up with her, began walking around the waiting room, then out into the hallway, Sophie continuing to cry.

"Where's Mommy? Let's go back and get her!" she cried.

They went back into the waiting room, Stuart now desperate to find some kind of distraction. He picked up Charlotte's Web, but she turned her face away. He picked up a puzzle and tried to get her to look at it, but she wouldn't do it.

Just when he was about to reach up and yank out his own hair in frustration, the waiting room door opened, and Jillian walked out. She looked pale and weak, but she ran to Sophie, gathered her in her arms, and held her, soothing her. Sophie's sobs morphed into a mild hiccup.

They decided that Sophie needed her own bed, so they checked out of the motel. Stuart drove them home, Sophie asleep in her car seat in the back. Back at the cabin, they put Sophie to bed, made a late dinner, and sat in Jillian's living room briefly. She seemed drained, but otherwise okay. They were both quiet except for talking about the next steps.

Two days later, Jillian called Stuart in a panic.

"Please, can you pick Sophie up from school? I—I had to stay home today. I'm so exhausted, I can barely move."

"Of course," Stuart told her. But when he got Sophie to the cabin, Jillian was sound asleep, so he made dinner, helped Sophie with her homework, played a game, and generally kept her occupied so she wouldn't disturb her mother.

The next day, it was more of the same. Jillian could barely move. Stuart took over and took care of Sophie. He brought food to Jillian in bed, and she managed to sit up and take a few nibbles, then pushed away the food. She looked drained and frightened, asking if Sophie was okay.

Later, Sophie crawled in bed next to her mother to get her

337

attention, opening one of her books and pointing to the pictures. Stuart explained to Sophie that the medicine Mommy was taking made her very sleepy and that they needed to let her rest. She mumbled okay and let Stuart lead her out of the bedroom.

And so, began Jillian's treatments. For Jillian's chemotherapy treatments, they worked out arrangements so both Stuart and Sophie could sit in the same room with Jillian, the I.V. line discreetly tucked under a blanket so as not to alarm Sophie. The room was cozy and calm. Jillian dozed under a dose of anti-anxiety medication, and Sophie contentedly read her books and played games.

Stuart watched over Jillian, interacted with nurses and doctors, took notes. He got juice and fed snacks to Sophie. He read books to Sophie, tucked in Jillian's blankets, called for an extra blanket when Jillian began to shiver.

On the second day following treatments, he showed up early in the day, urged Jillian to stay in bed and let him take care of things. She regarded him carefully, and at one point asked, "Why are you doing all of this, Stuart? I'm grateful, but ..." to which he replied gently for her to "shut up." She sighed, rolled over, pulled up the blankets, and was out for hours.

After the third treatment, Jillian's hair began to fall out. That was a very bad day. She couldn't stop leaking tears, though she tried, not wanting to upset Sophie. But Sophie looked at her Mom in alarm and asked her not to cry. Stuart, getting better at it, managed to distract her while Jillian calmed down.

The next day, Stuart packed her into the car, drove her to the local beauty shop, and got Jillian a complete buzz cut. He then surprised her with a handmade wig, the same color as Jillian's hair, but in a cute short style that he said made her look like Jennifer Lawrence. She rolled her eyes but tried it on and smiled at herself in the mirror for the first time in days.

⁂

Jillian wore her J-Law wig, and although she was visibly thinner, still looked stunning. Sophie was dressed in her best pink jeans with the purple sweater, hair pulled into a ponytail. Stuart was anxious, but it was time.

They all sat in a booth at one of the downtown restaurants. After the food was ordered, Jillian and Stuart sipping iced tea, Sophie slurping her root beer, they looked at each other, and Stuart nodded his head.

They'd consulted the best experts they knew—Dan and Karen Young.

"One thing I know seems to work well with kids, and that is the simple truth. Not a lot of complicated explanations that they're too young to understand. Just say it. After that, trust that over time, they will come to you—she will come to you—with her questions."

Karen agreed, adding that since every child was different, of course, pay attention to Sophie's reaction and get help if she didn't seem to handle it well.

Stuart had tapped the brakes on this meeting for a long time, more afraid of what would happen from this revelation than of anything he'd been through before. Sophie was just a kid—the adults had made big decisions that would affect her for the rest of her life. And he knew exactly what that felt like.

Were they making the best decisions for Sophie? Did she really need to know the details of how she came into the world? Would she understand any of it at this age? Were they doing this for themselves, or for her?

What if she didn't handle it well? What if she rejected the news? Rejected Stuart as her father?

Jillian had been patient, but finally, she'd persuaded Stuart it was the right thing to do.

"I think it's a mistake to put it off, especially with my, you know, because of the diagnosis. What if something happens to me? In the middle of that—to tell her then—I think it's too much. It's better to do this now." She was right, of course.

They'd decided Jillian should tell her, so she did.

"Sophie, I have something to tell you. It's a surprise."

Sophie perked up. "What, Mommy?"

"The surprise is that Stuart is your Dad."

Sophie's eyes widened, and she looked solemnly at Stuart, then back at her Mom. She slurped her root beer again. She slid her eyes to Stuart, then back to her Mom.

She smiled a little.

"Okay."

Jillian looked at Stuart, who shrugged his shoulders and shook his head, bewildered.

"Um, Sophie, are you really okay with this?" Jillian said, breaking one of the rules. She'd read that you're not supposed to give a child the impression that her feelings would change a situation that couldn't be changed.

"Sure, Mom."

They looked at each other again. Stuart couldn't believe how easy that was. He'd dreaded this moment, irrationally feared that Sophie would be upset, that she'd be unhappy somehow.

"You know, you don't have to call me Dad, or anything, not until you feel comfortable with all of this, or—or, never if you want," said Stuart awkwardly.

Sophie looked slightly alarmed.

"I can't call you 'Dad'?"

"Of course, you can! I just don't want you to feel like—uh, that is, I—I mean, this is all very new, and...," Stuart stumbled, at a loss. He stopped, dumbfounded.

"Oh," Sophie said. Then she grinned slyly.

"Okay, Daaaaaad!" she giggled, pointing at him.

His heart swelled, his throat choked up, and he beat back a tear.

When they arrived for Jillian's third treatment, a new nurse, much older than the usual receptionist, whispered to Stuart.

"The doctor wants to see the two of you today, without your little girl in the room," she said. "I don't want to alarm you, but it is important."

Stuart's heart thudded.

"Okay, what do I do with Sophie, though?"

"When you get in the room, I will come in and distract her with something to do outside of the room, and the doctor will come in to talk with you."

Stuart finished the conversation with the nurse, then turned to face Jillian and Sophie, putting on a stoic mask. After what seemed like an eternity, they were called back to the treatment room, but instead, were ushered into a doctor's office. Immediately, the nurse asked Sophie to help her pick out a surprise for Mommy. After looking at Jillian, who looked surprised, but who nodded, she went, and the doctor walked in.

"Hello, Jillian. Stuart, right? I'm Doctor Jorgensen," he said, shaking Stuart's hand. He was young—mid-30s—with an earnest expression. He had blond hair and wore wire-rimmed glasses that he pushed up his nose using the center bridge. "Please, sit down," he said, indicating the two chairs in front of his desk, which he circled to sit down opposite them. Stuart noted the numerous framed degrees and certificates of specialization on the wall. Maybe he looked younger than his actual age.

"I'm sorry to be so cryptic, but I thought it was best to have this conversation in person, so the nurses and I came up with this plan to have your daughter out of the room." He looked apologetic.

"The bad news is that your cancer has progressed, Jillian. It is now stage three. Don't panic. It is very treatable, but it means we will need to do surgery. We think it's in your lymph nodes, so we want to surgically remove those, send them to the lab, and then re-evaluate your treatment."

"Why didn't we know this sooner?" Stuart asked tersely.

"I'm sorry, but this these things are inexact, you see...," began Dr. Jorgensen, sounding academic, waxing into a lecture, but Stuart interrupted.

"An inexact science, right. And the practice of medicine...well, that's why they call it 'practice,' right?" Sarcastic. He was winding up for more, but then he got a glimpse of Jillian's face, white as a sheet. She was trembling.

He stuffed the rest of his ire.

"I understand how you feel," said Dr. Jorgensen, and Stuart thought, Yeah, I bet you do. Still wet behind the ears, probably never had anyone with cancer in your personal life.

"Let me go over the treatment plan. First, there won't be any chemo today. Instead, we will do the surgery in a couple of weeks, and that procedure...," he droned on, spewing out medical jargon and far too much information to take in. Stuart stopped him.

"Listen, Doc, this is way too much information right now. Slow down."

He started a voice recording on his smartphone, and the doctor started over, Stuart capturing every word so they could replay it all later.

"The bottom line is that we won't know what kind of treatment to do until we find out the extent of the cancer. There are actually levels of invasion in stage three cancer and depending on that...," he went on and on.

They went back to the waiting room, and the nurse brought out Sophie. Stuart announced that the doctors didn't need to give Mommy any medicine today, and wasn't that great? Instead, they were all going out to a great restaurant right there in Seattle to celebrate.

Jillian sat quietly, looking hollowed out. She faked a smile for Sophie's sake, but Stuart knew she wasn't feeling it. Dinner was mostly a bust. Neither Stuart nor Jillian felt like eating the five-star food placed in front of them. But Sophie ate a fair amount of the cheesy pasta dish they ordered for her.

Back at the hotel, with Sophie asleep in Jillian's bed, Stuart and Jillian tiptoed through the connecting door to his room, leaving it open, so they could hear her if she woke. They sat on the bed, leaning against the headboard, turned toward each other, talked softly.

Stuart got up at one point, opened his laptop, and did some research on the prognosis for stage three breast cancer. It wasn't good. The most advanced level of stage three was usually the precursor of stage four, and stage four was incurable. Stuart felt shell-shocked, couldn't imagine how bad Jillian was feeling inside.

They had major decisions to make. They talked into the night, ignoring the clock. As they did, Stuart's heart shifted, this time finding solid ground.

In every man's life there comes a moment when he must choose—between living in the past with anger and what should have been, or to have what he really wants now, and in choosing that, free himself of the past.

Three weeks later, after Jillian's surgery, they got the final news on her cancer.

CHAPTER THIRTY-ONE

"So, have you set the date?" Ben asked, heart in his throat. He and Michelle were sitting together at a dance event for Katie. Joe was out of town on business, and Liz had Jordan, so for once, he had time alone with her. Both stared ahead at the little girls prancing in tutus.

A small frown appeared on Michelle's forehead.

"Um, not yet. I have a trial coming up, and things are just so busy, it's hard to find the time."

She was quiet.

"Find the time?" he said.

This was his latest trick to keep Michelle talking. He'd read in a communication book that if you simply repeated the last few words the other person had spoken, it would get them to keep talking. It was a way of establishing "rapport," or so the book said.

Whatever it took.

Ben had found it tedious the first couple of times he'd tried it with Michelle, but lately, it seemed to be getting her to open up more.

"Right." She sighed.

He remained quiet.

"Actually, it's more me. I'm not sure...I'm not sure I'm ready for actually *being* married again. It didn't exactly turn out well for me the last time, and now it's much more complicated, with the kids, and...,"

And me, he thought.

Since her engagement to Joe, Michelle had gone even quieter.

When they were married, she wasn't exactly chatty, preferring instead to focus on getting things done, taking care of the kids, falling into bed exhausted at night and picking up a book to read, eyes drooping, book winding up on her chest. Ben removed her books at night and lay on his side, watching her sleep. Wondered what was in her head, what she thought about, what she dreamed about. Baffled about how to draw her out, he'd left her alone in her head, and allowed them to drift further and further apart.

That was then.

"It's complicated?" he offered.

"Yeah."

"How's that?" he said.

They continued to watch Katie's dance class, not looking at each other.

"It's hard to explain. I mean, I love Joe. Who wouldn't love Joe?"

Who wouldn't? He thought sarcastically.

"I mean, Joe is a great guy. He's—he's stable, he's kind, and he works hard. He's successful, he takes care of me, he's always there for me. Everyone—all his friends, his co-workers, even my friends now—*everyone* loves Joe."

Ben squirmed inside. This part of the conversation always drove him batshit crazy, but he'd learned to hide it. *Joe, Mr. Effing Wonderful.*

And the part she wouldn't say out loud to him, but he was sure it was there, was the part about how damn good looking he was, what a great lover.

"Everyone?" he said, unable to keep a little sarcasm out of his voice.

She slid her gaze sideways at Ben, which he observed out of the corner of his eye.

"Ben," she said.

"Well, you know, I tried to love him," he said in a flat but light-hearted voice, "but in the end, I had to give the rose to someone else."

She actually laughed.

They both watched Katie, smiling.

Back at Michelle's, Jordan lay sprawled between them across the sofa, and Katie sat on the floor cross-legged, eyes glued to the television. Post dinner and bath time, they were in pajamas. Michelle sipped red wine, and Ben sipped a beer.

"So, you don't have a date yet," he said, picking up the thread of their earlier conversation.

She looked at him over her wine glass.

"But we will, I'm sure," she said.

"I'm sure."

"Right," she said.

"Right."

She sighed.

"You know if you keep on saying that, at some point, it's going to be true," he said.

"I know," she said. She shook her head, gazing off into the corner of the room.

"What's wrong with me?" she asked the air as if Ben wasn't there. "I have this wonderful guy who adores me, and I can't seem to pull the trigger."

Ben couldn't think of what to say. *Pull the trigger? Wonderful guy? Wrong with you?* Nope, that wouldn't be right.

"Ben," she said.

He snapped back.

"What?"

"I asked, are you dating?" she said, that crinkle back in her forehead.

"Well, sure, of course, I am. I'm single, I'm a catch," his eyebrows up, his head nodding up and down, trying to make it sound real.

She smiled.

"You aren't dating," she said matter-of-factly, smirking.

"Yes, I am."

"Okay, tell me about your last date," she said smugly.

"Sure, I can do that," he said. "Just the other day, I..."

"What day?" she interrupted.

"Um, it was Friday," then realizing the error, because he'd had the kids on Friday night, "Nope, it was Thursday. Yeah, it was Thursday night, and I met this girl on match.com, and we met for drinks." He nodded his head once.

"Where?"

"Huh?"

"Where did you go for drinks?"

"Well, you know, that place, uh, downtown, right on the ..." he stumbled.

She waited.

He slumped. So embarrassing.

"Well, actually, I haven't been dating that much," he said.

There, *now you know*, he thought.

"Ben."

He looked up.

"What?"

"Why not?" she asked quietly. "Cause, you *are* a catch, and it's been long enough."

Why not? Why not date?

Michelle was engaged, even if uncertain about setting the date. He hadn't been with anyone since they separated. Sure, he'd gone on a handful of exploratory dates for coffee or drinks, but that felt awkward.

"The kids are done for the day, don't you think?" he said, picking up Jordan.

"Stalling?" Michelle said, rolling her eyes.

He carried Jordan to bed and tucked him in. He came back for Katie, now looking very droopy, and repeated the process. Yes, definitely stalling, but now it was time. His heart rate kicked up a notch.

Back in the living room, he sat down much closer to Michelle, gently took her wine glass as her eyes widened, set it down, and took her hands.

"Why am I not dating?" he said.

She said nothing, mouth slightly open.

"Because I'm still in love with you," he said, his heart feeling like it might pound out of his chest. *"I still love you,"* he whispered.

"I blew it with you, Michelle. I understand why you're marrying Joe. He's the guy who's never cheated on you, the faithful guy you can trust. I get it. I'm the guy you can never trust again."

He closed his eyes, raised her hands to his lips, kissed them both, rubbed his thumbs along them briefly, gently, then dropped them.

He stood, walked to the door, opened it, gently closed it behind him. The last glimpse he had of Michelle, she was still sitting there, head bowed, wiping away a tear.

They didn't see each other for a couple of weeks. Ben traveled to the wineries in Napa, focusing on new customer acquisition, and the time flew.

Alone in his hotel at night, he still felt raw, exposed, after that night with Michelle. He'd opened his heart, shown her exactly where he stood with her. Since then, she'd been awkward, polite, but no longer as warm and open as she'd been prior to that evening. He felt doubly raw, his confused feelings compounded by embarrassment.

Calling the kids at night, she'd answer the phone and almost immediately say, "Katie, it's your Dad," or "Jordan, come talk to Daddy." She handed the phone off to the kids, didn't bother to take it back to say good-bye.

Once, he tried to talk to her, over the phone from Napa, after quite a few wine tastings.

"Michelle, about that night," he began, but she interrupted him.

"I don't want to talk about it," she said. "Don't worry about it," she said, closing the door to that conversation.

But he wasn't worried about it. He was—what was he?

He'd been doing so well, getting emotionally centered. Learning how to listen to Michelle, how to get her to open up, even just in small ways.

He'd fooled himself into thinking he was making progress with her, finding a way back into her heart. What an idiot.

All he'd done was delude himself. Prolonged his own journey to finding a new relationship, someone to love him.

Then, just before he returned from Napa, she dropped the bomb. In a text message.

FYI, we have a wedding date. May 15th. Just wanted you to know.

May 15th—only one month away. Ben's heart dropped.

Ben grabbed a few shirts off of the rack in his closet. He rapidly folded them and placed them in a small travel bag. He stood in the middle of his bedroom, dazed. Went into the bathroom and grabbed a few items—toothbrush, razor, deodorant—stuffed them into a plastic baggie, went back into the bedroom, and threw it into the bag.

He pulled out his phone, tapped, scrolled. Flight in three hours. Not time to get an Uber, not yet. He paced around the apartment.

Someone knocked on the door. He flinched. Who could that be?

For sure, not Michelle. After all, tomorrow was her big day.

Someone banged on the door, calling out, "Ben! Open up."

Shocked, he pulled open the door, and Liz barged in, shoving past him, talking the whole time. "We have to do something about Michelle."

"What the hell are you talking about?" he said.

She looked up at Ben, the diminutive fury. "I'm talking about her so-called wedding!" She was breathing hard. "She has no business getting married tomorrow, not to that guy, anyway," she said. She paced.

"I mean, there's nothing really wrong with Joe. It's just that he's too, too..."

"Perfect?" said Ben.

"Right! And he's got this, this..."

"Hair?" said Ben.

"Yes! And his, his teeth are too..."

"White?" offered Ben.

"Right! You've got to *do* something," she finished, stopping in front of him, hand on her cocked hip, eyes blazing.

"Yeah, well, that's not my problem," said Ben, turning around and heading into the bedroom. He came back with his bag, dumped it by the door, and stood there, arms crossed.

"Are you kidding me?" she said, glaring at him. "If it wasn't for you, none of this would be happening!"

"And we have plowed that ground enough, haven't we? I know I'm a dirt-bag, I know I blew it with Michelle, I know she doesn't want anything to do with me except as a co-parent to the kids. I get it!" Ben couldn't believe he'd raised his voice.

"As she should!" yelled Liz. But she stopped pacing, stood still, and seemed to be working on ratcheting down her anger.

"Look, Ben, I'm sorry about that," Liz said. Ben was shocked. Liz *never* apologized, to anyone. *Ever.*

He softened.

"It's okay," he said, gesturing to the sofa. "Let's sit down for a minute. But I don't have much time. I'm heading out."

She raked her hand through her curls, shook her head, looked up at him intently.

"You can't leave. You have to stop this wedding," she said, in her usual cut-to-the-chase style.

"No, I don't, Liz. Michelle loves Joe, and it seems he loves her, and they're getting married tomorrow."

"You still don't have a fucking clue, do you?" she said, raising her eyes to Ben's and shaking her head.

He stared at her, confused once again. Fumbling around in the dark, trying to figure out his own life as if it were a map written in a foreign language.

"What are you talking about?"

"I'm talking about love, you idiot," she said, but softly, no longer venomous.

"Love," he said, puzzled.

"Yes, love. She still loves you."

"Loves *me*?" he was totally lost now.

"Yes, you. I have to admit, I didn't see it for a long time, even though I went along with your plan to win her back. I figured you'd give up fast, and that would be that. But you didn't," she said, looking in his eyes, surprised.

"Then she got engaged, and I just couldn't see that happening. I mean, Joe is a great guy, and all," she said.

"Yeah, I know, he's Mr. Effing Wonderful," said Ben sarcastically.

"Yes, he is," she said simply, staring at Ben.

"But he's not the man she really loves, the man she's loved for years."

Ben sat back, stunned.

"Wait a second, did she tell you this?" he asked, suspicious.

"No, she didn't, but there are some things that don't have to be said, that are so obvious. For one thing, she's about to get married, and you know what she said to me yesterday? She said she was, quote, *'ready for the whole thing to be over with.'* Said she hoped she could pick up her spirits once the wedding was over with, have a good time on the honeymoon. As if this was one of her court cases! She says things like that right before a trial because she's anxious about it or whatever. But this is her wedding!"

352

"Well, maybe that's normal. It is a lot to handle, planning a wedding, and she has a big job plus two kids to deal with along the way."

Liz looked at him like he was an idiot.

"Do you remember when you guys got married? Of course, you do. But you probably don't know what happened right before your wedding."

"What do you mean?" Ben asked, not sure he wanted to hear the answer.

"It was two weeks before, the night of her bachelorette party. Everyone else was gone, and it was just the two of us. Granted, we'd had a lot to drink, but you know Michelle. She doesn't really open up."

Two peas in a pod, thought Ben. Sisters.

He waited.

"So, we're sitting there, looking at all the crap everywhere from partying all evening, and she gets this ridiculous look on her face. All glowing, big silly smile, and I ask her what she's thinking about, and she says, *'I'm thinking about him, about tomorrow, and about how little I will miss being single.'*

"She turns to me and suddenly looks all serious, and says, 'Liz, it's so scary, loving someone so much. Sometimes I feel like my heart is just too full—like I can hardly stand it, but then he comes over, and he puts his arms around me, and we do this silly little swaying thing, staring into each other's eyes, grinning ridiculously. And then I feel like I'm home, home in the deepest possible way, in a place I never want to leave.'"

Liz looked astonished at the memory. "Michelle never talks about her feelings, you know that."

Ben nodded slowly, heart in his throat.

"And then, she says, 'Liz, I can't imagine my life without him. I'm afraid, afraid that someday, I could lose him. And I don't know how I would ever get over that.'"

Ben felt lost. He knew Michelle had loved him at one time, but this glimpse into her heart before their wedding rocked him to the core.

"There's something else," Liz continued. "Michelle acts so confident—she's a successful attorney, she's beautiful, she's all that. But deep down, she's insecure. It's an old story. She was the nerdy girl in school, always reading books, doing her writing, staying out of the limelight, even though guys wanted to date her. *But she never saw that.*

"She couldn't believe that a guy like you would ever choose her. She thought you were so good-looking, so sweet, and how could you want her, when you could have anyone? And then, when you cheated on her, it confirmed her worst fears. Woke up that nerdy, insecure girl."

They sat quietly, Ben stunned, Liz not speaking, staring at the floor.

"And now?" asked Ben quietly.

"And, after all this, she can't believe that you still love her, can't trust it."

"What can I do?" he asked, desperate.

"I don't know. Figure something out." Liz looked at him. Stood, went to the door, opened it, stopped.

"Ben?"

"What?"

"Don't let any grass grow," and she left.

Ben was frantic. After Liz had left the previous night, he'd canceled his flight, tried to get some sleep, but his mind had whirled. He'd tried to process what Liz had told him.

Michelle, still in love with him? Impossible! She'd moved on, she was engaged to Joe, getting *married* to Joe.

Michelle—gorgeous, smart Michelle—insecure? Afraid to believe he could love her? Going back to before they got married?

How could he not know this?

But he knew how. Because he'd never really tried to get her to open up. He'd taken her for granted, figured she would always be there. He'd been focused on his own inner world, a world populated with unlived alternate destinies.

He'd dwelled in that inner world most of the time, barely noticing the fact that Michelle was living in her own world as well. Until he'd begun to feel restless. Until he'd finally acted out one of those unlived alternate destinies.

He drove to Michelle's house and used his key to get in. The house was dark, quiet, and empty. Of course, it was. *Stupid, stupid*, he thought as he raced back to his car.

Why had he waited until this morning? Couldn't solidify his feelings, what he was going to do, until dawn. Too late, as always. She was probably walking down the aisle right now. Where, he couldn't say. Sacramento was a big city. Who knew where this wedding was taking place?

He pulled out his cell phone, texted Liz. No answer. Of course, not— her phone would be off. She would be standing at the front, next to her sister.

Michelle, walking down the aisle to another man, to Joe— undoubtedly grinning with happiness. Or, even worse, standing with tears brimming, overwhelmed by his love for this beautiful woman walking toward him.

Just as Ben had done years ago.

Michelle—lost to him forever.

This wasn't some Hallmark movie. He wasn't going to drive frantically to get to the church, arrive breathlessly, rush into the building, interrupt the ceremony just at the moment of the big question—"Does anyone here have any reason these two should not be wed?"—and make a scene. A dramatic, heroic scene—Ben declaring his undying love, Michelle turning around to him, throwing down her bouquet, running to him, jumping into his arms while Joe tried to engage him in a fistfight.

Stupid, stupid. He had no idea where she was.

Ben cried then—sobbed, head hunched over the steering wheel. Great gobs of tears, snot dripping. Like the time he'd had food poisoning and couldn't stop throwing up. Only this time, it was a purge of the deepest levels of pain he could imagine.

But the pain only ebbed. He didn't believe it would ever really stop.

Slowly he stopped crying. He sat, unmoored, drifting in thoughts, random, rambling memories of his and Michelle's life together. Life now permanently apart.

He motored the seat back, put his arm over his eyes. He was so tired. He drifted off to sleep.

Someone rapped on the driver's side window, startling him awake.

Michelle peered in at him. He peered back, confused.

She was dressed in her wedding dress. Not the white princess gown of their wedding years ago, but a simple, off-white suit.

"*Ben?*" she said.

Stupidly, he rolled down the window.

"Hi," he said.

"What are you doing here?"

"Uh, I'm—what are *you* doing here?" he said, suddenly sitting up.

She stood back, sighed. Gestured with her bouquet as she walked toward the front door.

Ben got out of the car, feeling like he was walking in soup, everything slowed down. There was a slight buzzing in his ears. He followed Michelle into the house.

He sat in the living room, across from Michelle, dazed. She gazed into the distance, then drew her eyes to Ben, said nothing, just stared with those beautiful blue eyes. Eyes that gradually misted with unshed tears. Her chin wobbled slightly.

"Michelle?"

"Yes?" softly, sadly.

"Are you married?"

"No." Softer.

"Are you getting married today?" Asked childlike.

"No." Almost a whisper. "I couldn't do it."

Huge breath in, huge breath out.

"Good."

He rose then, went to sit by her, took the bouquet away, and set it on the table. He put his arms around her, lifted her legs, and put them over his lap, held her close, in their old cuddle position. She melted into him, began to cry.

"Shh, baby, don't cry," he said softly. "I'm here. I'm never going away, ever again," he said with all his heart.

She sobbed. He held her even tighter.

"It's okay. I'm here. I'm sorry you couldn't trust me," he said. "I'm so sorry for everything."

She sniffed once, twice, wiped her nose on his shirt.

"That's not what did it," she said in a tiny voice.

"No?" he asked softly.

"No. Cheating on me—that was bad, horrible. But the thing that hurt the most was that you went away. You just...*gave up.* After that night, after you left me, left us."

She looked up at him, blue eyes still holding the pain.

He pulled a strand of her hair, tucked it behind her ear.

"I know. That was terrible. I can't even imagine how much that must have hurt. And, this doesn't excuse it—not in the slightest—but I didn't leave because I didn't love you. I left because I was so ashamed. I couldn't believe you would want me around ever again. And when I tried to call later, and you were so angry, I gave up because I didn't deserve you anyway."

They sat, holding each other. Michelle sighed, put her head on his chest.

"So, so wrong. Because all I really wanted was for you to want me enough to keep trying. I just wanted you to love me so much you'd never give up."

"And I never will again. *Ever.*"

He found her mouth, then. Kissed her, and she, deliciously, deeply endlessly, kissed him back.

CHAPTER THIRTY-TWO

The door of the restaurant opened. Ben looked up quickly as Stuart walked in, looked for Ben, and made his way to the table. Briefly, they embraced, slapping each other's backs, then shook each other's hands warmly.

"Hey, buddy. How are you?" said Stuart.

"I'm good," said Ben.

"How has your life since the island been?"

"Unbelievable," said Ben, smiling. "But not exactly what I thought it would be," he added more seriously.

"Mine neither," said Stuart.

Just then, the door opened again, and in walked Paul. They waved him over, and the greetings began again.

After putting in an order for drinks, they talked quietly.

First came the stories of family, lost loves, and recovered loves.

Paul held out his hand to Ben, who reached into his pocket for the ring. He handed it to Paul, who slipped it on his left ring finger gratefully.

"I'm so glad you didn't have to give this to my wife," he told Ben, who nodded.

"Yeah, me, too," he said. "So, how are you?" he asked.

Paul thought back over the past few months and tried to put it together for the guys. But there weren't enough words, or the right words, to summarize the many miracles he'd experienced.

Paul swam slowly out of the darkness to the sound of something beeping. He heard people talking softly and the sounds of movement, but it all sounded so far away. He felt heavy, sleepy. He closed his eyes, but someone wouldn't let him sleep.

"Hey, sleepy-head. Time to wake up," said a musical female voice with a bit of a laugh. He shivered. Hands moved a warm blanket to cover him. He snuggled in deeper, wishing away the bothersome voice.

"Paul, do you know where you are?" asked the voice.

"No," he said sleepily.

"You're in the recovery room. You just came out of surgery, and you're doing great. We just need you to wake up all the way."

Slowly, Paul's consciousness took over, and he opened his eyes groggily. He saw a face peering into his, smiling. Nurse.

"Hi," he said.

"Hi," she said. "I'm your nurse—Becky Thompson. Good, you're starting to wake up. You can sleep more later."

She bustled around his bed, adjusting things, checking things. She asked how he felt, and he gave her answers, slowly waking up more. He tried to move his left arm, but it felt impossibly restricted. She explained that he'd had surgery for the wound and that he would need a pressure bandage in place for a while.

He asked for water, and she gave him a few ice chips. "Don't want you getting sick to your stomach."

Finally, something registered. He tried to sit up.

"Nurse, is there—is there anyone here waiting for me?" He felt frantic for the answer, yet afraid to ask.

"Of course, there is," she said, "your wife is in the family room. She's been told you're out of surgery, and that you're fine. Just as soon as we get you out of recovery and into a regular room, she'll be there."

Paul lay back, exhausted with the effort, relief flooding his body. Sarah was there. She was waiting to see him. He let out a huge sigh. Felt for his wedding ring, found an empty finger, remembered he gave it to Ben.

Ben! The guys, the island, the boat. Memories cascaded—the boat sinking, almost not making it to the island, trying to find food and water, waiting for rescue. The long, hot days, restless nights. The storms.

Wait—he couldn't remember a rescue. In fact, he couldn't remember anything past—what was it? Oh, right—he remembered Tony coming to get him, telling him Stuart was hurt. Stuart! Was he okay? What happened? Why couldn't he remember anything after following Tony into the trees?

It was too exhausting, trying to remember everything. He closed his eyes.

He woke again later when they moved him into another bed. It was so bright in the room. Why on earth did hospitals feel the need to keep people awake at all hours of the day and night? He fell asleep again.

Paul slowly woke. It was semi-dark in the room. He pushed himself up, looked at the table by the bed, spotted what looked like a pitcher that might contain water. He was so thirsty. He reached for it, picked it up with his good arm, didn't bother looking for a glass. He opened the top and took a long, slow drink. After being dehydrated for long stretches of time on the life raft and the island, he thought he would never get enough water.

He lay back, trying to remember the sequence of events. The last thing he remembered was a conversation with the nurse about Sarah. Sarah! She'd been waiting for him to get out of recovery, according to the nurse. But she wasn't here now.

Of course, she wasn't here. She'd probably stayed long enough to determine that he was alive and recovering—because that's what decent people do. Sarah was a caretaker at heart—nothing activated that response more than someone who was down. She'd found out he'd come back and was injured, so she'd shown up long enough to make sure he was okay.

He fingered his empty left ring finger, feeling alone, and deserving of it. He'd messed things up with her so badly. And the fact that she'd been there and gone was evidence that she wasn't exactly yearning to take him back. He felt defeated, drained.

He'd set a goal on the island—to go and tell Sarah how sorry he was for driving her away. But what good would it do?

Then he felt a surge of energy. What good would it do? Who in the heck knew? But he knew one thing—he owed himself and Sarah an honest conversation. He needed to tell her everything in his heart, all the things he'd realized while on the island and gazing at the stars at night.

He sat up painfully, looked around. He gingerly crept out of the bed, conscious of the open hospital gown and the cool air hitting him on the backside as he did so. He spotted a small locker, opened it, and looked inside, dismayed. His clothes were there—the ones he'd worn on the island. Filthy.

Oh, well, better than a hospital gown. He pulled the clothes out, shook out his dirty jeans, started to pull them on awkwardly with his one good hand.

"Whoa, there, buddy. What do you think you're doing out of bed?"

Nurse Thompson, appearing from nowhere, now ushered him back toward the bed, but he resisted.

"I've got to get out of here. I need to get dressed."

"You haven't been discharged yet, and the doctor isn't due to make rounds for another few hours." She put on a steely look and pointed at the bed.

He tried to put on a leg of his jeans one-handed, almost fell.

"You don't want to put those dirty clothes back on," said the nurse firmly, this time gently nudging him toward the bed.

"You don't understand. I have to go see my wife. It's important."

"Your wife?" she said, puzzled.

"Yes, my wife," he said. Strange she was saying that in that way because she was the same person who'd told him Sarah was there.

"Well, in that case, sit tight," she said, smiling.

"No, I can't!" he said, again struggling to put on his pants.

The door of the room swung open, pushed by a woman's back, a woman who carried something in her hands. She turned around, faced Paul, and smiled.

Sarah.

"Hi," she said. "Finally, you're awake. I brought some food—real food, not hospital food. Your favorites."

She carried a tray, fully laid out with dinner—gourmet hamburger, side salad, and some kind of dessert. It smelled heavenly.

But food wasn't what he wanted. He stumbled toward her, took the tray, set it on the bedside table, and took her hands in his one good hand.

"Sarah," he breathed. "You're here."

"Paul, I—," she began, at the same time he started, "Sarah, I—"

They both laughed softly. He drew her into his arms, held her as close as he could using one arm, and the other one hanging stiffly.

The nurse chimed in at that point. "Okay, now you know she's here, would you please get back in bed?"

He did, settled under the covers, but insisted that Sarah sit close by so he could hold her hand.

"Sarah, I have so much to tell you. About the boat, and the island, but I don't know what happened at the end. But that's not it."

"I know. We have lots of time to catch up. You need to rest now. But first, eat something."

"I don't want to eat anything."

Seeing her pained look. "I mean, of course, I want the amazing food you brought, but first, I need to talk. Please."

"Okay, but just for a few minutes," she said. "I mean it."

When Sarah said those words, it usually meant she was in charge, and he might as well give up. But not before he'd said what was most important.

"Sarah, I made so many mistakes, and losing you was—I can't believe I ever let you walk out that door. And then, I was so full of righteousness, so convinced that I was right, and you were the one in the wrong. I let pride get in the way of what I really wanted to do."

"And what was that?" she said softly.

"Go and find you, get on my knees, and beg you to come home. I wanted to do that every single day."

"Why didn't you?" she asked, tears welling up.

"Because...for the same reason I wouldn't go see Nathan, stopped calling him. Because I felt so worthless, and I couldn't admit it. Because I convinced myself that everyone else had done me wrong, and that made me feel...like...,"

"Like a victim?" she said quietly.

"Yes. Exactly like that. But on the island, I could finally see the truth. Nathan didn't do anything to me. You didn't do anything to me."

He stopped, searching. He sighed.

Sarah squeezed his hand.

"I did something to me, and because you and Nathan loved me, I did it to you as well. I started hating myself. And I was so angry. Took it out on you mostly, but also on Nathan."

Tears coursed down Paul's cheeks.

"Sarah, can you forgive me?"

"Oh, Paul," she said, "I forgave you a long time ago."

She got on the bed next to Paul and curled into him. He wrapped his good arm around her, and they lay quietly together.

Paul's cracked heart began to heal. The fissure that had opened up months before pulled together. He felt it like a small burst of nuclear fusion, deep inside. Warmth spread throughout his body and his mind eased.

Redemption doesn't happen in large, sweeping events. It happens in the small ones, the moments that seem almost like nothing. You wouldn't see it on video if someone were filming the moment. Only the heart sees it.

⸙

"After that, the miracles kept happening. Nathan and his wife showed up the next day, and it was like old times again. I tried to apologize to him, but he wouldn't hear it. He just kept saying how happy he was to get me back, safe and on the mend."

Paul turned to Stuart. "So, what about you?"

Stuart pulled out his cell phone and scrolled through something on the small screen. He held it out to the guys and pointed proudly to the photos of his little girl.

"She's amazing," he said. "And smart? Wow! She is way beyond where I was at her age," he beamed.

"Hey, man, I'm so sorry about Jillian," said Ben sympathetically. He squeezed Stuart's arm, and they all looked down at the table momentarily.

They were quiet for a time, each taking sips of their drinks.

The food arrived, and they dug in. After a few minutes, they finished, and the plates were cleared away. They ordered another round of drinks.

Looking around the restaurant and lowering his voice, Paul said, "I guess it's time to talk about what happened on the island."

Ben spoke first. "Paul, you shouldn't have to hear this. We're all just grateful that you're okay."

"I know that, and I appreciate that. But I need to know what happened," said Paul, looking at the other two men in the eyes. "It's about me, after all, and the thing is, I have these glimpses, but I can't remember the whole thing. I need to fill in the gaps."

Stuart and Ben looked at each other, then looked away.

"If you're wondering, I can promise you I will not tell anyone what you tell me about the island, about Tony. Even Sarah," Paul said.

They told him.

Stuart showed them the pit, with Tony lying at the bottom. His body was bent unnaturally, and there was lots of blood. They stared down at him. He didn't move, and he didn't talk. His eyes were unfocused.

Jack clambered into the pit, put his hand on Tony's neck, and felt for a pulse. After a minute, he looked up.

"He's still alive, but barely. Let's get him out of here," he said.

"Wait. We have to stabilize Paul first," Stuart said urgently.

"What about Tony?" Ben asked. Stuart shrugged.

The men picked up Paul carefully and took him to a spot where they laid him on a makeshift bed under one of the shelters they'd built. They examined his wound and discussed it.

"It's probably not good to remove the stick," said Stuart, and Jack nodded his agreement. "But we can make him more comfortable."

Carefully, they broke off the ends of the branch, leaving a couple of inches on each side so that if they decided to remove it, they would have something to grab. Paul was still out, occasionally moaning as they manipulated the branch. They covered him with their only makeshift blanket and sat back.

"What about Tony?" asked Jack after a moment. They all looked at each other. "Let's go have a look."

They made their way back to the pit and looked down at Tony. The blood was no longer gushing; in fact, there appeared to be no blood flow at all. Tony lay completely still. His eyes were open but clouded.

"We'd better check again, just to be sure," said Jack, who began to climb down, but Stuart waved him back. "I'll do it. I've had paramedic training. I used to do volunteer fire work," he explained.

Stuart climbed down into the pit and crouched next to Tony. There was a large pool of blood under his neck and shoulders. Stuart felt for a pulse in his neck. He picked up a hand and felt for one in his wrist. Nothing. He looked up at the other guys.

"Dude is dead."

He climbed out of the pit, and they all sat on the ground nearby.

"What happened?" asked Ben. Stuart told them everything, from the moment Tony came to the beach looking for Stuart, all the way through the fight and Tony's fall into the pit.

"What do we do with the body?" asked Ben.

"We can just cover him up where he is," said Jack.

They thought about that.

"Only one problem," said Stuart.

"What's that?" asked Ben.

"Yesterday evening, I swear I heard a helicopter."

"That's great!" said Ben hopefully. "Maybe they're still looking for us! That would be a miracle—for Paul, and for us."

"So, what's the problem?" asked Jack.

"The problem is that whenever they rescue us, they're going to ask about Tony."

"It was an accident," said Ben, "right?"

"But will they see it that way?" asked Stuart. "I'm thinking they may want to investigate it, and who knows how that will turn out. I'm not even sure what jurisdiction we're in. We may be in international waters, or we may be in Mexican waters. I sure as hell don't want to end up in a Mexican jail."

They were all quiet for a moment.

"I think there's only one way to handle this," said Jack. "The guy is dead, and it's his own fault for trying to kill you, Stuart. I say we get rid of the body so it can't be found. We'll tell them he was lost at sea when the boat capsized. No reason to look for him then."

Ben nodded, and Stuart, after reflecting a moment, agreed.

They picked up the body, carried it to the other side of the island, far away from the cove and the beach, where they found a cliff overlooking the ocean. Beneath it, there was no beach, just crashing waves and rocks. They experimented with large rocks first, and after seeing how far and quickly they submerged when thrown in, they moved Tony's body to the edge of the cliff.

They sat for a moment.

"Should we do some kind of service?" asked Ben.

"Like what?" said Stuart. "Should we pray for his obviously damned soul?" he asked contemptuously.

"Hindus believe the soul comes back many times, always seeking enlightenment and redemption," said Jack. "We could ask for his soul to learn something from this lifetime."

"Sounds good to me," said Ben. "I'll start."

"God, please help this guy's soul find the way to enlightenment," he said, bowing his head. "Amen."

"Amen," said Jack.

"Amen," said Stuart, but he rolled his eyes.

"On the count of three," said Jack, taking hold of the body on one end. Stuart took the other end, and Ben took his place in the center of the body mass. Together, they rolled the body to the edge, counted three again, then heaved.

They all watched as Tony's body flew off the edge of the cliff, sailed outward very briefly, then plummeted into the waves below. They stood for a moment, watching the waves and seeing no evidence of the body.

"We'd better get back to Paul," said Jack.

The men made their way back to the beach and to Paul, who lay still. He was awake, but barely, and he croaked, "What happened?"

"You had an accident," said Stuart. "Your shoulder is injured, so be careful," he added, pointing at the stick.

Paul rolled his head over, looked at the stick poking out of his shoulder, and turned white.

Checking him carefully, Stuart said, "Your pulse is steady, and you're breathing well. The biggest issue is going to be the risk of infection."

Paul moaned. "What's wrong with my head?" he asked, trying to reach his other hand up to his head.

"You hit your head in the accident," said Jack. "Don't try to touch it. We're going to clean the wound."

They tore off strips from the bottom of their shirts, then used them to clean the wound on Paul's head. Halfway through the procedure, his eyes rolled up into his head, and he passed out again.

"Probably from pain," said Stuart. "But he may be going into shock."

He checked Paul's pulse again and shook his head.

"It's weaker now." He sat back on his haunches. "This isn't good. We need help, the sooner, the better."

Jack stood, facing the water. He peered at the horizon, shading his eyes with his hand.

"Hey, guys. We're in luck." He gestured.

Ben and Stuart looked up and toward the water. Far in the distance, there was a small black speck on the horizon.

"Is that a ship?" asked Ben hopefully.

"It is," said Jack. "But I can't tell yet if it's headed toward us. Let's build a fire. Wait, we still have that flare."

They started a fire on the beach, adding brush until it roared and sent a large spiral of smoke into the air. The smoke drifted above, and they prayed silently. They used the flare, sending it skyward.

The ship, or whatever it was, appeared to sit on the horizon, not moving. But after an hour or so of keeping the fire alive, Jack reported something new.

"I see something else moving. The men stood, staring and hoping.

Slowly, the smudge they saw grew, and as it did so, it became a helicopter, and the helicopter headed directly toward the island. They turned to each other and slapped each other on the back, whooping. Then, as one, they turned toward Paul, sobering up quickly. He lay quietly, not moving.

The next day, on the ship, Ben pocketed Paul's wedding ring.

Paul sat quietly as the story wound down.

"So, what happened on the ship? Did they ask you about Tony?"

"Sure, they did," said Ben. He looked at Stuart, who nodded.

"They asked, and we answered," said Stuart. "Tony never made it to the island. He was lost and presumably drowned after the wave sunk the boat."

"How do you feel about that?" asked Paul quietly, looking at them both.

Ben spoke first. "Not great, but I know it was the right thing to do. He tried to kill you and Stuart, and his death was accidental. It didn't make any sense to the rest of us to have an investigation that might have resulted in a bad outcome."

Stuart looked away first, then spoke. "The part of it that I don't like is that I had to lie to Jillian about what happened on the island. Granted, by omission, but still.

"Me, too," said Ben, "with Michelle. Here I am, coming clean for the first time in my life with her, opening up, getting her to open up with me, but I still had to keep that part back."

"It's worse than that," said Stuart. "You know there's more to this," he said, looking at Ben.

"What do you mean?" said Paul.

"Nothing. Shut up, Stuart," said Ben.

"No—I'm tired of pretending. You know what really happened," Stuart said to Ben. He turned to Paul. "When Tony was lying in the pit, bleeding to death, I'm the one who suggested we leave him there. *He was still alive*, and I could have done something about it, but I didn't. The truth is, I didn't care if he died."

He stopped, looked down at the table. "But now I feel bad about it. I wish—if I'd been less of a jerk, maybe..."

"Truth is, you have no idea if he would have pulled through. The dude was stabbed in the neck, a major artery or something, from the knife that he used to *try to kill you*," Ben said heatedly.

"Sounds like it's time to let this go," said Paul to Stuart. "You did what you did, and there's no going back. I'm grateful for what you did for me. Thank you."

They were quiet, staring at the tabletop for a moment.

"You know, we can still change this," said Stuart. "We don't have to continue with this lie hanging out there. What if we just go to the authorities and tell them what really happened, that Tony died on the island? Or, what if I do? Then you guys can be truthful with your wives."

Ben and Paul looked at each other.

"Why?" asked Ben. "Why open that back up? What good would it do for any of us?"

"It wouldn't stand in the way for you and Michelle," said Stuart. "Or for you and Sarah," he said, looking at Paul.

Ben shook his head. "I used to think that telling the truth, the whole truth, was always a good thing, good for everyone. But sometimes telling the truth is just selfish. It does no good; only hurts other people."

They were quiet, finishing their drinks.

Then, they talked about other things—their lives, where they stood, what it had been like, returning.

"I wonder what happened to Captain Jack," said Stuart. "Has anyone heard from him?"

"I had a trip to San Diego, so I went to the marina one day," said Ben. "He wasn't around, but there was someone in the main office who said he was off on an extended trip with his girlfriend."

"I wonder who that was," commented Paul.

"No clue," said Ben. "It's not like he confided in us. Real private guy."

They all nodded.

Ben called for the check, paid the whole thing over their protests. Turned to Stuart.

"And now, we have a wedding to go to, don't we? It appears that you have done an outstanding job of getting on with your life."

CHAPTER THIRTY-THREE

They'd chosen a venue in the Texas Hill Country. Overlooking a lake, bower with flowers covering it, white chairs—not that many since it was close friends and family only.

Stuart waited for his bride.

She walked slowly down the center aisle of the chairs as everyone stood. She was dressed in a pale green sleeveless gown, ribbon at the waist, holding a simple bouquet of white roses. She was radiant, smiling at Stuart.

It was his wedding day. The happiest day of his life, so far. But he couldn't help it. While he waited, he remembered all the painful moments with Jillian. Those days, weeks, and months had defined his life, after all, and made it possible for him to be here wholeheartedly, for this woman, today.

After tiptoeing out of the room where Sophie lay asleep, and going into the other room, Stuart and Jillian sat quietly on the bed, backs against the headboard, staring ahead at the blank flat-screen

television on the wall. He reached over and took her hand.

He felt her shoulders shaking, turned to her, alarmed, but she waved him away. Her eyes filled with tears.

"I'm so sorry, Stuart. I—I was so wrong about you. There's so much we haven't talked about, and it's so hard to even think about all of it."

"Jill, remember the doctor saying you don't need any stress? That cancer and immunity are linked to stress?"

"I know that, but this will help if you'll just let me get it out."

He was quiet.

"Remember that night we went to Ashley's? For couples game night?"

At his puzzled look, "Well, anyway, on the way there, we talked about getting married and our life after that. And that was the night, Stuart. I told you I wanted children, and you completely shut down. You barely spoke to me that whole night. You said, and I remember it exactly because it is burned in my memory. I'd said that maybe we could have children someday when we're ready, and you said, I will never be ready."

"I'm sorry about that, Jillian. It was a stupid thing to say."

"No, I'm not bringing this up because I'm still upset about it. I'm way past that. The way you are with Sophie, these past few weeks, watching you as a Dad—it's been the most eye-opening experience of my life. And—and the most shaming. Because I've never been brave when it comes to conflict of any kind. And I didn't challenge you back then because I was too afraid.

"But I short-changed you. I never thought about how things can

change, how people's attitudes can change over time. I didn't give you the benefit of the doubt. I just took those words, carved them in stone, and made my decisions, without you."

He sat still, stunned.

"I was pregnant that night, Stuart," she whispered.

"I thought it was later, maybe right before we broke up, or after," he said sorrowfully.

"No, it wasn't. Can you ever forgive me?"

Stuart felt heavy inside, crushed by the weight of their combined mistakes. How could two such seemingly intelligent people, so in love, screw things up so badly?

"Jillian, listen to me. I—I'm still struggling with the decision not to tell me about Sophie back then, but I also see how you'd not tell me. I was a jerk. I should have seen that we needed to talk about kids, have an actual discussion. I didn't exactly—well, you know how I am. I've always been quick to snap, make a judgment. Have things my way."

She drew a breath, let it out shakily, wiped her eyes.

"I think we have some decisions to make about Sophie. No, listen. It's not enough to have this shared custody thing. We need to move quickly and make sure you are established as her father, that there's no doubt she will be with you if something happens to me."

"Jillian, nothing's going to happen to you," he said firmly.

"You don't know that. We have to make sure you have Sophie, now and always."

"I'm still really new at this Dad stuff," he said doubtfully. "What if I mess it up?"

"No, you're a great Dad. You may not see it, but I do. And she feels safe with you. She's always been so shy—and look at how she's coming out of that. It's absolutely amazing to see her the way she is with you—not hiding behind me, really coming into her own personality." She had a slightly wonderstruck look.

"So, promise me, Stuart, that you'll always take care of her, be there for her. I know she will have a good life with you." She fixed him with an intense look, searching his expression.

"Jill, I, you...we don't need to...,"

"Please. Just promise me."

"Of course, I promise. I love Sophie. I'll always take care of her, do my best to give her a good life."

"Including—but you have to be picky, make sure it's someone who will cherish Sophie—a wife, a stepmother for Sophie, when you meet the right person."

"Jillian!"

"Promise me."

He sighed, played along.

"Okay, if it makes you feel better. I promise to run right out and get a mail order bride just as soon as you kick the bucket. There. Satisfied?"

She smiled a tiny bit.

"Okay," she said, blowing out a breath, turning back to stare at the television screen. Gradually, her lids lowered, and her breathing softened. She curled up next to Stuart, still in her sweats. He pulled a blanket over her gently, stretched out next to her, and watched her sleep until his eyes finally closed in exhaustion.

UNLIKELY RETURN

The next day, they drove home quietly, talking to Sophie but not each other. But the tension had gone out of the air between them, something had shifted, and Stuart felt calmer. Not euphoric, not madly in love, the way he'd felt before finding out about Sophie, but this was even better, somehow, in a way he didn't quite understand.

He found ways to touch Jillian, to brush her arm, to put three fingers gently against her lower back as they walked along. He reached out and tucked a strand of hair behind her ear, and she smiled up at him.

A few nights later, sitting in her living room in front of the fireplace, Stuart pulled out the engagement ring he'd given Jillian the first time. When he opened the box and showed it to her, sparkling in the firelight, she gasped.

"Oh, Stuart! You still have my ring," she said wondrously, and gently reached out to touch it, but pulled her hand back. Looked up at him sadly.

"We can't do this right now. It's a reaction—you're reacting to the news about the cancer."

"That's not true. I love you. I never stopped loving you, even when I was so hurt and angry. I want to marry you, Jillian. Say yes."

She looked away, didn't answer. He wavered for a moment, wondering.

"Jillian, there's one thing you haven't told me, and I guess—I want to hear it now. Do you love me? I was sure you loved me back when we were engaged the first time, but I haven't been sure since we— since lately. Crap, I sound like a needy girl," he said, brushing his hand through his hair, making it stick up.

She smiled. *"Of course, I love you. I'm sorry I haven't said it before, but yes, I love you with all my heart. But let's hold off on the ring until we know what's going to happen with the cancer."*

To hell with that, he thought. He picked up her left hand, slipped the ring on her third finger, folded up her fingers, and stared at her. She let him do it, then sighed, held out her hand to look at the ring. Snuggled up against him and gazed at the crackling fire.

He finally, after all these years, felt complete.

She gave it back to him for safekeeping on the day of her surgery, three agonizing weeks later due to getting a virus. They wouldn't go forward until she was completely over the illness that had struck suddenly, given her a fever, scared the wits out of Stuart.

Surgery was quick, one day in and out, and her recovery from the surgery was unremarkable. Then came the waiting for test results. That took far longer than it should have—ten days, though they'd been told it would be more like three days. Stuart threatened to personally drive to the laboratory—if only he knew where it was—and get the results.

Finally, the day came, the phone call came, and they both cried tears of relief. The cancer had spread to only two out of the six lymph nodes they'd removed. There was no evidence it had spread further.

Back to chemotherapy. It was rough, and Jillian had difficult days of exhaustion, nausea. Sophie began to react to the stress of the adults around her, whining at times, extra needy, wanting more attention at times when Stuart felt torn between taking care of Jillian and attending to his daughter.

No one could have prepared Stuart for the challenge. It was work, real work, to keep his game face on, not show his anger at the cancer itself—dumb, but he had those kinds of irrational feelings.

It was work, learning to parent a little girl who was too young to understand everything that was happening, while also being too sensitive and intelligent to be fooled into thinking nothing was happening.

She reacted to her mother's shifts in availability. One day, Jillian was playing games, cooking, and eating dinner with her. The next, she was asleep in bed during the day and all night as well.

On Jillian's bad days, Sophie struggled, uncharacteristically needy and demanding. At night, she insisted on sleeping with her mother, and sometimes, Stuart occupied the other side of the bed. Sophie seemed calmer on those nights, snuggled between her parents, safe and secure.

Jillian also fought depression, at times, welling up in tears for no apparent reason, talking darkly about the future. Stuart wanted to argue her out of it, blast away the dark clouds that assaulted Jillian's mind, but soon found out that made things worse. So, he waited out the dark moods, sometimes going for long runs to burn off his own pissed state of mind. Pissed at God, at the cancer. At himself.

He lay next to Jillian at night, listen to her breathing, and, although he wasn't a praying kind of guy, he sent up a short prayer. Thank you, God, for Jillian. Please, God, keep her safe, help her get well. I love her, you see, and me and Sophie—we need her. Thank you.

One night, after a particularly stressful day, sitting in Jillian's living room, twisting the ring slowly, she said, "I guess you've seen me at my absolute worst. I wouldn't blame you or be angry with you if you

decided this wasn't for you. We—we don't have to get married, and as long as we can still be together, I'm happy. But if you need to move on—I understand that, too."

That last sentence was spoken quickly, with a short intake of breath, not believable but said because that's what a person says to someone they love. Someone they don't wish to burden.

Stuart pulled her into his arms, whispered to her.

"Are you kidding me? I have a thing, you know, for bald ladies. And I don't want some boring relationship where everyone is fake happy, like a sitcom, and there's no screaming kid in the other room. Jeez." Huffed out a breath.

She smiled—he could feel it against his neck. He pulled her tighter.

The romance—the great sexual chemistry they'd shared years ago and for a brief night weeks ago—was submerged to the needs of Jillian's recovery. Stuart was a high testosterone guy, so being close to her but not making love was frustrating.

Dealing with an upset child every day was also frustrating. He was patient with Sophie, but he felt exhausted later. Dealing with the effects of illness every day was draining. Dealing with medical insurance was frustrating and took far too much time.

Stuart had never been happier.

He was glad they'd invited only their closest friends and family—Bob, Stuart's Dad, Dan and Karen from the hardware store, Ashley, and her current squeeze, plus a few other Austin friends of Stuart's and Jillian's. And, of course, the other guys from the island and their wives—Ben and Michelle, now living together and planning their remarriage; Paul and Sarah.

Stuart scanned the small audience and caught Samantha's eye. She smiled and gave him a little wave, then tucked her hand back into the arm of the guy by her side, who couldn't seem to take his eyes off of her. Stuart winked at her and gave her a "thumbs up."

He couldn't imagine getting married any other way than this small, intimate ceremony.

Sophie walked by her mother's side, holding one hand, in a dress that matched the pale green of Jillian's, tiny white roses woven in her upswept hair. She looked around shyly, then up at her mother, who whispered something that made her smile. She looked ahead, spotted Stuart, and tugged her mother's hand. Jillian laughed, then let her go. Sophie ran to Stuart, and when he turned her around to face the audience, she partially hid behind him, smiling.

Stuart tried so hard. But it was no use. Tears ran down his face as she approached, and he was unable to see anyone but Jillian at that moment. The world narrowed to just the two of them as she reached him, turned to him, and smiled.

They spoke their vows, carefully written by each of them. Everything slowed down to that moment, seared it in their memories forever.

At one point in the ceremony, they presented Sophie with a special necklace—a tiny antique gold locket suspended from a gold chain, a photo of each of them tucked inside. Stuart and Jillian spoke words of affirmation for their life together as a family while Sophie pulled at the locket, smiling.

Finally, the minister pronounced them husband and wife, but before they could kiss, Sophie whispered loudly, "Can we have some cake now?" to which everyone laughed.

They kissed, then turned to the audience, who gave them applause and cheers. Stuart grinning stupidly, Jillian smiling beautifully, the two of them went back down the aisle, Sophie swinging their hands in the middle. All beaming at the attendees and at each other.

Marrying Jillian, looking into her eyes while they spoke their vows, was the most powerful moment of his life, and nothing—no power on earth—could have dragged his attention away from her.

Her red hair—now a couple of shades darker—was short and curly. Jillian didn't like it. She'd wanted to cover it with a large, floppy hat, but Stuart wouldn't hear of it.

"Your hair is still beautiful, and I want to see your face, no hiding under a big hat."

So, she'd worn it the way it was, adorned with one small rose tucked over one ear, hippie style, but somehow not hippie on Jillian. Elegant, understated, lovely.

She'd cried over the few pounds she'd gained with all the treatments, her overall puffiness, *the fact that she no longer looked sixteen*, as Stuart put it.

And she'd never been more beautiful in his eyes than now. He kissed her hand, couldn't stop gazing at her. She finally told him to stop staring, self-conscious as always, so he bugged out his eyes even more, making her laugh and turn her head slightly away.

Stuart had his first father/daughter dance with Sophie. She giggled as she danced on top of his shoes, and his grin was so huge he thought his face would break. Then, he swung her up in his arms, holding one of her hands out ballroom style, rocking and rolling with her around the dance floor to Elvis Presley singing "*I'm in love...I'm all shook up.*"

Then, later, dancing slowly with Jillian to Rod Stewart crooning "The Way You Look Tonight."

EPILOGUE

He'd put it off for as long as he could, but it was time. Jack punched her number and called.

"Hello?"

"Hi, Amanda. It's me."

She screamed into the phone so loudly he had to pull it away from his ear.

"Jack!"

Then she lowered her voice.

"Are you okay? *Where are you?* Why haven't you called sooner?"

She began sniffling.

"I've been so worried! I saw you on the news, and I tried to call you, but I guess you lost your cell phone since this is a new number."

"I'm sorry it took so long. There's been a lot to handle."

He was quiet for a moment, then asked, "is it okay if I come over? If you're busy tonight, though, I totally understand," he added hastily.

"Busy? Of course not! Hurry up and come over! I can't wait to see you," she said breathlessly.

Jack sat for a moment, thinking. He went into the restroom and stared at himself in the mirror. He picked up the scissors and began clipping off the tight, dark beard. After that, he lathered his face and shaved. He showered and dressed.

As Jack made his way out of the house, he paused in the living room and looked around. As usual, it was charming and cozy, but without Melanie there, it seemed oddly empty. He wondered where she was, then shook his head at that. Why was he wondering about her whereabouts?

He left after taking one last look around.

Amanda's door flew open, and she threw herself at him, jumping up and wrapping her arms around his neck, legs around his waist, all while squealing with joy.

"Jack! I've missed you so much!"

She slid down his body, then tilted her head up for a kiss. When he hesitated, she pulled his head down to hers and gave him a full tongue, passionate kiss. His body responded. He kissed her back. They parted after a moment, and he led her into the living room.

Jack sat on the sofa, and Amanda threw herself into his arms again, this time straddling him on her knees, arms wrapped around his neck, pushing her pelvis into his while she delivered another steamy kiss.

"Oh, Jack," she breathed, pulling her lips away slightly. "I've missed you so much." She reached down and massaged his crotch. "Have you missed me, too?" she asked in a kittenish voice, her eyes half-closed. She pressed her lips and tongue into his and continued to arouse every testosterone-filled receptor in Jack's body.

He led her to the bedroom and gently pushed her onto the bed. She looked up at him, eyes shining. He unzipped her skin-tight jeans and peeled them off. She pulled up her tee-shirt over her head and tossed it on the floor, leaving her breasts tightly cupped in a lacy bra.

He peeled off her panties, then undid the clasp of her bra and pulled it away. He unzipped his jeans and hastily pulled them off, then his shirt. She gasped.

After that, he slowed down, teasing her with tongue, fingers, and other body parts, building the sexual intensity until she cried out in ecstasy. He had one hesitant thought but quickly brushed it away.

They lay wrapped around each other, but soon, she rolled away and padded into the bathroom. She called to him over the sound of running water.

"What do you want for dinner?"

"Nothing," he said as he lay staring at the ceiling.

"What?" she asked, coming back into the bedroom. She'd pulled on her underwear and a tee-shirt.

"Uh, I don't really care. Whatever you want," he said, propping himself up on one elbow.

"We could walk down to the marina since it's not far from here. It's happy hour for another two hours, with all you can eat shrimp. How does that sound?"

"It sounds great," he said, jumping up and pulling on his clothes. They dressed quickly, then strolled toward the hole-in-the-wall restaurant where they often ate flash-fried seafood.

It was another beautiful southern California evening, blue skies gradually giving way to hues of deep lavender. The crisp, clear air was perfectly still, a comfortable 65 degrees, plus or minus.

Walking along, Amanda grasped his hand in hers, twining her fingers with his. He allowed it but didn't exactly squeeze back. After a moment of that, she pulled her hand away and stopped on the street. He turned to look at her.

"Jack, what is it?" she asked, lips pouting.

"What?" he said, but he knew that was a cop-out.

"You know, it was really hard on me while you were gone," she said, tears welling in her eyes. "And now you're back, but you don't seem that...well, other than the fantastic sex, you don't act like you missed me all that much."

Jack stared at his beautiful girlfriend. Her tumbled brown curls fell past her shoulders, she was trim and taut, her golden eyes were framed by thick lashes and perfect brows, her face structured like a model, and man was the sex great. But his heart just wasn't on fire. What the heck was wrong with him?

"*Jack,*" she said, now beginning to get really upset. He reached out to take her hand, but she jerked it away. He stood there lamely, willing himself to do something demonstrative and unable to make it happen.

"I don't be*lieve* this!" she said, turning around and walking quickly back toward the apartments.

He watched her go, then began walking back slowly. Arriving a couple of minutes after her, he reached out to open the door, but it was locked. He rang the bell, but all he got was, "go away!" yelled from the other side.

"Amanda," he said loudly, "let me in. Come on, don't be this way."

The door flew open, and she stood there, furious.

"Don't be *what* way?"

He pushed past her, then pulled the door shut behind them.

"Shh, the neighbors," he said.

The flames of anger pulsed higher.

"I don't give a shit about the neighbors!"

She punched him in the chest with her forefinger as she spoke. Shocked, Jack took a step back.

"Amanda," he said softly. "I'm sorry."

She burst into tears.

"What are you doing?" she asked, face scrunched in pain, sobbing. "Are you breaking up with me? After being gone for weeks, and coming over here and having sex with me? Just like that?" She snapped her fingers.

"And don't think I didn't notice that when the reporters asked you about your personal life, you didn't even mention me. What am I to you, anyway? Convenient sex when you get back from your trips? Am I just a *booty call*?"

"Of course not," Jack said adamantly, shaking his head. "That's ridiculous."

He walked over to her, put his arms around her. She sniffled into his shirt for a minute or two. Her tears stopped.

"Jack," she said softly, in her little girl voice. "Let's skip dinner. I'm not hungry anyway. Let's just go to bed. I want you to hold me." She looked up at him, golden eyes glistening.

Steeling himself, Jack said gently, "I think we need to talk."

She pushed him away again and turned to stalk away, but he gently grabbed her wrist before she could.

"Amanda, please. Let's just sit down and talk."

She turned back, sat on the sofa, crossed her arms, and glared at him, chin wobbling and tears beginning to gather in her eyes. Jack felt like crap, but it was now or never.

"First off, I didn't come over here intending to break up with you. You are not a booty call, never were anything like that to me. I—I care deeply for you," he said.

"But you've never once in two years said, 'I love you,'" she whispered.

"You know how I feel about saying those words," Jack said.

"Yeah, I know, only too well. You don't want to say them unless you're sure you're with the woman you want to spend the rest of your life with," she said sarcastically. "Clearly, I am not that woman," she finished bitterly, rapidly wiping away a tear.

"But we agreed at the start of this that we weren't going to go marching down the aisle. Right, Amanda? We've had a good time together, and a lot of care. I thought that would be enough."

"You really don't know women all that well, do you," said Amanda angrily. "How many other girls have agreed to that plan—no promises, no future at all? Huh?"

Jack was quiet, thinking. He'd had that same agreement with several women in his past. Most of them he'd broken up with by drifting away—not calling as frequently, becoming more and more emotionally aloof with time. It was almost as if they hadn't noticed that he'd left.

Or cared. With a sudden pang, Jack realized that he wanted someone to care that he was there, care deeply about him while gone. He wanted someone whom he would miss terribly, who would miss him while apart, and with whom homecoming would be the most special part of his life.

He'd conducted his relationships in the past like someone passing through town, a visitor, not even bothering to rent long-term. Like someone who chooses casual motels, paying one night at a time, uncertain of the length of stay.

Jack didn't really see himself as a relationship guy. He enjoyed the company of women, for sure, but he'd never envisioned himself getting married, buying a house, having children with someone. He just wasn't wired that way.

Yet, if he was honest with himself, the reality was that he wasn't truly a loner. He could have been—it would be easy enough, with a boat on which he spent the majority of his time, a bedroom rental the rest of the time. He could have maintained that lifestyle indefinitely, going to bed for the most part, whether on the boat or on land, alone.

He could have filled the occasional night with casual, sexual liaisons. No emotional entanglements, swift exits.

But instead, he'd chosen to seek out and form intimate relationships with women, to spend time with them when not on the boat, exclusively with one woman at a time. For months, and even years, at a time.

He wasn't the kind of guy to go for casual relationships. He didn't want to find a willing partner for sex and nothing more. He found that distasteful and empty, like craving ice cream and buying fat-free frozen yogurt instead.

Not that women were like food cravings. Truth was, he enjoyed the closeness, the emotional as well as physical intimacy of a long-term, exclusive relationship. He enjoyed the anticipation of a fun evening with a beautiful woman after being at sea.

But with time came the inevitable waning of the spark of attraction. Sooner or later, conversations drifted into the routine of catching up on the latest events of their lives, or news, weather, and sports, but not much more. Mutual awareness of the temporal nature of the relationship precluded deeper conversations that might have provoked more intimacy.

Startled, Jack wondered to himself if he was shallow, if he lacked the ability to delve into deeper realms of emotional intimacy. He shook his head slightly, not wanting to believe that.

But if he was capable of more, why hadn't he gone there? And, to Amanda's point, why had he been setting up all his relationships for the inevitable breakup? Was that fair to him, or to them?

What was happening with Amanda? She'd provoked him into something deeper, taking him to a place that had prompted this soul searching. Something with which he was neither familiar nor comfortable.

Was she the one? Could he fall in love with her?

He knew what he had to do.

"Hey, Jack."

He re-focused on Amanda.

"You're right," he said, resigned.

"What?" she seemed surprised.

"You're right, I've been going about this all wrong. I set it up, in the beginning, to keep you at arms' length. It was stupid to think that one of us wouldn't feel something more, want more."

He paused, thought about what to say, knowing that there was no way to say it that wouldn't be a problem.

"I'm sorry, Amanda. I mean it. It was selfish and short-sighted of me," he said. "Truth is, I want more as well. I'm tired of having no real ties, no real home, and no partner to come home to."

Amanda's face lit up with hope, and it killed Jack to see that in her eyes.

"I'm sorry, Amanda, truly sorry, but that's not happening with us. You've pushed me to be honest with you. I respect you far too much to shortchange you. I'm bowing out, not because you aren't absolutely wonderful—you are. But if I'm being totally honest with you, I care deeply for you, but I'm not in love."

He stood up and pulled her to her feet. He wrapped his arms around her and held her close.

"Please, don't hate me, Amanda."

She held on for a couple of minutes, quietly sniffling, then pulled herself together.

"Don't worry, Jack. I don't hate you. I could never hate you. I just wish it had turned out to be me," she said.

She stepped back. He moved to the door, where he stopped and looked at her one last time. He was grateful for Amanda but saying that to her at this point would have been insulting and hurtful. Maybe someday he'd be able to tell her that she'd pointed him in a new direction in his life, one that he prayed would be what he hoped for.

"Good-bye," he whispered as he opened the door and left.

Jack waited in the living room, surveying his work. He heard the car drive into the small garage, listened closely as the engine turned off, the car door shut. His breath caught, and his heart rate accelerated. He'd never felt so vulnerable.

She walked into the living room, then stopped and gasped. Her eyes lit up with something—what was it? Joy? Surprise?

"Jack—you're back," she said.

Melanie was dressed for work—dark slacks, silky blouse in a turquoise color that caused her short blond hair to shimmer. She wore pearl earrings and a simple gold chain necklace. Her slender feet rested in gold sandals with low heels. Jack noticed her feet because he'd long thought they were the most beautiful feet he'd ever seen on a woman.

For the first time, he allowed himself to fully experience the attraction he'd been suppressing. She was elegant, self-possessed, yet oddly for her age, playful, sort of little girlish, but never immature.

She took a step toward Jack, smiling, then stopped.

"Jack, I'm so glad you're okay, that you're safe. I was—I was concerned about you," she said. Her voice held a note of something that reminded Jack of honey. It was golden, flowing, resonant of things he'd not felt in decades, things that reminded him of home, of the kind of love that anchors and holds gently. He wanted to literally taste her voice.

She carefully surveyed the room—the candles, the flowers on the coffee table, the tray with seared shrimp and seafood dip, the stemmed glasses next to a bottle of white wine.

He held his breath, hoping she wouldn't feel weird about it. Was it too much? Was it over the top? Was it too unexpected, out of the blue?

"What's going on?" she asked. She seemed surprised, in a good way perhaps, but then her expression shifted to something else, a slightly sad and resigned look.

"Oh. I guess Amanda's coming over," she said. "I'll just take something to eat in my room so you guys can have the place to yourselves. I'm sure she's missed you." She turned to leave the room but paused.

"I'm really glad you're home, Jack," she said softly over her shoulder.

"Melanie?" he said.

She turned back slowly.

"Amanda's not coming over," he said.

Her brows crinkled in puzzlement.

"She's not?"

"No, she's not. In fact, she won't be coming over anymore, and I won't be going to see her. We broke up," he finished.

"Oh, Jack, I'm so sorry," said Melanie in a rush of empathy. "And just after getting home."

"Melanie, can you come over here? I really need to talk to you," Jack said, feeling his heart rate move up another notch.

"Of course! I'm all ears, you know that," said Melanie, sitting on the sofa across from Jack, who occupied a wing chair.

"I know that," said Jack. "In fact, you've been a wonderful listener for me, not that I've shared all that much."

"Well," said Melanie, laughing softly, "it's true you are kind of a quiet guy, but I like that about you. I sometimes feel like the quiet spaces with you are filled with," she fluttered her hands a bit in the air, "with something special. This sounds silly, but I really like it when we just sit here with the fireplace going, me reading a book, and you listening to music."

Melanie blushed and looked down.

"I'm sorry—that sounded so—so lame," she said with embarrassment.

Jack smiled as he gazed at her, watched her self-consciously tuck a strand of hair behind one ear. She looked up at him, surprised to find him staring.

"Um, Jack, what happened with Amanda? You must be shocked that she would break up with you. I mean, how are you?"

Melanie gazed at Jack, concern in her eyes.

"It's a long story, but she didn't break up with me. I broke up with her, and it was one of the hardest things I've ever done. She's a great girl. She wasn't happy about it," Jack said, looking miserable. "But I know it was the right thing to do," he said.

Leaning forward, Jack said, "I hope you don't think too poorly of me. I sound like a jerk, don't I?"

He waved away her protestations.

"No, really. I've done a little soul searching lately, and I realize that I haven't done the right things when it comes to my relationships with women. What I mean is, I've been in this relationship with Amanda, and it's not the first time I've done this."

"Done what?" she asked.

"Carried on a relationship with someone I'm not in love with. Told myself it's okay to do that because, after all, I made it clear to her upfront not to expect the ring, the church, and all of that. So, if I tell a woman not to expect any kind of commitment, it's okay, right? I mean, that's what everyone does."

She was quiet, listening intently. She didn't try to stop him or persuade him he wasn't that bad. Jack rushed on.

"But it didn't really feel great to me, you know? I told myself all these short-term relationships were great, a lot of fun for both of us, but later, I just felt a sour taste. There was something missing."

"Something missing?" she said, eyebrows slightly raised, her eyes locked on his, a touch of candlelight reflected in them.

"Yes, something missing. You see, while I was on that damn island, I got to have these conversations with the other guys, and believe me, I don't go around having heart-to-hearts with guys."

Her eyes were glued to Jack's. She'd moved to the edge of the sofa, leaned slightly toward him.

"But there wasn't anything else to do, so we talked, or at least they did—about their lives, about their past relationships, about how they'd screwed things up with their women. They really opened up, and I just sat there on the sidelines." Jack paused, now up and pacing the room, back and forth a few feet away from her.

"The whole time, I kept thinking to myself how lucky I am, how much easier my life is because I don't have these emotional entanglements. At one point, they asked me about my life—who was waiting for me and hoping I would return. I didn't answer. I brushed it off—didn't say anything."

Jack stopped pacing and looked at Melanie with an intensity that he'd never shared with a woman. His arms hung by his sides, but his muscles were bunched, his fists closed as if preparing for fight or flight.

"But what I was thinking was, the person who was waiting for me wasn't the person I wished was waiting for me," Jack spoke quickly now as if by rushing out the words, he could get to the end of the story faster and find out how it ended.

"I was thinking of you. Were you, Melanie?" he asked, staring into her eyes with something close to a combination of desperation and fear.

He moved over to her, knelt on the floor, took her hands in his, bent his head and put his forehead on top of their hands. He felt himself shaking inside.

"Were you waiting for me?" he finally gasped, not daring to look up for the answer.

Time seemed to stand still after that. He was completely out on a limb for this spectacular woman who probably only saw him as a younger brother.

He heard nothing, only silence. His heart was like a caged animal, beating against the bars, trying to escape. He let out a breath, sighed in resignation.

Slowly, he looked up at Melanie, ready to see embarrassment, ready to hear the painful rejection of his awkward advances.

And looked into the eyes of love, the shining, adoring eyes of a deeper love than he'd ever experienced. His heart stopped.

Then began beating again, but now pulsed with something new, something unlike anything before. The caged animal was a beautiful bird, free and soaring.

"Jack," she breathed, her face filled with joy. "I *was* waiting for you. I will always wait for you," she said.

THE END

ACKNOWLEDGMENTS

Writing a book is a solitary venture. Part of the writer's job is to infuse the book, as much as possible, with elements that ring true, even though they are often about subjects that are outside the author's expertise. That is why we rely on the kindness of others to fill in the gaps, and we give them a shout out in the acknowledgments.

But first, the inevitable caveat: while these people assisted me with their knowledge and wisdom, they are not responsible for the literary license that I utilized or any mistakes, shortcuts, or lack of resemblance to reality. The responsibility for that is solely mine.

Many thanks to Mark Hay, Ph.D., Regents Professor at Georgia Tech and renowned experimental marine ecologist. Thank you for giving me insight that informed the men's experience on the island and helped shape the island and its inhabitants. And a very warm thank you, Candace, for allowing me to hang out with the two of you in your beautiful home and pick Mark's brain!

Warm acknowledgments to Jeff Crilley, media consultant extraordinaire, who provided insight and glimpses into the world of reporting in the field, both from an experiential standpoint as well as a motivational one. Your insight helped bring Heather Steel to life and gave her the motivating factors that fueled her drive, resulting in her impact on our heroes' journey. Many, many thanks and much gratitude to you, Jeff, for the media boosts you've given me over the years as an author!

Thank you to Wes Witt, former aviation electrician and C-130 flight engineer, who provided insight into search-and-rescue as well as naval training exercises. That gave rise to the very brief but pivotal character, Admiral Janet Steel.

Thanks to my editor, Nicole d'Entremont, for making the book so much better!

Most of all, my deepest love and gratitude to my husband, Mark, for supporting me in the authors' journey. I recognize the sacrifices you make—in less "presence" together as I wander off into my characters' universes, and in the forfeited pursuit of other life experiences for which there is less time.

ABOUT THE AUTHOR

Nina Atwood is a licensed psychotherapist with over 30 years' experience as an expert in the field of human relationships. She wrote and published five self-help books before turning her pen to fiction.

Nina's "day job" is executive coaching. She spends her weekends and evenings in the company of two adorable cats, writing, while her husband Mark brings water and hot tea, and provides much-needed shoulder rubs, periodic manuscript reviews, and encouragement.

Drawing from her extensive expertise, Nina crafts rich, vibrant relationship and life transformation stories. *Unlikely Return* is her first fiction book, soon to be followed by her second, *Free Fall*.

Sign up for Nina's email list to keep informed as she writes and publishes more stories. Visit her website:

www.ninaatwoodauthor.com

Please leave a review on amazon.com or any other place where you purchased the book. It makes a huge difference to an author when you do. Thank you!

Keep going to get a preview of Nina's next book.

Free Fall

by Nina Atwood

FREE FALL

CHAPTER ONE

Hannah Lee breathed in once, twice, and felt excruciating pain. It began in her lower back and extended into her abdomen. It was dark, but that was only because her eyes were closed, or so she thought. She vaguely thought, *don't bother opening your eyes; you won't like what you see*, so she lay there for a while, drifting in and out.

Later, she swam out of the darkness behind her eyes and into real darkness. It was cold. Her brain couldn't register her location in space. She focused, concentrated as hard as she could through waves of pain. She wiggled her fingertips, felt dirt, tiny pebbles, and some type of plant matter. She moved her arms like a snow angel—first sweeping upward toward her head on the ground, then sweeping back to her sides. *I'm outside, lying down, on the ground*.

What happened to me? How did I get here?

She focused on her body, trying to assess the extent of her injuries. She moved her feet slightly, and that gave her a tiny ray of hope.

Weren't you supposed to be unable to move if your spine was severed?

She could move her hands and feet. She raised her right arm in the air, but that seemed to generate another wave of pain in her abdomen. She raised the left, gritting her teeth with the pain. She could move her arms, so she definitely wasn't going to be quadriplegic. But what about her legs?

She was afraid to try lifting a leg. Something was terribly wrong in her lower back and abdomen. *Not a spinal injury*, she commanded her body, as if by saying that to herself it wouldn't be true.

Hannah Lee lay still for a while, letting her mind drift to the possibilities. *Was I thrown from a car?* She listened but couldn't hear any sounds of traffic. She might be in a ravine beside a highway, the road too far above for her to hear the traffic. Maybe someone would notice the place where her car left the road.

Wait. She slowly rotated her head, looked around. There was no sign of her vehicle. There was, however, some kind of tent-like, large piece of fabric or canvass lying nearby. That brought a faint glimmer of memory, but not enough.

If she lay somewhere with no roads, the likelihood of another driver noticing her didn't exist. If that was true, she could lie here slowly dehydrating, or worse, bleeding out internally.

It was up to her to get herself out of there. That brought a shiver of anxiety that traveled from her scalp down her spine. But the alternative was far worse.

Time to try.

She tried to roll over on her side, hoping to get into position to sit up, maybe stand. That tiny bit of attempted movement set off another wave of unbearable pain. She felt herself slipping away from consciousness. This time, she fought the darkness, sensing that she needed to wake up, be alert.

It was so cold. She began shivering, couldn't stop. She tried again to figure out where she was, what had happened. She looked around and saw purple velvet dusk. Her view encompassed rocks and scree, hillside, and scrub. But where? *And how did she get here?*

She noticed a sense of altitude. Even though she couldn't see beyond the immediate surroundings, she sensed a nearby canyon, that she was at the top of it, perhaps on a ridge or the side of a mountain.

Hannah Lee lay silently in the darkness, watching the stars slowly wheel overhead, glowing brilliantly. Every movement brought heightened pain, so she lay still. She heard night birds calling, their whispery ululations echoing in the canyon below. Insects chirped and buzzed nearby. She wondered absently if there might be snakes, poisonous snakes.

An owl hooted as it swooped overhead. Owls were such beautiful night creatures—swift, silent, beautiful, and deadly to the small creatures that scurried futilely to escape. She felt so small, so feeble, so vulnerable.

"Hello?" she called out, for the umpteenth time. Her voice cracked, a whisper in the wilderness. She didn't believe anyone could hear her, but she tried anyway, at least every hour. She swallowed dryly, wishing she had a bottle of water within reach. Every so often, she tried again to roll over, but the pain was unbearable.

The rocks and scree under her body made it impossible to lie completely still. She moved her head slightly to try to get off of the small rock that punched a hole in her scalp. Like a pebble in the shoe that won't move, this one stayed firmly underneath the back of her head. Slowly, she reached up with one hand and brushed away the pebble under her head. That brought scalp relief but increased her other pain.

She wondered how many broken bones she had. A terrible thought occurred to her—what if her initial assessment was wrong? What if she'd broken her spinal column? Dread filled her mind and her heart began to race. What if she could never walk again, never do anything on her own power? She tried again to wiggle her toes but couldn't tell if she succeeded. Her sneakers bound everything tightly and the cold removed sensation. Panic rose.

Stop it, she admonished herself. She made herself take dee breaths. She began to pray. Please God, bring help. Bring it fast. I don' ask for much, but this time, I'm asking.

Her thoughts drifted, searching for answers. What is the last thin I remember? Basics—start with basics. Breakfast? What do I normall eat? Granola, yogurt, and fresh coffee with just a trace of real cream Yes, that's it. Where is my favorite place for breakfast?

She visualized her spacious wood deck, cantilevered on the side c the hill, hummingbirds darting around the potted geraniums an impatiens, the morning sun hovering just below the horizon. A cush deck chair with a light throw, a small, round table with multi-colore glass on the top, her coffee mug sitting within reach. And the view— Carmel Valley, filled with lush, rolling green hills.

A memory surfaced. Breakfast on the deck, interrupted by he husband, Ryan, asking her something. What was it? She couldn't pu up the entire memory. It was as if she saw a brief movie that suddenl faded away, leaving...a blank screen, a huge, empty space where he morning once existed. She couldn't remember the rest of it, and, ever more disturbing, had no idea if that was this morning, yesterda morning, or a month ago.

Ryan! He must be so worried. She never went anywhere withou letting him know. She had no sense of the passage of time bu minimally she'd been on the side of this mountain for several hours Her hands and lower arms were cold, and she couldn't feel her feet.

How long can someone lie injured outside and survive? She vaguel recalled stories she'd read in the media of people who were lost in th wilderness, who survived on water they found and food the scrounged. But that wasn't her. She'd never find water if she couldn' move, couldn't stand, couldn't even crawl. Forget food.

The pain in her lower back and abdomen began to spread. It wa unbearable, and after a couple of minutes, she felt herself slippin away. She didn't fight it, sensing that there was no point. Darknes descended, and it wasn't the dark of the night.

Hannah Lee swam out of the darkness. She heard a loud *whump, whump, whump* overhead. It grew louder, but then faded away. What was that sound? It was familiar, but she couldn't place it.

Mind swirling in confusion, she tried again to recall where she was, recent events. *What day is it?* She wondered. She felt as if a black curtain had fallen, obscuring everything in the recent past. Impressions emerged—the clear blue sky, the wind, the utter quiet, and, suddenly, the sensation of falling. Then, the impressions quickly receded behind the black curtain.

Fingers of crimson spread gradually in the sky—dawn's early light. She peered around, saw that she was on a ridge, on the side of a small mountain, as she'd theorized. But where? The horizon lay far away, shrouded in low clouds. Nothing looked familiar.

Fear gripped her. How could she not know where she was, or how she got there? It was far too difficult to stay focused, so she began fading. Faintly, in the distance, she heard voices calling out. She fought the blackness, but it didn't matter.

Light penetrated the darkness and voices swelled. *Why don't they turn out the lights, be quiet and let me sleep?* She wanted only to fade away, to go back into the darkness where there was far less pain.

"Mrs. Winn? Hannah Lee Winn? Can you hear me? Make a sound if you can hear my voice," said someone. His voice was soothing, calm, and somewhat melodious, distinctly male.

She moaned.

"Over here!" Someone shouted, a deeper male voice nearby.

"She's semi-conscious, possibly in shock," said the melodious voice.

"She's hypothermic. Let's get her warmed up," said the other voice.

Someone wrapped something around her. She shivered uncontrollably.

"Let's stabilize her neck with a brace."

Something was wrapped firmly around her neck. Then something hard slid underneath her body. It was even more uncomfortable than the ground had been.

"Hang in there, Mrs. Winn. We're getting you onboard. In just a short time we will get you to the hospital where you will be in great hands. They know you're coming because we've radioed ahead. You are going to be fine." The melodious voice again.

She felt movement, the hard platform on which she lay in motion. *They're taking me somewhere.* She could hear the sounds of breathing nearby. There was jostling for a moment, awkward movements, and the hard surface tilted, all of which elicited another moan.

"Sorry, Mrs. Winn. We just need to get you settled, and then it will be less uncomfortable."

The shivering decreased. She was still, could hear voices around her, and then a loud engine began, increased in volume, and she could feel the entire vehicle— what was it?—take off, move rapidly upward. *I must be in a helicopter*, said her brain, just before she lost consciousness again. She vaguely heard someone say, "check her blood pressure—it's dropping like a rock," and then, "she's bleeding internally—she's bleeding out!"

After that, the darkness was complete.

Hannah Lee heard soft laughter in the distance. An odd, rhythmic pumping sound whirred away on a regular beat. Several beeping noises alternated with the pumping sound. At first, it was nothing more than white noise. Then her brain registered the source of the sound and she began to stir.

Then she felt it—a tube inserted in her nostril, snaking impossibly down her throat. She began to squirm. She reached up with her hand

and tugged at the tube. Her heart rate zoomed—*she was choking*. Panic struck swiftly.

"Oh, my God—she's waking up. Nurse! She's trying to pull out her breathing tube. Hurry!" shouted a familiar male voice.

Sounds of rapidly swishing footsteps, and suddenly Hannah Lee felt a dropping sensation as drugs were pumped into the I.V. line that connected through a port in her hand. She tried to fight it, but it did no good. Darkness descended.

The next time Hannah Lee's eyes opened, she looked into a man's concerned face. She remembered the tube and swiftly put her hand on her face, but it was gone.

"It's okay, there's no tube this time," he said. He sat close to the bed, which was surrounded by some kind of curtain, holding her left hand. His sandy hair fell over his forehead, and he was slightly disheveled. His jawline was clenched.

Ryan, her husband. She lay in a narrow bed with siderails. Tubes snaked into her arms and her chest. Machines measured her every bodily function. The hospital—*why was she in the hospital?*

"What happened? What's going on?" she pleaded, panic striking. "Why can't I move?"

She struggled to move, to sit up, but her body refused to cooperate. Her heart thudded and her chest tightened. She managed to push herself up with her left arm, but not far before pain shot through her lower back and abdomen.

"You have to calm down, Hannah Lee," Ryan said, as he gently pushed her back against the bed. "You've been injured but you're going to be okay. It was an accident."

"No, help me sit up! I don't want to be here," she said, throat tightening. Ryan stroked her arm and spoke soothingly.

"It's okay, I'm here. Calm down, it's okay."

But it wasn't okay. Nothing was.

"Let's go home, please," she heard herself plead. She'd never felt so trapped, so helpless.

"You can't go home yet. You have some broken bones and you need time for things to set before you can move around. Please, baby, settle down." He sounded almost panicky.

Hannah Lee forced herself to lie back down. She focused on her husband's eyes, took a deep breath. His fear transferred itself to her, so she closed her eyes, took another deep breath.

She opened her eyes again. Ryan looked concerned but no longer panicky.

"What happened?" she asked him.

"What do you remember?" he asked slowly.

"I don't remember anything...just images," she said, eyes cutting rapidly to the left. A cascade of images: deep blue sky punctuated by clouds, white on top, dark on the bottom; the ocean; mountain tops.

She shivered with the memory of the chill wind. Then, the memory of panic, of a far-too-rapid descent. Her heart rate accelerated suddenly, and her breath caught in her throat. She reached out and gripped Ryan's arm, tightly.

Her air passages tightened, her eyes flew open wide, and she squirmed, tried again to get out of the bed.

"I have to get out of here!" she cried out, but she felt so weak, unbelievably tired.

"Nurse!" yelled Ryan. "We need help in here!"

Rapid, swishing footsteps approached, a curtain around the bed opened, and this time Hannah Lee saw the nurse—young, probably in her early thirties, long dark hair, calm features. She reached out and touched Hannah Lee's arm soothingly.

"It's okay, Mrs. Winn," she said as she injected something into the I.V. line. "I'm Becca, your nurse. This is a mild sedative, just to help you relax. We don't want you pulling out your lines or re-breaking any fractures."

Hannah Lee felt the panic loosen its grip, felt herself begin to float.

he felt a deep sense that all was well. Then she thought about the
nemories and a flutter of fear emerged. A tiny alarm bell tried to sound
n her brain, but it was too far away. Not important. Her eyes closed,
nd she gradually drifted off, fell into a deep sleep.

Hannah Lee's eyelids felt heavy, so she kept them closed. She was
onscious, but barely. She breathed softly, not moving. Gradually, she
noticed low voices nearby. One of them was her husband, and that
rought a tiny smile to her lips.

"You shouldn't be here! What were you thinking? Are you crazy?"
whispered Ryan urgently. Then he murmured something indistinct.

"I'm telling you, I had nothing to do with it," said a female
whisperer.

Hannah Lee's breath hitched. *Who was that?* She didn't recognize
the voice. *Was it the nurse?*

"I find that hard to believe," whispered Ryan. "It was your
equipment," spoken harshly.

"I didn't do anything! How can you even *think* I would do something
ke that?"

"Wait! Don't leave. No, let's step outside. I'll go first so it doesn't
ook so weird."

Was that her husband? Who was he talking to? What were they
alking about?

Hannah Lee felt distant, fuzzy, sleepy. It was so difficult to
oncentrate, to make rational sense out of what her ears detected.
Who would be here, with Ryan? Someone she didn't know, but that
nade no sense. She knew all of Ryan's business acquaintances, and he
lidn't really have friends.

She heard the curtain swish. Then silence for a heartbeat or two.

Someone stepped closer to the bed. Hannah Lee lay still, keeping
her breathing steady and long. She felt it was important to give the
ppearance of deep sleep. Someone stopped at the side of the bed.

Straining to listen, Hannah Lee could just barely hear soft breathing. She caught the faint scent of perfume.

Fingers brushed her hair. Hannah Lee froze, made herself continue breathing, steady, long breaths.

"Why?" Big sigh. "Why didn't you just die on the mountain?"

Hannah Lee's heart rate kicked up. Who was that? *Who wanted her to die?* Her mind swirled in confusion, foggy in the narcotic soup.

The curtain swished again, and Hannah Lee heard the nurse, Becca, ask "who are you and what are you doing here?"

"Oh, I'm so sorry. I thought this was my mother's bed. I got lost," said the sheepish, apologetic voice. "I'll go ask for the information again."

The curtain opened and closed again.

The nurse bustled around the bed, did something to the I.V. line and smoothed the blanket over Hannah Lee, who now felt drowsiness rapidly descend. She tried to speak before she drifted off but wasn't sure her actual voice made it into the air.

She tried to say, "Wait," feeling the urgency to tell the nurse, or someone, something. *What was it?* She knew it was important. But she couldn't remember. Her breathing slowed and she slept.

Look for Free Fall in late 2020 through Amazon and other booksellers

Made in the USA
Las Vegas, NV
26 August 2024

94425997R10246